The
Bach English-Title Index

The
Bach English-Title Index

Ray Reeder

Fallen Leaf Press
Berkeley, California

Published by Fallen Leaf Press
P.O. Box 10034
Berkeley, CA 94709 USA

Library of Congress Cataloging–in–Publication Data

Reeder, Ray, 1931-
    The Bach English-title index / Ray Reeder.
        p. cm. -- (Fallen Leaf reference books in music; no. 20)
    For use with the 1st and 2nd eds. of Wolfgang Schmieder's Thematisch-
systematisches Verzeichnis der musikalischen Werke von Johann Sebastian
Bach.
    Discography:
    Includes bibliographical references.
    ISBN 0-914913-23-9
    1. Bach, Johann Sebastian, 1685-1750--Indexes. 1. Bach, Johann Sebastian,
1685-1750. Vocal music. I. Schmieder, Wolfgang. Thematisch-systematisches Verzeichnis der musikalischen Werke von Johann Sebastian Bach.   II.
Title.   III. Series.
ML134.B1R43 1993
016.7822'2'0268--dc20   92-37177
                                                                    CIP
                                                                    MN

Contents

Preface

This index had its genesis in a telephone call to the Music Library at California State University, Hayward. A patron wanted the score for a Bach cantata that she could identify only by an English title. My efforts to equate her title with a recognizable German title were without success. There were only general indexes to go to for additional help. Should there be an exclusive Bach resource? The idea to create an index of English titles seemed to have some merit. I discussed the plan with colleagues from the University of California at Berkeley, who agreed that the project was worth pursuing.

Many years and innumerable frustrations later, the work has stopped; it can never be complete, and I offer it with the hope that it will be of help to those who need to identify a line that is set to Bach's music. To that unknown caller who started this quest: Forgive me for not having the information when you needed it.

This publication is not the work of my hands alone. The kindness, cooperation and generosity of many people made this index possible. With genuine gratitude, I acknowledge their contributions. Thanks to the staff members who granted exceptional privileges and courtesy to me in using the music resources at:

> Oakland Public Library
> San Francisco Public Library
> Stanford University
> University of California at Berkeley
> University of California at Los Angeles.

Thanks to Peter Chamberlain, Academic Computer Consultant, California State University, Hayward, for his extraordinary patience and contribution of time far beyond the circumscriptions of his job description in leading me through the computer maze. In words from BWV 212:8, he is "Our most excellent Chamberlain."

Thanks to those indispensable ones who endured the mind-numbing persecution of multiple proof readings,

> Norma Byrd
> Ruth Reeder
> Richard Riffer.

Introduction

The Bach English-Title Index (BETI) is a compilation of English-language words and phrases used as translations, paraphrases, and original texts for the titles and separate movements of the vocal works of J.S. Bach, as well as for the chorales and chorale preludes that bear the titles of the hymn tunes from which they derive. I have also included some instrumental works derived from vocal works and a few rare examples of vocal works derived from instrumental music. I have not included numerous examples attributed to Bach that I could not match with any musical incipits.

The information, gathered over several years, comes from scores, librettos (including those published with recordings), and analytical and critical works found in the music collections at four universities and two large public libraries. There are 13,804 entries representing 16,029 titles and textual incipits. Many other English-language versions exist, but no copies were available for my examination.

The index is intended for use with Wolfgang Schmieder's *Thematisch-systematisches Verzeichnis der musikalischen Werke von Johann Sebastian Bach* (first edition Leipzig: Breitkopf & Härtel, 1961), hereafter referred to as BWV. Because the numbers in the first edition have become the international standard, they are used in this index. A concordance identifies and correlates variations in numbers that differ from those given in Schmieder's second edition of 1990.

I have imposed a few editorial procedures upon the titles and phrases:

- Words with variant spellings are spelled according to current American usage.
- I have retained capitalization of pronouns referring to the Deity for consistency with the style of the earlier published texts. This procedure was complicated by the ambiguous and peculiar natures of some of the paraphrases and original English texts. I have not generally applied capitalization to extended metaphors such as "Morning Star."
- All incipits beginning with "Blest" have been changed to "Blessed."
- All incipits beginning with "O" and "Oh" are interfiled as "O."
- Some questionable words, such as misused archaic forms, appear to be editorial errors in the original sources. I have identified these by a single asterisk and have reproduced them as found. (For example, "Thou are*.")

- Other words seem definitely to be errors; I have changed these and marked them with two asterisks. (For example, "adorn**" [originally "adorne."])
- Some incipits vary only by one letter or word. I have combined these if the alphabetical order of the text is not affected. The variant letter or word is given in parentheses immediately after the letter or word it should replace:

  Jesu(s) = Jesu and Jesus

  awaits thee (you) = awaits thee and awaits you

- Many incipits begin with the same words even though the text varies considerably farther into the phrase. I have shortened these and entered them only once with multiple BWV references.

How to use BETI

Look up the English-language phrase in the main (alphabetical) section. To the right of the entry are BWV numbers.

- A number following a colon indicates a portion of a larger work.

  6:1 = BWV 6, movement 1.
- A movement number with a decimal indicates the number of a stanza.

  43:11.1 = BWV 43, movement 11, stanza 1.
- Some published scores and librettos make distinctions that are not separately numbered in BWV. These are designated by a lower-case letter following the final digit.

  244:76c = BWV 244, movement 76, subsection c.

A concordance at the end of this index identifies subsection c, in case there is any question.

- The letter A preceding a BWV number indicates Anhang.

  A160 = BWV Anhang 160.

Because some phrases occur with various musical settings, the user may have to refer to the musical incipits in BWV for precise identification.

The user should keep in mind that identifying a chorale phrase in BWV does not necessarily provide the original title of the chorale. Because Bach used various stanzas of chorales as well as variant texts, it may be necessary to consult an additional source for the original title of the complete text.

Title and First Line Index

A

Abide, O Lord, in me, 148:5

Abide with me, 508

Abide with us, for it is toward evening, 6:1

Abide with us, for it will become evening, 6:1

Abide with us, O blessed Lord, 6:3

Abide with us, our blessed Lord, 6:3; 253; 649

Abide with us, our Saviour, 281

The abyss of many a former sin, 102:7

Accept me, Lord, as Thine, I pray, 65:6

Accept, O Lord, the praise outpoured, 346

Acclaim God in all lands, 51:1

According to Thy name, O God, 171:1

Accursed knave, what's on your mind, 246:3

The ache and pain of childbirth, 246:58

Acknowledge me, my keeper, 244:21

Acknowledge will I His name's honor, 200

Acknowledging the Godhead's might, 62:5

An Adam, full of terror, may hide himself, 133:3

An Adam may, full of fears, from God's, 133:3

An Adam may when filled with terror, 133:3

Adam must be dead within me, 31:6

Adam must in us decay, 31:6

Adam must in us now perish, 31:6

Adam's fall entirely corrupted human nature, 18:5; 637

Admire, all ye people, this mystery's grandeur, 62:2

Adorn thyself, dear soul, 654

Adorn thyself, O dear soul, 180:1

Aeolus appeased, 205

The afflicted shall eat, 75:1a

Affliction is there none, 20:2

Affright not thyself, my heart, 111:2

Affrighted be, 102:5

Affrighted be not, 15:4

Affrighted pause, 102:5

After my tribulation Thou wilt comfort me, 103:4

After three days I will rise again, 244:76c

After weary days of sadness, 150:7

Again as evening's shadow falls, 253

Again the day is past and done, 396

Again we keep this solemn feast, 6:6

Against Thee their faces have grown hard, 102:1c

Agreed, O favored Vistula, 206:4

Agreed, O lucky Vistula, 206:4

Agreed that our master, 212:7

Ah: *see also* O

Ah, a child of sin am I, 78:3

Ah, ah, alas! How much Thy will, 73:1b

Ah, all too well we know our guilt, 116:4

Ah, but ah, how much lets me Thy will, 73:1b

Ah, but to see Thee lying in Thy cradle, 121:5

Ah, Christians too much heed, 186:4a

Ah, comfort sweet, 138:4

Ah, constant refuge, 16:4

Ah, could it to me then soon, 95:3

Ah, dear Christians, be comforted, 114:1; 114:7; 256

Ah, dearest God, Thou lettest me, 13:2

Ah, dearest Jesu, Child Divine, 248:9

Ah, dearest Jesu, Holy Child, 248:9

Ah, dearest Jesu, what was Thy transgression, 245:27.1

Ah, dearest Jesus, Holy Child, 248:9

Ah, do not pass by me, 23:2

Ah, do not pass me by now, 23:2

Ah, do stay, 11:4

Ah, draw close my spirit with bonds of affection, 96:3

Ah, draw the soul with cords of love, 96:3

Ah, draw Thou my spirit with cords of affection, 96:3

Ah, ever perverse is the heart, 73:3

Ah, faithful refuge, 16:4

Ah, faithful shield, 16:4

Ah, fellow Christians, be consoled, 114:1

Ah, go Thou not far from me, 23:2

Ah, God and Lord, 48:3; 255; 692; 692a; 693

Ah, God, from Heaven look anew, 2:1; 77:6

Ah, God, from Heav'n look down and see, 741

Ah, God, from Heaven look down and view, 2:1; 2:6; 77:6; 153:1; 741

Ah, God, from Heaven look into it, 2:1

Ah, God, from Heaven look on us, 2:1

Ah, God, from Heaven look therein, 2:1; 77:6; 153:1

Ah, God, from Heaven look thereto, 2:1

Ah, God, from Heav'n look down anew, 741

Ah, God, full many a heartbreak, 3:6; 44:4; 58:1; 153:9.3

Ah, God, hear my sighing, 254

Ah, God, how many a heart pang, 3:1; 58:1

Ah, God, how many a heartfelt woe, 44:4

Ah, God, how many pains of heart, 3:1

Ah, God, how many pains of heart trouble me, 44:4

Ah, God, how much affliction, 58:1

Ah, God, how much heart-sorrow, 3:1; 58:1

Ah, God, how oft a heartfelt grief, 3:1; 44:4; 58:1

Ah, God, how sad and sick at heart, 3:1; 44:4; 58:1

Ah, God, in mercy, 741

Ah, God, in mercy look from Heav'n, 2:1

Ah, God, look down from Heaven and see, 2:1

Ah, God, my Lord, 255; 692; 692a; 693; 714

Ah, God, my way is weary, 155:1

Ah, God, our master good and true, 101:3

Ah, God, when shalt Thou, 98:2

Ah, God, where may I find relief, 98:2

Ah, Golgotha, 244:69

Ah, good Lord, Thine own dear angel send, 149:7

Ah, grieve not so, nor so lament, 384

Ah, happy are ye, steadfast spirits, 442

Ah, head so pierced and wounded, 244:63.1

Ah, heal me, Lord, 135:2

Ah, heal me now, Thou soul's physician, 135:2

Ah, heal me, Thou physician, 135:2

Ah, heal Thou me, Thou soul-physician, 135:2

Ah, holy and great God, 32:4

Ah, holy and most mighty God, 32:4

Ah, holy Jesu(s), how hast Thou offended, 244:3; 245:27.2

Ah, holy Jesus, how have You offended, 244:3

Ah, how brief, a thing of nothing, 26:1; 26:6

Ah, how cheating, ah, how fleeting, 644

Ah, how cheating, hollow, fleeting, 26:6

Ah, how cheerful a place is my coffin, 157:4b

Ah, how doth ease my heart, 57:2

Ah, how empty; ah, how fleeting, 26:1; 26:6

Ah, how fleeting; ah, how cheating, 26:1

Ah, how fleeting; ah, how empty, 26:1; 26:6

Ah, how fleeting; ah, how fading, 26:1; 26:6

Ah, how fleeting; ah, how futile, 26:1; 26:6; 644

Ah, how fleeting; ah, how invalid, 26:6

Ah, how fleeting; ah, how transitory, 26:1

Ah, how fleeting, frail and cheating 26:1

Ah, how futile, ah, how fleeting, 644

Ah, how hungry is my spirit, 180:3b

Ah, how I long to die at peace, 502

Ah, how I will glory, 146:7

Ah, how inconstant are we all, 73:3

Ah, how my mind hungers, 180:3b

Ah, how perverse our will remains, 73:3

Ah, how pleasant to me is my death-casket, 157:4b

Ah, how Thy comfort sweet restores, 57:2

Ah, how weary; ah, how fleeting, 26:1; 26:6

Ah, human will, perverse art thou, 73:3

Ah, I am a child, 78:3

Ah, I am a sinning child, 78:3

Ah, I have already perceived, 162:6

Ah, I have already witnessed, 162:6

Ah, I see now, as I go, 162:1

Ah, if I now in Heav'n could be, 146:4

Ah, if it could for me now, 95:3
Ah, if it only soon might happen, 249:8b
Ah, if only it could happen soon, 249:8b
Ah, it tastes really very good, 212:4
Ah, Jesu Christ, with us abide, 6:1; 253; 649
Ah, Jesu, comforter, 21:7
Ah, Jesu, dost Thou leave us so soon, 11:3
Ah, Jesu, is Thy going then so near, 11:3
Ah, Jesu, my rest, 21:7
Ah, Jesus Child, my heart's delight 248:9
Ah, Jesus Christ, with us abide 649
Ah, Jesus dear, what precept hast Thou broken, 244:3
Ah, Jesus, is the time of Your departure, 11:3
Ah, Jesus, is Thy parting now so near, 11:3
Ah, Jesus mine, I grieve indeed for Thee, 159:3
Ah, Jesus mine, what agony, 487
Ah, Jesus, must Thou go away so soon, 11:3
Ah, Jesus, my Jesus, no more will I leave, 154:7b
Ah, Jesus, my repose, 21:7
Ah, King of Heaven, 245:27.1
Ah, lay down the Sodom of sinful limbs, 48:4
Ah, lay the Sodom of sinful members, 48:4
Ah, lead me, gracious Lord, 96:4
Ah, lead me, O God, 96:4
Ah, lead Thou me, O God, 96:4
Ah, leave me not, my dearest Savior, 11:4
Ah, leave me not, my dearest treasure, 11:4
Ah, leave us not, beloved Jesu, 11:4
Ah, let us through the stinging lashes, 116:5
Ah, little Jesu, my heart's love, 248:9
Ah, Lord, come Thou soon to us, 249:8b
Ah, Lord, confirm and guide me, 194:12
Ah, Lord, forgive all our guilt, 127:5
Ah, Lord, forgive us all, 127:5
Ah, Lord God, through Thy faithfulness, 101:3
Ah, Lord, how can I hope, 39:6
Ah, Lord, how sad and sick of heart, 44:4
Ah, Lord, how shall I meet Thee, 248:5

Ah, Lord, let this Thine angel dear, 149:7
Ah, Lord, let Thy beloved angels, 149:7
Ah, Lord, let Thy dear angels come, 149:7; 245:68
Ah, Lord, let Thy little angel, 245:68
Ah, Lord, me a poor sinner blame not, 135:1
Ah, Lord, me poor sinner do not punish, 135:1
Ah, Lord, me poor sinner punish not, 135:1
Ah, Lord, my God, forgive me, 113:7
Ah, Lord, my God I come to Thee, 65:7
Ah, Lord, our many sins forgive, 127:5
Ah, Lord, since I am wholly Thine, 92:7a
Ah, Lord, spare Thou this sinner, 135:1
Ah, Lord, teach us, 106:2c
Ah, Lord, what is a child of man, 110:4
Ah, Lord, what then indeed is man, 110:4
Ah, Lord, when comes that final day, 149:7; 245:68
Ah, Lord, when comes that last sad day, 149:7
Ah, Love, thou base deceiver, 203:1
Ah, many deny Thy word and faith, 18:3d
Ah, many word and faith renouncing, 18:3d
Ah, may the sharp rods, 116:5
Ah, may we soon behold in glory, 249:8b
Ah, melt indeed with Thine own radiant love, 164:4
Ah, melt then through Thy love-beam, 164:4
Ah, melt Thou, Lord, with love's hot-burning ray, 164:4
Ah, men deny word and faith, and fall, 18:3d
Ah, might but the hour of dying, 439
Ah, might I reach the heavenly shore 27:4
Ah, mighty God, 35:6
Ah, mighty King, 245:27.1
Ah, Mister Tax Collector, 212:6
Ah, mitigate these cruel purges, 116:5
Ah, mortals, we may not escape it, 198a:2
Ah, my failings sorely grieve me, 78:3
Ah, my heart-beloved little Jesus, 248:9
Ah, my Jesus has gone now, 244:36a
Ah, my mind, where finally willst thou go, 245:19

Ah, my Savior, 248:29
Ah, my Savior, I entreat Thee, 248:39
Ah, my soul, how futile is thy goal, 245:19
Ah, my soul, where wilt thou fly, 245:19
Ah, my soul, whither wilt thou fly 245:19
Ah, now is my Jesu(s) gone, 244:36a
Ah, now is my Savior gone, 244:36a
Ah, now, my God, I fall here thus, 65:7
Ah, now, my God, thus do I fall, 92:7a
Ah, now my Jesus is gone, 244:36a
Ah, now, so will I even, 138:6
Ah, now would I to Heaven go, 146:4
Ah, ought not this most awful day, 70:9
Ah, our own will remains perverse, 73:3
Ah, our will remains perverted, 73:3
Ah, pass Thou not now by me, 23:2
Ah, past all telling is our woe, 116:2
Ah, plant then the spirit of joy, 73:2
Ah, pour Thou yet Thy joyful spirit, 73:2
Ah, powerful God, 35:6
Ah, put off that Sodom, 48:4
Ah, remain with us, Lord Jesus Christ, 6:3
Ah, return again soon; end at last, 11:8
Ah, sad mind, where canst thou comfort find, 245:19
Ah, sanctified and mighty God, 32:4
Ah, Savior mine, 16:4
Ah, shall not this great day, 70:9
Ah, shall not this terrible day, 70:9
Ah, shall not thought of Judgment Day, 70:9
Ah, shallow all man's vain profession, 18:3d
Ah, should not this great day, 70:9
Ah, sleepy soul, 115:2
Ah, slumbering spirit, 115:2
Ah, slumbering watchman, why sleepest thou, 115:2
Ah, some deny Thy word and faith, 18:3d
Ah, some have disavowed Thy doctrine, 18:3d
Ah, sorely dreaded is the call, 116:2
Ah, soul that art drowsy, 115:2
Ah, stay, my dearest life, 11:4
Ah, stay with me, my dearest life, 11:4

Ah, stay with us, Lord Jesus Christ, 6:3; 253
Ah, strike then soon, 95:4
Ah, strike thou then soon, happy hour, 95:4
Ah, strike you now soon, blessed hour, 95:4
Ah, sweet comfort, 138:4
Ah, take flight away from human sight, 245:19
Ah, that a Christian so much, 186:4a
Ah, that a Christian so should for his body care, 186:4a
Ah, that my faith is still, 38:4
Ah, that the curse, 136:2
Ah, there bideth in my loving, 77:5
Ah, there remains in my love, 77:5
Ah, Thine own hand, Thy blessing, 41:3
Ah, think not the Lord delayeth, 263
Ah, this blessed hope revives, 57:2
Ah, this sweet comfort, 57:2
Ah, tidings doubly blessed, 147:2
Ah, today, now today, dearest Father, 211:8
Ah, toll for me now, chimes so mournful, 95:4
Ah, toll for me soon, 95:4
Ah, unspeakable is the misery, 116:2
Ah, unspeakable is the need, 116:2
Ah, we acknowledge all our guilt, 116:4
Ah, we are speechless in our dread, 116:2
Ah, we confess our guilt, 116:4
Ah, well we know our grievous blame, 116:4
Ah, were I but in Heaven now, 146:4
Ah, what a cruel parting, 244:72
Ah, what a precious gift the blessed communion, 180:3a
Ah, what a wav'ring faith is mine, 38:4
Ah, what a wonderful taste coffee has, 211:4
Ah, what am I, a sinner, to do, 259
Ah, what delight to me, 157:4b
Ah, what longing fills my spirit, 180:3b
Ah, what rapture mine at last to gain, 161:3
Ah, what? God clearly careth for the kine, 138:3b
Ah, when comes to us salvation, 248:51
Ah, when on that great day, 70:9
Ah, when shall the time appear, 248:51

Ah, when shall we see, 248:51
Ah, when the last dread hour, 70:3
Ah, when upon that last great day, 70:9
Ah, when will the time, 248:51
Ah, where, 245:48b
Ah, where can I, poor man, 25:3
Ah, where in this sad vale of sorrow, 114:2a
Ah, where shall I, 25:3
Ah, where shall this wretch find help, 25:3
Ah, whither may I fly, 89:6; 646
Ah, who then already in Heaven would be, 146:4
Ah, who were then already in Heaven, 27:4
Ah, who would be already in Heaven, 27:4
Ah, who would dare to smite Thee 245:15.1
Ah, why hast Thou, my God, 21:4
Ah, why such distress, 138:1
Ah, with hunger doth my spirit, 180:3b
Ah, woe, how trembles His tormented heart, 244:25a
Ah, woe is me! How sorely by Thy will, 73:1b
Ah, woe is me, of little faith, 38:4
Ah, woe is me; what grief is mine past measure, 400
Ah, would I were already in Heaven, 146:4
Ah, would I were in Heaven, 27:4
Ah, would that I had a thousand tongues, 69a:2
Ah, would that soon, 95:3
Ah, wounded Head that bearest, 244:21; 244:63.1
Ah, ye who sinneth daily, 122:2
Ah, yea, my heart will ever cherish, 248:32
Ah, yes, I hold to Jesus closely, 157:4a
Ah, yes, so come Thou soon again, 11:8
Aid to praise God's goodness, 613
The air? A dirge, 210:7
Alack, I know how weak is man, 30:9
Alas, at righteous men the evil rabble, 70:6
Alas, come soon again to us, 11:8
Alas, dear Lord, what evil hast Thou done 244:3
Alas, dear Lord, what law, 245:7

Alas, dear Lord, what law then hast Thou broken, 244:3; 244:55
Alas, for the soul that no longer recognizes, 102:3
Alas, Golgotha, hapless Golgotha, 244:69
Alas, how heavy is the care, 124:4
Alas, I had forsaken thee, 103:6
Alas, my God, 48:3; 692; 692a; 693; 714
Alas, my God, my sins are great 255
Alas, my heart is bathed in tears, 244:18
Alas, my Jesus now is gone, 244:36a
Alas, my Jesus now is taken 244:33a
Alas, now is my Savior gone 244:36a
Alas, our human will is still corrupt, 73:3
Alas, our Princess lies in death, 198:5
Alas, the town were Neisse flows, 216:2
Alas, what grievous toil and woe, 124:4
Alas, when my sad heart reflects, 113:3
Alas, where shall I Jesus seek, 154:2
Alive today, today repent, 102:7
All beings now are under Thee, 454
All breathing life, sing and praise ye the Lord 225:5
All care and doubt defying, 108:2
All darkness flies before Thy face 248:46
All depends on our possessing, 263
All Earth doth sound Thy praises, 16:6
All earthly power doth pass away, 188:4
All enemies are in Thy hand, 178:1
All evil deeds begin with Satan, 54:3
All expect of Thee that Thou give them, 187:1
All eyes wait, Lord, Thou Almighty God, 23:3
All foes to humble, destruction to deal them, 215:7
All generations, 243:4
All glories of Earth gladly I forgo, 47:5
All glorious doth the day-star shine, 1:1
All glory be to God, 192:3
All glory be to God most high, 117:1
All glory be to God on high, 260; 662; 663; 663a; 664; 664a; 675; 676; 676a; 677; 711; 715; 716; 717; 771; A48

All glory, laud, and honor, 29:8; 245:52; 415

All glory, laud, and praise be giv'n, 106:4a

All glory, might, and blessing 29:8

All glory, praise, and blessing, 29:8; 51:4

All glory, praise and honor, 415

All glory, praise(s), and majesty, 106:4a

All glory, thanks, and blessing, 167:5

All glory to our God, 117:2b

All glory to the Father, 135:6; 382

All glory to the Lord, eternal God, 129:4

All glory to the Lord of Lords, 117:1; 251

All glory to the Lord, our comfort, 129:3

All glory to the Lord, our God, 129:1

All glory to the Lord, the God, 129:2

All glory to the sov'reign good, 117:1

All glory to Thee, Jesus Christ, 91:1

All glory, worship, thanks, and praise, 248:23

All good gifts are in His hand, 16:3b

All gracious God, 244:60

All hail, 244:62b

All hail! Right honored guests, 30a:10

All hail, the new regime, 71:7

All hail, Thou, heart's delight, 36:5

All hail! Thy name shall all alone, 248:40a

All He who doth search the heart knows, 226:3

All hearts are moved, 202:4

All hearts with joy are filled, 36b:4

All heavens rejoice, the glad earth and all, 31:2

All Highest, make Your gifts anew, 51:3

All Highest, renew Thy favors, 51:3

All honor, laud and glory be, 6:6; 121:6; 153:9.1; 248:21; 326; 327

All honor, praise, and blessing, 29:8

All honor, praise, and glory, 51:4

All human will and might, 126:3

All I long for, all my heart's desire, 161:3

All is but borrowed wealth, 168:2

All is fulfilled 245:58

All joyous I, this day to die, 82:5

All laud and praise with honor, 28:6; 29:8; 51:4; 167:5

All mankind alike must die, 643

All mankind fell in Adam's fall, 18:5

All men alike must die, 643

All men born of God our Father, 80:2a

All men living are but mortal, 643

All men must die, 262; 643

All men's eyes, 23:3

All must be as God doth will it, 72:1

All my days, Lord, I adore Thee, 25:6

All my days, O God, I'll praise Thee 25:6

All my days which pass in sadness, 150:7

All my failings and misdoing, 168:3

All my heart doth ask of Heaven, 108:5

All my heart this night rejoices, 248:33; 422

All my heart today rejoices, 248:33; 422

All my hope is in the Lord, 93:6

All my life from Jesus springeth, 490

All my life shall be employed, 25:6

All my tears, 244:61

All my thoughts to Heav'n are turning, 166:2

All one gets from plaguey daughters 211:2

All only according to God's will, 72:1

All our joy is turned to sadness, 26:3

All people at this hour, 479

All people sing Thy praises, 16:6; 28:6

All people that on Earth do dwell, 130:6.2; 326

All praise and glory with honor, 51:4

All praise and thanks to God, 192:3

All praise and thanks to God most high, 117:1; 251

All praise be to God, 30:3

All praise, Lord Jesus Christ, to Thee, 314

All praise to God enthroned on high, 33:6

All praise to highest Heaven, 135:6

All praise to Jesus' hallowed name, 91:1; 91:6; 314; 604; 697; 722; 722a; 723

All praise to Thee, eternal God, 604; 697; 722; 722a; 723

All praise to Thee, O Jesus Christ, 64:2

All praise to Thy great merit, 135:6

All praises to the Lord, 129:1

All ready was she for death's coming, 198:6

All such things of Thy goodness, 28:6

All such Thy goodness we praise, 16:6

All temporal praise would I glad forsake, 47:5

All the skies tonight sing o'er us, 248:33

All that hath life and breath, 190:1b

All that hath life and breath, praise ye the Lord, 225:5

All that hath life now give praise, 63:5

All that He has done for us, 91:6

All that I call mine own, 168:2

All that I have and all I am, 72:2c

All that is by God created, 80:2a

All that of God is born, 80:2a

All that which breath doth own, 190:1b

All that which of God is fathered, 80:2a

All they from Saba shall come, 65:1

All things are by God ordained, 72:1

All things are Thine, 332

All things but as God is willing, 72:1

All things move as God doth will them, 72:1

All things move as God hath made them 263

All things now lie beneath Thy throne, 11:6

All things now that ye wish, 24:3

All things that live and breathe, 190:1b

All things that live and breathe, sing to the Lord, 225:5

All things, then, 24:3

All things wait for Thee, 187:1

All things wait on our possessing, 263

All things wait upon Thee, 187:1

All this did He for us freely, 64:2; 91:6

All this for us did Jesus do, 64:2; 91:6

All this for us He has done, 64:2

All this for us our God hath done, 64:2; 91:6

All this hath He done for us 248:28

All this He did that He might prove, 64:2; 91:6

All this He has done for us, 248:28

All this He hath for us achieved, 91:6

All this our God for us hath done, 91:6

All Thy goodness, all Thy mercy, 189:5

All thy sins will be forgiven, 31:6

All uncharted is the country, 188:3

All ye righteous, joyful praise, 195:1b

All ye stars and winds of Heaven, 248:53; 366; 476

All ye stars, ye winds of heaven, 476

All ye thoughts and all ye senses, 110:2

All ye with breath in ye, praise ye the Lord, 225:5

Alleluia: *see also* Hallelujah

Alleluia, 143:7a; 230:2

Alleluia, alleluia, 51:5

Alleluia, alleluia, all praise to God, 110:7

Alleluia, alleluia, alleluia, 66:6

Alleluia, alleluia, give praise to God, 110:7

Alleluia, alleluia, give thanks to God, 110:7

Alleluia! Alleluia! Hearts to Heaven, 453

Alleluia, alleluia, praise be to God, 110:7

Alleluia, alleluia, praised be God, 110:7

Alleluia, alleluia, sing thanks to God, 110:7

Alleluia, fairest morning, 248:53

Alleluia, give praise to our God, 142:8

Alleluia, oh, praised be God, 142:8

Alleluia! Power and might, 29:3; 29:7

Alleluia, praise be unto God, 142:8

All's well, for Jesus now awakes, 81:6

All's well; guards us from disaster, 67:6b

All's well; Jesus guards us, 67:6b

Almighty, continue to renew Your kindness, 51:3

The Almighty Father, 232:13b

Almighty God, continue to make Thy goodness, 51:3

Almighty God forgets us not, 188:2a

Almighty God, I Thee obey, 32:4

Almighty God, look graciously, 63:7

Almighty God, may this Thy tender love, 149:5

Almighty God, preserve us still, 225:3

Almighty God, Thy word endue with might, 34a:7

Almighty God will send a golden era, 134a:6

Almighty God's divine abode, 198a:8a

The Almighty Lord our God remain, 120a:7

Almighty, send on all who love Thee, 181:5

The Almighty's will, 45:2

Almost has thou persuaded me, 205:6
Almost my will thou hast persuaded, 205:6
Alone in Jesus' hands paternal, 114:2b
Alone in Thee, Lord Jesu Christ, 33:6; 261
Alone in Thee, Lord Jesus Christ, 33:1, 261
Alone on Thee, Lord Jesu Christ, 33:1
Alone Thy Father's fond affection, 114:2b
Alone to Jesu's Father-hands, 114:2b
Alone to Jesus I'll commend me, 114:2b
Alone to Thee, Lord Jesus Christ, 33:1
Already within my soul I feel, 76:11
Also with subdued weak voices, 36:7
Although among us is sin abundant, 38:6
Although, beloved Musica, 210a:5
Although both heart and eyes o'erflow, 244:18
Although from Hell Satan would place, 107:4
Although I have not Peter's boldness, 68:3
Although I have strayed from Thee, 244:48
Although I have turned aside from Thee, 55:5
Although in tears dissolves my heart, 244:18
Although inconstancy in man has been his curse, 30:9
Although mine eyes with tears o'erflow, 244:18
Although my broken voice, 51:2b
Although my heart in tears, 244:18
Although my heart swims in tears, 244:18
Although my needs be sore, 89:6
Although our eyes with tears o'erflow, 244:18
Although our falt'ring lips, 51:2b
Although our feeble tongues, 51:2b
Although our feeble voice(s), 51:2b
Although our sin be great, 38:6
Although our souls for Heav'n are yearning, 70:4
Although soon from Hell's cavern, 107:4
Although the fools say with their mouth, 308
Although the mouths are feeble, 51:2b
Although the wicked world may persecute, 58:2

Although yearning for Heaven, our life, 70:4
Always, whenever I am rejected, 52:3
Am I not to sing to my God, 413
Ambitious, men contrive and plan, 207:3
Amen, amen, 61:6a; 196:5b; 232:20b
Amen at ev'ry hour I'll say, 148:6
Amen! I cleave to Thee though earth and sky, 197a:4
Amen! Jesus with us fighting, 67:6b
Amen. Laud and honor, A160:3
Amend your ways while yet you may, 102:7
Amidst these pains of grief, 199:5
Amusement and mirth, 197:8
The ancient dragon raging lurks, 130:3
The ancient law departs, 878
The ancient serpent burns with spite, 130:3
And a superscription also was, 246:63
And abiding in the field, 248:11
And after making sport of Him, 244:64
And after that they had mocked Him, 244:64
And after they had mocked Him, 244:64
And after they had worshipped Him, 11:9
And after this, Joseph, 245:66
And after this there came Joseph, 245:66
And again He came and found them sleeping, 244:32
And all His acquaintance, 246:75
And although all devils Thee would withstand, 153:5
And although inconstancy, 30:9
And although usually the inconstancy, 30:9
And are you so bold as now, 201:2
And are you thus so bold, 201:2
And as eight days were past, 248:37
And as the angels went from them, 248:25
And as the angels were gone, 248:25
And as they led Him away, 246:57
And as they looked at Him, 11:7
And as they watched Him going heavenwards, 11:7
And as they were eating, 244:17
And as Thou, Lord, hast said, 171:5
And as thy days, so shall thy strength be, 71:3

And ask that Thou shouldst ever wish, 130:6.2

And became incarnate, 232:15

And before their eyes He was taken, 11:5

And behold, He rose, 11:5

And behold, one of them, 244:34

And behold, the veil of the temple, 244:73a; 245:61

And being in an agony, 246:26

And being warned of God, 248:60

And bide, my God, in me, 148:5

And bowed down His head, 245:59

And even if the world were full of devils, 80:5

And even though the fickle heart, 30:9

And forget not to show us, 29:6

And from that hour, 245:57

And from that time, 245:57

And from the sixth hour there was, 244:71a

And from then on, 245:57

And gather'd he together all the chiefs, 248:50

And gathering together all the chief priests, 248:50

And God spoke to them in a dream, 248:60

And grant me, Lord, to do, 45:7

And hast Thou, Lord, not said, 171:5

And He answered and said, 244:17

And He bowed His head, 245:59

And He came again and found them sleeping, 244:32

And He came and found them asleep again, 244:32

And He came to His disciples, 244:30

And He came to. the disciples, 244:30

And he cast down the pieces of silver, 244:50

And he cast down the silver pieces, 244:50

And He cometh unto the disciples, 244:30

And he gathered together all the chief priests, 248:50

And he promised, and sought, 246:6

And He said, Go into the city, 244:15a

And He said unto them, 246:43c; 246:45a; 246:55e

And He shall Israel deliver, 131:5b

And He shall redeem Israel, 131:5b

And he shall show you a large upper room, 246:10

And He that searcheth the hearts, 226:3

And he took it down, 246:77

And He was visibly raised, 11:5

And He was withdrawn from them, 246:24

And He went a little farther, 244:27

And He went yet farther, 244:27

And He will redeem Israel, 131:5b

And his gracious lady, 212:11

And His mercy is from generation, 243:6

And His mercy is on them (those), 243:6

And how? How may I well discern, 213:2

And I appoint to you a kingdom, 246:20

And I appoint unto you a kingdom, 246:20

And I await the resurrection, 232:20a

And I believe in the Holy Ghost, 232:18

And I look for the resurrection, 232:20a

And I look forward to the resurrection, 232:20a

And I were the lady so fair, 212:17

And if a longer life, 71:2b

And if Christ be in you, 227:8

And if man's feeble notes, 51:2b

And if the world were full of devils, 80:5

And if Thou wish me not to suffer, 156:5

And in Earth peace, 232:4b

And in Him we die at His good time, 106:2b

And in one Lord, 232:14

And in our souls take up Thy rest, 631; 631a

And in the evening of that very Sabbath, 42:2

And in the Holy Ghost, 232:18

And in those same days it came to pass, 248:2

And it came to pass, as the angels were gone, 248:25

And it came to pass at this time, 248:2

And it came to pass in those days, 248:2

And it came to pass, the veil of the temple, 244:73a

And it came to pass, when Jesus, 244:2

And it was about the sixth hour, 246:69
And Jesus, perceiving it, 244:8
And Jesus said to him, 246:67
And Jesus said unto him, 246:67
And Joseph took the body, 244:76a
And kingly pilgrims, long foretold, 65:2
And last, since Thou didst, Lord, 119:8
And lead us not into temptation, 246:35
And let that be enough, 212:21
And likewise also did the chief priests, 244:67c
And likewise also the chief priests, 244:67c
And lo, all Christendom the love of God, 76:13
And many other things, 246:43a
And many women were there, 244:73c
And meanwhile, sighing, we here burn, 249:8a
And mindful of His mercy, 10:5
And mine eyes shall look to Him, 150:6
And my spirit hath rejoiced, 243:2
And my spirit rejoices, 243:2
And ne'er suppose, ye godless, 46:4
And now, behold the happy father, 211:9
And now behold, the veil of the temple, 244:73a
And now I ask you all, 212:11
And now I think we've had enough, 212:21
And now, my Lord, I come to Thee, 65:7
And now our little play is done, 211:10
And now the Lord is laid to rest, 244:77a
And now the Lord to rest is laid, 244:77a
And now the Paschal Lamb see, 4:6
And now the Paschal Victim see, 4:6
And now 'tis time to go, 212:22
And now to search goes forth, 211:9
And now, when they had sung a hymn, 244:20
And on Earth peace, 191:1b; 232:4b; 234:2b
And on the same day were Pilate and Herod, 246:53
And one of the malefactors, 246:65
And one of them when he saw, 17:4
And others care but for their wine, 18:3e

And our gracious mistress, 212:11
And our right worthy dame, 212:11
And peace on Earth, 232:4b
And Peter remembered, 246:38
And Peter remembered the word, 245:18
And Peter then began to curse and to swear, 244:46b
And Pilate asked Him, 246:45e
And Pilate said to them, 244:76d; 245:37
And Pilate said unto Him, 245:28
And Pilate saith unto them, 245:37
And Pilate then answered them, 245:51,
And Pilate then set Barabbas free, 244:59e
And Pilate thus made answer, 245:37
And she brought forth her first-born son, 248:6
And shouldst Thou will me not to perish, 156:5
And show your neighbor, too, 169:6
And Simon Peter followed, 245:12
And since in my mind, 131:4b
And since Thou, Lord, hast said, 171:5
And since Thou, Lord, hath said, 171:5
And so, as pilgrims here we wander, 198a:9b
And so, as Thou, O Lord, 119:8
And so come forth, 194:11
And so, dear Lord, I Thee entreat, 111:6
And so I live, 84:5
And so Love also seeks, 202:4
And so Love seeks also, 202:4
And so may the bond of pure love, 202:8
And so, my God, I come to Thee, 65:7; 92:7a
And so my heart and my mouth, 45:6
And so my soul may rest content, 150:3
And so our sin(s) will fall asleep, 244:26b
And so shall thy light ever break forth, 39:1b
And so that you all know, 212:22
And so through all my mortal days, 112:5
And so throughout my length of days, 112:5
And so throughout my mortal days, 112:5
And so we sob and sigh and pray to God, 249:8a
And some lead lives of gluttony, 18:3e

And still did he deny with cursing, 244:46b
And straightway one, 244:71d
And suddenly appeared with the angel, 248:20
And suddenly there was with the angel(s), 248:20
And surely, who e'er on Thee trusteth, 176:4b
And that same day, when evening had fallen, 42:2
And that same day, when the evening had fallen, 42:2
And the angel said, 248:13
And the angel spoke, 248:13
And the chief priests, 246:51
And the governor said, 244:56
And the high priest answered and said, 244:42a
And the high priest gave Him answer, 244:42a
And the Lord, after He had spoken, 43:4
And the Lord, as soon as He had spoken, 43:4
And the Lord, once that He amongst them, 43:4
And the Lord said, 246:22a
And the Lord, so soon as He had these words, 43:4
And the men that held Jesus, 246:41a
And the same day Pilate and Herod, 246:53
And the shepherds hastened, 248:30
And the shepherds returned, 248:34
And the soldiers also mocked Him, 246:61c
And the soldiers plaited, 245:33
And the third day He rose, 232:17
And the whole multitude, 246:45c
And the Wise Men, when they heard the king, 248:58
And then began he to curse and to swear, 244:46b
And then behold, the veil, 245:61
And then behold, the veil of the temple, 244:73a
And then did he begin to curse and to swear, 244:46b

And then did the soldiers, 245:53
And then did the soldiers of the governor, 244:62a
And then did they spit in His face, 244:43a
And then did they that laid hold on Jesus, 244:37
And then he delivered Him, 245:47
And then he spake the third time, 246:55e
And then I will many hunters send, 88:1b
And then it is Love, 202:4
And then shall thy light, 39:1b
And then the four soldiers, 245:53
And then with their hands, 245:35
And there appeared an angel, 246:26
And there crucified they Him, 245:49
And there she brought forth her first-born son, 248:6
And there they crucified Him, 245:49
And there was also a strife, 246:18
And there was written over Him, 246:63
And there were in the same country, 248:11
And there were many women there, 244:73c
And there were shepherds, 248:11
And thereafter, I will send out many hunters, 88:1b
And thereafter I'll send hunters, 88:1b
And thereafter send for many a hunter, 88:1b
And thereafter will I many hunters, 88:1b
And thereupon they prayed to Him, 11:9
And they all grew very sad, 244:15b
And they came with haste, 248:30
And they crucified Him there, 245:49
And they grew exceeding sad, 244:15b
And they parted His raiment, 246:61a
And they smote Him with their hands, 245:35
And they that had laid hold of Jesus, 244:37
And they that had laid hold on Jesus, 244:37
And they that laid hold on Jesus, 244:37
And they took counsel, 244:52
And they were exceeding(ly) sorrowful, 244:15b
And they were glad, 246:4
And they were the more fierce, 246:49a

And they, when they had heard the king, 248:58

And they who had so laid hold on Jesus, 244:37

And they worshipped Him and returned, 11:9

And this happy course of life, 197:9

And this is good fortune, 202:6

And this is the good fortune, 202:6

And this is the happiness, 202:6

And this is the sign to you, 248:16

And this joyful life will continue, 197:9

And this shall be a sign to (unto) you, 248:16

And this thy happy course of life, 197:9

And this you will have for a sign, 248:16

And though I wander in darkness' vale, 112:3

And though I wander in death's dark vale, 112:3

And though I wander in the dark valley, 112:3

And though now all the devils, 153:5

And though with muted, feeble voices, 36:7

And three kingly pilgrims, 65:2

And thus at peace with God I'm living, 84:5

And thus I live in God at peace, 84:5

And thus, through all my earthly days, 112:5

And too are wisdom and judgment, 92:4

And too, our gracious dame, 212:11

And unto Israel forgiveness, 131:5b

And unto Israel redemption, 131:5b

And was crucified also, 232:16

And was crucified for us, 232:16

And was incarnate(d), 232:15

And was lifted up manifestly, 11:5

And went a little farther, 244:27

And were the world with devils filled, 80:5

And what is that to us, 244:49b

And what the ever gracious God, 86:3

And what the everlastingly good God, 86:3

And when at last Death sounds his call, 219:5.2

And when eight days were accomplished, 248:37

And when eight days were fulfilled, 248:37

And when he had gathered all the chief priests, 248:50

And when He rose up from prayer, 246:28

And when Herod the king heard it, 248:48

And when in thiswise they were come, 244:67a

And when Jesus had cried, 246:71

And when Joseph had taken, 244:76a

And when Pilate heard, 245:43

And when Pilate heard of Galilee, 246:49c

And when Pilate heard that, 245:39

And when Pilate saw that all, 244:59c

And when the angels had departed, 248:25

And when the angels were gone, 248:25

And when the centurion saw, 246:73

And when the cruel stroke of death, 124:3

And when the dreaded stroke of death, 124:3

And when the fatal blow of death, 124:3

And when the hard death-stroke, 124:3

And when the hard stroke of death, 124:3

And when the king had gathered all the scribes, 248:50

And when the morning came, 244:49a

And when the soldiers had plaited, 245:33

And when they came unto a place, 244:67a

And when they had heard the king, 248:58

And when they had kindled a fire, 246:36

And when they had sung a(n) hymn, 244:20

And when they saw which were about Him, 246:32a

And when they were come to a place, 244:67a

And when they were come unto a place, 244:67a

And while He yet spake, 246:30

And while they looked steadfastly, 11:7

And while they looked up steadfastly, 11:7

And whither? Where is the right path, 213:2

And why are you thus shaken, 248:49

And why are* thou, my soul, 8:2

And why art thou, my soul, 8:2

And willst Thou, that I shall not be ill, 156:5

And wilt thou, cruel Aeolus, 205:8

And wilt Thou pardon, Lord, 878

And with that—enough, 212:21

And yet amid this unmannerly generation, 70:6

And yet amidst this savage generation, 70:6

And yet, enchanting melody, 210a:5

And yet, O Lord, my spirit knows no calm, 67:5

And yet thou must, O sinner, 46:4

And your hearts shall evermore flourish, 75:1b

Anew I dedicate myself to Him, 31:5

The angel band, who did from man of old, 122:3

The angel choir, which once avoided us, 122:3

The angel hosts give thanks to Thee, 117:2a

The angelic host from Heaven came down, 607

The angels all who did before shun you, 122:3

Angels at the Savior's birth, 262

The angels, who previously shunned you, 122:3

The angels, who themselves formerly from you, 122:3

An angry judge thou need not fear, 127:4d

Another heeds alone his paunch, 18:3e

The appearance of heinous sins, 54:2

Appeared is now the glorious day, 67:4

Appeared is the glorious day, 67:4

Appeasement of Aeolus, 205

Approve, Lord, my endeavor, 194:12

Approve my works when shown Thee, 194:12

Are lightning and thunder, 244:33c

Are my weeping and my wailing, 244:61

Are not Thine eyes, Lord, fixed on perfection, 102:1a

Are you so bold as now, 201:2

Arise, arise and shine, 878

Arise, arise, the moment now is here, 440

Arise, arise, the time, 440

Arise, away with care and sadness, 110:6

Arise, believers; sing lovely songs, 134:2

Arise my brothers, this day is holy, 479,

Arise, my soul, thy Savior comes, 180:2

Arise, my soul, thy voice employ, 248:46

Arise, O daughter of Jerusalem, 46:2

Arise, O Lord, our God, 332

Arise thee now, thy Savior knocks, 180:2

Around God's throne in Heaven, 309

Around Thy tomb here sit we weeping, 244:78

Arouse thee, O halting and timorous spirt, 176:5

Arouse thee, then, my soul, 31:5

Arouse thee, thou timid and fainthearted spirit, 176:5

Arouse thyself, my feeble spirit, 454,

Arouse thyself, thy Savior knocks, 180:2

Art Thou Christus? Tell it us, 246:43b

Art Thou He who bring'st relief, 186:3

Art Thou He who shall help me, 186:3

Art Thou, Lord Jesus, from Heaven to Earth now, 650

Art thou not also one of His disciples, 245:17

Art thou not one of His disciples, 245:17

Art Thou the Christ? Tell us, 246:43b

Art Thou then Son of God, 246:43d

Art Thou then the Son of God, 246:43d

Art truly Christ's, thy will alway submitting, 72:2a

As a bird at dawning singeth, 32:6; 70:7; 154:3

As a father has mercy on his little children, 17:7

As a father has taken pity, 225:2

As a father is merciful, 225:2

As a father pities his small children, 17:7

As a father takes pity, 17:7; 225:2

As any father pities, 225:2

As are thy days, so shall thy strength be, 71:3

As cat for mouse is on the watch, 211:10

As doth the hart, 148:3

As fades the daylight splendor, 244:16; 392

As far as the full banks of the Vistula, 198:9b

As far as Thou hast allotted excellent peace, 41:4

As far as Thou hast decided noble peace, 41:4

As far the brimming Vistula, 198:9b

As fast as rushing waters gush, 26:2

As from your infancy, 197:7

As God has watched and cared, 197:7

As hath a father mercy for all, 17:7

As he promised to our forefathers, 243:11

As He spake to our fathers, 243:11

As He spoke to our fathers (forefathers), 243:11

As head and members belong, 31:7

As here today, O honored Hennicke, 30a:4

As I stand in God's good graces, 503

As in a vision bright, 43:9

As it was in the beginning, 191:3; 243:12b

As it was written in the Holy Scriptures, 9:4

As long as God eternal reigns, 20:7

As long as there's a drop of blood, 124:2

As long as yet a drop of blood, 124:2

As members by the head are guided, 31:7

As mice to cats, the coffee craze, 211:10

As often as I my tobacco pipe, 515

As Peter once, I'll not now boast, 68:3

As quick to pass as lightest summer, 166:4

As quickly as rushing water gushes (shoots), 26:2

As silver's in the furnace tried, 2:5

As sure as day follows night, 30:9

As sure as I live, my maker saith, 102:7

As swift as rushing waters flow, 26:2

As swift as water's mad career, 26:2

As swift in channels waters whirl, 26:2

As the hart panteth, 148:3

As the hart pants, 148:3

As the hart with eager yearning, 32:6

As the Lord Christ was at supper, 285

As the rain and snow fall from heaven, 18:2

As the rain and the snow come down from heaven, 18:2

As Thou, O Lord, with peace hast blest us, 41:4

As to thee bides My heart's devotion, 49:5b

As true as I live, says thy God, 102:7

As we are members all of Christ, 31:7

As we were members all of Christ, 31:7

As willed the Three: Father, Son and Holy Ghost, 291; 520

As with gladness men of old, 384

As your years are multiplying, 36c:9

Ascension Day Oratorio, 11

Assail my fainting heart, 8:3

Assert Thy power with all speed, 6:6

Assurance will my faith afford me, 37:2

Assured is Heaven now to me, 64:6

At even, hour of calm and rest, 244:74

At even, sweet, cool hour of rest, 244:74

At evening, hour of calm and peace (rest), 244:74

At evening, when it was cool, 244:74

At eventide, cool hour of rest, 244:74

At last, at last my yoke, 56:3

At last, at last will my yoke fall, 56:3

At last, beloved Savior mine, 248:3

At living waters, crystal clear, 112:2

At that feast the gov'nor, 244:54a

At the Lamb's high feast we sing, 262; 355

At the manger stand I, 469

At the rivers of Babylon, 653; 653a; 653b

At the side of Your tomb, 247:132

At the supper, Christ the Lord, 373

At this painful repentance, 199:5

At Thy right hand on high, 128:5

Attend, my loyal subjects, 205:2

Augustus' birthday brilliant breaketh, 207a:3

Augustus guards our pleasant pastures, 207a:6

Augustus guards the pastures, 207a:6

Augustus protects the fertile fields, 207a:6

Augustus protects the happy fields, 207a:6

Augustus' welfare, 207a:4

Authority is God's endowment, 119:5

Authority proceeds from Heaven, 119:5

Avert from us, Lord, Thou faithful God, 101:7

Awake, all ye people, 15:5

Awake, awake, poor wandering mortal, 20:8
Awake, awake! the watchman calls, 140:1
Awake, awake, ye sheep that wander, 20:8
Awake, awake, ye souls unnumbered, 20:8
Awake! cries to us the voice, 140:1
Awake, my fainting soul, 43:11.2
Awake, my heart, and sing, 194:12
Awake, my heart; be roused from sloth, 268
Awake, my heart, rejoicing, 194:12
Awake, my heart, with gladness (joy), 441,
Awake, my powers and all within me, 110:6
Awake, my soul, and sing ye, 194:12
Awake, my soul, thy maker praising, 110:6
Awake the sound of harp and string, 36:4
Awake! the voice is calling to us, 140:1;
140:7
Awake! the voice of watchmen calls us, 140:1
Awake thou wintry earth, 129:5
Awake us, Lord, and hasten, 22:5; 96:6;
132:6; 164:6
Awake us, Lord, we pray Thee, 22:5; 96:6;
132:6; 164:6
Awake us Lord, we pray to Thee, 96:6
Awake, ye senses consecrated to God, 480
Awake ye souls; this is the day, 248:46
Awake, ye veins and ye limbs, 110:6
Awaken! calls to us the voice, 140:1
Awaken, happy heart, 441
Away: *see also* 'Way
Away, all you that work evil, 135:5
Away and gone is sweet contentment,
198a:3a
Away, away with Him, 245:44
Away, begone, idolatrous band, 76:5
Away has flown the peace of Eden, 198a:3a
Away, idolatrous tribe, 76:5
Away lamentation, affliction and terror,
66:1b
Away, my heart, with the thoughts, 19:7;
25:6; 30:6; 32:6; 39:7; 194:6
Away now, away now, ye winds wildly whirl-
ing, 201:1
Away now, my heart, haste away from the
world, 124:5

Away now with lessons, 209:5
Away then led they Jesus, 245:22
Away, then, with dismal repining, 209:5
Away then, ye cares that so vainly beset me,
8:4
Away, thou world of fleeting pleasure, 64:3
Away with all earthly treasure, 227:7
Away with all riches (treasures), 227:7
Away with care, O troubled mortal, 103:5
Away with Him, away (crucify), 245:44
Away with sorrow, 187:5b
Away with this man, 246:55b
Away with your sadness and hesitance, 209:5
Away, ye forebodings and fearing, 209:5
The awful aftermath of Adam's base, 165:2
Awful thought of endless doom, 36:8
Ay, what then has been His wrong, 246:54

B

A Babe is born in Bethlehem, 603,
Back, back, winged winds, 205:11
Ballads sung with sweet devotion, 210:2;
210a:2
The band then, together, 245:10
Banish fear and sadness, 227:11
Banish fears and forebodings, 209:5
Banish, Lord, all preaching, 2:3
The banquet now is spread, 49:3a
Barabbas, 244:54c
Barabbas he set free, a robber, 245:30
Barabbas was a thief, 245:30
Be ashamed, O spirit not, 147:3
Be at pains in this time, soul, 185:3
Be at peace with yourself, 510; 511; 512
Be calm, though the serpent's tongue, 244:41
Be cheerful, my spirit, 55:5
Be comforted, 72:3
Be comforted; a holy body, 133:2
Be comforted, my heart, 153:7
Be comforted, ye troubled spirits, 103:5
Be concerned within this life, 185:3
Be content, 210a:10

Be content and be silent, 315; 460; 510; 511; 512

Be content now, my spirit, 21:9

Be contented, O my soul, 155:1

Be contented once more, my soul, 21:9

Be dumb, sweet music; cease ye, 198:3

Be dumb, ye gentle strings, 198:3

Be faithful; all pain, 12:6

Be faithful; all suffering, 12:6

Be faithful; every woe, 12:6

Be fearful, ye hardened sinners, 70:2

Be fortunate, noble pair, 210:10

Be fortune e'er lucky, 208:15

Be frightened not, my heart, 111:2

Be frightened, O my bosom, not, 111:2

Be frightened, O ye stubborn sinners, 70:2

Be frightened yet, 102:5

Be glad, 133:2

Be glad, and sing how Christ your king, 248:35

Be glad, my heart, for now all pain, 151:2

Be glad, my heart, thy Savior calls, 180:2

Be glad, my soul, 55:5; 146:8; 154:3; 244:48

Be glad now, all ye Christian men, 388; 734; 734a; 755

Be glad, O my spirit, be glad, 21:10

Be glad; rejoice, 184:3

Be glad the while that your Savior, 248:35

Be glory and praise with honor, 167:5

Be glory, praise, and honor, 29:8; 51:4; 167:5; 231

Be gone, then, evermore, 123:6

Be happy; God has thought of you, 134:3

Be His, my soul, for ever, 13:6; 44:7; 97:9

Be honor, praise and glory, 167:5

Be joyful, glad and gay, 243:14

Be joyful meanwhile that our Savior, 248:35

Be joyful now, my heart, 151:2

Be joyful; sing praise to your king, 248:35

Be joyful then, all ye elected, 184:3

Be laud and praise and honor to God, 51:4

Be laud and praise with honor, 167:5

Be lively now; thy Savior knocks, 180:2

Be loyal; all torment, 12:6

Be my weeping and my wailing unavailing, 244:61

Be near me, Lord, when dying, 244:72

Be not afraid, 153:3

Be not afraid, for I am near, 228

Be not afraid, for I am with thee, 228

Be not annoyed, O my soul, 186:1

Be not ashamed, O soul, 147:3

Be not disheartened, 315

Be not cast down when He delays, 9:7; 155:5

Be not dismayed, fear not, thou ailing spirit, 99:3

Be not dismayed, for I am near, 228

Be not dismayed; I am with thee, 153:3

Be not dismayed, my heart, 111:2

Be not so sad, my soul, 384

Be not solicitous therefore, 187:4

Be not troubled, 489

Be not troubled, O my heart, 384

Be not troubled, O soul, 186:1

Be now again contented, my soul, 21:9

Be now again satisfied, my soul, 21:9

Be now once more contented, O my spirit, 21:9

Be of courage; hope on ever, 155:2

Be of good cheer, good Christians all, 114:1

Be of good comfort, Christians all, 114:1

Be patient; for that delightful day, 30:11

Be patient; the long expected day, 30:11

Be pleased, exalted chieftain, 215:8

Be praise and honor to the Highest Good, 117:1

Be praised now, O Lord Jesus, 41:1

Be quiet, towering sea, 81:5

Be quieted and contented, 460

Be silent, all good people, 211:1

Be silent, army of Hell, 5:5

Be silent; do not chat, 211:1

Be silent; do not talk, 211:1

Be silent, flutes; be silent tones, 210:6

Be silent, host of Hell, 5:5

Be silent, hounds of Hell, 5:5

Be silent, just be silent, staggering reason, 178:6

Be silent; not a word, 211:1
Be silent now, tottering reason, 178:6
Be silent, silent all, 211:1
Be silent; stop chattering, 211:1
Be silent, thou raging ocean, 81:5
Be silent, you flutes, 210:6
Be steadfast, ev'ry pain, 12:6
Be steadfast in your faith, 443
Be steadfast, sure of purpose, 244:53; 247:67; 270; 271; 272; A79
Be still, and wait on God's good pleasure, 93:3
Be still, towering ocean, 81:5
Be still, ye lovely lyres, 198:3
Be still, yea if lying lips assail, 244:41
Be strong; endure, if ye be reproached, 244:41
Be sure that awful time will come, 307
Be Thee greeted, 768
Be therefore never troubled, 187:4
Be thou content, and repose, 510; 511; 512
Be thou content, my soul, 510; 511; 512
Be thou content, my soul; never fear, 460
Be thou contented, 510; 511; 512
Be Thou exalted, O my God, 438
Be Thou hailed, O Christ, my treasure, 499
Be Thou our guide and beacon light, 225:4
Be thou true, 12:6
Be Thou welcome, gentle Jesus, 768
Be thou with me, 508
Be Thou with them, 508
Be very quiet and don't talk, 211:1
Be wakeful, ye heavenly watchmen, 149:6
Be wakeful, you holy watchers, 149:6
Be watchful, O ye holy watchmen, 149:6
Be watchful, ye guardian angels, 149:6
Be watchful, you holy watchmen, 149:6
Be welcome, O Jesus, 499
Be welcome, thou great angel, 27:3
Be ye true; all your pain, 12:6
Be yours the path of love, 197:9
Bear in mind, dear heart, 482
Bear up, my heart, 153:7
Bear we then our woes and cares, 115:6
Beat, kettledrums! Blow trumpets!, 214:1

Beautify thyself, my spirit, 180:1
Because all who on Thee believe, 176:4b
Because all, who only believe in Thee, 176:4b
Because he hath regarded the humility, 243:3
Because He that is mighty, 243:5
Because of love my Savior now is dying, 244:58
Because of Thine anger is there no soundness, 25:1
Because the wool-rich herds, 208:13
Because then the head its limb, 31:7
Because this is the Christian's crown, 132:2b
Because Thou art my God and Father, 138:7
Because Thou from death art arisen, 95:6
Become cheerful, my spirit, 147:6
Befooled world, 94:4
Before God's awful throne I place me, 179:6
Before God's presence here we come, 117:9
Before God's throne I prone do place me, 179:6
Before God's throne in Heaven, 309
Before Jehovah's awful throne, 326
Before me lies a weary road, 58:5
Before the day draws near, 321
Before the Father, our Redeemer falling, 244:28
Before the throne in Heaven, 309
Before Thy throne I come, 327; 668
Before Thy throne I herewith come, 327
Before Thy throne I now appear, 327; 668
Before Thy throne I stand, 668
Before Thy throne, my God, I stand, 327; 432; 668
Before Thy throne, O Lord, 668
Before we go off, 212:13
Begone, all ye (you) evildoers, 135:5
Begone; enough, my treasure still, 248:61
Begone, idolatrous band, 76:5
Begone, world! Have only what is thine, 64:3
Begone, world! Just keep your possessions, 64:3
Begone, worries, 187:5b

Behold, a sinner poor and low, 179:6

Behold, alway blessed is he, 34a:3

Behold, and see if there be any sorrow, 46:1a

Behold around us on ev'ry side, 6:4

Behold, dear God, how all (enemies), 153:1

Behold, He brings a year of praise, 122:6

Behold here, there in a dark stable lies, 248:17

Behold Him, how His mortal pain, 245:32

Behold how His bloodstained back, 245:32

Behold, how still, how calm, 244:41

Behold, how throbs the heavy-laden breast, 244:25a

Behold, I come, 182:3

Behold, I stand at the door, 61:4

Behold, I stand beside Thee, 247:58

Behold, I will many fishers send out, 88:1a

Behold, I will send out many fishermen, 88:1a

Behold, in gloomy stable stall, 248:17

Behold, in yonder gloomy stall, 248:17

Behold, Jesus has stretched out His hands, 244:70a

Behold my desire, I know, 17:6

Behold, my Jesus now is taken, 244:33a

Behold, my Savior now is taken, 244:33a

Behold my will, I recognize, 17:6

Behold, O gods; this is an image, 213:12

Behold, O Lord, the many foes, 153:1

Behold, our hero comes, 43:6

Behold, the Bridegroom, 248:3

Behold, the glorious day of days, 67:4

Behold, the happy faces, 36b:2

Behold, the Lamb of God, 416

Behold the temple of the Lord, 402

Behold the victor Christ, 43:2

Behold then and see if there is any sorrow, 46:1a

Behold then how each livid (living) stripe, 245:32

Behold then, one of His disciples, 244:34

Behold, there in the gloomy stable lieth, 248:17

Behold, there lies in darkened stall, 248:17

Behold, Thou, Jesus, Thou alone, 248:40a

Behold, thy Savior Christ, O man, 403

Behold, we are going up to Jerusalem, 159:1a

Behold, we go up to Jerusalem, 159:1a

Behold, what happy change I see, 206:2

Behold, what Isaiah did once foretell, 65:3

Behold, what manner of love, 64:1

Behold, what wondrous thing is this, 248:17

Behold, ye sinners, 408

Behold ye; what you now have heard, 213:12

Belief bestow upon me, 37:6

Belief creates the soul's (spirit's), 37:5

Belief doth guarantee the love now, 37:2

Belief is the pledge of love, 37:2

Belief provides the soul with pinions, 37:5

Believe not those who say, 878

The bells' repeated thrilling sound, 198:4

The bells' repeated tolling records, 198:4

Beloved God, have Thou pity, 179:5

Beloved God, my thanks I bring, 149:5

Beloved God, when shall I die, 8:1

Beloved God will heed, 744

Beloved God will heed my cry, 188:5

Beloved God, with pity do Thou hear me, 153:2

Beloved Immanuel, duke of the faithful, 485

Beloved Immanuel, Lord of the righteous, 123:1

Beloved Jesu, how hast Thou defaulted, 244:3

Beloved Jesu, how hast Thou offended, 244:3

Beloved Jesu, see us here, 633; 634; 706; 730; 731; 754

Beloved Jesu, we are here, 633; 634; 730; 731

Beloved Jesu, what hast Thou done wrong, 244:3

Beloved Jesu, You alone, 16:5

Beloved Jesus, my desire, 32:1

Beloved Jesus, Thou, 157:3

Beloved Jesus, Thou alone, 16:5

Beloved Jesus, Thou art alone, 16:5

Beloved Savior, hear my question, 245:60a

Beloved Savior, wilt Thou answer, 245:60a

Beloved sir, relax not, 210:9

Beloved Son of God, Thou hast for me, 151:4

Beloved soul, thy thoughts withdraw now, 494

Beloved spirit, take desire and sin, 494

Beloved virtue, thou alone shalt be, 213:10

Beloved virtue, 'tis thine arm, 213:10

Beloved virtue, you alone shall for ever, 213:10

Beneath: *see also* 'Neath

Beneath his purple hem, 173a:4

Beneath Thy protection I am freed, 81:7

Beneath Thy shield, 227:3

Beneath your protection, 227:3

Beseech and implore Heaven, 63:5

Beside Him there will He prepare, 43:10

Beside the flood of Babylon, 267

Beside the streams of Babylon, 267; 653; 653a; 653b

Beside the waters of Babylon, 653; 653a; 653b

Beside Thee, Lord, 244:23

Beside Thy cradle here I stand, 248:17; 248:59

Beside Thy cradle, see, I stand, 248:59

Beside Thy manger here I stand, 469

Beside Thy tomb I shall abide, 247:132

Best of princes, loved of all men, 213:13

Bestir thee then, my soul, 31:5

Bestir thyself, my feeble soul, 248:12; 454

Bestir thyself, the Bridegroom knocks, 180:2

Bestir ye then, ye holy company, 194:11

Bethink, Lord Jesu, on Thy ministry, 143:7b

Bethink Thee, Jesu, that indeed, 143:7b

Bethink Thee, Jesus of Thy charge, 143:7b

Bethink thee now, O favored land, 134a:5

Bethink thee, O my soul, 245:31

Bethink ye not nor worry, 187:4

Bethink you now, you favored place, 134a:5

Beware, I say unto you, 127:4b

Beware thou now, 102:5

Bide with us, 6:1

Bide with us, Lord Jesu Christ, 649

Bide, ye angels, bide with me, 19:5

Big wedding, much joy, 524:7

Birthday Cantata, 36b; 36c; 173a; 193a; 206; 207a; 208; 208a; 213; 214; 249a; 249b

Bitter Passiontide begins, 450

Black darkness flies before Thy face, 248:46

The blandishments of earthly pleasure, 204:4

Bleed and break, thou loving heart, 244:12

Bleed on, dear heart, 244:12

Bleed thou must, beloved heart, 244:12

Bless the Lord, my soul, 196:4

Bless the Lord, O my soul, 69:1; 69:4

Bless the Lord, O my spirit, 69:1

Bless thou the Lord, O my spirit, 69:1; 69a:1

Bless us, Lord, by word and deed, 193:5

Blessed am I that I have Jesus, 147:6

Blessed are the dead, 60:4b

Blessed are the dead men, 60:4b

Blessed are they who feel compassion, 39:7

Blessed are they who from pity, 39:7

Blessed are they whose founts of mercy, 39:7

Blessed are they, with God's word, 80:7

Blessed are those who with compassion, 39:7

Blessed are ye by fortune favored, 34a:5

Blessed be my Lord and God, 129:1

Blessed, blessed are we, 130:4

Blessed Christ hath risen, 306

The blessed Christ is ris'n today, 306; 628; A51

Blessed Christians, blissful flock, 184:2

Blessed country, 119:2

Blessed flock that Jesus herds, 104:5

Blessed he, who for his help hath Jacob's God, 143:3

Blessed he who hath for his help, 143:3

Blessed he who praise* God, 80:7

Blessed he who praises God, 80:7

Blessed he who self can to his God, 139:1

Blessed he who thinks on Christ, 498

Blessed he who thinks on Jesus, 498

Blessed Holy Trinity, 172:3

Blessed is He that cometh, 232:23

Blessed is He who comes (cometh), 232:23

Blessed is he who thinks, 498
Blessed is the man, 57:1
Blessed is the soul (spirit), 87:7
Blessed Jesu, at Thy word, 373; 633; 634; 706; 730; 731; 754,
Blessed Jesu, priceless treasure, 32:1
Blessed Jesu, we are here, 730; 731
Blessed Jesus, at Thy (Your) word, 373
Blessed Jesus, here we stand, 373
Blessed Jesus, my desire, 32:1
Blessed Jesus, my salvation, 32:1
Blessed Jesus, priceless treasure, 32:1
Blessed Jesus, see us here, 730; 731
Blessed Jesus, we are here, 373; 633; 634; 706; 730; 731
Blessed morn, when Jesus was born, 151:1
Blessed mouth, Mary makes her innermost soul, 147:2
Blessed of men are they beyond all telling, 405; 406; 495
Blessed Ressurection Day, 70:10a
Blessed state of faithful souls, 442
Blessed they who from compassion, 39:7
Blessed they who perish, 60:4b
Blessed those who through compassion, 39:7
Blessed though is he who doth his bonder know, 105:4
Blessed truly is he, 87:7
Blessed word, Mary makes known, 147:2
Blessed ye hearts whom God has chosen, 34:3
Blessed ye who live in faith, 198a:8b
Blessed ye who live in faith unswerving, 405; 406; 495
Blessed ye who think on Him, 498
Blessed ye whose lives on faith were founded, 198:a:8b
Blessing and honor and glory, 21:11b
Blessing, glory, and wisdom and thanks, A162:1
The blessings God bestows today, 36b:5
Blessings shower from His hand, 16:3b
Blest: see Blessed
Blissful are the pious, 495

Blithe bells, 208:9
The blood which Thou hast shed for me, 78:4
Bloom, ye lindens in Saxony, 214:9
Blossom, ye lindens of Leipzig, 214:9
Blow the well held flutes, 214:3
Blow, ye flutes and clash, ye timbrels, 214:3
The blows of fate come thick, 139:4
The body, earth-committed, 161:6
The body, indeed in the earth, 161:6
The body Joseph took, 244:76a
The body of soldiers with their captain, 245:10
The body, truly in the earth, 161:6
The bond God sealed and ratified, 99:4
Book of books, our people's strength, 373
Both Heaven and the Earth as well, 178:7.2
Both high and low, and rich and poor, 26:5
The bounteous God casts His abundant store, 39:2
The bounteous God on us bestows, 39:2
Bow before our Savior, keeping our faith, 182:5
Bow, city of our hearts beloved, 120:3
Bow Thine ear, O Lord, 372
Bow to thank Him, 248:36
Bow ye, thankful kneel and praise, 248:36
Bow your heads before your Savior, 182:5
Bowed with grief, deeply repentant, 199:4
A Boy born in Bethlehem, 65:2
A Boy is born in Bethlehem, 603
Bread of Heav'n, on Thee we feed, 384
Bread of life, all grace conveying, 180:7
Bread of the world in mercy broken, 321; 517
Break and die, thou dearest heart, 244:12
Break apart, my poor heart, 444
Break bread for the hungry, 39:1a
Break for the hungry man thy bread, 39:1a
Break forth, O beauteous, 248:12
Break forth, O bright and rosy morn, 248:12
Break forth, O lovely morning light, 248:12
Break forth, thou beautiful morning light, 248:12

Break in grief, thou loving heart, 244:12
Break in twain, my poor heart, 444
Break in two, my heart so saddened, 444
Break in woe, O loving heart, 244:12
Break, my heart, in bitter grieving, 444
Break out, O beauteous morning light, 248:12
Break through, O lovely light of morn, 248:12
Break with hungry men thy bread, 39:1a
Breath of God, life giving, 445
Breathe on me, breath of God, 878
Brethren, take to you this comfort, 7:6
Brethren, when this day comes, 479
Bridegroom, all mine own, 409; 496
Bridegroom of my soul, 496
Bridegroom of the soul, 409; 496
Brightest and best of the sons, 123:6; 485
Bring Him back, is all my prayer, 244:51
Bring me cross and cup, 244:29,
Bring the hungry man thy bread, 39:1a
Bring to the Lord honor, 148:1
Bring to the Lord the honor of His name, 148:1
Bring ye to God honor, 148:1
Broad as the heavens above, Thy mercy ever stands, 17:3
Broken, broken is my yoke, 56:3
Broken is the grave, 66:2
Brood o'er us with Thy shelt'ring wing, 321
Brooks of salted tears flow always, 21:5
But a gesture from His hands, 248:57
But a merciless judgment will surely be, 89:3
But as our enemies, 41:5
But at the same time, 169:6
But, beautiful shepherdesses, 249a:6
But behold, the hand of him that betrayeth, 246:16
But cried they out yet more, 244:59a
But death abides to human nature, 60:4a
But God, amid a sinful generation, 70:6
But God indeed must pity me, 199:3
But God must be gracious, 199:3
But God must have mercy on me, 199:3

But God to me shall gracious be, 199:3
But God to me will surely bend, 199:3
But happy he who his Redeemer knows, 105:4
But he denied and said, I am not, 245:18
But He said to them, 246:43c
But He that searches the hearts, 226:3
But Heaven and Earth, O Lord, are Thine, 178:7.2
But here doth work the Savior's hand, 48:5
But how doth it regard Thee in Thy cradle, 121:5
But how happy he who his surety knows, 105:4
But how shall I look upon Thee, 121:5
But if Christ is in you, 227:8
But if more days on Earth, 71:2b
But if the Spirit of Him that raised up Jesus, 227:10
But if Thou look on me in love, 172:6
But it also means by this, 169:6
But Jesus, turning unto them, 246:59
But Jesus will in hours of trial, 46:5
But keep us, faithful Father, keep us, 18:3c
But listen now, 212:13
But lo, the Lord indeed protects His flock, 138:3b
But lo, the Spirit prays for us and pleadeth, 226:2
But make way, you senseless, vain worries, 8:4
But must I walk the vale of death, 92:9
But now no human wit or might, 178:2
But now Thy healing word assures, 113:4
But oh, what grave discomfiture, 124:4
But oh, what sore distress and woe, 124:4
But oh, what sorrow, grief, and pain, 124:4
But one of the malefactors, 246:65
But one of them, when he saw, 17:4
But one thing, O Lord, do I require of Thee, 111:6
But Peter denied it and said, 245:18
But Pilate answered, 245:51
But Pilate gave answer, 245:51

But Pilate made answer, 245:51
But Pilate replied to them, 245:51
But Pilate saith unto them, 245:37
But praise to God, His might hath closed, 14:5
But pray too therewith, 115:4
But put Thy grace into our mouths, 134:5
But rouse, Thyself, the thanks within our voices, 134:5
But seriously, listen, 212:13
But shouldst Thou, Lord, mark our misdoing, 131:2a
But since the foe, 41:5
But somehow was the law to have fulfillment, 9:4
But still it seems that certain of my foes, 67:5
But thanks to God, the Savior's hand, 48:5
But the eyes of God see in us, 90:4
But the Jews cried out, 245:41
But the law had to be fulfilled, 9:4
But the Spirit itself, 226:2
But the time will come, 44:2
But then the Jews did cry, 245:41
But there is mercy, Lord, with Thee, 131:4b
But there will come a time, 44:2
But they comprehended not, 175:5
But they cried out the more, 244:59a
But they did not understand, 175:5
But they understood Him not, 175:5
But they understood not His meaning, 22:1b
But Thy reviving Gospel-word, 113:4
But 'tis not so, 210a:7
But to do good and communicate, 39:4
But to Jesus' fatherly hands, 114:2b
But well for him who knows his surety, 105:4
But what is that to us, 244:49b
But when He, the Spirit of Truth, is come, 108:4
But when in our hearts God searcheth, 226:3
But when Pilate heard them, 245:39
But where, 245:48b
But who gives heed, 76:4

But who hears, 76:4
But who will hear, 76:4
But why wast thou looking for Me, 32:2
But ye are not in the flesh, 227:6
But ye are not of the flesh, 227:6
But yet, O frightened heart, 168:4
But yet the Spirit doth make intercession, 226:2
But yield, ye mad, vain cares, 8:4
But you must also love, 169:6
By Adam's fall is all corrupted, 637
By all confessed, 212:7
By all generations, 243:4
By Antichrist 'tis sought, 44:5
By death we may not punish, 245:25
By faith and power from on high, 7:7
By faith and power spiritual, 7:7
By God are none forsaken, 107:2
By His cross I am saved from sin and loss, 244:26b
By His great love for Him who died, 198a:9a
By law we cannot kill Him, 245:25
By mortals renowned, 134a:8
By our love and tender mercy, 164:3
By our might is nothing done, 80:2b
By praise offered, 17:1
By sin's dark stain our soul's disfigured, 136:5
By strength alone we do nothing, 80:26
By tares life's strength is choked, 181:4
By the rivers of Babylon, 267
By the waters of Babylon, 653; 653a; 653b
By these is the strength choked, 181:4
By these will all our strength be choked, 181:4
By Thine agony and bloody sweat, 246:27
By Thine atonement make me strong, 113:8; 168:6
By Thy capture, O God's Son, 245:40
By waterside in Babylon, 267
By waters of Babylon, 653b

C

Call and cry to Heaven now, 63:5

Call and implore the heavens, 63:5
Call out and pray to Heaven, 63:5
Call thou on God; He will in blessing, 88:5
Call ye on God, so gain His blessing, 88:5
Callousness can blind the powerful, 147:4
The calm and peace of Heaven, 123:2
Calm and tranquil lie the sheepfolds, 208:9
The calm Pleisse is playing, 207a:2
The calm Pleisse plays, 207a:2
Calm ye; calm your anxious seeking, 197:3
Calmly abide; wait thou, my spirit, 93:3
Calmly then I wait my ending, 249:7
Can God indeed be in us, 102:2
Can I this world esteem, 64:4
Can it be, Jesu, from highest Heaven, 650
Can man indeed ascend to God, 194:9
Can my tears not move Thy pity, 244:61
Can the tears of my cheeks, 244:61
Can the world not cease, 58:4
Cannot the red cheeks, 205:7
Cantata in burlesque, 212
Capital and interest of my debts, 168:3
Capital and int'rest payment, 168:3
Captain of Israel's host, 377
The care, the woe, 156:3
Cast me not from Thy presence, 105:2
Cast, my heart now, cast thyself, 155:4
Cast, oh cast thyself, my heart, 155:4
Cast thy doubts, my spirit, hence, 186:1
The cat does not leave mousing, 211:10
Cats must have their mice, 211:10
Cats won't give up mice, 211:10
Cease, music, cease, 210:3
Cease now, doubting reason, cease, 178:6
Cease, sad eyelids, cease, 98:3
Cease thy weeping, cease thy wailing, 98:3
Cease, ye eyes now, all your weeping, 98:3
Cease ye eyes to weep, 98:3
Cease, you eyes, from weeping, 98:3
Cease your anguish, sorrowful voices, 103:5
Cedars must before the tempest, 150:5
Cedars on the mountain swaying, 150:5
Cedars tall, their branches growing, 150:5
Celebration of the spirit, 249b

Certainly Augustus' name, 215:3
Certainly does August's name, 215:3
Certainly such a room for the heart, 248:53
The chamberlain collects ten thousand ducats, 212:16
The chamberlain has become our new squire, 212:2
The chamberlain is now our squire, 212:2
Chaotic sin hath me not merely stained, 5:2
Charming fair one, 216:3
The chase, 208
Cheer the heart with sweetest music, 201:15
Cheer Thou, O Jesus, me in sadness, 135:3
Cheer up, fearful and timid minds, 176:5
The chief priests then, 246:51
The chief priests, therefore, 245:64
The Child, born in Bethlehem, 603
A Child born in Bethlehem, 65:2
A Child is born in Bethlehem, 65:2; 603
A child is born to us this day, 414
The Child that Isaiah of old foretold, 65:3
Children are a source of countless troubles, 211:2
Children oftentimes are headaches, 211:2
The children whom He loves and rears, 225:2
Chimes, ring out the moment longed for, 53
The choice of Hercules, 213
Chorale prelude, 609
Christ baptized was in Jordan's flood, 7:1, 7:7, 176:6; 280
Christ, by heav'nly hosts adored, 262
Christ, by whom we are saved, 245:21
Christ, by whose all-saving light, 283; 620; 620a
The Christ Child shall be still my hope, 702
Christ, desire of ages, 337
Christ did our Lord to Jordan come, 7:1
Christ, everlasting source of light, 274
Christ has arisen, 627
Christ has risen, 627
Christ have mercy, 233:1b; 234:1b; 235:1b; 236:1b
Christ, have mercy on us, 232:2
Christ, have mercy upon us, 232:2

Christ, He is my life, 95:1a
Christ in the bands of death was laid, 4:2
Christ in the bonds of death was laid, 4:2; 158:4; 277; 278; 279
Christ is arisen, 276; 627; 746
Christ is my life, 281; 282
Christ is my light and treasure, 95:1a
Christ is now risen (rysen), 276; 627
Christ is now risen again, 746
Christ is risen, 66:6; 276; 627
Christ is risen, has conquered, 284
Christ is the only Son of God, 96:1; 601; 698; A55; A156:1
Christ is the world's true light, 45:7; 479
Christ Jesus, God's only Son, 4:4
Christ Jesus is arisen, 67:2
Christ Jesus lay in Death's strong bands, 4:8; 277; 278; 279; 625; 695; 695a; 718
Christ Jesus now is risen, 67:2
Christ Jesus, our Redeemer born, 688; 689
Christ Jesus praise we ev'ry one, 121:1
Christ, Lamb of God, 619
Christ lay by death enshrouded, 4:2; 277; 278; 279; 625; 695; 695a; 718; A171
Christ lay enshrouded by death, 4:2
Christ lay fast bound, 4:2
Christ lay in bonds of death, 4:2
Christ lay in death enshrouded, 277; 278; 279
Christ lay in death's bonds, 158:4
Christ lay in death's dark prison, 4:2; 277; 278; 279; 625; 695; 695a; 718; A171
Christ lay in Death's embrace, 625
Christ lay in death's grim prison, 4:2; 4:8; 277; 278; 279
Christ lay in the bonds of death, 4:2; 277; 278; 279; 625; A171,
Christ lay in thralls of death, 4:2
Christ lay to death in bondage, 4:2
Christ lives, and is from death today arisen, 160:2
Christ, our helper and life-giver, 475
Christ, our hope, 670; 673

Christ our Lord came to the Jordan, 7:1; 176:6; 280
Christ our Lord is risen, 284
Christ our Lord is risen today, 306; 628; A51
Christ our Lord to Jordan came, 7:1; 684; 685
Christ our Savior hath redeemed us, 363
Christ the image of God's glory, 474
Christ the Lord has risen, 628
Christ the Lord is risen, 284
Christ, Thine atoning blood, 136:6
Christ, Thou Lamb of God, 23:4; 233:1b; 233a:2; 619
Christ, Thou support of Thy followers, 275
Christ, Thou the champion of the band, 275
Christ, through whom we all are blessed, 245:21
Christ, Thy wounds and bitter Passion, 19:7
Christ today is risen, 284
Christ was the Word who spake, 194:12
Christ we praise, in duty bound, 611
Christ, we praise Thee as the son of the spotless, 121:1
Christ we should certainly praise, 121:1
Christ, we would meetly praise Thee, 611; 696
Christ, who art clear day, 273
Christ, who art day and light, 274
Christ, who art my very life, 281; 282
Christ, who brought us to the light, 245:21
Christ, who died mankind to right, 245:65; 283; 620; 620a
Christ, who freed our souls from danger, 363
Christ, who gave (gives) us life and light, 245:21
Christ, who is my life, 95:1a
Christ, who knew no sin or wrong, 245:21; 283; 620; 620a; 747,
Christ, who makes us blessed, 245:21; 245:65; 283; 620; 620a,
Christ, who saves us by His cross, 245:21
Christ, who the cross has mounted, 347

Christ, whom all the world praises, 611

Christ, whom the Virgin Mary bore, 611; 696

Christ, whose all-redeeming might, 620; 620a

The Christ-child brings the year of real jubilee, 122:6

Christendom today is in a sad way, 179:2

Christian brothers, joyful be, 40:7

Christian children, 40:7

Christian, courage take and say, 40:6

Christian, myrrh and precious spices, 249:5

Christian, ne'er let sin o'erpower thee, 54:1

Christian people, clear bethink ye, 132:5

Christian people, ever ponder, 132:5

Christian people, joyful be, 40:7

Christian, stand with sword in hand, 115:1

The Christian world today, 179:2

Christians all, this happy day, 63:1

Christians, be joyful and praise your salvation, 248:1

Christians, engrave this day in metal, 63:1

Christians, engrave this glad day, 63:1

Christians, etch ye now this day, 63:1

Christians ever must be patient, 44:3

Christians, grave ye this glad day, 63:1

Christians, hold this rite for comfort, 7:6

Christians, mark ye all this day, 63:1

Christians, mark ye well this day, 63:1

Christians must be Christ's disciples, 44:3

Christians must on Earth Christ's true disciples, 44:3

Christians must, while on Earth, 44:3

Christians, on this happy day, 63:1

Christians, show your love through deeds, 76:12

Christians, show your lovely deeds, 76:12

A Christian's spiritual life, 456

Christmas oratorio, 248

Christmas pastorale, 248:9

Christmas song, 469

Christ's church shall glory in His power, 80:8; 302; 303

Christ's example we must follow, 481

Christ's own members, ah, consider, 132:5

Christus, our God's own Son, 4:4

Church concerto, 42

Clash now, crash now, judgment call, 70:10b

Cleanse thee, O my soul, from sin, 244:75

Close in sleep, O weary eyelids, 82:3

Close the doors of Janus' temple, 206:3

Close the temple doors of Janus, 206:3

Close, tired eyes, 82:3

Close ye now, ye weary eyelids, 82:3

Cloudless, serene and splendid, 448

Coffee and Cupid, 211

Coffee cantata, 211

Coffee my one and only bliss is, 211:4

Coffee my one, only bliss is, 211:4

Coffee's far nicer than riches, 211:4

Come again and be rested, O my spirit, 21:9

Come again from out the dark tomb, 480

Come all and hail this day of days, 67:4

Come, all men, praise ye our God, 391

Come, Almighty God, Holy Ghost, 631; 631a

Come and abide with me, 80:4

Come and hear our blessed Savior, 39:7

Come and let us go up to Jerusalem, 159:1a

Come and thank Him, 248:36

Come, be glad, rejoice, O my soul, 70:7

Come be joyful, 16:3a

Come, be of cheer, 109:4

Come, blessed cross, 244:66

Come, celebrate this morn, 479

Come, Christian folk, 40:3; 110:7; 248:35; 612; 710

Come, Christians all (greet), 479

Come, come; I will give myself to Thee (You), 229:2

Come, come; I will surrender (yield), 229:2

Come, come, my heart, 74:2

Come, come, my voice, 508

Come, come, that I my all may give Thee, 229:2

Come, come; to Thee, O Christ, I yield me, 229:2

Come, dazzle to blindness, 208:12

Come, Death, brother of Sleep, 56:5
Come dwell within my heart, 80:4
Come, enter in with Me, 140:5
Come, enter Thine own portal, 417; 418; 419
Come, enter to Thy dwelling, 183:5
Come fairest, let me now embrace, 49:3c
Come, fairest linden-bordered town, 120:3
Come fairest one, come and let me kiss, 49:3c
Come, Flora, come quickly, 249a:9
Come, follow me, the Savior spake, 377
Come, follow my path, 213:4
Come, for in my heart will I receive Thee, 248:38c
Come forward, judges both, 201:8
Come, gentle death, 478
Come, gladness all borrow, 66:1a
Come, God, Creator, Holy Ghost, 218:5; 370; 631; 631a; 667,
Come, God, the Creator, Holy Ghost, 218:5; 370
Come, gracious Spirit, heav'nly dove, 370
Come, hasten and hurry, 249:3
Come, hasten and run, 249:3
Come, hasten and show us, 249:3
Come, hasten, impatient, 249:3
Come, hasten, tune, 74:5
Come, healing cross, 244:66
Come, help me praise God's goodness, 613
Come here to me, says God's Son, 42:4
Come hither, happy folk, 207a:8
Come, Holy Ghost, 651; 651a; 652; 652a
Come, Holy Ghost, Creator blessed, 631; 631a; 667
Come, Holy Ghost, Creator, come, 631; 631a
Come, Holy Ghost, draw near us, 96:6
Come, Holy Ghost, eternal God, 218:5
Come, Holy Ghost, help Thou me, 175:7; 651; 651a; 652; 652a,
Come, Holy Ghost, Lord God, 59:3; 226:4; 651; 651a; 652; 652a
Come, Holy Ghost, Lord our God, 59:3

Come, Holy Ghost, O Lord my God, 59:3
Come, Holy Ghost, our souls inspire, 218:5; 370
Come, Holy Spirit, come apace, 59:3; 651; 651a; 652; 652a
Come, Holy Spirit; come, Lord our God, 59:3
Come, Holy Spirit; come, O Lord, 59:3
Come, Holy Spirit, God and Lord, 59:3; 122:6; 175:7; 226:4
Come, Holy Spirit, God the Lord, 59:3
Come, Holy Spirit, Lord our God, 59:3
Come, Holy Spirit, most blessed Lord, 651; 651a; 652; 652a
Come, hurry and run, 249:3
Come, hurry, tune strings and songs, 74:5
Come, hymn with me God's goodness, 613
Come, I will embrace Thee with joy, 248:38c
Come, I will with delight (joy), 248:38c
Come in my heart's abode, 80:4
Come into my heart's house, 80:4
Come into the house of my heart, 80:4
Come, Jesu, come, 229:1; 229:4
Come, Jesu, come, Thy church awaits Thee, 61:3
Come, Jesu, come to Thy church, 61:3
Come, Jesu, with me stay, 80:4
Come, Jesus, come, 229:1
Come, Jesus, come to Thine elected (own), 61:3
Come, Jesus, come to this Thy church, 61:3
Come, Jesus, come to Thy (Your) church, 61:3
Come, Jesus, revive and gladden my soul, 21:8
Come, join with us, 208:10
Come, joyful voices raise, 36:1; 36c:1
Come kindle, thou heavenly bright, 1:3
Come, kindly cross, 244:66
Come, kindly death, 478
Come, Kitty, will you choose your mate, 212:3
Come, lead me hence, 175:2
Come, lead me, Lord, 175:2

Come, lead me, my spirit, 175:2
Come, lead me out, 175:2
Come, lead Thou me, 175:2
Come, let me no longer wait, 172:5
Come, let me wait no longer, 172:5
Come, let the Lord teach you, 39:7
Come, let us all this day, 479
Come, let us all with fervor, 16:6; 28:6; 613; A54
Come, let us go up to Jerusalem, 159:1a
Come, let us hail this day of days, 67:4
Come, let us hail this happy year, 122:6
Come, let us join in a song of thanksgiving, 66:3
Come, let us praise our mighty Lord, 130:1
Come, let us to the bagpipe's sound, 212:24
Come, look thee now, my heart, 159:1b
Come, look ye now, and say, 159:1b
Come, Lord, direct my feeble will, 158:3a
Come, Lord, haste Thee, 61:6b
Come, Lord Jesus, 106:2f
Come, Lord Jesus, and restore me, 21:8
Come, loved one, come, 49:3c
Come, lovely crown of joy, 61:6b
Come, make me no longer tarry, 172:5
Come, make my heart Thy home, 80:4
Come, Midas, 201:10
Come, Miecke, give me a kiss, 212:3
Come, mortals, laud ye God's perfection, 167:1
Come, mortals, now ponder a mystery wondrous, 62:2
Come, most beautiful one, come, 49:3c
Come, my heart, behold, 159:1b
Come, my heart, throw wide thy portals, 61:5a
Come, my Jesu, and refresh me, 21:8
Come, my Jesus, and refresh me, 21:8
Come, my Jesus, and restore me, 21:8
Come, my Jesus, and revive and rejoice, 21:8
Come, my Jesus, with refreshment, 21:8
Come, my Savior, and restore me, 21:8
Come, my soul, thyself prepare, 115:1
Come, my soul, today prepare, 115:1

Come, my spirit, come (raise), 189:1
Come, no longer let me wait Thee, 172:5
Come, now attend, 212:13
Come now, dear Lord, O Spirit blessed, 218:5
Come now, let us not divide, 245:54
Come now, Savior of mankind, 61:1; 62:1
Come now, Savior of the Gentiles, 61:1; 599; 659; 659a; 660; 660a; 660b; 661; 661a; 699
Come now, Savior of the world, 599
Come now, sweet death, 478
Come now, the nations' Savior, 36:2
Come, oh come, in pious lays, 146:8; 262
Come, O Creator, spirit blessed, 631; 631a; 667
Come, O daughters, swell my mourning, 244:1
Come, O Death, and end my voyage, 56:5
Come, O Death, brother of Sleep, 56:5
Come, O Death, kind brother of Sleep, 56:5
Come, O Death, O brother of Sleep, 56:5
Come, O Death, of Sleep the brother, 56:5
Come, O Death, soft Sleep's kind brother, 56:5
Come, O Death, thou blessed healer, 161:1
Come, O Death, thou Sleep's brother, 56:5
Come, O death, thou sweetest hour, 161:1
Come, O Death, thou twin, 56:5
Come, one and all, 194:11
Come order thy house, 106:2d
Come out from yonder cave in there, 480
Come, people, on this day, 479
Come, Polly, give your swain, 212:3
Come, ponder well, my mind, 159:1b
Come praise the Lord, 479
Come praise ye all our mighty Lord, 326
Come, praise ye God, our mighty Lord, 76:14
Come pretty maid, come let me kiss, 49:3c
Come, pure hearts, in joyful (sweetest), 263
Come quickly, come fill me with holiest ardor, 1:3
Come quickly, now come, 140:3

Come, Redeemer of our race, 36:2; 36:8; 61:1; 62:1; 62:6; 599; 659; 659a; 660; 660a; 660b; 661; 661a

Come, rejoice, ye faithful, come, 30:1

Come, rejoice, ye nations all, 30:12

Come, rejoice, ye ransomed souls, 30:1; 30:12

Come, right gladly will I embrace Thee, 248:38c

Come, roar ye, tornadoes, 205:1

Come, Savior of nations wild, 599; 659; 659a; 660; 660a; 660b; 661; 661a; 699

Come, Savior of the Gentiles, 599; 659; 659a; 660; 660a; 660b; 661; 661a,

Come, Savior of the heathen, 599

Come, shatter to pieces, burst open the lair, 205:1

Come, sing all ye faithful ones, 134:2

Come sing for joy, 249:10a

Come, sing, ye little children, 613; A54

Come, soothing death; come, sweet repose, 478

Come soul, thyself adorning, 180:1

Come, souls, behold today, 479

Come, sweet cross, 244:66

Come, sweet death; come, blessed rest (sleep), 478

Come, sweet death; come, blissful (heavenly), 478

Come, sweet Death, thou blessed healer, 161:1

Come, sweet hour of death, 161:1

Come, sweet repose, 478

Come, sweetest death, 478

Come then, and let us go up to Jerusalem, 159:1a

Come then, Flora, come quickly, 249a:9

Come, then, into His presence, 117:9

Come then, lovely joy-crown, 61:6b

Come then, my heart, behold, 159:1b

Come then, Thy name alone shall be, 248:40a

Come, thine hour, kind Death is striking, 161:1

Come, thou beautiful crown of my joys, 61:6b

Come, thou blessed hour of parting, 161:1

Come, Thou blessed Savior, come, 61:1

Come, Thou Creator God, 218:5

Come, thou crown of all rejoicing, 61:6b

Come, thou fair crown of joy, 61:6b

Come, thou fairest crown of Heaven, 61:6b

Come, Thou Holy Three-in-One, 172:3

Come, thou lovely crown of gladness, 61:6b

Come, thou lovely hour of dying, 161:1

Come Thou now to save mankind, 61:1

Come, Thou of man the Savior, 36:2; 61:1; 62:1

Come, Thou, oh come, 60:5

Come, Thou Savior of mankind, 36:2; 61:1; 62:1; 599; 659; 659a; 660; 660a; 660b; 661; 661a; 699

Come, Thou Savior of the Gentiles, 61:1

Come, thou source of life and glory, 61:6b

Come, Thou Spirit which caresses, 172:5

Come, thou sweet death's hour, 161:1

Come, thou sweet hour of death, 161:1

Come, thou sweet rest, 478,

Come Thou, the world's Redeemer, 62:1; 659; 659a; 660; 660a; 660b; 661; 661a,

Come to me, speaks the Son of God, 74:8; 108:6

Come, tread the path I show, 213:4

Come unto Me, ye heavy laden, 57:6

Come, welcome Death, and close my eyes, 31:8

Come what may, 52:3

Come where, 245:48b

Come with haste, you hours, 30:10

Come, with joy I will embrace Thee, 248:38c

Come with shouting, 16:3a

Come with us, O blessed Jesus, 147:6; 147:10

Come ye, and praise Him, 322

Come ye and thank your God, 120a:2a

Come, ye Christians, praise and pray, 63:5

Come ye, come before His face, A160:1b

Come, ye daughters, 244:1

Come, ye faithful, raise the strain, A57

Come ye forth, ye troubled souls, 30:5

Come ye, our way is up to Jerusalem, 159:1a

Come, ye people, list and mark ye, 39:7
Come, ye sinners, sorely (wayworn), 30:5
Come, ye sorely tempted sinners, 30:5
Come, ye souls, 245:48a
Come, ye tempted sinners, 30:5
Come, you daughters, help me lament, 244:1
Come, you tempted sinners, 30:5
Come, you troubled sinners, 30:5
Come, your hearts to Jesus open, 175:6
Come, joyful voices raise, 36:1
Comes a day of reckoning, 45:3
Comes death apace with footfall eager, 156:2a
Comest Thou, Jesu, from Heaven to Earth, 650
Comest Thou now, Jesu (Jesus), 650
Comfort, comfort my love, 30:6
Comfort, comfort ye, my people, 13:1; 30:1; 30:6; 146:8
Comfort for me, Jesus, my mind, 135:3
Comfort me, Jesu, in my sadness, 135:3
Comfort me, Jesu (Jesus), 135:3
Comfort my soul, Jesus, or I sink, 135:3
Comfort, O Jesu, Thou my spirit, 135:3
Comfort, sweet comfort, my spirit, 145:5
Comfort sweet, Lord Jesus comes, 151:1
Comfort sweet, my Jesus comes, 151:1
Comfort sweet that Jesus came, 151:1
Command Thy blessing from above, 245:40
Commend thy ways, 153:5; 244:53
Commend your way, 244:53
Commit thou all that grieves thee, 244:63.1; 270; 271; 272
Commit thou all thy going, 270; 271; 272
Commit thou all thy griefs, 244:53; 466
Commit thou every grievance, 244:53; 270; 271; 272
Commit thy way, confiding, 244:53
Commit thy way to Jesus, 244:53
Commit thy ways, O pilgrim, 244:53
Commit thy ways to Jesus, 153:5; 244:53; 244:72
Compared to the splendor that awaits us, 59:4
Compose thyself, 109:4

Comrade of my soul, 409; 496
Conceals my shepherd Himself too long, 104:3
Concerning them which are asleep, 244:31
Concerto in dialogue, 57; 58
Conduct thyself, beloved, according to My pleasure, 57:8
Confer Thou faith upon me in Jesus, 37:6
Confess thy God with hearty, 45:5
Confine, ye wise men of this world, 443
Confront me, Moses, if thou wilt, 145:4
Confused by guilt and shame, 507
Congratulatory cantata, 134a
A conscience clear hath God provided, 75:6
Consider, child of God, 80:3
Consider how His bloodstained back, 245:32
Consider how His body, blood-bespatter'd, 245:32
Consider Jesus' bitter death, 101:6
Consider, my soul, 245:31
Consider, my soul, and reflect, 509
Consider, O my soul, 245:31
Consider then, child of God, 80:3
Consider then, my soul unwary, 509
Consider well, O child of God, 80:3
Consider, ye mortals, the wonderful myst'ry, 62:2
The constant goodness, 10:3
Content am I in mine affliction, 58:3
Content am I to leave thee, 95:2b
Content am I with life, 204:1
Content is ours, 30:2
Content, my God, 65:7
The contented Aeolus, 205
Contented rest, beloved inner joy, 170:1
Contented rest, beloved joy of the soul, 170:1
Contentedness, in this life it is a treasure, 144:5
The contention between Phoebus and Pan, 201
Contentment is a treasure in this life, 144:5
The contest between Phoebus and Pan, 201
Contrition and repentance, 244:10
Cool shadows, my joy, 205:5

Couldst thou be with me, 508

Courage then, for He will give all, 115:6

Cradle song, 248:19

The crafty world would fain devise, 244:38

Crash and crackle, roar and knell, 70:10b

Crash down in ruin, arrogant bombast, 126:4

The crash of cannon sounds, 214:4

The crashing guns we hear, 214:4

Creator, God, and Holy Ghost, come, 218:5; 370; 631; 631a; 667,

Creator Spirit, Holy Dove, 218:5

Cross and crown are bound together, 12:4

Cross and crown are connected, 12:4

Cross and crown are joined together, 12:4

Cross and crown are one together, 12:4

The cross shall be Thy kingly throne, 246:64

Crown and blesseth if His hand, 16:3b

Crown and prize of crowned ladies, 214:7

Crowns and blesses His hand, 16:3b

Crucify, crucify, 244:54d; 244:59b; 245:36

Crucify Him, 246:55d

Crucify Him; crucify Him, 245:36

Crucify, off with Him, 245:36

Cursed for thy sake, 136:2

D

Damnation befalls not those who are in Christ, 227:2

The dangerous thorns' countless harvest, 181:3

Dark and cold the heart within me, 248:53

The darkness has gained, 6:4

The darkness has in many places, 6:4

Darling of the people and your loved ones, 213:13

Darling, that's a very sensible remark, 212:23

Daughters! Plague upon their fancies, 211:6

Day and night are Thine, 71:4

Day by day we magnify Thee, 248:53

The day has passed; the sun at last, 447

The day hath dawned, the day of days, 67:4; 145:7; 629

The day hath now an ending, 244:16

The day is done, and left alone, 404

The day is done; the sun again descending, 297

Day is done; the sun is setting, 447

The day is o'er; the sun is setting now, 447

The day is over; night descends, 396

The day is past and over, 67:7

The day is past; no more the sun shines, 447

Day of doom, the Lord's great day approacheth, 310

Day of judgment! Day of wonders, 41:8

The day of judgment is at hand, 307

The day, so full of joy, 605

The day that gave thee happy birth, 36c:5

The day that is so joyful, 605

The day, which is so joyful, 605

The day will come when truth at last, 136:3

Day with its light, 448

The day with its light is gone, 448

The days of old were days of might, 245:40; 247:44

Days which here are filled with sadness, 150:7

Deal not according to Thy law, 101:2

Deal the hungry ones thy bread, 39:1a

Deal with me, Father, 514

Deal with me, God, at Thy good pleasure, 514

Deal with me, God, in mercy now, 156:2b; 377

Deal with me, God, of Thy good will, 156:2b

Dear Aeolus, pray do not spoil, 205:10

Dear Christians, let us now rejoice, 388; 734; 734a; 755

Dear Christians, one and all rejoice, 388; 734; 734a

Dear, dear, sweet holy name, 299

Dear face with pain transfigured, 244:63.1

Dear Father, pray Thee, stem, prevent, 18:3c

Dear friends, the loss we feel this day, 118

Dear heart, consider yet, 482

Dear honored sir, 210:9

Dear Jesus shall my comfort be, 702

Dear Jesus, where do you tarry so long, 484

Dear kind taxman, pray be kind to us, 212:6
Dear Lord and Father of mankind, 376
Dear Lord, forgive us all our guilt (ill), 127:5
Dear Lord, have mercy; give me consolation, 179:5
Dear Lord, oh quickly come again, 11:8
Dear love, lend us thy grace, 169:7
Dear Master, in Thy way, 264
Dear Mister Taxman, 212:6
Dear Savior Thou, if Thy disciples, 244:9
The dear sun's light and splendor, 446
Dearest God, have mercy, 179:5
Dearest God, I cry to Thee, 179:5
Dearest God, when shall (will) I die, 8:1; 483
Dearest God, when will my death be, 8:1
Dearest God, when wilt Thou call me, 8:1; 483
Dearest Immanuel, guide of the simple, 123:6
Dearest Immanuel, Lord of the devout, 123:1; 485
Dearest Immanuel, Lord of the faithful, 123:1; 123:6; 485
Dearest Immanuel, Lord of the pious, 485
Dearest Immanuel, Lord of the righteous, 123:1
Dearest Jesu, Lord, where doest Thou stay, 484
Dearest Jesu, my desire (longing), 32:1
Dearest Jesus, how hast Thou transgressed, 244:3; 244:55; 245:7; 245:27.2
Dearest Jesus, my desiring, 32:1
Dearest Jesus, sore I need Thee, 32:1
Dearest Jesu(s), we are here, 373; 633; 634; 706; 730; 731
Dearest Jesus, we are Thine, 373; 633; 634; 706; 730; 731; 754,
Dearest Lord Jesu, where art Thou remaining, 484
Dearest Lord Jesus, how long wilt Thou tarry, 484
Dearest Lord Jesus, oh why dost Thou tarry, 484

Dearest Lord Jesus, where art Thou remaining, 484
Dearest Lord Jesus, where dost Thou tarry, 484
Dearest Lord Jesus, why now so belated, 484
Dearest Lord of my salvation, 491
Dearest Lord, when wilt Thou summon, 8:1; 8:6; 483
Dearest Master, Shepherd, Pastor, 497
Dearest one, depend upon My favor, 57:8
Dearest Savior, priceless treasure, 32:1
Dearest Savior, should reflection, 248:39
Dearest Savior, whom I long for, 32:1
Dearest soul, withdraw thy senses, 494
Dearly I love Thee, O Lord, 174:5; 245:68; 340
Dearly loved Son of God, 6:2
Death, I do not fear thee, 227:5
Death none could command, 4:3
The death of Jesus Christ, our Lord, 321
Death remains yet to human nature hateful, 60:4a
Death sounds its solemn knell, 161:4
Death still remains hateful to human nature, 60:4a
Death's a sleep; I fear no longer, 249:7
Deceiver, thou dost hope to find the Lord, 248:56
Deck thee, O my soul, with gladness, 180:7
Deck thyself, beloved soul, 654
Deck thyself, dear soul, 180:1; 180:7
Deck thyself, my soul, in gladness, 180:1
Deck thyself, my soul, with gladness, 180:1; 180:7; 654; 759; A74
Deck thyself, O my soul, with gladness, 180:1
Deck thyself, O soul beloved, 180:1
Deck yourself, soul, with gladness, 180:7
Deep concealed is His wisdom, 188:3
Deeply bowed and filled with remorse, 199:4
Deeply bowed and filled with sorrow, 199:4
Deeply bowed and full of regret, 199:4
Deeply bowed and full of remorse, 199:4

Deeply my soul doth long, 727
Defend me, Holy Father, guard me, 18:3c
Defy the old dragon, 227:5
Delight and pleasure, prosperity, 197:8
Delight the heart, O gentle strings, 201:15
Delight the heart, you lovely strings, 201:15
Delight us both with your joyful beams, 208:12
Delight us both, you rays of joy, 208:12
Delightful rest, beloved desire of the soul, 170:1
Delights and pleasures, well-being, 197:8
Deliver not to the multitude of the wicked, 71:6
Delivered he Him therefore, 245:47
Deluded world, 94:4
Depart; enough, my treasure, 248:61
Depart now, dark shadows, 202:1
Depart now, gloomy shadows, 202:1
Depart? Oh no, my treasure stays, 248:61
Descend, O Spirit, purging flame, 6:6
Descending from His throne on high, 91:2
Desired day, 31:3
Despair not, O little band, 42:4
Despair not, O little flock, 42:4
Despair ye not, 42:4
Despise Thou not, Thou sunshine of my soul, 65:5
Despised am I, 138:2
Despisest thou the riches of His goodness (grace), 102:4
Despisest thou the riches of His mercy, 102:4
Despiseth* thou the riches of His goodness, 102:4
Despite the ancient dragon, 227:5
Despite the old dragon (serpent), 227:5
Destroy if Thou wilt, 48:4
Destroy, O God, the doctrines, 2:3
Destroy the old Adam, 48:4
Destroy ye me, 245b
Devotion, such as never known, 174:3
Dialogue, 49
Dialogue between Fear and Hope, 60
Die in me, Earth (world), 169:5

Diligently will I guard Thee, 248:33
Direct for me my way, 148:6
Direct me, then, O God, 96:4
Direct my heart and mind, 148:6
Direct Thou, Lord, my actions, 194:12
Direct thyself, dearest, according to My pleasure, 57:8
Direct yourself, most beloved, 57:8
Discard ye this frantic and profitless sorrow, 8:4
Disdain not, O light of my soul, 65:5
Disdain not, Thou, my soul's light, 65:5
Disdain then not, Thou light unto my soul, 65:5
Dispelled and gone today's, 63:4
Disperse ye, disperse ye, 205:11
Disperse ye, lords of Hell, 5:5
Dissolve now, my spirit, 245:63
Dissolve, O my heart, 245:63
Disturb thyself not, discouraged spirit, 99:3
Do justice to all men, 163:1
Do not be afraid, my heart, 111:2
Do not be downcast, my soul, 489
Do not be shocked, despondent soul, 99:3
Do not deal according to Thy law, 101:2
Do not deal by Thine own justice, 101:2
Do not despair, O little flock, 42:4
Do not despise, Thou my soul's one true light, 65:5
Do not forget us for long, 29:6
Do not murmur, dear Christian, 144:2
Do not punish me in Thy wrath, 246:74
Do not quaver so, dishearted soul, 99:3
Do not think in thine extreme hardship, 93:5
Do not turn your foot back, 207:4
Do thine alms and have compassion, 39:4
Do thou good and help thy neighbor, 39:4
Do Thou, O Lord, appease my conscience, 78:6
Do Thou, our God, beside us stand, 2:6
Do with me as Thy goodness prompts Thee, 245:40; 377

Do with me, God, according to Thy goodness, 156:2b

Do with me, O God, according to Thy will, 514

Do with me what Thou wilt, 514

Do ye not know that I must be about my Father's, 154:5

Do ye not know that I must be busy, 154:5

Do you no longer take pleasure, 208:4

Does not one have with his children, 211:2

Does Thy name, my Savior, 248:39

Don't children cause a hundred thousand troubles, 211:2

Don't our children give us a hundred thousand, 211:2

Don't tell anyone that our taxes, 212:10

Don't we have a hundred thousand troubles, 211:2

The door of Heaven He opened wide, 151:5

Dost think thy prayers He doth not heed, 138:3a

Dost thou despise the riches of His goodness, 102:4

Dost thou despise the riches of His grace, 102:4

Dost thou disdain the riches of His goodness, 102:4

Doth Thy name, my Savior, 248:39

Down, thou ancient dragon, 227:5

Down with the haughty, arrogant, 126:4

Draw near, O Lord and give Thy blessing, 120a:6

Draw us to Thee, 255

Draw us to Thee, and draw Thou near, 43:11.2

Draw us to Thee and we shall run, 43:11.2

Draw us to Thee, Lord Jesus, 281; 282

Draw us to Thee without delay, 43:11.2

Due praises to th' incarnate love, 248:28; 314

Due time for joy He knoweth truly, 93:4

Dull care, away, 210a:3

Dumb sighs, quiet moans, 199:2

Dumb sighs, secret laments, 199:2

Dust art Thou now, 246:78.2

The duteous day now closeth, 244:16; 392; 393; 394; 395,

Dwell not upon the morrow, 187:1

The dwelling is ready, 74:3

E

Each hour of ev'ry day, 477

Each righteous soul adds light, 195:2

The earth and the heavens, 134a:8

Earth, thy pleasures are burdens, 161:2

An earthly brilliance, 1:4

An earthly gleam, a worldy light, 1:4

An earthly ray, 1:4

An earthly shimmer, a physical light, 1:4

Earth's dazzling lure I'd all resign, 47:5

Earth's frail pomp and vanities, 426

Earth's glittering lure I would fain resign, 47:5

Earth's proudest dignities, 26:5

The Easter Lamb for us was slain, 4:6; 158:4

Easter oratorio, 249

E'en: see also Even

E'en as the billows, wildly crashing, 178:3

E'en as the grain to earth doth fall, 114:4

E'en as the rain from heaven, 166:4

E'en as to earth the grain doth fall, 114:4

E'en now is He above a mansion bright preparing, 43:10

E'en the cruel cross' journey, 123:3

E'en though the world refrain not, 58:4

E'en with our muted, feeble voices, 36:7

E'er: see also Ever

E'er bide with us, O Savior dear, 6:3

E'er will the Lord the poor deliver, 186:8

Empty heads and swollen, 201:13

Enchant us both, you rays of joy, 208:12

Enclose my heart, this blessed wonder, 248:31

The end has come, 245:58

The end is come; the pain is over, 159:4

The end is nigh, 245:58

The ending is already made, 161:4

Endless time, thou mak'st me anxious, 20:3
Endure! endure, 244:41
Endure, faint heart, 153:7
Endure, faint heart; though men falsely, 244:41
Endure for a little quietly, 93:3
The enemies are all in Thine hand, 178:7.1
Engrave this memorial, 207:9
Enlighten also our mind and heart, 116:6
Enlighten my dark mind, 248:47
Enlighten Thou my blinded senses, 248:47
Enlighten Thou our ev'ry heart, 116:6
Enlighten too my dark thoughts, 248:47
Enough have I, 82:2
Enough! I prithee hold thy tongue, 212:21
Enough of him, 212:7
Enough! We each have had our chance, 212:21
Enraged, the Prince of Hell, 44:5
Enrich, Lord, with Thy joy and radiance, 73:2
Enter not into judgment with Thy servant, 105:1a
Enter now into my heart, 80:4
Enter these courts with Me, 140:5
Enter Thy gates, 28:6; 183:5
Entrust thy ways, 161:6; 270; 271; 272; A79
Entrust thy ways unto Him, 153:5; 244:53
Erase, O God, the teachings, 2:3
Especially that in my heart, 131:4b
Esteem of the whole wide world, 204:4
Etch this day in our remembrance, 207:9
Eternal as is God on high, 20:7
Eternal God, whom we dare Father name, 173:5
The eternal mansions of our God, 198a:8a
Eternal mighty God, 194:2
Eternal One, our hearts go out to Thee, 173:5
Eternal peace, 244:78
Eternity, dread word of terror, 20:3
Eternity, most awful word, 20:1
Eternity, terrific word, 20:1
Eternity, thou awful word, 20:1; 60:1a

Eternity, thou mak'st me anxious, 20:3
Eternity, thou thunder-word, 20:1; 20:11; 60:1a; 397; 513
Eternity, thou thunderous word, 20:1; 20:11; 60:1a
Eternity, trememdous word, 20:1; 20:7; 20:11; 60:1a; 397
Eternity, you make me fearful, 20:3
Eternity's sapphire house, 198:8
Even: see also E'en
Even as He promised to our forefathers, 243:11
Even as the hart, 148:3
Even as the rain and the snow from heaven fall, 18:2
Even as the rainwaters soon flow away, 166:4
Even as the wild sea waves, 178:3
Even if this evil world does persecute, 58:2
Even in heavenly longing, our body holds, 70:4
Even in our heavenly longing, our body holds, 70:4
Even so, come, Lord Jesus, 106:2f
Even the Earth's foundation, 246:70
Even the edifice of the world trembles, 246:70
Even the hard cross-journey, 123:3
Even the hard journey of the cross, 123:3
Even today, Father, please do that, 211:8
Even with subdued and weak voices, 36:7
The evening, though, of the very same Sabbath, 42:2
Ever: see also E'er
The ever bounteous God, 192:2
Ever charming Zephyrus, 205:9
Ever God doth justice, 45:3
Ever God shall have my heart, 93:6
Ever hopeful raise your prayer, 115:4
Ever shining, guide my spirit, 180:5
Ever tender, see I press thy form, 201:5
Ever the name of God I honor with praise, 142:4
Ever think I of that day, 329
Evermore, with dread I quiver, 20:3

Every: *see also* Ev'ry
Every billow of my waves, 206:5
Every creature born of God, 80:2a
Every man that God created, 80:2a
Every mortal soon must perish, 262; 643
Every ripple of my stream (waters), 206:5
Every soul by God created, 80:2a
Everyone who is born of God, 80:2a
Everything according to God's will, 72:1
Everything born of God, 80:2a
Everything is awaiting You, 187:1
Everything is on God's blessing dependent, 263
Everything now that you wish, 24:3
Everything that has breath, 190:1b
Everything the heart can wish for, 30a:5
The evil, sinful world is past, 248:63b
Evil world, thy flatt'ring kisses, 247:53
Ev'ry: *see also* Every
Ev'ry blessing, ev'ry pleasure, 30a:5
Ev'ry day I sing Thy praises, 25:6
Ev'ry day my thanks redoubles*, 25:6
Ev'ry eye now awaiteth, Lord, 23:3
Ev'ry hour I think of Thee, 246:66
Ev'rything He comprehends, 245:56
Exalt the Lord, the God of Israel, 167:2
Exalted flesh and blood, 173:1
Exalted lord, whom Anhalt sovereign, 173a:5
Exalted one, as Anhalt's father, 173a:5
Examine me God, and discover my heart, 136:1
Examine me, God, and inquire of my heart, 136:1
Exterminate, O God, the teaching, 2:3
Extinguish with haste will the judge, 90:3
Exult, rejoice! Awake, praise the days, 248:1
Exultantly upspringing, 313
The eye alone doth water see, 7:7
The eye alone the water sees, 7:7
The eye sees only the water, 7:7
The eyes alone the water see, 7:7

F

The fading sun has from the heavens descended, 297
Fain would I give myself, O God, 163:4
Fair city thou among the lindens, 119:3
Fair fields, your green showing, 208:14
Fair town among the linden, 119:3
Faith creates the soul's wings, 37:5
The faith is the pledge of the love, 37:2
The faith lend me in Thy Son, 37:6
Faithful Christians, God confessing, 173:2
Faithful Echo, 213:5
Faithful God, I lay before Thee, 25:6; 194:6
Faithful God, I must complain, 194:6
Faithful God, I must complain to Thee, 25:6
The faithful shepherd I, 85:1
Faithful soul, thy spices dainty to the living, 249:5
Faithless world, I trust you not, 52:2
Fall asleep, weary eyes, 82:3
Fall asleep, ye cares and troubles, 197:3
Fall asleep, ye weary eyes, 82:3
Fall asleep, you eyes so weary, 82:3
Fall asleep, you weary eyes, 82:3
Fall down with thanks, 248:36
Fall with praises and thanksgiving, 248:36
Fall with thanks; fall down, 248:36
Fall with thanks; fall with praising, 248:36
False hypocrites' likeness, 179:3
False love, thou traitor perjured, 203:1
False world, hypocritical kisses, 247:53
False world, I do not thee trust, 52:2
False world, I trust you not, 52:2
Fame and honor and praise, 21:11b
Far beyond all other pleasures, 211:4
Far from me put I off all empty pleasure, 123:6
Far off I see my fatherland, 58:5
Fare thee well for ever, 64:8
Fare thee well, O pleasure, 64:8; 227:9
Fare thee well; of thee I'm weary, 27:6
Fare thee well that errest, 227:9

Fare thee well that's mortal, 64:8
Fare thee well, thou world of sorrow, 27:5
Fare thee well, thou worldly tumult, 27:5
Fare ye well, all passions, 227:9
Fare ye well, ye joys that wither, 27:5
Farewell, farewell for ever, 95:2b; 245:52; 415
Farewell, henceforth for ever, 95:2b; 415; 735; 735a; 736
Farewell I gladly bid thee, 95:2b; 245:52; 415; 735; 735a; 736
Farewell I gladly give thee, 735; 735a; 736
Farewell, O weary, broken body, 245:67
Farewell then, O world of sorrow, 8:5
Farewell, thou who choosest Earth, 64:8
Farewell to the being that chooses, 227:9
Farewell will I give thee, 95:2b; 735; 735a; 736
Farewell will I to thee give, 95:2b
Fast my bitter tears are flowing, 21:5
Father, all I bring Thee, 39:5
The Father Almighty, 232:13b
Father, by Thy love and pow'r, 40:8
Father, dwell in ev'ry heart, 317; 748; 748a
Father, give us still Thy favor, 51:3
Father, give us Thy favor, 51:3
The Father gives to Him an everlasting, 43:8
The Father has for Him yea an eternal, 43:8
The Father has to Him a crown, 43:8
The Father hath appointed Him, 43:8
The Father hath crowned the year, 28:5
The Father hath Him, yea, a lasting kingdom, 43:8
Father in eternity, 669; 672
Father in Heaven, we thank Thee, 28:6
Father, in high Heaven dwelling, 263
Father, Lord of mercy, 292
Father, may Thy blessing fall, 63:7
Father, may Thy loving mercies fall, 51:3
Father, merciful and holy, 154:3,
Father, O gracious heavenly Lord, 103:6
Father of empires, great ruler of rulers, 215:9
Father of mercies, God most high, 103:6

The Father there above, 292
Father, we thank Thee who has planted, 321
Father, what I proffer, 39:5
The Father's voice has clearly spoken, 7:4
The Father's voice itself resounded, 7:4
The Father's voice let(s) itself be heard, 7:4
Fear and trembling, shame and anguish, 246:1
Fear and trembling, shame and grief, 246:1
Fear God with dread, 45:5
Fear have thou none, 153:3
Fear not; compassion was of God, 198a:5
Fear not, for I am with thee, 228
Fear not, I am with thee, 153:3; 228
Fear not, little flock, 42:4; 176:5
Fear not, my soul, 461
Fear not, O little flock, 42:4
Fear not, thou faithful Christian flock, 402
The fear of death, how doth it fright me, 60:3
Fear then, thou too, 102:5
Fear thou not, for I am with thee, 228; 153:3
Fear thou not; I am with thee, 153:3
A fearful end awaits thee (you), 90:1
Fearful falter my steps, yet Jesus hears, 33:3
The fearful suffering endured by Israel, 63:4
Feeble is our puny might, 14:2
A feeble soul, 198a:4b
A feeble soul, a feeble sinner, 179:6
A feeble soul, a slave of sin, 55:1
Feed and nourish me, I plaint, 246:9
Feel I the fear and pains of Hell, 3:3
Fellow, that's just wind, 201:3
Fervent is my longing, 727
Fervently do I long for, 727
Fie, thou roaring lion, 227:5
Fifty dollars, 212:12
Fifty florins seem a lot, 212:12
Fight and triumph, mighty hero, 62:4
Fight, conquer, strong hero, 62:4
Fight on, vanquish, hero bold, 62:4
Fight victorious, hero strong, 62:4
Fill, O Lord, with Thy rich blessing, 120a:3
Fill, thee heavenly, godly flames, 1:3

Fill, ye heavenly, divine flames, 1:3
Filled with the Spirit's grace and love, 295
Filled with yearning, to thy side, 201:5
The final day will soon arrive, 310
Final hour, break now forth, 31:8
Finally my yoke must (will), 56:3
The fire doth make the silver pure, 2:5
Firm faith undoubting grant me, 37:6
Firm in Thy truth retain us, 79:6
Firm me with Thine own spirit's joy, 113:8
Firmly enshrine, my heart, 248:31
First comes need; Oh Lord, this one thing, 453
First innocence of Paradise, 198a:3b
The fitting time of joy He knoweth, 93:4
Flee, disappear, give way, ye cares, 249a:3
Flee, you worries, 187:5b
The flesh in earth now lying, 161:6
The flesh must even be crucified, 244:65
Flocks and herds may graze (safely), 208:9
Flocks in pastures green abiding, 208:9
Flourish like cedars, lime trees of Saxony, 214:9
Flow gently, fair rivers, 206:1
Flow gently, playful rivers, 206:1
Flutes be silent; cease your piping, 210a:6
Flutes be silent; stay your piping, 210:6
Fly, begone, vanish, O cares, 249a:3
Fly hence, ye godless crew, 76:5
Fly, my soul, this doleful mood, 489
Fly, oh where, 245:48b
The foam-crested billows of Belial's waters, 81:3
The foaming and ravening billows of Belial, 81:3
The foaming waves of Belial's rivers (streams), 81:3
The foaming waves of the floods of the ungodly, 81:3
The foe are all within Thine hand, 178:7.1
Follow God and His will, 197:4
Fond heart, ever faithful, 68:2
Fond heart, full of mercy, with love, 185:1
The font of grace, sin-cleansing, 165:6

Fool is he that with fate as his master, 203:3
The fool on Mammon sets his heart, 18:3e
Foolhardy lover, truly fate is thy master, 203:3
For all mankind is He the light, 83:5; 125:6
For all men who in Thee believe, 176:4b
For all that believe in Thee shall not perish, 176:4b
For all the good Thou gave us, 16:6
For all ye whose faith is steadfast, 176:4b
For as a loving father hath pity, 17:7
For as a tender father, 225:2
For as a tender father hath pity, 17:7
For as the rain and snow from heaven fall, 18:2
For as the rain cometh down, and the snow, 18:2
For before Thee becomes no living person, 105:1b
For before Thee no living person, 105:1b
For behold, all generations, 243:4
For Christ my Savior live I, 95:1a; 281; 282
For dancing, for leaping, so shaketh the heart, 201:7
For dancing, for leaping, so trembles the heart, 201:7
For Elijah's voice is crying, 30:6
For ever to sever the shackles that bind me, 57:7
For ever with the Lord, 466
For every time I had great heaviness of heart, 21:2
For God forsakes no one, 107:2
For God forsaketh no one, 107:2
For God has loved the world so well, 68:1
For God has wondrous love to show, 68:1
For God His wondrous love to show, 68:1
For godly folk this light upspringing, 195:2
For God's angels ne'er depart, 149:4
For God's eye looks on us, 90:4
For hath God the world so loved, 173:4
For He has regarded the low estate, 243:3
For He hath regarded the humility, 243:3

For He hath regarded the low (lowliness), 243:3

For He is the help of my countenance, 21:6b

For he must release one of necessity, 246:55a

For He that is mighty, 243:5

For he, when trouble comes, 186:4b

For He who is mighty, 243:5

For His ends God designed thee, 107:5

For I am sure, 95:5

For I can naught accomplish, 97:3

For I know this, 95:5

For I look upon myself, 189:2

For I say to you, 246:12

For I say unto you, 246:12

For if He hath decided, 97:7

For if I look at myself, 189:2

For if I think upon my days, 189:2

For in Him we live and move, 106:2b

For in my mind, as I have earlier, 131:4b

For in Thy sight no man living, 105:1b

For in Thy sight no man that liveth, 105:1b

For in Thy sight shall no man living, 105:1b

For just as Thou hast noble concord, 41:4

For love my Savior now is dying, 244:58

For love my Savior will die, 244:58

For love, O my Savior, for love of me, 244:58

For love of man the Savior dieth, 244:58

For love of me my Lord is dying, 244:58

For love of us my Savior suffered, 244:58

For love unending He came down to us, 182:4

For love will my Redeemer die, 244:58

For man liveth and moveth, 106:2b

For me a table Thou dost spread, 112:4

For me a table Thou hast spread, 112:4

For me the untrue world hath set with lie, 244:38

For me to live is Jesus, 95:1a; 281; 282

For my erring, my misdoing, 245:11

For my salvation Thou wast sent me, 68:4

For my soul is longing for the Lord, 131:4a

For no man shall in Thy sight, 105:1b

For now the law of the Spirit hath given, 227:4

For of necessity he must release, 246:55a

For out of necessity he must release, 246:55a

For see, here in a manger lies, 248:17

For since the head his limbs, 31:7

For so the Father willed, 73:5

For so to do's the Christian's crown, 132:2b

For such His will who made us, 73:5

For that Thine advent glory be, 121:6

For the Baptist's voice is crying, 30:6

For the beauty of the Earth, 344

For the brave of every race, 262

For the covenant from the beginning, 106:2e

For the heart's pleasure to cling, 26:4

For the inmost heart-recesses, 248:53

For the law of the Spirit of life, 227:4

For the law of the Spirit, which gives (lives), 227:4

For the Lord God is a sun and shield, 79:1

For the Lord has made me full of lamentations, 46:1b

For the Lord hath made me full of lamentation, 46:1b

For the Lord hath me with sorrow, 46:1b

For the meek shall not go empty, 75:1a

For the righteous, 196:2

For the righteous light is sown, 195:1a

For the righteous must the light ever new, 195:1a

For the righteous the light hath awakened, 195:1a

For the time is at hand, 44:2

For Thee, Jehovah, are our praises, 299; 452

For Thee, Lord, I long, 150:2

For Thee, Lord is my desire, 150:2

For thee, O dear, dear country, 369

For then no man alive may Thou acquit, 105:1b

For this I know, 95:5

For this is appeared the Son of God, 40:1

For this is the Christian's crowning honor, 132:2b

For this is the crowning honor, 132:2b

For this shall be the Christian's crowning, 132:2b

For this there was sent us, 40:1
For this we give Thee willing praise, 130:6.1
For Thou alone art holy, 232:10; 233:5; 234:5; 235:5b; 236:5
For Thou around my path wilt be, 112:5
For Thou hast promised, Lord, 128:5
For Thou only art holy, 232:10; 233:5; 234:5; 235:5b
For thou shalt die the death, 106:2e
For though we wake and though we sleep, 114:7
For 'tis our Father made us, 73:5
For today shalt thou be with Me, 106:3b
For today thou wilt with Me, 106:3b
For unto us a Child is born, 142:2
For unto us a Child's born, 142:2
For us a Child is born, 142:2
For us all killing is unlawful, 245:25
For us He left His throne in Heaven, 68:4
For us he naught but good, 244:57
For us the Easter Lamb was slain, 4:6
For us the Lord great things hath done, 119:7
For us to Earth He cometh poor, 248:7a
For what art Thou so angry, Lord, 101:4
For what purpose is this waste(d), 244:7
For what the eternal God of peace, 86:3
For who blessed passeth thither, 146:8
For ye are the blessed ones, 196:5a
For you, the most loving glances, 208:15
For you 'tis best that I should go hence, 108:1
For you 'tis best that we be parted, 108:1
Forbear, the lovliest of days, 30:11
Forbear Thy vengeance, O Lord, 463
Forever blessed be His name, 69:2
Forget me not, 505
Forget me not that I may not forget Thee, 504
Forget not further still, 29:6
Forget not to do well and to share, 39:4
Forget us not, O Lord, 29:6
Forgive me Jesus my transgressions, 48:6
Forgive me, Lord my God, I pray, 113:8

Forgive, O Father, all our sin, 87:3
Forgive, O Father, forgive our sin, 87:3
Forgive, O Father, our default, 87:3
Forgive, O Father, our guilt, 87:3
Forgive, O Father, our offense, 87:3
Forgive, O Lord, our severing ways, 377
Forsake me not, my dear beloved God, 505
Forsake me not, my God, 45:7
Forsake me not, O dearest God, 505
Forsake me not that I may not forsake, 504
Forsake, O man, the delights of this world, 20:9
Forsake, O man, the pleasure of this world, 20:9
Forsake, O man, the vices of the world, 20:9
Forsake this vile earth, 494
A fortress strong is God, our God, 80:1
A fortress sure is God our King, 80:1
Fortunate are the souls who trust, 442
Fortunate flock, Jesu's sheep, 104:5
Fortunate flock, Jesus' sheep, 104:5
Fortunate is he who knows who stands, 105:4
Fortune and blessing are ready, 184:4
Forty** days had passed since Christ arose, 266
Forty days and forty nights, 745
Foundation of the empire, bearer of the crown, 215:9
Foundation of the realm, king of kings, 215:9
Founder of empires, dispenser (ruler), 215:9
Fount of all goodness, 445
Fount of ev'ry blessing, 445
Fountain of all blessings, 445
Fountainhead of all virtues, 445
Four* days had passed since Christ arose, 266
The four seasons, 206
Fret not, my soul, 153:7
Fret not, my soul, nor be downhearted, 155:3
Fret not, my soul, on God relying, 315; 460; 510; 511; 512
Fret not, soul, that God give thee fame, 384; 489
Fret thee not, thou mortal soul, 186:1

Friend Aeolus, pray, 205:10
Friend of man, our souls possessing, 180:3b
From all that dwell below the skies, 174:5; 326
From all the world goes up the cry of woe, 25:2
From all who on the world do dwell, 195:6
From Bethany the Master comes down, 245:52
From blemish Heaven itself's not free, 136:4
From Caiaphas they led him, 245:22
From Christ, who is the head and founder, 31:7
From deep distress to Thee I pray, 38:1
From deep need I cry to Thee, 38:1; 38:6
From depths of woe cry I to Thee, 38:1
From depths of woe I call on Thee, 38:1
From east to west, 121:6
From God a ray of joy comes to me, 172:6
From God comes to me a joy-light, 172:6
From God do all our blessings flow, 194:8
From God I will not depart, 73:5; 417; 418; 419
From God I will not leave, 73:5
From God I will not wander, 73:5; 417; 418; 419
From God I'll not be parted, 417; 418; 419; 658; 658a
From God my all deriving, 107:6
From God naught shall divide me, 658; 658a
From God shall naught divide me, 73:5; 220:1; 417; 418; 419; 658; 658a
From God to me comes joyful light, 172:6
From God will I not depart, 658; 658a
From God will nothing part me, 417; 418; 419; 658; 658a
From God's house they will expel you, 44:1
From hardness of our hearts, 18:3b
From Heaven above I come here, 248:9
From Heaven above I hither come, 248:9; 248:17

From Heaven above to Earth I come, 248:9; 248:17; 606; 700; 701; 738; 738a; 769; A63; A64; A65
From Heaven came the angel host, 607
From Heaven high I come to Earth, 243:13
From Heaven high the Lord, 90:4
From Heaven on high I come to you, 606
From Heaven the angel troop come near, 607
From Heav'n a song is falling, 95:2b
From Heav'n above, 248:23
From Heav'n the angel host come near, 607
From heights above I hear its tones, 198a:4a
From high Heaven, 769
From high Heaven do I come, 606
From ill do Thou defend me, 244:21
From lands that see the sun arise, 121:1
From lofty towers bells are tolled, 198a:4a
From love unbounded, yes, all from love, 244:58
From me take me, make me Thine, 163:5
From my eyes salt tears are flowing, 21:5
From my eyes salt tears are raining (streaming), 21:5
From my eyes the salt tears show'ring, 21:5
From my guilty soul, I pray Thee, 105:6
From out my heart I praise, 269
From out the Heaven high, from off God's throne, 62:3
From out their temples they cast you, 183:1
From Sheba shall many men be coming, 65:1
From Sheba to Thee shall all men come, 65:1
From Sheba will they all arrive, 65:1
From the bondage of transgression, 245:11
From the deep I cry to Thee, 246:40
From the deep, Lord, cried I, Lord, to Thee, 131:1a
From the deep, Lord, cried I out to Thee, 131:1a
From the depths I call to Thee, 745
From the depths now do I call Lord, to Thee, 131:1a

From the depths of my heart, 269

From the depths of woe I call on Thee, 686; 687

From the depths to Thee I call, 745

From the shackles of my vices' bondage, 245:11

From the snare of my sins, 245:11

From the tangle of my transgressions, 245:11

From the world I demand (long), 64:7

From today, dearest Father, 211:8

From trouble deep I cry to Thee, 38:6

Fruiting branches, 205:13

Fruits and flowers, 205:13

Fugue on the choral, 700

Fulfill me with Thy spirit's glow, 113:8; 168:6

Full forty days past Easter Day, 266

Full fourscore years am I, 71:2a

Full of longing, I press your tender cheeks, 201:5

Funeral cantata, 53; 198; 198a; 244a

The future is full of the promise, 134a:4a; 134a:4b

G

The gates of Heaven open wide, 151:5

Gaze upward, for our God hath built, 198a:8a

The gentle Pleisse see, 207a:2

Gentle shall my dying labor, 249:7

Gentle Shepherd, Thou has stilled, 472

Gentle Shepherd, watch Thou o'er us, 184:6

Get hence, idolatrous band, 76:5

Get thee gone, vanity, 123:6

Get thyself, my soul, prepared, 115:1

Get you gone, vanity, 123:6

Girls have difficult dispositions, 211:6

Girls who are of hard disposition, 211:6

Girls with strong minds, 211:6

Give ear, O Lord, and mark my sore complaining, 254

Give ear, O Lord, Thou light, 65:5

Give, fair one, many sons, 212:18

Give glory, praise and honor, 231

Give heed and listen, 211:1

Give him, oh fair one, many handsome, 212:18

Give honor, praise and glory, 51:4

Give honor to the Lord, 129:1; 129:2; 129:3; 129:4

Give laud and praise the Highest Good, 117:1

Give, Lord, Thy church and this our land, 219:5.1

Give me back my dearest Master, 244:51

Give me back my Jesus (Lord), 244:51

Give me Jesus, I implore ye, 244:51

Give me still Thy shelter, 81:7

Give me that heart of thine, 518

Give me thereby, my God, 77:4

Give me thy heart, 518

Give, mighty God, Thy word increasing, 34a:7

Give, oh, give me back my Lord, 244:51

Give praise and sing, 248:35

Give praise, glory and honor, 231

Give praise to God enthroned on high, 33:6

Give praise to God whose might doth close, 14:5

Give praise! With us all's well, 29:4

Give thanks; sing praises, for God's love, 286

Give thanks to God; His friendship, 286

Give the hungry man thy bread, 39:1a

Give thought, Lord, now unto Thy work, 143:7b

Give thought, my soul, 245:31

Give thought, my spirit, 509

Give to our God all honor, 117:2b

Give to our God the glory, 117:2b

Give to the Lord glory due the Master, 148:1

Give to the winds thy fears, 466

Give unto the Lord the glory due unto His name, 148:1

Give us peace, 232:25

Give way, ye foolish, fruitless cares, 8:4

Give way, you spirits of sadness, 227:11

Glad am I to die, 82:5

Glad rejoice, my spirit, today, 70:7; 246:68; A52; A53

Gladly I clasp Thy hand extended, 229:4

Gladly will I agree to take cross, 244:29

Gladly will I, all resigning, 244:29

Gladly will I, fear disdaining, 244:29

Gladly will I too accept them, 244:29

Gladly would I be enduring, 244:29

Gladly would I take upon me, 244:29

Glide gently, ye waters, 206:1

Glide, playing waves, 206:1

Gloria be sung to Thee (You), 140:7

Gloria, hark, Heav'n is singing, 140:7

Gloria, sing all our voices, 140:7

Gloria to Thee be sung now, 140:7

The glorious company of the apostles, 246:21

The glorious day has appeared, 67:4; 145:7

The glorious day has dawned, 67:4; 145:7; 629

The glorious day hath dawned, 629

Glory and honor to God the Father, 10:7

Glory and praise eternally, 106:4a

Glory be in Heaven's throne, 135:6

Glory be sung to Thee (You), 140:7

Glory be to God, 248:43

Glory be to God in the highest, 110:5; 232:4a; 248:21

Glory be to God on high, 110:5; 191:1a; 232:4a; 243:15; 248:21; 662; 663; 663a; 664; 664a; 675; 676; 676a; 677; 711

Glory be to God on the highest throne, 33:6

Glory be to God the Father and the Son, 10:7

Glory be to God upon the highest throne, 33:6

Glory be to the Father, 191:2; 243:12a

Glory be to the Father and to the Son, 10:7

Glory be to Thee, 140:7; 232:22

Glory be to Thee, O Lord, 248:43

Glory, laud, and honor be to God, 51:4

Glory, laud, and honor to God, 51:4

Glory, laud and thanks be sung to Thee, 121:6

Glory, laud, praise and majesty, 106:4a

Glory now to Thee are singing, 140:7

Glory now to Thee be given, 140:7

The glory of Augustus' saint's day, 207a:3

The glory of God are the heavens declaring, 76:1a

The glory of our God most high, 91:2

The glory of these forty days, 6:6

Glory, praise, and honor be to God, 51:4

Glory, praise, honor and majesty, 106:4a

Glory, praise, honor and splendor, 106:4a

Glory to God for all His wonders, 225:4

Glory to God in highest Heaven, 33:6

Glory to God in the highest, 110:5; 191:1a; 232:4a; 233:2; 234:2a; 235:2; 236:2; 248:21; 662; 663; 663a; 664; 664a; 675; 676; 676a; 677; 711; 715; 716; 717; 771; A48

Glory to God on high, 232:4a; 233:2; 234:2a; 235:2; 236:2

Glory unto God the Father, and the Son, 10:7

Glory unto Thee be given, 140:7

Go and leave us behind in sorrow, 209:3

Go away, atheist company, 76:5

Go forth, O Jesus, to suffer death, 500

Go forth then, you shepherds, 248:18

Go from me, world, 169:5

Go hence; it is enough that my treasure, 248:61

Go in then with Me, 140:5

Go, Jesu, go Thy path of pain, 247:1

Go, my Jesus, fulfill Your destiny, 247:1

Go then and with pain, 209:3

Go then; enough, my dear (treasure), 248:61

Go thy way, and grieving leave us, 209:3

Go 'way, earthly treasure, 227:7

God above desires me to believe, 45:2

God, ah God, forsake Thine own never-more, 79:5

God, ah God, forsake Thy faithful (people), 79:5

God, ah God, leave Thy people nevermore, 79:5

God all alone my heart shall master, 169:2a; 169:3

God alone my heart shall have, 169:2a

God alone shall (will) have my heart, 169:2a; 169:3

God and man, 147:6

God, as Thy name is, 171:1

God, as Thy name, so is Thy fame, 171:1

God be gracious and merciful to us, 323

God be merciful to me, 199:3

God be merciful unto us, 76:7

God be praised and blessed, 322

God be praised; now goes the year to its end, 28:1

God be praised; now the year goes to its end, 28:1

God be praised! The dragon falls, 19:2

God be praised! The dragon has fallen, 19:2

God be praised, who hath in His love for us, 79:4

God, be with us furthermore, 225:3

God bless and keep His faithful band, 76:9

God bless still the faithful host, 76:9

God bless then all the faithful throng, 76:9

God bless Thy ever faithful flock, 76:9

God, bless Your church with strength, 466

God, blot out all teachings, 2:3

God, by Thy strong protection, 14:4

God cares for the birds and beasts, 138:3b

God casts down and exalts in time, 75:4

God casts on us His kindly glance, 76:7

God casts the strong down from their seat, 10:4

God certainly helps, 86:5

God chooses for Himself the holy dwellings, 34:4

God chooseth out His holy places, 34:4

God cometh in poor human guise, 91:5

God does not even as the world, 86:4

God doth not act as doth the world, 86:4

God e'er is just, 20:5

God ever is man's best provider, 197:2

God ever of His mercy, 10:5

God ever will concern Him to mould, 107:5

God fairly deals with everyone, 188:2a

God faithful is, 52:4

God for us hath crowned the old year, 28:5

God for us, ye sons of Adam, 173:3

God, for whom Earth's orb is too small, 91:3

God for whom the Earth is too small, 91:3

God, for whom the Earth's orbit is too small, 91:3

God from the heavens blessing uttered, 7:4

God full of justice, alas, if Thou, 89:5

God gave His Gospel, 319

God gave the Gospel, 319

God gave to us a law, 9:2

God gave to us His law, 9:2

God gave to us the law, 9:2

God gave us a commandment (law), 9:2

God gives each of us his station, 75:4

God gives us each his station, 75:4

God goes up with rejoicing, 43:1

God goeth up with exultation, 43:1

God goeth up with shouting, 43:1

God grant that I, while here below, 156:2b

God guideth us with tender care, 188:2a

God has a heart, 98:4

God has adorned the earth with beauty, 187:7

God has all things done well, 35:4

God has arranged the Earth, 187:7

God has arranged this world, 187:7

God has blessed us by His grace, 194:10

God has blessed us in the new year, 28:5

God has blessed us in the past year, 28:5

God has blessed us in the present year, 28:5

God has done everything well, 35:4

God has my heart and there abideth, 169:3

God has my heart; there He abideth, 169:2a

God has ordained that man should stand, 115:3

God has provided for us all, 187:7

God has seated Himself high, 189:3

God hath a care for all living things, 187:5a

God hath a heart, 98:4

God hath all so well achieved, 35:4
God hath all things wisely done, 35:4
God hath done all things well, 35:4
God hath forsaken no one, 369
God hath set Himself on high, 189:3
God hath the Earth in fullness set, 187:7
God hath us in this very year, 28:5
God, have mercy on us, 225:3
God hearkens to His people's crying, 115:5
God helps certainly, 86:5
God Himself hath given His promise, 13:3
God His faithful word hath given, 13:3
God, Holy Ghost, to Thee I pray, 175:7
God, how great Thy goodness is, 462
God, how wonderful Your favor, 462
God humbleth and exalteth, 75:4
God in Heaven, almighty, 292
God in His wrath is like the tempest, 46:3
God in plenty e'er provideth, 187:5a
God, in Thy great goodness, 600
God is a fount, 28:4
God is a spring, 28:4
God is alive, 461
God is and bides the best provider, 197:2
God is aye our sun and shield, 79:2
God is e'er true, 52:4
God is ever just and right, 35:4
God is ever sun and shield, 79:2
God is faithful, 52:4
God is just in His works, 20:5
God is living; God is here, 461
God is my friend, 139:2
God is my joy; He my delight, 162:5
God is my King, 71:1
God is my ruler, 71:1
God is my shield and helper true, 85:6
God is my sov'reign, 71:1
God is my strong salvation, 245:52
God is not such as I and you, 86:4
God is our confidence, 197:1
God is our fortress and our rock, 80:8; 302; 303
God is our friend and helper true, 122:4a
God is our good providence, 197:1

God is our hope and strength, 24:6
God is our hope; we put our trust, 197:1
God is our refuge and defense, 377
God is our refuge in distress, 80:1
God is our sun and shield, 79:2
God is our true confidence, 197:1
God is our true sun and shield, 79:2
God is reconciled to us and is our friend, 122:4a
God is still our sun and shield, 79:2
God is the city of our strength, 80:1
God is thy keeper, 71:1
God is true; His word endures, 167:3
God, keep us ever in Thy thought, 225:3
God kindles His fire, 456
God, like a kindly father hath pity, 225:2
God lives; He's near, 320
God lives still, 461
God liveth aye, 320; 461
God liveth still, 320; 461
God liveth yet, 320; 461
God made it clear by word and deed, 7:3
God, man praiseth Thee in the stillness, 120:1
God meaneth well for ev'ryone, 188:2a
God means it well with everyman, 188:2a
God my shepherd walks beside me, 208:9
God now prosper you, 196:4
God, O God, forsake Thy people nevermore, 79:5
God of eternity, Lord of the ages, 123:6
God of Heaven and Earth, 248:53
The God of Israel slumbers not, 193:2
God of love, forgive and bless us evermore, 79:5
The God of love my shepherd is, 376
God of love, to Thee I call, 33:5
God of the earth, the sky, the sea, 153:9.1
God of the living, in whose eyes, 321
God of truth, eternal good, 373
God, one praises Thee in the stillness, 120:1
God our Father evermore, 669; 672
God our Father, send Thy spirit, 74:8
God, our hope, be ne'er forgetting, 79:5

God our Lord is sun and shield, 79:1
God owes nothing to me, 84:2
God praise and thanks who did not let, 14:5
God, praise waiteth Thee in the temple, 120:1
God preserveth all that liveth, 187:5a
God provides all life that breathes, 187:5a
God provides for all, 187:5a
God pushes the powerful from their seat, 10:4
God puts down the mighty from their seat(s), 10:4
God raiseth and down casteth, 75:4
God really owes me nothing, 84:2
God reigns for ever, 71:1
God safely Israel doth shield, 193:2
God send us to Mahanaim, 19:3
God sends Mahanaim us to us, 19:3
God sends to us His angel hosts, 19:3
God sends us Mahanaim here, 19:3
God sends us to Mahanaim, 19:3
God shall alone my heart have, 169:2a; 169:3
God shall, O ye mortal children, 173:3
God, show us grace and loving kindness, 323
God showers blessings on us, 90:2
God so loved the world and man, 173:4
God so loved the world His pity, 173:4
God so loved the world that He gave, 68:1
God so loved this world of sin, 173:4
God still lives, 320; 461
God supplieth ev'ry being, 187:5a
God surely owes me nothing, 84:2
God the Father and God the Son, grant it, 290
God the Father, be our stay, 317; 748; 748a
God the Father, dwell with us, 317
God the Father everlasting, 672
God the Father, send Thy spirit, 108:6
God the Father, with us be, 317
God the Lord is sun and shield, 79:1
God the Lord my king is, 71:1
God, the might of Thy protection, 14:4
God this hath told by word, 7:3

God, Thou hast all well accomplished, 63:3
God, Thou hast it well ordained, 63:3
God, Thou hast ordained what we now receive, 63:3
God, Thou hast us well accommodated, 63:3
God, Thou who art called love, 33:5
God, Thou who art love now called, 33:5
God, through Thine own strong protection, 14:4
God throws down the mighty from their seats, 10:4
God thrusts the mighty from the seat, 10:4
God, Thy goodness knows no bounds, 462
God we praise Thee now in the stillness, 120:1
God, we thank Thee for our Savior, 63:3
God, we thank Thee for the blessings, 120:4
God, we thank Thee for Thy kindness, 193:3
God, we thank Thee; not in vain, 472
God we thank Thee; Thy protection, 193:3
God, we thank Thy goodness, 193:3
God, who art Thyself the light, 316
God, who for this thy soul doth watch, 115:3
God, who for thy soul watches, 115:3
God, who has promised me, 13:3
The God who has promised me His aid, 13:3
God, who is watching us so well, 115:3
God who madest Earth and Heaven, 248:53
God, who ordained the Earth so fair, 187:7
The God who promised me His support, 13:3
God who regards the Earth so small, 91:3
God, who to me has promised, 13:3
God, who upon thee watch e'er keeps, 115:3
The God whom earth and sea and sky, 377
God, whose power never faileth, 149:2
God, whose very name is love, 33:5
God whose wide realm doth fill the skies, 91:3
God will its purity defend, 2:6
God will not fail, 86:5
God will, O ye men's children, 173:3

God will sustain everything, 117:3
God, with your powerful protection, 14:4
God works His will, and best it is, 72:5; 244:31
God, yet adorn** this Earth below, 187:7
God, You who are love, 33:5
God's a mighty sun and shield, 79:2
God's almighty and heavenly power, 147:8
God's angels never waver, 149:4
God's angels watch do o'er us keep, 19:3
God's anger is outpoured, 165:2
God's blessing on His faithful flock, 76:9
God's bright angels never sleep, 149:4
God's dear angels watch do keep, 149:4
God's deep purpose no man knoweth, 188:3
God's ensample thus to follow, 39:3
God's eternal shining light, 194:3
God's flock so ill do fare, 2:4
God's font of grace, sin-cleansing, 165:6
God's grace and strength will never fail, 80:8
God's help is sure, 86:5
God's love alone my heart possesseth, 169:3
God's mighty armies never cease, 19:3
God's mighty throne surrounding, 309
God's name for ever I'll be praising, 142:4
God's outstretched arms would clasp, 186:8
God's own angels never go, 149:4
God's own angels never yield, 149:4
God's own Son appeareth, 318; 600; 703; 724
God's own time, His time is ever best, 106:2a
God's own time is ever, now and evermore the best, 106:2a
God's own time is the best, 106:2a
God's own time is the hour, 106:2a
God's own time is the very best of times, 106:2a
God's own word can ne'er decieve, 167:3
God's own word is ever sure, 167:3
God's praises sounding, all worthy Christian folk, 391
God's providence and love alone, 194:8
God's self alone my heart possesses, 169:2a
God's self alone my heart possesseth, 169:2a

God's Son has come, 600
God's Son hath come, 703
God's time is best, 106:2a
God's time is the best of all, 106:2a
God's time is the ever best time, 106:2a
God's time is the very best time, 106:2a
God's true word deceiveth not, 167:3
God's ways who understandeth, 128:4
God's word He'd have us e'er defend, 2:6
God's word, that does not deceive, 167:3
God's word, that doesn't deceive, 167:3
God's word unshaken e'er shall stand, 80:8
God's word will remain with us, 80:8
God's works are manifold, 187:2
Goest Thou now, Jesu, from Heaven to Earth, 650
Gold from Ophir, 65:4
Gold of Ophir, 65:4
Golden and glorious the heaven's, 451
Golden season, happy moment, 173a:2
The golden sun, 451
Golden sunshine, happy leisure, 173a:2
Gone is sorrow, gone is sadness, 32:5
Gone is the day, 447
Good and faithful shepherd He, 85:2
Good cause have we to thankful be, 212:10
Good cheer, from God forgiveness came, 198a:5
Good cheer, ye, ye with faith shaken, 122:4b
Good Christian men, rejoice, 40:3
Good Christians all, rejoice ye, 313
Good fellows, be merry, 212:20
Good fortune and wealth, well-being, 197:8
A good man, too, 204:7
Good Midas, 201:14
Good neighbors all, come join with us, 212:2
Good news from Heav'n, 248:9
Good night, confused business of the world, 27:5
Good night, O being, 227:9
Good night, O elect of this world, 227:9
Good night, O existence, 64:8
Good night, thou world-confusion, 27:5
Good night, thou worldly tumult, 27:5

Good night, way of life, 64:8

Good Shepherd, comfort of Thy people, 184:6

Good sir, that's boast, you know, 201:3

The good things that God showers, 36b:5

Goodly without appearing, 246:31

The goodness and constancy, 10:3

Goodness and mercy follow, 112:5

The goodness and mercy of the Highest, 10:3

The goodness of God comes fresh, 10:3

The goodness of the Most High, 90:2

The Gospel God has given you, 319

The Gospel promise standeth fast, 99:2

The government is God's gift, 119:5

The governor answered, 244:56

The governor asked them, 244:56

The governor said, 244:56

The governor's soldiers then took, 244:62a

The gov'nance from on high is given, 119:5

Grace by the Holy Ghost bestowed, 295

The grace of God is all unbounded, 121:3

Gracious God, when wilt Thou call me, 8:1; 8:6

Gracious Lord of all our being, 147:1; 147:10

Gracious Lord of our being, 147:10

Graciously grant us peace, 126:6

Grant, Highest, to us at all times, 181:5

Grant in the bottom of my heart, 245:52

Grant, Lord God, grant that hope's bright ray, 198a:1

Grant, Lord, my soul to grow, 71:2b

Grant, Lord, that I may well forgive, 177:3

Grant, Lord, to us through all the ages, 181:5

Grant, Lord, unto us, 190:6

Grant me to find the task, 45:7

Grant, O Jesu, blessed Lord, 245:65

Grant, O our Father, 190:6

Grant that I do eagerly that which becometh me, 45:7

Grant that I do with care (diligence), 45:7

Grant that I find the task, 45:7

Grant that I from heart's depth, 177:3

Grant that Thy angel warrior band, 130:6.2

Grant them, O beloved father, 215:8

Grant this, that we Thy people, 176:6

Grant to us peace most graciously, 126:6

Grant unto me, O God, 77:4

Grant us graciously, Lord God, 126:6

Grant us, Jesu, God's dear Son, 245:65

Grant us, O Lord, Thine angel band, 219:5.1

Grant us, O Lord, to keep the faith, 2:6

Grant us peace, 232:25

Grant us peace graciously, 42:7

Grant us, Savior, God's dear Son, 245:65

Grant us Thy peace, 232:25

Grant us Thy peace, we pray Thee, 42:7

Grant us to do with zeal, 94:8

Granted that the torment of the damned, 20:4

Granted the damned's torment lasted, 20:4

Grasp and hold onto salvation, 174:4

The grave is broken, 66:2

The grave is foiled, 66:2

Great David's Lord and greater son, 23:1

Great God, have mercy, 246:74

Great God, I own Thy heavenly might, 345

Great God, in Thee I put my trust, 244:38

Great God of nations, 332

Great God of wonders, 416

The great God throws His abundance, 39:2

Great judge of all men, 33:2

Great King of Heaven, 245:27.1

Great Lord and almighty king, 248:8

Great Lord and mighty king, 248:8

Great Lord, O strong king, 248:8

Great love of God come in, 45:7 with 466

A great many splendid and fine, sturdy sons, 212:18

Great Master of Creation, 120a:1

A great mysterious light hath filled the orb, 125:4

Great One, what I treasure, 39:5

Great patron, your pleasure, 210:8

Great sponsor, your pleasure, 210:8

Great things our God for us hath done, 69:2

Great Thy love, Lord, 182:4

The greatest brilliance and pomp, 26:5
Greatest Lord, O mighty king, 248:8
The greatest lord, the meanest clod, 26:5
The greatest splendor, 26:5
Green and peaceful are the pastures, 208:9
Greetings, Jesus, Thou my treasure, 499
Grief and pain rend repenting hearts, 244:10
Grief and pain wring the guilty heart in twain, 244:10
Grief for sin rends the guilty heart, 244:10
Grief for sin sure acceptance finds, 244:10
Grief, now is my Jesus gone, 244:36a
Grief's lowest deeps he soundeth, 209:2
Grief's lowest depth he soundeth, 209:2
Grief's shadow now be gone, 202:1
Grieving's vain, and vain repining, 13:5
Grim death is most of all foes feared, 60:4a
Grip fast, grasp salvation, 174:4
Grip fast; sieze salvation, 174:4
Groaning and miserable wailing (weeping), 13:5
Groaning and piteous weeping, 13:5
Groaning and pitifully weeping, 13:5
Groaning, woe and vain repining, 13:5
Groans and piteous weeping, 13:5
Grow silent, host of Hell, 5:5
Grumble not, fretting soul, 144:2
Guard, dear angels, guard my ways, 19:5
Guard, O my glory, this marvelous wonder, 248:31
The guard of Israel doth sleep, 193:2
Guard thy soul, 54:1
Guard your faith; hold it fast, 174:4
Guide also my heart and mind, 148:6
Guide also my heart and thought, 5:7
Guide, O God, with loving kindness, 120a:3
Guide Thou my heart Thyself to own, 153:9.3
A guilty man, 198a:4b
Gush forth in abundance, thou fount, 5:3

H

Ha-ha! The longed-for hour, 205:2

Ha-ha! Just blame the wind, 201:3
Had God not come, may Israel say, 14:5; 257
Had God the Lord not remained with us, 178:1; 258
Had I now what most I wish for, 439
Had not the Lord been on our side, 14:1; 178:1; 178:7.2; 258
Hail, all hail now, mighty King, 245:34
Hail, all hail, Thou King of Jews, 244:62b
Hail Augustus, mighty sovereign, 207a:9
Hail, hail, King of the Jews, 244:62b
Hail, Jesu Christ, blessed for aye, 67:4; 314
Hail, King of the Jews, 245:34
Hail my Lord, in Your distress, 499
Hail our master, guide and teacher, 207:11
Hail the Almighty with songs of rejoicing, 66:3
Hail the day so rich in cheer, 605
Hail thou day when I may dwell, 70:10a
Hail, thou most precious of blisses, 211:4
Hail to the Lord's annointed, 415
Hail to Thee, Jesus kind, 410; 499
Hail to Thee, my Jesu holy, 768
Hail, true Body born of Mary, 484
Hair-splitting erudites insist that friendship, 443
Hallelujah: see also Alleluia
Hallelujah, 143:7a; 230:2
Hallelujah, hallelujah, 51:5
Hallelujah, hallelujah, praised be God, 110:7
Hallelujah! Let strength and might, 29:3; 29:7
Hallelujah! Power and might, 29:7
Hallelujah! Strength and might, 29:3; 29:7
The hand of God, 109:2
The hand of the Almighty works, 147:8
Hands in charity extended, 164:5
Hapless sinners are we, 407
Happiness and blessing are ready, 184:4
Happy am I; my Jesus has spoken, 81:6
Happy am I that possess Jesus, 147:6
Happy and fortunate are the pious, 442
Happy are we, 130:4

Happy be ye, wedded pair, 197:6
A happy change indeed, 206:2
Happy day, darling Father, 211:8
Happy day, noble couple, 210:10
Happy day, O noble couple, 210:10
Happy flock(s), 208:9
Happy he who thinks on Christ, 498
Happy he whose home is yonder, 146:8
Happy hours of golden sun, 173a:2
Happy I, to find my Jesus, 154:7a
Happy I, who have my Savior, 147:6
Happy is he who knows his surety, 105:4
Happy is he who puts his trust, 119:3
Happy is my soul to find Thee, 154:7a
Happy is the land ruled by a kindly hand, 212:8
Happy 'neath his princely sway, 173a:4
Happy shepherds, haste; ah, haste, 248:15
Happy shepherds, hurry, ah, hurry, 248:15
Happy souls chosen by God, 34:3
Happy souls, your voices rouse, 194:10
Hard the way the cross invites me, 123:3
The hardened race of sinners, 54:2
Hark, a solemn voice is calling, 30:6
Hark, a voice saith, All are mortal, 162:6; 262; 643
Hark, faithless world! Henceforth no more, 95:2a
Hark, I hear the voice that crieth, 30:6
Hark, my soul; it is the Lord, 36:8
Hark now, soft strains of flutes, 206:9
Hark, the glad sound, the Savior, 376
Hark, the song of jubilee, 262
Hark, the sound of holy voices, 423
Harken: see Hearken
Harmonious clashing of answering viols, 207:2
Harp and viol, voices blending, 1:5
Harps and lutes, and voices raising, 1:5
Has a father with his children, 211:2
Has a man with children round him, 211:2
Has He then ordained it, 97:7
Hast Thou, Lord Jesus, Thy countenance far, 57:8; 137:5

Hast Thou then, Jesus, hidden Thy countenance, 57:8
Haste, slow moments; hither fly, 30:10
Haste thee, soul, right joyfully, 83:3
Haste Thou then, my joy, my glory, 61:6b
Haste, ye deeply wounded spirits, 245:48a
Haste, ye hours, 30a:9
Haste, ye hours; come (get), 30:10
Haste, ye moments, 30a:9
Haste, ye mortals sin-beladen, 245:48a
Haste, ye shepherds, haste, 248:15
Haste, ye souls forlorn and weary, 245:48a
Haste, ye troubled souls, 245:48a
Haste, ye victims, 245:48a
Haste ye with a joyful heart, 83:3
Hasten, heart, full of joy (joyfulness), 83:3
Hasten, heart, with joyfulness, 83:3
Hasten, Immanuel, prince of the lowly, 123:1; 123:6; 485
Hasten thee now, my feeble soul, 454
Hasten, ye hours; come along (hither), 30:10
Hasten, you hours, 30a:9
Hate me then, hate me, 76:10
Hate only, hate me well, 76:10
Hate then, hate me wholly, 76:10
Hate ye me well, foul fiends, 76:10
Hatred on me do ye pour, 76:10
Have courage now, fearful and timorous, 176:5
Have done with thy raging, 15:6
Have faith in God, 72:3
Have faith in God, nor e'er distress thee, 315
Have Him crucified, 244:54d; 244:59b
Have hope, my heart; do not despair, 247:41
Have I e'er from Thee departed, 55:5; 244:48
Have I to tread the road of death, 198a:7b
Have lightnings and thunders, 244:33c
Have lightnings, has thunder, 244:33c
Have mercy; but now I will comfort, 55:4
Have mercy, God, 244:60
Have mercy; let tears, 55:3
Have mercy; let the tears, 55:3
Have mercy, Lord, 55:3; 131:2b

Have mercy, Lord, and hear our prayer, 101:1

Have mercy, Lord, for the sake, 244:47

Have mercy, Lord! However, I now hope, 55:4

Have mercy, Lord, my God, 244:47

Have mercy, Lord; my sin forgive, 305; 721

Have mercy, Lord, on me, 244:47

Have mercy Lord! See, hope's to me restored, 55:4

Have mercy, my God, 244:47

Have mercy, O God, 244:60

Have mercy on me, 55:3; 131:2b

Have mercy on me in such grief, 113:2

Have mercy on me, my God, 244:47

Have mercy upon me, 55:3; 131:2b

Have mercy upon me, O Lord, 244:47; 721

Have mercy upon me, O Lord God, 305

Have mercy upon me! Yet ever I'll be comforted, 55:4

Have mercy; yet now I comfort myself, 55:4

Have not people with their children, 211:2

Have patience; the welcome day, 30:11

Have pity, God, 244:60

Have pity, Lord, on my distress, 113:2

Have pity, Lord, Thy servant pleads, 305; 721

Have pity, O God, for the sake, 244:47

Have pity on me, 131:2b

Have pity on me in such trouble, 113:2

Have pity on my heart's, 131:2b

Have pity then, for now I hope again, 55:4

Have pity, Thou whose heart, 185:2

Have pity, ye whose hearts, 185:2

Have thunder and lightning, 244:33c

Have thy armor on, my soul, 115:1

He answered and said, 244:17

He answered them and said, 244:17

He answered to them and said, 244:17

He answers not to lying tongues, 244:40

He bids us comfort take, 248:27

He blesseth them who fear their God, 196:3

He blesseth those the Lord fearing, 196:3

He brings the year of jubilee, 122:6

He calleth all His sheep by their name, 175:1

He calleth for Elias, 244:71c

He calleth for Elijah, 244:71c

He calleth His own sheep, 175:1

He calleth His sheep by name and leads them, 175:1

He calls His sheep by name, 175:1

He came among us meek and poor, 248:7a

He came poor upon Earth, 248:7a

He came to Earth in poverty, 248:7a

He can and will not leave thee, 138:3a

He can and would thee not forsake, 138:3a

He comes, He comes, He comes (is), 247:49

He comes! the bridegroom comes, 140:2

He comes, the Lord of Hosts, 43:6

He comes, the Lord of Lords, 43:6

He comes to Earth in poverty, 248:7a

He denied it, and said, 245:18

He does not know what his pain is, 209:2

He does not know what pain is, 209:2

He guides my path to waters clear, 112:2

He guilty is of death, 244:42b

He has come to Earth poor, 248:7a

He has comforted His people, 248:27

He has done good to us all, 244:57

He has filled the hungry, 243:9

He has helped His servant Israel, 243:10

He has put down the mighty, 243:8

He has shown strength, 243:7

He hath come upon Earth poor, 248:7a

He hath comforted His people, 248:27

He hath done only good to all, 244:57

He hath filled the hungry, 243:9

He hath helped His servant Israel, 243:10

He hath His nation blessed, 248:27

He hath His people comforted, 248:27

He hath holpen His servant Israel, 243:10

He hath my course ordained, 97:7

He hath others saved, 246:61b

He hath put down the mighty, 243:8

He hath received Israel His servant, 243:10

He hath showed strength, 243:7

He hath shown might, 243:7

He hath shown strength, 243:7

He helps us all, 212:9

He holds His peace, to not a word replying, 244:40

He, however, who searches our hearts, 226:3

He is gone beyond the skies, 262

He is guilty of death, 244:42b

He is of death deserving, 244:42b

He is salvation's blessed light, 83:5

He is that grace and blessed light, 125:6

He is the health and happy light, 83:5; 125:6

He is the heathen's saving light, 83:5; 125:6

He is the help of my countenance, 21:6b

He is the hope, the saving light, 83:5

He is the salvation and blessed light, 83:5; 125:6

He is the salvation and the blessed light, 125:6

He is the true Easter Lamb, 4:6

He is worthy of death, 244:42b

He it is that doth uphold me, 21:6b

He it is, who quite alone, 43:7

He knows the hour when happiness (joy), 93:4

He knows the proper time for gladness, 93:4

He knows the right hours for joy, 93:4

He knows the right joy-hours, 93:4

He knows the time when joy is seemly, 93:4

He lives; from out the grave He is arisen, 160:2

He lives; from the dark grave He has arisen, 160:2

He of everything took heed, 245:56

He opens unto us the door, 151:5

He ordains it to His honor, 107:5

He promised, and sought, 246:6

He remembering His mercy, 10:5

He remembers His mercy, 10:5

He remembers mercy, 10:5

He said, Go into the city, 244:15a

He said, Go ye into the city, 244:15a

He said unto them, 246:45a

He saith, Go ye hence to the city, 244:15a

He saved others, 246:61b

He saved others, Himself He cannot save, 244:67d

He sent His word, His holy word, 376

He sets all for His honor, 107:5

He shall not to damnation come, 127:4d

He showeth to thee, man, what is right, 45:1

He stirreth up the people, 246:49b

He that believeth and baptized is, he shall, 37:1

He that believeth and is baptized shall be saved, 37:1

He that believeth shall not be condemned, 68:5

He that believeth will escape damnation, 68:5

He that hopeth in God steadfastly, 109:6

He that is down, 396

He thinks of mercy, 10:5

He to the heathen hath brought light, 83:5; 125:6

He took all into His care, 245:56

He took care of all things, 245:56

He took it down, 246:77

He troubles Himself about our crying, 115:5

He was crucified also, 232:16

He was reviled also by the robbers, 244:68

He went a little farther, 244:27

He who believes in Him will not be judged, 68:5

He who believeth and is baptized, 37:1

He who Christ's would fain be throughly, 47:2

He who commits sin, 54:3

He who does not believe in Jesus' name, 133:4b

He who exalts himself shall be humbled, 47:1

He who holds naught within his soul, 94:7

He who in Jesus bides, 75:11

He who is in the protection of the Highest, 339

He who is the same within, 179:4

He who lets God alone rule him, 434

He who lets only beloved God rule, 84:5; 88:7; 93:7; 179:6; 197:10; 434

He who looks from inside, 179:4

He who looks into our hearts, 226:3

He who loves Me, 172:2

He who loves Me keepeth My commandments, 59:1; 74:1

He who loves Me to My counsel heedeth, 59:1; 74:1

He who loves me will keep My commandments, 59:1; 74:1

He who ne'er so feebly striveth, 39:3

He who offers thanks praises Me, 17:1

He who owneth God with sincerity, 45:5

He who relies on God's command, 642

He who relies on God's compassion, 93:1

He who self exalteth shall soon with contempt be, 47:1

He who still loveth, 203:3

He who suffers God to guide him, 642; 690; 691; 691a; A68

He who trusteth and is baptized, 37:1

He who trusts God has built well, 433

He who trusts in God to guide him, 642; 647

He who wants to sail to India, 524:3

He who will only let God guide him, 642

He who will suffer God to guide him, 88:7; 93:1; 93:7; 197:10; 434; 642; 647; 690; 691; 691a; A68

He who would be called true Christian, 47:2

He who would in Christ be living, 31:6

He who would seek the joys of Earth, 94:7

He who would truly be known as a follower, 47:2

He whom God has not befriended, 248:57

He who's sincere, 179:4

He whose hand of mercy's empty, 164:5

He whose life was as the light, 245:21

He whose nature's pure and holy, 173:2

He will for me, near Himself, 43:10

He will not come into judgment, 127:4d

He will not come to judgment, 127:4d

He will not leave thee in thy need, 138:3a

He will not speak; He heareth, 244:40

He withdrew Himself from them, 246:24

He would beside Himself, 43:10

He yearneth after all our crying, 115:5

Health and blessing, 216:7

Health and blessing shall and must, 120:4

Hear, faithless world, for me thy empty joys, 95:2a

Hear, King of Angels, 248:24

Hear me, though my song be faulty, 25:5

Hear, Mighty One, 134a:7

Hear my pleading, Jesu, treasure, 410

Hear, O God, the eternal Father, 669; 672

Hear, O God, the Holy Ghost, 671; 674

Hear then, the choir of gentle flutes, 206:9

Hear Thou, O Lord, my sighs and lamentation, 254

Hear ye, I'll send for many fishers, 88:1a

Hear ye my lusty laughter, 205:3

Hear, ye nations, God's voice calling, 76:3

Hear, ye people, God is calling, 76:3

Hear, ye people, God's voice, 76:3

Hear, you nations, the voice of God, 76:3

Hearken, all ye sinful mortals, 247:126

Hearken to my halting praises, 25:5

Hearken, when with trembling accents, 25:5

Heart and lips, thy whole behavior, 147:1

Heart and mouth and deed and life (living), 147:1

Heart and mouth to Thee are open, 148:4

Heart and voice and all our being, 147:1

Heart and voice and thought and action, 147:1

A heart, aroused by tender feeling, 36c:2

Heart, break free of Mammon's fetters, 168:5

The heart I ask from thee, 518

The heart is wicked and deceitful, 176:1

The heart of God, 98:4

Heart, rend Mammon's chains, 168:5

Heart, tear away Mammon's chain, 168:5

A heart that its Jesus living knows, 134:1

A heart that its living Jesus knows, 134:1

The heart that knoweth Jesus still doth live, 134:1

A heart that knows his Jesus lives, 134:1

A heart that knows its Jesus to be living, 134:1

A heart that knows that Jesus lives, 134:1

The heart that thou hast given, 518

A heart which doth its Jesus clearly know, 134:1

Heartily dear have I Thee, 174:5

Heartily do I love Thee, 174:5

Heartily do I love Thee, O Lord, 149:7

A heart's chamber such as this, 248:53

The Heaven above, the Earth below, 178:7.2

Heaven and Earth are full, 232:21b

Heaven and Earth are full of the majesty, 246:46

Heaven and Earth were both created, 178:7.2

Heaven crumbling, mountains tumbling, 245a:1a

Heaven is my certainty, 64:6

Heaven is my goal, 146:3

Heaven laughs; the Earth rejoices, 31:2

Heaven nor Earth are my delight, 70:11

The heaven proclaimeth abroad God's glory, 76:1a

Heaven remains to me assured, 64:6

Heaven-given sweet content, 204:8

Heavenly cheerfulness, the heart, 204:8

Heavenly contentment, 204:8

Heavenly fire, sweet consolation, 226:4

The heavenly foresight of eternal goodness, 206:11

Heavenly gift, O sweet content, 204:8

The heavenly host gives thanks to Thee, 117:2a

Heavenly King, be welcome, 182:2

A heavenly light falls from the sky, 172:6

The heavenly shepherd for me cares, 104:2

The heavenly word proceeding forth, 377

Heaven's angels watch will keep, 149:4

The heavens are telling the glory of God, 76:1a

The heavens are themselves not pure, 136:4

The heavens declare the glory of God, 76:1a

The heavens declare Your (Thy) glory, 68:2

The heavens laugh, 31:2

The heavens proclaim the glory of God, 76:1a

The heavens rejoice; the earth, 31:2

Heavens resound! Earth, rejoice, 134:6

The heavens shout, the earth with praise, 31:2

The heaven's sweetness, 123:2

The heavens tell of God's glory, 76:1a

The heavens themselves are not pure, 136:4

Heavenward like an eagle soaring, 213:7

A heavy load of sin, 199:6

Hellish serpent, 40:4

Hell's despite, nay, nor Satan, 107:4

Hell's very serpent, 40:4

Help, God, that I may achieve (triumph), 624

Help, God, that we succeed, 194:5

Help, God, that we this achieve, 194:5

Help, God, the former of all thing*, 343; 624

Help, Highest, help, 134a:7

Help, Jesu, help, 147:7

Help, Jesus, help, 147:7

Help, Lord, help; behold we enter, 248:42

Help, Lord, in my endeavor, 624

Help, Lord Jesus, let it succeed, 248:42

Help, Lord Jesus; send good speed, 248:42; 344

Help, Lord, that I may prosper, 624

Help me, for I am weak; I fight, 177:5

Help me, God, that I may succeed, 624

Help me, God, to succeed, 343

Help me, Jesus, that I prosper, 344

Help me my life to meet forthright, 153:9.2

Help me praise God's goodness, 16:6; 28:6; 183:5

Help me to do my task aright, 153:9.2

Help me to glorify God's goodness, 613

Help me to praise God's goodness, 16:6

Help, O Christ, Son of God, 245:65

Help, O Christ, that through the pain, 245:65

Help, O Christ, Thou Son of God, 245:65

Help, O Jesus, God's own Son, 245:65

Help, O Lord; behold we enter, 344
Help, O Lord; our souls inspire, 194:5
Help Thy people, Lord Jesus Christ, 119:9
Help us, Christ, Almighty Son, 245:65
Help us, O Lord; behold we enter, 344
Help us, O Lord, from age to age, 119:9
Help us, Son of God most high, 245:65
Hence, all fears and sadness, 227:11
Hence, all thoughts of sadness, 227:11
Hence, all ye evildoers, 135:5
Hence, all ye sons of evil, 135:5
Hence, dismal shadows, 202:1
Hence, hence with Him, 245:44
Hence, my heart, and cease such thinking, 32:6
Hence, repining, 187:5b
Hence, then, sorrow; hope I'll borrow, 87:6
Hence, thou imp of sorrow, 227:11
Hence with earthly treasure, 227:7
Hence world! Retain only (then), 64:3
Hence, world! Thyself keep Earth's poor riches, 64:3
Hence, ye earthly riches, 227:7
Hence, ye fiends ferocious, 227:5
Henceforth I flaunt the fiends of Hell, 139:6
Henceforth I will hate and desist, 30:8
Henceforth your people, 249a:11b
Her life let the art of dying, 198:6
Her living let the art of dying, 198:6
The herald comes, 30:4
Hercules at the crossroads, 213
Here at Thy grave sit we all weeping, 244:78
Here, before the face of God, I am a poor man, 179:6
Here can I take my ease and pleasure, 207a:5
Here doth the Savior's mighty hand, 48:5
Here hath the darkness now, 6:4
Here, however, does the Savior's hand, 48:5
Here I beside Thy cradle stand, 248:59
Here I lie, O merciful Father, 519
Here I stand before Thy manger, 248:59
Here I stand, ready and willing, 56:4
Here in My Father's abode, 32:3

Here in My Father's house, My dwelling, 32:3
Here is the crypt, and here the stone, 249:6
Here is the grave, and see the stone, 249:6
Here is the place, and here the stone, 249:6
Here is the proper Easter Lamb, 4:6; 158:4
Here is the real Easter Lamb, 4:6
Here is the spotless Easter Lamb, 4:6
Here is the tomb, and here the stone, 249:6
Here is the true Easter Lamb, 4:6; 158:4
Here is the true Passover, 158:4
Here is the true Passover Lamb, 4:6
Here is the vault, and here the stone, 249:6
Here, laid to rest, in tears we leave Thee, 244:78
Here lies he now, 519
Here look now all men to Thee, 187:1
Here My Father God abideth, 32:3
Here my soul is waiting for the Lord, 131:4a
Here, O God, Thy healing presence, 439
Here ready and prepared I stand, 56:4
Here, sad at heart for Jesu's bitter smart, 159:3
Here see the victor, 43:2
Here stands the true Paschal Lamb, 158:4
Here to test me, good and ill opposing face me, 162:1
Here wait, Lord, all things on Thee, 187:1
Here will I stay beside Thee, 244:23
Here within My Father's dwelling (mansions), 32:3
Here would I stand beside Thee, 159:2b; 244:23
Here yet awhile, Lord, Thou art sleeping, 244:78
Herewith today the anguish, 63:4
The hero's hero comes, 43:6
He's blessed who the Lord feareth, 196:3
He's blessed whom Jacob's God, 143:3
He's helped us all, 212:9
He's my countenance's helper, 21:6b
Hey derry, down derry, 212:18
Hey, what a sour face, 524:6
Hide anxiety and fear, 209:5

The high feast thus we celebrate, 4:7
High in the heav'ns, eternal God, 72:5; 244:31
High-exalted Son of God, 6:2
The high Mass, 232
The highest Almighty's wonder-hand, 147:8
Highest comforter, Holy Ghost, 183:4
Highest, contemplate in mercy, 63:7
Highest helper, Holy Ghost, 183:4
The highest herdsman cares for me, 104:2
The Highest informeth me of His will, 45:2
The Highest lets me know His will, 45:2
Highest, look with mercy now, 63:7
The highest majesty and pomp, 26:5
Highest, make Thy goodness, 51:3
Highest, make Thy gracious goodness, 51:3
Highest, my possessions, 39:5
Highest of all, look kindly, 63:7
Highest One, make Thy goodness, 51:3
Highest One, what I have is merely Thy gift, 39:5
The highest shepherd cares for me, 104:2
Highest, what I have is only Thy gift, 39:5
Highest wished-for feast (joyous), 194:1
The Highest's goodness and faithfulness, 10:3
The Highest's goodness is renewed, 90:2
The Highest's gracious love, 10:3
The Highest's kindness is from day to day, 90:2
The Highest's presence here alone, 194:8
Highly honored Son, 6:2
Highly praised Son of God, 6:2
Him shall my laurel(s), 207:6
Him to whom we now with joy sing, 129:5
Himself doth God leave not unproven, 76:2
His blood be on all (us), 244:59d
His blood be upon us, 244:59d
His boundless might to fathom, 128:4
His face my shepherd long is hiding, 104:3
His first care those who did Him wrong, 246:60
His goodness and His mercy shall attend, 112:5

His gracious wife isn't proud, 212:11
His hand crowns and blesses, 16:3b
His head bowed, He gave up, 245:59
His is no empty word, 207:8
His name I shall confess, 200
His omnipotence to fathom, 128:4
His own God ne'er neglecteth, 369
His pow'r, His might, who knows them, 128:4
His servant Israel He hath holpen, 243:10
His spirit, whom God sends at need, 108:6
His very first concern was, 246:60
His word, baptism, and sacrament, 165:6
His word, baptism, supper all help, 165:6
His word believing, thou will* find salvation, 68:5
His word, His baptism, His communion, 165:6
His word is truth beyond all doubt, 99:2
His word of truth doth stand secure, 99:2
His word of truth stands fast, 99:2
His work is done, 159:4
Hither, Jesus' outstretched arm, 244:70a
Hitherto have you nothing asked in My name, 87:1
Hitherto you have prayed for nothing in my name, 87:1
Ho there! Where lies th'appointed way, 213:2
Hold I only fast to Him, 187:6
Hold in affection Jesus Christ, 67:1
Hold in remembrance Jesus Christ, 67:1
Hold my endeavor broad and high, 153:9.2
Hold thou firm against all evil, 54:1
Hold thou forever this blessing, 248:31
Hold ye your heads now high, 70:8
Hold your tongue, heady Reason, 178:6
Holiest, look with favor now, 63:7
Holiest Trinity, great God, 172:3
Holy ardor, sweet consolation, 226:4
The Holy Child my hope shall be, 702
Holy day of rebirth, lead me, 70:10a
Holy Father, we Thy children, 147:6
Holy Ghost, dispel our sadness, 8:1
Holy Ghost, enthroned in Heaven, 194:6

Holy Ghost, of equal honor, 194:6
The Holy Ghost's abundant grace (mercy), 295
Holy, holy, holy, 325
Holy, holy, holy, Lord God of Hosts, 283
Holy, holy, Lord God of Sabaoth, 325
Holy, Lord God of Hosts, 232:21a
Holy, Lord God of Sabaoth, 232:21a
The holy Passiontide now brings to mind, 450
The holy Son of God most high, 248:17
The holy Son, the new-born Child, 122:1; 122:6
Holy Spirit, comfort sweet, 183:4
The Holy Spirit helpeth our infirmities, 226:1
Holy Spirit, Lord of love, 262
Holy Spirit, throned in Heaven, 194:6
The holy twelve in Thee rejoice, 246:21
Homage cantata, 210a
Honor alone to God on high, 662; 663; 663a; 664; 664a
Honor be chanted to Thee, 248:43
Honor be in Heaven's throne, 135:6
Honor be to God on the highest throne, 33:6
Honor to Thee, O Christ, be paid, 121:6
Honor, Zion, this thy God, 190:3
Hope and light of man's endeavor, 147:10
The hope awaits the right time, 86:6
Hope looketh for the dawning day, 86:6
Hope, though deferr'd, let none destroy, 86:6
Hosanna in the highest, 232:22
Hosanna in the highest! Our eager hearts, 245:52
Hosanna to the living Lord, 345
The host of Heaven their thanks upraise, 117:2a
The hosts of darkness in many places, 6:4
The hour is come, O Lord, 378
Hour of parting, come to me, 31:8
House preserved by our God, 134a:3
The house which God does not protect, 438

How am I gladdened in my heart, 1:6
How am I now so truly glad, 49:6a,
How am I so heartily happy, 1:6
How amazing is this punishment, 244:55
How beauteous beams the morning star, 1:1
How beautiful shines the morning star, 739
How beautifully gleams the morning star, 1:1; 172:6
How beautifully shines the morning star, 1:1; 36:4
How better to robe innocence, 246:52
How blessed are then they, 80:7
How blessed are they who carry God, 80:7
How blessed are they whose faith unshaken, 442
How blessed are we in Him believing, 122:4b
How blessed is he who trusteth in the Lord, 105:4
How blessed then are they, 80:7
How blessed though are those who God, 80:7
How bright and fair the morning star, 1:1; 436; 739; 763; 764
How bright appears the morning star, 1:1; 36:4; 436
How brightly beams the morning star, 1:1; 1:6
How brightly glows the morning star, 1:1
How brightly shines the morning star, 1:1; 1:6; 36:4; 172:6; 436; 739; 763
How brightly shines yon morning star, 1:1; 1:6; 36:4; 172:6; 436
How brightly shines yon star of morn, 1:1
How brilliantly shines the true Christian life, 456
How can a house be pleasing, 194:4
How can a man ascend to God, 194:9
How can I best admire Thee, 248:5
How can I e'er, dear Lord, 39:6
How can I fitly greet Thee, 248:5
How can I, my dear one, my joy, comprehend Thee, 152:6
How can I rightly greet Thee, 248:5

How can I, straining sight and expectation, 245:27.2

How can the pow'r of noble love, 34a:2

How can we, almighty August, 215:2

How can we now, Augustus, 215:2

How can we stubborn mortals, 102:2

How can you be so arrogant, 201:2

How cheerfully the heroine died, 198:5

How comforting is now the thought, 95:3

How costly are the holy banquet's off'rings, 180:3a

How could from Thee, Thou highest, 194:4

How dangerous is delay, 102:6

How dang'rous to delay, 102:6

How dearly could I wish, 95:3

How deep the darkness falls, 6:4

How delusive, how conclusive, 26:6

How died our lady, 198:5

How difficult does flesh and blood, 3:2

How difficult it is for flesh and blood, 3:2

How do the thoughts of sinners quiver, 105:3

How doth the world dismay, 94:5

How doubting is my hope, 109:3

How doubting is my hoping, 109:3

How easily could then the Highest, 88:2

How easily might God dispense, 88:2

How easily, though, could the Highest do without, 88:2

How fair thou art, beloved town, 119:4

How, fairest goddess, how, 208:3

How fairly shines the morning star, 1:1

How false a part the world doth play, 244:38

How false the world its part doth play, 244:38

How falsely doth the world accuse, 52:6; 244:38

How fearful and uncertain, my steps, 33:3

How fearful wavered then my paces, 33:3

How fearful were my faltering steps, 33:3

How fearfully did my stride falter, 33:3

How fearfully do my footsteps falter, 33:3

How fearfully faltered my steps, 33:3

How fierce and dreadful was the strife, 4:5

How filled with doubting is my hoping, 109:3

How frail a thing is man, 19:4

How frail, in truth, is man, 19:4

How* frightened, trembling steps I seek Him, 33:3

How glad am I that my dear Lord, 1:6

How glad is my heart, 199:8

How gladly would we that our flesh and blood, 244:65

How good, Lord, to be here, 878

How graciously doth shine afar, 1:1

How great is God's dear kindness, 69:2

How great, O Lord, is Thy goodness, 462

How great soe'er our sin may be, 38:6

How great the wisdom of our God, 92:4

How great then is God's goodness, 69:2

How grieve me then the perverted hearts, 170:3

How grievous do these hearts perverse, 170:3

How happy am I, O friend of souls, 517

How happy am I that my beloved, 49:6a

How happy am I that my guard, 49:6a

How happy are those who bear, 80:7

How happy he, he who is firm assured, 105:4

How happy he who on his God, 139:1

How happy I, O soul companion, 517

How happy I with God in Heaven, 35:7

How happy is my heart, 199:8

How happy then are they who carry, 80:7

How happy they with God abiding, 35:7

How hard for flesh and blood to fight, 3:2

How hard it is for flesh and blood, 3:2

How hard to teach our flesh and blood, 3:2

How hardly allows itself flesh and blood, 3:2

How hardly can my flesh and blood, 3:2

How hast Thou then, my God, 21:4

How heartily glad am I, 1:6

How heartily glad am I that my treasure, 49:6a

How heartily glad I am that my treasure, 49:6a

How I am so heartily glad, 1:6

How I lament still for those perverse hearts, 170:3

How I shall myself rejoice, 146:7

How I will rejoice, 146:7

How ill content me now Earth's hollow pleasures, 123:6

How is it love's so wondrous might, 34a:2

How is it that ye sought Me, 32:2

How is the world dismayed, 94:5

How is't that ye here do seek Me, 32:2

How jovial is my laughter, 205:3

How joyful is my heart, 199:8

How justly might our God, 88:2

How, Lord, does now my reck'ning stand, 89:5

How lovely does it resound in the ears, 133:4a

How lovely it rings in my ears, 133:4a

How lovely shines the morning star, 1:1; 1:6; 436

How lovely to my ears it ringeth, 133:4a

How many, and how mighty, Lord, 153:1

How many, and how mighty rail, 153:1

How many creatures, 187:2

How many they, how mighty rail, 153:1

How marvelous that the heart, 125:3

How may I, beloved, inherit salvation, 152:6

How may I, in sin forsaken, 259; 770

How may we, all-powerful August, 215:2

How merrily will I laugh, 205:3

How miraculous indeed is this punishment, 244:55

How now is it that ye sought Me, 32:2

How now, most beautiful goddess, 208:3

How now, my soul, why makest sore complaining, 425

How now, thou spirit, why art so full of woe, 435

How, O Lord, may I fitly repay, 39:6

How painful is life to me, 170:5

How perverse are the mighty ones, 147:4

How perverted hearts grieve me, 170:3

How poor's my life indeed, 89:6

How precious are the gifts, 180:3a

How precious are the holy feast's gifts, 180:3a

How profitless our dreary sorrow, 93:2

How rarely blessed is man, 173:1

How rich the store of blessing, 189:4

How sad am I for that perverted mortal, 170:3

How selfishness deceives itself, 185:4

How shall I, beloved of souls, embrace Thee, 152:6

How shall I fitly meet Thee, 248:5

How shall I give thee up, Ephraim, 89:1

H. hall I meet my Savior, 248:5

H. hall I now renounce thee, Ephraim, 1

How shall I, O lover of souls, now embrace Thee, 152:6

How shall I receive Thee, 248:5

How shall I thee surrender, Ephraim, 89:1

How shall I then, O Lord, 39:6

How shall I then receive Thee, 248:5

How shall I to Thee, O Lord, 39:6

How shall I understand you, Ephraim, 89:1

How sleep the brave, 416

How strange, how wondrous strange, 244:55

How sweetly echo in my hearing, 133:4a

How sweetly in mine ear is ringing (singing), 133:4a

How sweetly rings it in my ears, 133:4a

How the sinner's faults do quaver and waver, 105:3

How the thoughts of the sinner quake, 105:3

How, then, to Thee whose clear unerring sight, 194:4

How those perverted hearts arouse my pity, 170:3

How those souls who have gone astray, 170:3

How tremble and totter the sinner's thoughts, 105:3

How tremble and waver the sinners' intentions, 105:3

How tremble and waver the sinners' thoughts, 105:3

How vacillating is my spirit, 109:3

How weary and dreary, this mortal existence, 57:7

How well am I, O friend of souls, 517
How will I be joyful, 146:7
How wonderful, O God, 120a:2
How wondrous are the holy gifts, 180:3a
How wondrous God's affection, 96:2
How wondrous is the light that faint Earth's, 125:4
How wondrous strange is forsooth this punishment, 244:55
Howbeit when He, of truth the spirit, 108:4
Howbeit when that the spirit is sent down, 108:4
However great our failings be, 38:6
However sore my need, 89:6
However, they understood nothing, 22:1b
A hundred thousand adorations well up, 249a:5
A hundred thousand flatteries now well up, 249a:5
The hungering shall be nourished, 75:1a
Hunting cantata, 208,
Hunting is the delight of the gods, 208:2
Hunting is the joy of gods, 208:2
Hunting is the pleasure of gods, 208:2
Hunting is the sport of gods all, 208:2
Hunting joy to princes offers, 208:2
Hurl them down headlong, 126:4
Hurl to ground, arrogant, proud ones, 126:4
Hurry, anguished souls, 245:48a
Hurry, hurry, ye wild whirling winds, 201:1
Hurry, make the hours fly, 30:10
Hush, hush then, giddy intellect, 178:6
Hush, my dear, 259
Hypocrisy is a brood, 24:4
Hypocrisy is a foul spawn, 24:4
Hypocrisy is of the brood, 24:4
Hypocrisy, this is a brood, 24:4
Hypocrites, who thus ignore, 179:3
Hypocritic souls we see, 179:3

I

I acknowledge one baptism, 232:19
I adore Thee, my most exalted Lord, 449
I already see in my spirit, 43:9
I am a good shepherd, 85:1
I am a shepherd true, 85:1
I am after all only the tiniest part, 5:6
I am amazed, for everything, 35:3
I am and shall be e'er content, 150:3
I am averse to living longer, 170:5
I am content in my good fortune, 84:1
I am content in my sorrow, 58:3
I am content in myself, 204:1
I am content in this my sorrow, 58:3
I am content to fill the station, 84:1
I am content with my good fortune, 84:1
I am content with my place in life, 523
I am contented with my good luck, 84:1
I am despised, 138:2
I am from sighing weary, 135:4
I am glorious, I am beautiful, 49:4
I am glorious; I am fair, 49:4
I am happy in my good fortune, 84:1
I am happy in my suffering, 58:3
I am ill; come, strengthen me, 246:62
I am ill; strengthen me, my force, 246:62
I am in conflict and doubt, 177:5
I am indeed, Lord, in Thy power, 345; 464
I am indeed only the smallest part, 5:6
I am, indeed, so truly glad, 1:6
I am, indeed, the world's mere smallest part, 5:6
I am joyous; I am glad, 49:4
I am lacking much indeed, 89:6
I am like Peter not mistaken, 68:3
I am like Peter not presumptuous, 68:3
I am looking forward to my death, 82:5
I am not skilled to understand, 255
I am prepared; come, summon me, 128:2
I am prepared; come, take me (Thou), 128:2
I am prepared my blood and poor existence, 183:3
I am prepared my cross, 146:6
I am prepared my life now to surrender, 183:3
I am quiet and love my God, 466
I am ready; come fetch me, 128:2

I am ready, my blood and poor life, 183:3
I am ready my cross patiently to bear, 146:6
I am ready to bear my cross, 146:6
I am satisfied, 82:1; 82:2
I am saved from sin and loss, 244:26b
I am splendid; I am fair, 49:4
I am the good shepherd, 85:1
I am tired of sighing, 135:4
I am weak; come, strengthen me, 246:62
I am weary with my groaning, 135:4
I am well content, 204:1
I am with sighing weary, 135:4
I am wonderful; I am pretty, 49:4
I am yours; you are mine, 213:11
I ask for no more, 82:1; 82:2
I ask Thee Lord, again in Jesus' name, 177:2
I ask Thee, Lord Jesus Christ, 166:3
I ask yet more, O Lord God, 177:2
I ask your pardon, elders, 206:8
I believe, dear Lord, help my unbelief, 109:1
I believe in but one true God, 437
I believe in one God, 232:12; 232:13a
I believe in one Lord, 232:14
I believe in the Holy Spirit, 232:18
I believe; in Thee believing, 78:7
I believe, Lord; help my frailty, 78:7
I believe, Lord; help my unbelief, 109:1
I beseech, O Lord, from the bottom of my heart, 18:5
I bring to Thy crib, 469
I call on Thee, Lord Jesus Christ, 177:1
I call to Thee in my distress, 117:4
I call to Thee, Lord Jesu(s) Christ, 177:1; 177:5; 185:6; 639; A73
I call to You, Lord Jesus Christ, 639
I call upon Thy name, O Jesus, 639
I called to God in my distress, 117:4
I called to God with my last breath, 117:4
I called to Thee in my distress, 117:4
I called upon the Lord in my need, 117:4
I can lack nevermore, 92:2
I care not, even if I am, 52:3
I carry my sorrow with joy in my heart, 21:2; 75:5

I certainly feared the grave's darkness, 66:5
I clasp and cling to Christ my master, 157:2
I clasp my dear Lord Jesus closely, 157:2
I cleave, O Lord, to Thee, 133:6
I cling to my Jesus, now and for evermore, 157:2
I come from highest Heaven above, 243:13; 700; 701
I come with joy to meet my Lord, 255
I confess one baptism, 232:19
I could not do without Thee, 244:53; 369
I crave of Thee, Lord Jesus Christ, 166:3
I cried to the Lord in my distress, 117:4
I cry on Thee, Lord Jesus Christ, 177:1
I cry to Thee, Lord Jesus Christ, 177:1; 639; A73
I cry to Thee, my dearest Lord, 177:1; 177:5; 185:6; 639; A73
I dedicate my life, my whole behavior, 183:3
I desire nothing of this world, 64:7
I desire sincerely a blessed ending, 153:5
I desire to follow Your way, 147:6; 147:10
I desire with God to live, 35:7
I do not boast with Peter, 68:3
I do not leave Jesus from me, 124:6
I do not leave my Jesus, 157:5
I do not let go of mine Jesus, 157:5
I do not let go of Thee unless Thou blessest me, 157:1
I do rejoice in all my sorrow, 58:3
I doubt not, dearest Lord, 109:1
I eat my meager bread with joy and gladly grant, 84:3
I eat now with gladness my humblest of bread, 84:3
I eat with delight the little bread, 84:3
I eat with gladness my scanty bread, 84:3
I eat with joy my scanty bread, 84:3
I end swiftly my earthly life, 57:7
I entrust myself into Thy hands, 229:4
I fain would know, 502
I falter not, in simple child-like faith, 187:6
I fear indeed the grave's darkness, 66:5
I fear me not, 149:3

I fear not a thousand, 149:3
I fear not death, despise its terror, 183:2
I fear not death's terror, 183:2
I feared in truth the grave and all its darkness, 66:5
I feel already in my spirit, 76:11
I feel Hell's anguish and pain, 3:3
I feel now in my soul, 76:11
I feel the wrack and pains of Hell, 3:3
I feel within my breast my soul, 76:11
I fight, Lord Jesus, and withstand, 177:5
I find my joy in Thee, 133:1
I follow after Christ, 12:5
I follow after Thee through spittle and shame, 159:2a
I follow Christ always, 12:5
I follow Christ; I will not abandon, 12:5
I follow Christ till death, 12:5
I follow God with happy footsteps, 111:4
I follow Thee also, 245:13
I follow Thee likewise, 245:13
I follow Thee my love to show, 159:2a
I follow Thee now, 159:2a
I follow Thee still, 159:2a
I follow Thee through spitting and shame, 159:2a
I follow Thy footsteps, 245:13
I follow Thy path, 159:2a
I follow with gladness, 245:13
I give myself into Thy pleasure, 229:4
I give myself unto Him, 97:8
I give Thee thanks, Almighty God, 149:5
I give Thee thanks, O my dear God, 149:5
I give Thee thanks unfeigned, 244:63.1
I give to thee farewell, 735; 735a; 736
I give you My hand, 57:4
I gladly bear my cross, 56:1
I gladly content me with scantiest fare, 84:3
I gladly end my earthly life with joy, 57:7
I go and search for thee with longing (yearning), 49:2
I go and search with longing for thee, 49:2
I go and seek with longing, 49:2
I go away and come again, 74:4

I go from hence, 74:4
I go from here and come again, 74:4
I go hence and come again, 74:4
I got me flowers, 319
I greatly fear the grave's dark desolation, 66:5
I had a great affliction in my heart, 21:2
I had great fear of heart, 21:2
I had great heaviness of heart, 21:2
I had much sorrow in my heart, 21:2
I had much worry in my heart, 21:2
I had perchance forgotten thee, 103:6
I had so much distress and woe, 21:2
I hasten right cheerful, 148:2
I hasten, the teaching of life to hear, 148:2
I hasten to fathom the secret, 148:2
I hasten to hear now, 148:2,
I hasten to hear the teachings, 148:2
I have a difficult journey before me, 58:5
I have against God acted, 55:2
I have against just God offended, 55:2
I have against my God offended, 55:2
I have before me a heavy journey, 58:5
I have enough, 82:1; 82:2
I have faith, O dear Lord, 109:1
I have in God's heart and mind, 65:7; 103:6
I have, in truth, O bridegroom of my soul, 165:4
I have, indeed, my soul's bridegroom, 165:4
I have into God's heart and being (mind), 92:1
I have left thee a moment, 103:6
I have left you for a moment, 103:6
I have lived eighty years, 71:2a
I have loved thee for ever and ever, 49:6b
I have loved you now and for ever, 49:6b
I have many afflictions, 21:2
I have my confidence on the faithful, 188:1
I have no fear, 149:3
I have no fear of death's dread terror, 183:2
I have now all my confidence, 188:1
I have now enough, 82:1; 82:2
I have, O Death, no fear to cross thy portal, 114:5

I have placed all my affairs in God's hands, 351

I have stood up against God, 55:2

I have surrendered myself to Him, 97:8

I have thee but a little while, 103:6

I have to God's own heart and mind, 92:1

I have transgressed against God, 55:2

I have turned my confidence, 188:1

I have waited for the Lord, 93:6

I hear amidst my very suff'ring, 38:3

I hear in the midst of suffering(s), 38:3

I hear my last hour knell, 161:4

I hear the accents of my Master, 154:6

I hear the voice of my Redeemer, 154:6

I hear when I am brokenhearted, 38:3

I hold my Jesus fast; I leave Him not, 157:2

I hold the world as naught, 64:4

I hold Thee fast; be Thou my Jesus ever, 467

I hold to the dear God, 52:5

I hold with my dear God, 52:5

I hurry, the lessons of life to hear, 148:2

I, I and all my sins, 246:17

I, I and my sins, 245:15.2; 246:17

I, I with sin encumbered, 246:17

I in truth would roses gather, 86:2

I into God's own heart and mind, 65:7

I into God's own heart and mind, 92:1

I joyfully eat my scanty bread, 84:3

I know God's justice, 45:3

I know God's true justice, 45:3

I know, my God, and I rejoice, 345

I know that my Redeemer lives (liveth), 31:9; 160:1

I know that Thou wilt still my conscience, 105:6

I know the things of Earth, 169:2b

I know with full assurance, 245:52

I lay myself in these wounds, 199:7

I lay myself into these wounds, 199:7

I leave all things to God's direction, 642; 647; 690; 691; 691a

I leave Thee not except Thou bless me, 157:1

I leave Thee not; Thou blessest me then, 157:1

I left thee for a moment, dear child, 103:6

I let Thee not go except I be blessed, 157:1

I lie midst strife and now resist, 177:5

I live meanwhile content in Thee, 84:5

I live meanwhile in Thee contented, 84:5

I live, my heart, for thy delight, 145:3

I live, my heart, for thy glorification, 145:3

I live now, my dear one, but for thy well-being, 145:3

I live now, my spirit, to thy purest pleasure, 145:3

I live, O beloved, but for thy salvation, 145:3

I live that my sorrow as joy may appear, 75:5

I longed for rest in death, 57:3

I look forward to my death, 82:5

I love and serve my God, 466

I love Jesus always, 468

I love Jesus at all hours, 468

I love my Jesus day and night, 468

I love my Jesus ev'ry hour, 468

I love the Almighty with all of my spirit, 174:2

I love the Almighty with deepest devotion, 174:2

I love the Highest with all my might (mind), 174:2

I love the Highest with my whole mind, 174:2

I love the Supreme One with all my soul, 174:2

I love Thee Lord, with all my heart, 174:5; 340

I love you still, but today, 208:5

I marvel for all that one sees, 35:3

I may enjoy the sweet silence, 207a:5

I may not hear you, 213:9

I must and will obedience show, 206:10

I must, I will obey, 206:10

I my Jesus shall not leave, 98:5

I need Thee, precious Jesu, 244:63.1

I nimbly end my earthly life, 57:7

I nothing fear while God doth reign, 52:5

I only live to give Thee worship, 248:41
I, poor man and sinner, stand, 179:6
I poor man, I poor sinner, 179:6
I poor man, I servant of sin, 55:1
I pray, Lord, from my heart to Thee, 18:5
I pray, O Lord, from heart's depth, 18:5
I pray, O Lord, to be, 77:4
I pray, O Lord with all my heart, 18:5
I pray, O Lord, with inmost heart, 18:5
I pray still more, O Lord my God, 177:2
I pray Thee from my deepest heart, 177:3
I pray Thee, Lord Jesus Christ, 166:3
I pray to Thee, Lord Jesus Christ, 166:3
I pray to You, Almighty God, 449
I pray with all my heart, O Lord, 18:5
I profess one baptism, 232:19
I reach My hand to thee, 57:4
I reach out to thee My hand, 57:4
I reach to thee My hand, 57:4
I rejoice and bid Thee welcome, 465
I rejoice at my death, 82:5
I rejoice in my death, 82:5
I rejoice in myself, 204:1
I rejoice in Thee, 133:1; 133:6; 465
I remain steadfast and love my God, 466
I saw the city of the Lord, 349
I scatter my tears with anxious heart, 146:5
I see already in spirit, 43:9
I see, though, that the world, 169:2b
I see within my soul, 43:9
I seek alone with God to live, 35:7
I seek thee daily, yearning ever, 49:2
I seem to see Thee come to meet me, 175:4
I send my cries unto the Lord, 18:5
I sense that the world, 169:2b
I shall all my days extol Thy strong hand, 25:6
I shall hold to my Jesus firmly, 157:2
I shall look to the Lord, 93:6
I shall my tears of sorrow, 146:5
I shall not leave my Jesus, but go always, 157:5
I shall not leave Thee, 467
I shall on the Lord look, 93:6

I shall remain faithfully silent, 466
I shall then forsooth gather roses, 86:2
I should have wished for death, 57:3
I should wish for me death, 57:3
I sought Him in my hour of need, 117:4
I sought the Lord in my sore need, 117:4
I sow my bitter teardrops, 146:5
I sow my tears with an anxious heart, 146:5
I sow the tears of sorrow, 146:5
I stand at the threshold, 156:2a
I stand before a toilsome road, 58:5
I stand beside Thee ever, 159:2b
I stand beside Thy cradle here, 248:59; 469
I stand beside Thy crib, 469
I stand beside Thy manger here, 469
I stand here at Thy crib, 248:59
I stand here beside Thy manger here, 248:59
I stand here by Thy cradleside (crib), 469
I stand here by Thy manger, 248:59
I stand here close beside Thee, 244:23
I stand here, Lord, beside Thee, 159:2b
I stand here ready and prepared, 56:4
I stand in awe and with amazement, 35:3
I stand ready and prepared, 56:4
I stand unworthy at Thy throne, 131:4b
I stand with one foot in the grave, 156:2a
I step before Thy throne, O Lord, 668
I stretch to thee My hand, 57:4
I suffered greatly, 21:2
I suffered with great heaviness, 21:2
I take my sorrow with joy upon me, 75:5
I take thee now in My protection, 49:5b
I take up my sadness with gladness, 75:5
I take upon myself my sufferings with joy, 75:5
I thank my God in Heaven, 287
I thank Thee, dear Lord, 37:6
I thank Thee, dear Lord, 347; 348
I thank Thee dearly through Thy Son, 349
I thank Thee, God, for all Thy benefits, 346
I thank Thee, indeed, through Thy Son, 349
I thank Thee, Lord, that Thou afford, 346
I thank Thee Lord, through Thy dear Son, 349

I thank Thee, my beloved God, 149:5
I thank Thee, O God, upon Thy throne, 350
I thank Thee, Savior dearest, 37:6; 347; 348
I, the accustomed god, 208:6
I therefore scorn the host of Hell, 139:6
I think I can see Thee coming, 175:4
I think it very shy, 176:2
I think, really timid, 176:2
I think, right timidly, 176:2
I, though I be a god, 208:6
I, Thy sore-troubled child, 199:6
I, Thy troubled child, 199:6
I to Heaven would now be gone, 146:3
I too claim a part in this rejoicing, 206:6
I too in your rejoicing, 206:6
I too must have a share in your delight, 206:6
I too will stand beside Thee, 244:23
I tremble with horror beholding the wicked, 105:3
I trust His grace which shields, 97:4
I trust His mercy surely, 97:4
I trust in God's good will, 503
I trust in His dear mercy, 97:4
I trust in His mercy, 97:4
I trust Thee, dearest Lord, 109:1
I wait for the Lord, 131:3
I want to sing of Jesus' wounds, 147:9
I want you all to know, 212:22
I was glad they came to call me, 147:10
I welcome Thee in joy, 465
I, who have ever been a god, 208:6
I, who of old do rule, 208:6
I will acknowledge His name, 200
I will all my days forever glorify, 25:6
I will carry the cross with gladness, 56:1
I will confess His name, 200
I will detest now and all avoid, 30:8
I will endeavor, both now and ever, 30:8
I will even with dimmed eyes, 125:2
I will even with dimming eyes, 125:2
I will ever in my gladness, 25:6
I will give my heart to Thee, 244:19

I will give thanks with my whole heart, 332
I will give Thee my heart, 244:19
I will gladly bear the cross, 56:1
I will gladly carry the cross, 56:1
I will gladly dispense with temporal honor, 47:5
I will gladly submit myself, 244:29
I will glorify Thee, O God, 117:7
I will guard with diligence here, 248:33
I will henceforth my whole life, 117:7
I will here by Thee tarry, 159:2b
I will here with Thee stand, 159:2b
I will hold you, 30a:7
I will keep Thee diligently in my mind, 248:33
I will keep Thee with diligence, 248:33
I will know that the world, 169:2b
I will learn from this, 246:33
I will lift up mine eyes unto the hills, 37:1
I will live only to glorify Thee, 248:41
I will live only to Thy honor, 248:41
I will look unto the Lord, 93:6
I will look upon my (the) Lord, 93:6
I will my cross-staff gladly carry, 56:1
I will, my God, make full confession, 132:4
I will, my God, openly confess to Thee, 132:4
I will, my God, to Thee make free confession, 132:4
I will my whole life long, 117:7
I will not fear, 149:3
I will not hear you, 213:9
I will not leave my Jesus, 98:5; 124:6; 154:8; 379
I will not leave my Jesus, since He gave, 157:5; 380
I will not let Thee go, my Jesus, A159:1
I will not let Thee go until Thou bless me, 157:1
I will not regard thee, 213:9
I will now hate and everything (leave), 30:8
I will, O God, to Thee make full confession, 132:4

I will, O my Jesus, now nevermore leave Thee, 154:7b
I will of Jesu's wounds sing, 147:9
I will on Heaven think, 166:2
I will only live to honor Thee, 248:41
I will praise the strength of Thy hand, 25:6
I will search within my heart, 246:33
I will sing of Jesu's wounds, 147:9
I will sing of the wonder of Jesus, 147:9
I will stand beside Thee here, 244:23
I will stand by You, 247:58
I will stand here beside Thee, 244:23
I will stand here by Thee, 159:2b
I will stay here beside Thee, 244:23
I will suffer, I will be silent, 87:6
I will suffer, I'll keep silent, 87:6
I will suffer uncomplaining, 87:6
I will suffer yet with meekness, 87:6
I will the cross with gladness carry, 56:1
I will the cross-staff gladly carry, 56:1
I will Thee all my life's extent, 117:7
I will Thee, my Jesus, now nevermore leave, 154:7b
I will to the Lord now look, 93:6
I will towards the heavens go, 146:3
I will try if I can, 203:2
I will uphold thee, 30a:7
I will wake with Jesus mine, 244:26a
I will watch beside my Jesus, 244:26a
I will watch with Jesus, 244:26a
I wish for a peaceful end, 502
I wish I were living with God, 35:7
I wish to bid you farewell, 95:2b; 245:52; 415
I wish to go to Heaven, 146:3
I wish to prove, if I can, 203:2
I with my cross-staff gladly wander, 56:1
I worship Thee, my God most high, 449
I worship Thee, my highest God, 449
I would beside my Jesus be, 244:26a
I would beside my Lord, 244:26a
I would e'en with my broken vision, 125:2
I would gladly bear the cross, 56:1
I would have wished death, 57:3

I would live my life for Jesus, 490
I would long for death, 57:3
I would now yearn for death, 57:3
I would stand here beside Thee, 244:23
I would to Thee, O God, my (the) heart, 163:4
I would unto Heaven go, 146:3
I would wish death for myself, 57:3
I wrestle and pray, A159:1
I, wretched man; I, slave of (to) sin, 55:1
I, wretched man; who will deliver me, 48:1
I, wretched mortal; who will deliver me, 48:1
I, your grieving child, 199:6
I, your troubled child, 199:6
I'd fain heavenward instant fly, 146:3
I'd quit now so quickly mine earthly existence, 57:7
If a man love Me, he will keep My words, 59:1
If all the world with devils swarmed, 80:5
If all the world with fiends were fill'd, 80:5
If but Thou, Jesus, be my dear companion, 105:5
If by His Spirit, God, that upraised Jesus, 227:10
If e'er the hirelings slumber, 85:4
If fortune had made me the master, 212:16
If from Thee I ever stray, 55:5
If glorious peace our land hath dowered, 41:4
If God, appeased, is now our friend, 122:4a
If God commands, then must His blessing, 88:5
If God does not bestow His grace, 438
If God doth choose the holy shelters, 34:4
If God Himself calls, must the blessing, 88:5
If God Himself calls, then must the blessing, 88:5
If God is my protection and true shepherd, 85:6
If God is my shield and helper (shepherd), 85:6

If God is our friend and helper, 122:4a
If God is reconciled and our friend, 122:4a
If God makes me a present, 84:2
If God the Lord does not hold with us, 178:1
If God the Lord hold not with us, 178:1
If God the Lord is not on our side, 178:1
If God were not upon our side, 14:5; 178:1; 257; 258
If God were not with us at this time, 14:1
If God were not with us this time, 14:1; 14:5; 257
If God withdraweth, all the cost, 438
If He were not a malefactor, 245:23
If His hand crowns and blesses, 16:3b
If I am to pass the course, 153:8
If I but cling to Him, 187:6
If I but Jesus as my friend, 105:5
If I but recollect, 69a:4
If I can just make Jesus my friend, 105:5
If I can make Jesus my sole source, 105:5
If I can only cleave to Him, 187:6
If I can only make a friend of Jesus, 105:5
If I can only make Jesus my friend, 105:5
If I feel fear of Hell and torment, 3:3
If I feel Hell's anguish and pain, 3:3
If I have Jesus as my friend and Savior, 105:5
If I have wandered from Thee, 244:48
If I hold fast to God, 187:6
If I know God's commandments, 45:3
If I know God's laws, 45:3
If I lay myself down late, 97:6
If I see coffee here about, 211:5
If I should e'er forsake Thee, 244:72
If I should in this world, 71:2b
If I stand by my God, 503
If I then, too, the way of death, 92:9
If I to God be true, 503
If I were King of Portugal, 524:13
If in your hearts still God's Spirit, 227:10
If it be God's will and pleasure, 161:5
If it is my God's intention (will), 161:5
If it is the will of my God, 161:5

If it need be that judgment's pain, 48:3
If it seems as though He does not want, 9:7
If Jesus Christ abide in thee, 227:8
If Jesus forgives me, my sins, 48:6
If Jesus has my sins forgiven, 48:6
If Jesus thou wilt trust, 72:4
If, Lord, Thou keep me well and thriving, 156:5
If man will be restored anew, 31:6
If my God today shall will it, 161:5
If my Lord Jesus only deigns to love me, 105:5
If my shepherd hides himself too long, 104:3
If my tears be unavailing, 244:61
If my weeping may not reach Thee, 244:61
If now Christ Jesus be in you, 227:8
If now in you God's Spirit dwelleth, 227:10
If now, O Lord, it pleases Thee, 65:7; 92:7a
If now the Spirit of Him who raised, 227:10
If now thy heart be mine, love, 518
If only God be still thy friend, 58:2
If our God were not on (upon) our side, 14:1
If our lips are feeble, 51:2b
If pain and woe must follow sin, 48:3
If pain and woe with sin must go, 48:3
If so, from out my heart anger, 89:4
If still for coffee you insist, 211:5
If such be Thy will, Lord, 48:4
If that be so that pain and woe, 48:3
If the cross' bitterness with the flesh's weakness, 99:5
If the Lord but raise His finger, 248:57
If the tears on my cheeks, 244:61
If the world cannot cease, 58:4
If therefore Christ abide in you, 227:8
If this mad thirst, 211:5
If this man were not a malefactor, 245:23
If this man were not an evil-doer, 245:23
If thou art near, gladly I'll follow, 508
If thou art near, I will with gladness, 508
If Thou art to bring me help, 186:3
If Thou be King of Jewry, 246:61d
If thou be near, go I with gladness, 508
If thou be near, I go rejoicing, 508

If Thou be the King of the Jews, 246:61d
If thou but suffer God to guide thee, 88:7; 197:10; 434; 642; 647; 690; 691; 691a; A68
If thou but sufferest God to guide thee, 93:1
If Thou dost, Lord, my reckoning keep, 89:5
If Thou dost then, my hope, intend, 30:7
If thou, in open fashion acknowledge, 145:2
If thou let* this man go, 245:42
If thou lettest this man go, 245:42
If Thou, Lord, shouldst mark all our failings, 131:2a
If Thou, Lord, shouldst mark iniquities, 131:2a
If Thou my heart in faith keep pure, 3:6; 153:9.3
If Thou, O Lord, shouldst mark iniquities, 131:2a
If thou shalt confess with thy mouth, 145:2
If thou thy heart wilt give me, 518
If thou, thy sins confessing, 145:2
If thou wilt call thyself a child, 132:2a
If thou wilt give me thy heart, 518
If Thou wilt, Lord, mark what is sinful, 131:2a
If thou wilt suffer God to guide thee, 93:1
If thou wilt sufferest God to guide thee, 642
If thou, with true devotion, 145:2
If thou wouldst call thyself God's child, 132:2a
If Thy disciples, 244:9
If to Thy throne, 87:4
If we but be a little quiet, 93:3
If with thy mouth Lord Jesus thou art confessing, 145:2
If you are near, 508
If you are there, 508
If you are with me, 508
If you be with me, with joy go I, 508
If you desire to call yourself a child of God, 132:2a
If you don't give up, 211:5
If you won't give up, 211:5

If you would give me your heart, 518
If you would offer me as a gift, 518
I'll be unto Heaven mindful, 166:2
I'll bide there where I shall be dwelling, 158:3b
I'll follow after Christ, 12:5
I'll follow Thee also, 245:13
I'll leave You not; You must remain my Jesus, 467
I'll not despair, though deep my sorrow, 58:3
I'll not leave Thee; Thou must remain my Jesus, 467
I'll not let Him go, 188:2b
I'll not let Thee free, 188:2b
I'll not let Thee go, 197a:3
I'll not let Thee go till blessed by Thee, 157:1
I'll side with my dear God above, 52:5
I'll stand beside my Jesus watchful (watching), 244:26a
I'll to thee not listen, 213:9
I'll walk, then, with emboldened paces, 111:4
I'll wash me in that stream, 199:7
I'll watch with my dear Jesu alway, 244:26a
Illumine my darkened senses, 248:47
Illumine now my darkened senses, 248:47
Illumine too my darkened senses, 248:47
Illumine too our minds and hearts, 116:6
Illumine, ye heavenly fires all inflaming, 1:3
Illustrious Leopold, 173a:1
I'm blessed; my Jesus speaks, 81:6
I'm laughing and shouting, 15:7
I'm sick to death of living, 170:5
I'm sure of this, 212:7
I'm thine alway, 213:11
I'm weary of my groaning, 135:4
The image of false hypocrites, 179:3
Imagine not, ye sinners, 46:4
Imagine that His blood-bespattered body, 245:32
Immanuel, accept with grace my adoration, 142:6
Immanuel, beloved name, 248:38a

Immanuel, blessed name, 248:38a

Immanuel, I know how far is my shortcoming, 142:6

Immanuel, O blessed name, 248:38a

Immanuel, O sweet word, 248:38a

Immanuel, O sweetest word, 248:38a

Immanuel, O word so sweet, 248:38a

Immanuel, oh, give to me in Thy great mercy, 142:6

The immeasurable source of grace, 121:3

Immortal love, 492

In Adam's fall, 705

In all my deeds, 13:6; 44:7; 97:1; 244:16; 367

In all my undertakings, 97:1

In all that I am doing, 13:6; 44:7; 97:1; 367

In anger and fury the judge will avenge him, 90:3

In banishment they will cast you, 44:1; 183:1

In chorus now to Thee we raise, 248:23

In Christ my life is hidden, 95:1a

In death my glassy eyes are turning, 125:2

In death there is no sorrow, 161:6

In death's dark vale I fear no ill, 95:1c

In death's strong grasp the Savior lay, 4:2; 4:8; 277; 278; 279; 625; 695; 695a; 718; A171

In deep distress I cry to Thee, 38:1

In deepest need, 668

In deepest need I cry to Thee, 686; 687

In distress ye are provided and are filled daily, 75:1a

In earnest, one word, 212:13

In exultation my soul rejoices, 243:1

In faith I grasp Thy hand, 229:4

In faith I quiet wait, 466

In furious anger the Lord will extinguish, 90:3

In gentle fashion love endeavors, 36:3

In glory, through Heaven's, 249:10c

In God above, my soul, rejoice, 162:5

In God I place my faith and trust, 188:1

In God I will confide, 188:5

In God, my faithful God, 5:7; 646; 744

In God, my faithful God, I trust, 188:5

In God my ways repose, 351

In God the Lord I put my trust, 138:5; 188:1

In God the Lord most just, 188:5

In God the Lord my trust I place, 92:1

In God's most holy name, 378

In gracious mercy grant us peace, 42:7; 126:6

In grief and penitence, 199:5

In happiness see how this day, 202:9

In Heaven above one day I'll rest, 64:6

In Heaven God high enthroned, 189:3

In Heaven's throne be glory, 135:6

In Hell the serpent, hot with hate, 130:3

In Him is understanding deep, 92:4

In Him live we, 106:2b

In Him living, moving, 106:2b

In Him we live, act, and are, 106:2b

In Him we live and move, 106:2b

In His final hour did He, 245:56

In hope we wait the joyful day, 86:6

In Jesu's arms my spirit resteth, 127:3

In Jesus' grace may we alone, 38:2

In Jesu's humility can I find, 151:3

In Jesus' humility I can find, 151:3

In Jesus is my hope and trust, 151:3

In Jesus is my only joy, 702

In Jesus' life to live with joy, 66:4a

In Jesus lowly is my trust, 151:3

In Jesus' meekness can I strength (trust), 151:3

In Jesu's meekness I find hope, 151:3

In Jesus' meekness is my hope, 151:3

In Jesus' mercy will alone, 38:2

In Jesu's mercy will alone the comfort, 38:2

In Jesu's mercy will we trust, 38:2

In joy and peace I go my way, 95:1c

In joy and peace I pass away, 125:1

In life, this then is what I crave, 27:2

In like manner the chief priests, 244:67c

In love my Savior now is dying, 244:58

In many things I am wanting, 89:6

In Me thou shall* find peace and rest, 57:6

In Me thou shalt find peace and rest, 57:6

In might and majesty sublime, 91:2
In my beloved God I trust, 188:5
In My bosom lies peace and life, 57:6
In My bosom lies rest and life, 57:6
In My breast there is rest and life, 57:6
In my dear God, 5:7; 188:5
In my despair I cry to Thee, 38:1; 686; 687
In My Father's house thou'lt find Me, 32:3
In my God am I rejoiced, 162:5
In my God will I confide, 93:6
In my heart of hearts the chamber, 248:53
In my heart's inmost kernel, 245:52
In my jewels fair am I, 49:4
In my sore misery, 199:5
In my trouble call I, Lord, on Thee, 131:1a
In our hour of deepest need, 668
In our own strength we were undone, 80:2b
In Paradise may Adam tremble, 133:3
In peace and joy away I go, 616
In peace and joy do I depart, 125:1; 616
In peace and joy from life I part, 95:1c
In peace and joy I go away, 125:1
In peace and joy I go hence, 616
In peace and joy I go my way, 125:1; 382; 616
In peace and joy I now depart, 83:5; 95:1c; 125:1; 125:6; 382; 616
In peace and joy I pass away, 95:1c
In peace thy sheep may graze, 208:9
In peace we pause, 30:2
In peril thou dost wait, 102:6
In pity look upon my need, 113:2; 131:2b
In poverty to Earth He came, 248:7a
In praise we lift our voices, 29:8
In prayer we now Thy temple face, 51:2a
In probity maintain us, 79:6
In quiet faithfulness, 466
In sin's dark ways we had downfallen, 9:3
In soft delights I take no pleasure, 206:2
In sore perplexity I lie, 177:5
In sorrow Thou, O Lord, 300
In spite of all our heav'nly longing, 70:4
In sweet jubilation, 368; 608
In tears of grief, 244:78

In thankful praise sing ev'ry one, 121:6
In thanks the songs of angel throngs, 117:2a
In that dread hour when God shall chasten, 70:3
In that fateful garden, 247:56
In that last hour when fear and dread, 127:2
In the bonds of death He lay, 4:2
In the depths of my heart, 245:52
In the dust, bowed down with weeping, 199:4
In the evening when it was cool, 244:74
In the hour of trial, 407
In the Lord put thou thy trust, 40:6
In the midst of life we all (are), 383
In the sweat of my brow I still (will), 84:4
In the sweat of my face I will meanwhile enjoy, 84:4
In the tomb? The grave?, 210:7
In the waiting is danger, 102:6
In the world have ye woe, 87:5
In the world there is woe, 87:5
In the world ye have fear (tribulation), 87:5
In the world you are afflicted, 87:5
In the world you have tribulation, 87:5
In Thee alone, Lord Jesus Christ, 33:1; 261
In Thee alone, O Christ, my Lord, 33:1; 261
In Thee do I rejoice, 133:1; 133:6; 197a:4; 398
In Thee have I hoped, Lord, 52:6
In Thee have I put my trust, O Lord, 640
In Thee I trust, God Father, Son, and Holy Ghost, 520
In Thee is bliss, 615
In Thee is gladness, 615
In Thee is joy, 615
In Thee I've placed my hope, O Lord, 52:6
In Thee, Lord, have I put my trust, 52:6; 244:38; 640; 712
In Thee, my God and Savior, 245:52
In Thee, O Lord, I put my trust, 52:6; 244:38; 640
In thee, of heroines the greatest, 198:7
In thee, thou example of great women, 198:7
In thee, thou model of great women, 198:7

In Thee will I rejoice, 133:1
In these our days so perilous, 42:7; 126:6
In Thine arm(s) I rest me, 81:7; 227:3
In Thine honor will I risk all, 246:19
In this celebration your glorification, 208:12
In this grace believe, O mortals, 7:6
In this remorseful sorrow, 199:5
In this, Thy bitter Passion, 244:63.2
In this wise, filled with fright, 176:2
In three days I will rise again, 244:77c
In Thy faithful help confiding, 25:6; 194:6
In Thy most bitter passion, 159:2b
In truth and love abiding, 79:6
In truth can man to God ascend, 194:9
In truth hath God the world so loved, 68:1
In truth I say to thee (you), 127:4b
In truth, to bear the cross our flesh, 244:65
In truth to me 'tis very clear, 113:3
In truth, when I before me see, 113:3
In vain the world around, 169:2b
In vision Christ I see, 43:9
In waiting danger lurks, 102:6
In waiting is danger, 102:6
In waking or in slumbering, 114:7
In warm devotion here on New Year's Day, 16:2
In You alone, Lord Jesus Christ, 33:1
Incline, O Lord, Thine ear to me, 48:7
An inconceivable light fills the whole orbit, 125:4
Inconstancy, I must admit, 30a:8
Indeed defies August's name, 215:3
Indeed God owes me nothing, 84:2
Indeed, good news, 212:10
Indeed I lack very much, 89:6
Indeed, I love thee (you) still, 208:5
Indeed my weak heart feels fear, 8:3
Indeed, myself I bid you join, 205:14
Indeed now, my God, thus fall I, 92:7a
Indeed, Thy people's lives, 119:8
The infamous wiles of sin, 54:2
Infinite grace, and boundless loving, 121:3
Inflated ardor, but few brains, 201:13
Injurious thorns in their infinite toll, 181:3

The inner life of the Christians is shining, 456
Insincere and fickle spirits, 181:1
Inspired by purest love's emotion, 202:8
Instruct my darken'd understanding, 248:47
Integrity, a gift direct from God, 24:2
Into my heart's foundation, 245:52
Into the hands of sinners, 246:56
Into Thine hand I commend my spirit, 106:3a
Into Thine hand I commit my spirit, 106:3a
Into Thine hands now do I commit my soul, 106:3a
Into Thy hands I commend my spirit, 106:3a
Into Thy hands my spirit I commend, 106:3a
Into Thy keeping do I commit my soul, 106:3a
Into Thy keeping my spirit I commit, 106:3a
Into Thy keeping my spirit I confide, 106:3a
Is it not to deal thy bread, 39:1a
Israel, hope thou in the Lord, 131:5a
Israel, hope ye in the Lord, 131:5a
Israel, trust now in the Lord, 131:5a
Israel, trust thou in the Lord, 131:5a
Is't true indeed that music's art, 210:5
It angers all the worldlywise, 152:5
It brings the year of jubilee, 122:6
It can never fail me, 92:2
It cannot fail me anytime, 92:2
It disgusts me to live longer, 170:5
It does taste good, 212:4
It has been told to thee, man, what is good, 45:1
It hath thee been told, man, 45:1
It is: see also 'Tis
It is a true saying, 141:1
It is accomplished, 159:4
It is admittedly difficult, 204:5
It is all my heart's delight, 473
It is always distressing to Christian souls, 75:9
It is an obstinate and hopeless thing, 176:1
It is and bides the Christians' hope, 44:6
It is and continues to be, 44:6

It is and remains the consolation, 44:6
It is certainly time, 248:59; 307
It is complete, 159:4
It is enough, 82:1; 82:2
It is enough! Lord, brace me to the test, 60:5
It is enough! Lord, by Thy wise decree, 60:5
It is enough! Lord, call my spirit home, 60:5
It is enough! Lord, if it be Thy will, 60:5
It is enough! Lord, if it pleases Thee, 60:5
It is enough! Lord, let it please Thee so, 60:5
It is enough! Lord, when it pleases Thee, 60:5
It is enough! So take, Lord, 60:5
It is enough, so take my soul to Thee, A157:5
It is enough! So take my spirit, 60:5
It is enough! Then take my spirit, 60:5
It is finished, 245:58; 472
It is finished; do not forget, 458
It is for you, 36c:4
It is for you that I depart now, 108:1
It is for your good that I go away, 108:1
It is for your good that I now leave you, 108:1
It is fulfilled, 159:4; 245:58
It is fulfilled; do not forget, 458
It is fulfilled; do not mistake, 458
It is good for you that I go away, 108:1
It is He, who quite alone, 43:7
It is I, I should atone, 244:16
It is I, it is, should make atonement, 244:16
It is I who must atone, 246:48
It is I who should atone, 246:48
It is indeed my purpose, 203:2
It is my heart and mouth, 45:6
It is not lawful for us, 245:25
It is not mine to be high-minded, 68:3
It is only borrowed property, 168:2
It is our joy your heart to please, 36c:8
It is the ancient law; Man, thou must perish, 106:2e
It is the Christian's sure belief, 44:6
It is the end; do not mistake, 458
It is the heart and mouth, 45:6

It is the law of old; Man, thou must perish, 106:2e
It is the Lord who all the world, 119:4
It is the old covenant, 106:2e
It is the old decree; Man, thou art mortal, 106:2e
It is the old decree; Man, you must die, 106:2e
It is the old oath; Man, thou art, 106:2e
It is the salvation to us come hither, 9:1
It is Thy promise, Lord, 128:5
It is to thee declared, Man, what good is, 45:1
It is unlawful to put a man to death, 245:25
It is very difficult, 204:5
It is well for me that I have Jesus, 147:6
It remains to say, 212:7
It seems as though the remnant, 67:5
It seems to me I see Thee come, 175:4
It seems to me I see Thee coming, 175:4
It shall be always my delight, 30a:6
It should certainly be so, 48:3
It strickens me to live any longer, 170:5
It takes much sacrifice to be a Christian, 459
It was a curious war, 4:5
It was a strange fight (war), 4:5
It was a wonderful array (battle), 4:5
It was a wondrous battle (fight), 4:5
It was an amazing war, 4:5
It was an awesome thing that strife, 4:5
It was in the cool of eventide, 244:74
It was the Father's pleasure, 73:5
It will: see 'Twill
It's dancing and leaping that stir the heart, 201:7
It's for thy good that I depart, 108:1
It's obvious our squire, 212:7
I've naught here of my own, 39:6

J

Jehovah, let me now adore Thee, 299
Jehovah, now I would adore Thee, 299, 452
Jesu: see also Jesus

Jesu, all Thy bitter pain, 159:5; 182:7
Jesu, all Thy loving kindness, 11:10
Jesu, bend then my heart, 47:4
Jesu, best and dearest, 227:1; 227:11
Jesu, bring us all who own Thee, 40:8
Jesu, by His bitter cross, 159:5; 245:20; 245:56
Jesu Christ, of Heaven King, 159:5
Jesu, come let us praise Thee, 41:1; 41:6; 362
Jesu, comfort of all, 670; 673
Jesu didst deliverance bring me, 78:1
Jesu, do Thou then bend my heart, 47:4
Jesu, fondest, dearest treasure, 154:3; 359; 360
Jesu, fount of consolation, 475
Jesu, fount of every blessing, 162:3
Jesu, give solace to my mind, 135:3
Jesu, guard and guide Thy members, 40:8
Jesu, guide my ev'ry action, 248:42
Jesu, hope of men, 475
Jesu, hope of souls faint-hearted, 141:4
Jesu, humble make my heart be, 47:4
Jesu, I never can forget, 267
Jesu, in Thy love and pity, 165:3
Jesu, in Thy love enduring, 165:3
Jesu, Jesu, be Thou mine, 357
Jesu, Jesu, Thou art mine, 357; 470
Jesu, Jesu, You are mine, 470
Jesu, joy and balm of soul, 497
Jesu, joy and treasure, 64:8; 81:7; 87:7; 227:1; 227:11; 358
Jesu, joy for everlasting, 147:10
Jesu, joy of all my heart, 246:11
Jesu, joy of man's desiring, 147:6; 147:10
Jesu, joyaunce of my heart, 246:11; 361
Jesu, joyaunce of the living, 353
Jesu, knit in closer union, 40:8
Jesu, lead my footsteps ever, 248:42
Jesu, let me find Thee, 154:4
Jesu, let us gaze on Thee (You), 6:5
Jesu, lifespring of the living, 353
Jesu Lord, my dearest Master, 248:38b
Jesu, Lord of life and death, 355

Jesu, lover of my soul, 159:5; 470
Jesu mine, I leave Thee not, 380
Jesu, my beloved Savior, 78:1
Jesu, my chief pleasure, 64:8
Jesu, my delight and pastor, 248:40b
Jesu, my faith, 728
Jesu, my friend, 227:1
Jesu, my joy, 227:1; 610; 713; 713a; 753; A58; A59; A76
Jesu, my joy and bliss, 248:40b
Jesu, my joy and delight, 248:40b
Jesu, my joy and rapture, 248:40b
Jesu, my Lord; Jesu, my God, 505
Jesu, my Lord, my God, 342
Jesu, now let us praise Thee, 41:1
Jesu, on Thy features gazing, 6:5
Jesu, on Thy happy birthday, 142:3
Jesu, our comfort and our life, 475
Jesu, paths of weal and woe, 182:6
Jesu, praise to Thee be given, 142:7
Jesu, priceless treasure, 64:8; 81:7; 227:1; 227:7; 227:11; 358; 610; 713; 713a; 753; A58; A59; A76
Jesu, refuge, dearest Savior, 154:3
Jesu, sacred name, 496
Jesu, Savior, heed my greeting, 410; 768
Jesu, Savior of Thy flock, 143:6
Jesu, shine on us from yonder, 6:5
Jesu, smite** in closer union, 40:8
Jesu, source of bliss eternal, 147:1
Jesu, source of our desire, 147:6
Jesu, spring of all mercies, 162:3
Jesu, still lead on, 409
Jesu, sweetest, loved, and best, 361
Jesu, Syon's King, we greet Thee, 263
Jesu, take Thee thy members further, 40:8
Jesu, thanks to Thee be given, 142:5
Jesu, that last glance of kindness, 11:10
Jesu, the bliss of my soul, 147:6
Jesu, the sore Passion is to me, 159:5
Jesu, Thou my dearest treasure, 356
Jesu, Thou my joy, 610
Jesu, Thou my soul, 105:6
Jesu, Thou my wearied spirit, 78:1

Jesu, Thou source of ev'ry good, 334
Jesu, Thou wast overpowered, 475
Jesu, Thou who knewest death, 245:60b
Jesu, through weal and woe, 182:6
Jesu, Thy wounds of Love, 471
Jesu, to my enjoyment, 17:7
Jesu, treasure passing price, 472
Jesu, who deliv'rance bought me, 78:1; 78:7; 352; 353; 354
Jesu, who didst ever guide me, 248:42
Jesu, who hast by Thy bitter death, 78:1
Jesu, who in sorrow dying, 78:1; 352; 353; 354
Jesu, who my soul eternal, 78:1
Jesu, who wast killed, 245:60b
Jesu, Zion's King, we greet Thee, 263
Jesus: see also Jesu
Jesus accepts sinners, 113:5
Jesus accepts the sinners, 113:5
Jesus, all my gladness, 227:1; 227:11
Jesus, all my joy, 248:40b
Jesus all my joy remaineth, 147:10
Jesus answered again, 245:6
Jesus answered and said, 245:6
Jesus answered, I have, 245:6
Jesus answered them, 245:6
Jesus, be my firm foundation, 248:42
Jesus, be with me and lead me, 248:42
Jesus, bliss of my soul, 154:3
Jesus, Bread of Life, 180:7
Jesus, by my side protect me, 248:42
Jesus, by Thy cross and Passion, 78:1; 78:7; 352; 353; 354
Jesus called to Him the twelve, 22:1a
Jesus calling then the twelve, 22:1a
Jesus Christ, God's Son, 4:4
Jesus Christ is God's own Son, 4:4
Jesus Christ, my sure defense, 365; 728
Jesus Christ, our blessed Savior, 665; 665a; 666; 688; 689
Jesus Christ, our God's own Son, 4:4
Jesus Christ, our great Redeemer, 626
Jesus Christ, our Lord and Savior, 363; 364; 626; 665; 665a; 666; 688; 689

Jesus Christ, our Lord Redeemer, 363; 364; 626; 665; 665a; 666; 688; 689
Jesus Christ, our Redeemer, 626; 665; 665a; 666; 688; 689
Jesus Christ, our Savior, 363; 364; 626; 665; 665a; 666
Jesus Christ, our Savior, our King, 364
Jesus Christ, our Savior true, 688; 689
Jesus Christ redeemed mankind, 141:2
Jesus Christ, Son of God, 4:4
Jesus Christ, the only Son of God, 4:4
Jesus Christ, the Son of God, 4:4
Jesus Christ, who art our Savior, 688; 689
Jesus Christ, who came to save us, 364
Jesus cried aloud and said, 246:71
Jesus, dearest Master, 227:1; 358; 610; 713; 713a; 753; A58; A59; A76
Jesus' death by bitter pain, 245:56
Jesus' death in bitter pain, 245:56; A57
Jesus, death of mine own death, 165:5
Jesus, direct my beginning, 248:42
Jesus e'er, in grief and joy, 182:6
Jesus e'er my joy abideth, 147:10
Jesus, ever filled with pity, 11:10
Jesus, ever shining light, 247:56
Jesus, first I speak Thy name, 171:4
Jesus for His dear ones careth, 42:6
Jesus forgets not His elected, 109:5
Jesus, fount of every blessing, 162:3
Jesus, fountain of all mercy, 162:3
Jesus from the grave is risen, 4:4
Jesus, from Thy Passion came, 159:5; 182:7
Jesus, from Thy Passion I gain, 182:7
Jesus, grant us Thy assistance, 248:42
Jesus, guide my actions, 248:42
Jesus, guide my beginning, 248:42
Jesus, guide my ev'ry action, 248:42
Jesus hath the world redeemed, 141:2
Jesus, heart's delight to me, 473
Jesus, hope of them who falter, 141:4
Jesus, humble yet my spirit, 47:4
Jesus hung there on the cross, 621
Jesus I will never leave, 70:11; 380
Jesus, I'll not let leave me, 124:6

Jesus is a gem of price, 365
Jesus is a good shepherd, 85:2
Jesus is a jewel fair, 474
Jesus is a shepherd true, 85:2
Jesus is a shield of His own, 42:6
Jesus is a shield to His own, 42:6
Jesus is my all in all, 190:5
Jesus is my heart's delight, 473
Jesus is my joy, my all, 498
Jesus is my only life, 490
Jesus is my shepherd true, 85:2
Jesus is my soul's true need, 75:10
Jesus is the eternal light, 474
Jesus is the fairest light, 474
Jesus is the light supreme, 474
Jesus is the sinner's friend, 113:5
Jesus is this dark world's light, 474
Jesus, Jesus, Thou art mine, 357; 470
Jesus, jewel of my faith, 472
Jesus, joy of my heart, 361; 473
Jesus, joy of my soul, 359; 360
Jesus, joy of our desiring, 147:6; 147:10
Jesus, just bend my heart, 47:4
Jesus, keep me ever by Thy side, 182:6
Jesus, keep our sights upon Thee, 6:5
Jesus, keep us for Thee yearning, 6:5
Jesus, King of Glory, 227:1
Jesus, lead my footsteps ever, 248:42
Jesus, let me find Thee, 154:4
Jesus, let Thou Thine elected, 40:8
Jesus, let through weal and woe, 182:6
Jesus, let Thyself be found, 154:4
Jesus, let us look to Thee, 6:5
Jesus, let us Thee see, 6:5
Jesus, light of my existence, 356
Jesus lives! The victory's won, 365
Jesus lives; thy sorrows now can no more, 379
Jesus, longed-for consolation, 491
Jesus, Lord, through weal and woe, 182:6
Jesus, make my heart to submit, 47:4
Jesus makes me spiritually rich, 75:10
Jesus makes my spirit rich, 75:10
Jesus mine abides with me, 98:5; 379

Jesus, mine, the wounds You suffered, 471
Jesus, my beloved Savior, by Thy death, 78:1
Jesus, my confidence, 365
Jesus my dear joy remaineth, 147:10
Jesus, my death's death, 165:5
Jesus my first word shall be, 171:4
Jesus, my great pleasure, 227:1
Jesus, my guardian, 728
Jesus, my joy, 64:8; 81:7; 87:7; 227:1;358; 610
Jesus, my Lord, Thou art the fountain, 445
Jesus, my most precious pleasure, 359; 360
Jesus, my refuge and rescuer, 154:3
Jesus, my shield and Redeemer, 154:3
Jesus, my strength, my hope, 466; 878
Jesus, my sure defense, 728
Jesus, name all names above, 146:8
Jesus, never leave I Thee, 98:5; 124:1; 380
Jesus never will I leave, 124:6; 244b
Jesus now be praised, 41:1; 41:6; 171:6; 190:7; 362
Jesus, now we shall praise You, 41:1
Jesus, now will we praise Thee, 41:1; 362
Jesus, O Lamb of God, 496
Jesus of Nazareth, 245:3; 245:5
Jesus, of Thy flock the Savior, 143:6
Jesus, on this joyous day, 171:4
Jesus, ornament of my faith, 472
Jesus, our comfort and life, 475
Jesus, our life and our consolation, 475
Jesus, part Thou not from me, 124:6; 154:8; 157:5; 244b
Jesus, praise I bring with singing, 142:7
Jesus, priceless treasure, 227:1; 358
Jesus raised His hands and blessed, 11:2
Jesus remains all my joy, 147:10
Jesus remains my joy, 147:10
Jesus, safely guide me, 154:4
Jesus said to Simon, 88:4
Jesus said to them, 245:4
Jesus saith to them, 245:4
Jesus saith unto them, 245:4
Jesus, Savior, I am Thine, 244:19

Jesus, Savior, loving, tender, 143:6
Jesus, Savior of my soul, 165:5
Jesus, Savior of Thy flock, 143:6
Jesus, Savior, of Thy people, 143:6
Jesus shall be my first word, 171:4
Jesus shall be the first word, 171:4
Jesus shall my all be, 190:5
Jesus shall my all now be, 190:5
Jesus shall my first word, 171:4
Jesus shall now shield His people, 42:6
Jesus shall remain my gladness, 147:10
Jesus, shepherd, be Thou near me, 208:9
Jesus should be my first word, 171:4
Jesus, show me my beginning, 248:42
Jesus, since Thou hast, through Thy bitter death, 78:1
Jesus sinners doth accept, 113:5
Jesus sleepeth; what hope have I, 81:1
Jesus sleeps; I am forsaken, 81:1
Jesus sleeps; vain all my hoping, 81:1
Jesus sleeps; what am I to hope for, 81:1
Jesus sleeps; what hope is there for me, 81:1
Jesus sleeps; what hope remaineth, 81:1
Jesus sleeps; what shall I hope for, 81:1
Jesus sleeps; what should my hope be, 81:1
Jesus sleeps; wherein is my hope, 81:1
Jesus sleeps; who then will save me, 81:1
Jesus' sorrows, pain and death, 159:5
Jesus, source of ev'ry blessing, 147:10
Jesus, source of heavenly light, 245:21
Jesus, source of precious pleasure, 248:40b
Jesus spake to Simon, Be not afraid, 88:4
Jesus spake to Simon, Fear have thou none, 88:4
Jesu's suffering, pain and death, 159:5
Jesus' suffering, pain and death, 159:5; 245:20; A57
Jesus, take my heart and mold it, 47:4
Jesus, take now these Thy members, 40:8
Jesus, take unto Thyself Thy members, 40:8
Jesus, thanks I bring with singing, 142:5
Jesus, the death of my death, 165:5
Jesus the first word shall be, 171:4
Jesus then said to the chief priests, 246:34

Jesus, this is Thy Passion, 182:7
Jesus, this Thy Passion, 159:5
Jesus, Thou art the joy of my soul, 497
Jesus, Thou hast suffered death, 245:60b
Jesus, Thou joy of loving hearts, 443
Jesus, Thou my all shalt be, 190:5
Jesus, Thou my blessed Redeemer, 154:3
Jesus, Thou my comfort art, 365; 728
Jesus, Thou my constant gladness, 147:1
Jesus, Thou my dearest life, 248:38b; 356
Jesus, Thou my dearest Master, 248:38b
Jesus, Thou my heart's delight, 361; 473
Jesus, Thou my heart's great joy, 361
Jesus, Thou my joy, 248:40b
Jesus, Thou my refuge, 227:3
Jesus, Thou my soul's delight, 472
Jesus, Thou my soul's enchantment, 154:3; 359
Jesus, Thou my very soul, 352; 353; 354
Jesus, Thou my wearied spirit, 78:1
Jesus, Thou that for me livest, 248:38b
Jesus, Thou who knowest death, 245:60b
Jesus, Thou who my soul, 78:1
Jesus, Thou who once was* dead, 245:20
Jesus, Thou who once wert dead, 245:60b
Jesus, Thou who saved my soul, 78:1; 352; 353; 354
Jesus, Thou who suffered so, 355
Jesus, Thou who this my spirit, 78:1
Jesus, Thou who Thyself indeed hast tasted death, 355
Jesus, Thou who were* dead, 245:60b
Jesus, through weal and woe, 182:6
Jesus, Thy boundless love to me, 416
Jesus, Thy dear mercy's glances, 11:10
Jesus, Thy dear wounds, 471
Jesus, Thy deep wounds, 25:6; 30:6; 32:6; 39:7; 194:6
Jesus, Thy humiliation, 471
Jesus, Thy looks of mercy, 11:10
Jesus, Thy Passion is for me pure joy, 159:5; 182:7
Jesus, Thy Passion is unmixed joy, 159:5
Jesus, Thy Passion uplifts me, 159:5

Jesus, Thy wounds of love, 471
Jesus to Him sinners calls, 113:5
Jesus today rose triumphing, 342; 630
Jesus took to Him the twelve, 22:1a
Jesus took to Himself the twelve, 22:1a
Jesus took unto Him the twelve, 22:1a
Jesus triumphant rose today, 342; 630
Jesus, true Bread of Life, help, 180:7
Jesus, turning unto them, 246:59
Jesus, we now must laud and sing, 121:1
Jesus went forth with His disciples, 245:2
Jesus went with His disciples, 245:2
Jesus, who by Your bitter death, 78:1
Jesus, who didst ever guide (love) me, 248:42
Jesus, who for love most mighty, 165:3
Jesus, who from great love, 165:3
Jesus, who has loved me dearly, 165:3
Jesus, who me my beginning, 248:42
Jesus, who salvation gave us, 475
Jesus will I never leave, 98:5; 124:1; 124:6;
    154:8
Jesus will I not let go, 124:6
Jesus will protect His people, 42:6
Jesus works in wondrous ways, 75:10
Jesus, Your look of grace I can see, 11:10
The Jews came therefore, 245:64
The Jews therefore, because, 245:64
John, filled with joy, 121:4
John's joyful leaping, 121:4
John's premature leap for joy, 121:4
The journey through life, 56:2
Joy and blessedness untold, 184:4
Joy and blessing are prepared, 184:4
Joy and blessing rest upon our city state,
    120:4
Joy and blessing shall be theirs, 184:4
Joy be yours, 210:10; 210a:10
Joy becomes sadness, 26:3
Joy my soul, with joy exceeding, 246:68
Joy of the people, joy of your own, 213:13
Joy turns to mournfulness, 26:3
Joyful be, O hallowed throng, 30:12
Joyful be, O ransomed throng, 30:1
Joyful flourish like the fields, 216:7

Joyful, joyful now am I, for the yoke, 56:3
Joyful shepherds, haste, oh, haste(n), 248:15
Joyful shepherds, hasten, 248:15
Joyful shout in happy chorus, 120:2
The joyful tidings angels gave us, 133:4a
Joyful time in the new covenant, 83:1
Joyful time in the new dispensation, 83:1
Joyful we hail this glorious day, 145:7; 629
Joyfully rise aloft, 36:1
Joyfully shall my heart leap, 248:33
Joyous all, ye hallowed souls, 30:12
Joyous all, ye ransomed souls, 30:1
A joyous gift God's promise holdeth, 83:1
The joyous golden sun, 451
Judge us not as base defaulters, 101:2
A judgment stern in condemnation, 89:3
A judgment stern without compassion, 89:3
Just as a father is loving, 17:7
Just as a father showereth, 17:7
Just as cats prey on mice, 211:10
Just as God hath towards thee, 197:7
Just as I'm my waters lending, 30a:11
Just as the cat always preys, 211:10
Just as the rain and snow from heaven falls,
    18:2
Just as the showers and snow from heaven
    fall, 18:2
Just as the wild sea-waves, 178:3
Just begone, sad shadows, 202:1
Just behold and see whether any other sor-
    row, 46:1a
Just keep, O world, what is mine, 8:5
Just one thing grieves a Christian, 75:9
Just storm, storm, sadness-weather, 153:6
Just the same, 52:3
Just this, Lord, will I ask of Thee, 111:6
Just through love and through compassion,
    164:3
The just year of jubilee has arrived, 122:6

K

Keep it quiet is the watchword, 246:7
Keep my heart pure in faith, 3:6

Keep, my heart, this blessed wonder, 248:31
Keep, O my spirit, this blessing, 248:31
Keep to thyself, O world, my treasure, 8:5
Keep up your courage, Christian folk, 114:1; 256
Keep us in the truth, 79:6
Keep us, Lord, in Thy word, 6:6; 126:1
Kill us by Thy goodness, revive, 132:6
Kill us of Thy goodness, arouse, 132:6
Kindly muses, hear thy mother, 214:5
King and Master, I will love Thee, 248:33
King Augustus, loud we hail thee, 215:3
King of Glory, King of Peace, 361; 473
King of glory, strong defender, 31:4
King of Heaven, be Thou welcome, 182:2
King of Heaven, come in triumph, 182:2
King of Heaven, ever welcome, 182:2
King of Heaven, Thou art welcome, 182:2
King of honor, Jesus Christ, 246:44
The King of Love my shepherd is, 255; 349
King we hail Thee, King of Jews, 245:34
The kings from out Sheba came then forth, 65:2
The kings from Sheba came along (there), 65:2
The kings have come out of Sheba, 65:2
The kings out of Saba came, 65:2
Klein-Zschocher must always be, 212:14
Klein-Zschocher must be as tender, 212:14
Klein-Zschocher must be e'er blithe, 212:14
Klein-Zschocher, our little town, 212:14
Knight of Habsburg's noble blood, 206:7
Know me, my keeper, 244:21
Know, O child, thy full salvation, 248:53
Know thou, beloved one, naught will I ever, 57:8
Know ye then not that I must be there, 154:5
Know'st thou not, I must be about my Father's, 154:5
Kyrie, Father in eternity, 669; 672
Kyrie, God our Father ever more, 371; 669; 672
Kyrie, God the Father eternally, 371

Kyrie, O God, Holy Ghost, 671; 674
Kyrie, Thou spirit divine, 671; 674

L

A lamb goes forth; the sins he bears, 267
The lamb is dumb before his shearers, 246:50
The lamb lies still before the shearer, 246:50
Lamb of God, 232:24
The Lamb of God for mortals' sakes, 267
Lamb of God, I fall before Thee, 244:48
The Lamb of God is delivered, 246:56
Lamb of God, Lord Jesus, 23:4
Lamb of God, O Jesus, 23:4
Lamb of God, our Savior, 23:4; 619
Lamb of God, pure and holy, 618
The lamb that is slaughtered, 21:11a
The lamb that was sacrificed is worthy, 21:11a
The lamb that was slain is worthy, 21:11a
The lamb which is slaughtered, 21:11a
A lambkin goes and bears the guilt, 267
Lament, lament, God's city now in dust, 46:2
Lament thee now, thou ruined town of God, 46:2
Last hour, break herein, 31:8
Last hour, break in, 31:8
The last hour of my life, 381; 488
The last part of my life is here, 488
The last period of my life, very soon, 488
A last request, O Lord, me grant, 502
Laud and honor and praise, 21:11b
Laud and praise be God the Father and the Son, 10:7
Laud and praise be to God the Father, 10:7
Laud and thanks bide, O Lord, 249:10b
Laud, honor and praise be to God, 192:3
Laud, honor, praise to God, 192:3
Laud, praise and honor be, 231
Laud, praise, and thanks to Thee be given, 121:6
Laud to God in all His kingdoms, 11:1
Laud we the name of God most holy, 142:4

Lead also my heart and mind, 5:7; 148:6
Lead both my heart and mind, 163:6
Lead e'en my heart and will, 5:7
Lead me to pasture and feed me, 246:9
Lead on! I follow, 212:23
Lead on; 'tis my desire to cleave, 133:6
Lead Thou me in paths of wisdom, 150:4
Lead Thou me in Thy true pathways, 150:4
Lead Thou me in Thy truth, 150:4
Lead Thou my heart and will, 5:7; 148:6; 163:6
Lead us with Thine own righteous hand, 90:5; 101:7
Lead us with Thy right hand, 90:5; 101:7
Leader of faithful souls, 122:6
The learned world, 36b:6
The least event occurring, 97:3
Leave fear and pain, 248:35
Leave, Highest One, to us at all times, 181:5
Leave Him; bind Him not, 244:33b
Leave Him, leave Him; bind Him not, 244:33b
Leave Him; stop, 244:33b
Leave me, O world, out of contempt, 123:5
Leave me, world, for thou dost scorn me, 123:5
Leave me, world, in detestation, 123:5
Leave, O man, the lusts of this world, 20:9
Leave off your tears, 146:8
Leave to mocking tongues their scorning, 70:5
Leave us then despite our sorrow, 209:3
Leave us then with sadness, 209:3
Lend Thou Thy spirit and power, 18:3b
Lengthened shadows, leaves descending, 205:5
Leopold's excellences, 173a:3
Leopold's most courtly graces, 173a:3
Leopold's outstanding virtues, 173a:3
Lest evil tempt my steps astray, 244:26b
Lest I forget, do not, O Lord, forget me, 504
Let a song of thanks resound, 66:3
Let all creation bless the Lord, 261

Let all creatures now adore Thee, 140:7
Let all give thanks to Thee, 79:3
Let all men praise the Lord, 79:3
Let all the Earth with songs rejoice, 248:9
Let all the multitudes of light, 86:6
Let all together praise our God, 375; 376; 609; 732; 732a
Let all with gladsome voices, 64:4
Let be; let us see whether Elias, 244:71e
Let constancy and truth, 24:5
Let every region in the wide world, 214:8
Let everything that hath breath, 190:1b
Let everything that hath breath praise the Lord, 225:5
Let ev'ryone beware, 166:5
Let fear and pain, 248:35
Let God be blest, be praised, 322
Let God inspire and rule your life, 197:4
Let grief and woe on earth below, 48:3
Let high glory and praise be to the Father, 135:6
Let Him be crucified, 244:54d; 244:59b
Let Him be; hold, do not bind Him, 244:33b
Let him hold with the blind world, 94:7
Let him tend to the world so blind, 94:7
Let Israel hope in the Lord, 131:5a
Let it strike, the long-awaited hour, 53
Let me but live to tell my story, 248:41
Let me but once, but once more, 246:76
Let me find grace for Thee, 246:29
Let me find grace in Thine eyes, 246:29
Let me find Thy favor ever, 246:29
Let me kiss Him but once more, 246:76
Let me no desire nor fear, 177:4
Let my heart be pure as Thine, 244:75
Let my heart my tribute be, 163:3
Let my heart the coin be, 163:3
Let my heart the coinage be, 163:3
Let my heart the tribute be, 163:3
Let my life be hid in Thee, 159:5
Let my soul be content, 204:6
Let naught, my soul, affright thee, 13:6; 44:7; 97:9
Let naught, my soul, distress thee, 13:6

Let no desire or fear, 177:4
Let no sorrow, soul separate thee, 186:10
Let not, Lord, greed or fear, 177:4
Let not our God be unattested, 76:2
Let nothing thee dismay, O fainting spirit, 99:3
Let now all honor due be done, 121:1
Let, O prince of holy cherubs, 130:5
Let, O prince of the cherubim, 130:5
Let one pay attention, 166:5
Let our choir new anthems raise, 159:5
Let our hearts e'er be joyful, 110:1
Let our mouth be full of laughter, 110:1
Let our voice and strings resounding, 1:5
Let, Princess, let another gleam, 198:1
Let, Princess, let one more ray, 198:1
Let, Princess, let still one more glance, 198:1
Let songs of rejoicing be raised, 149:1
Let sorrow ne'er try thee, 186:10
Let soul, no sorrow from Jesus, 186:10
Let sound the strings in Cythara, 36:4
Let thank, God, and praise Thee Thy people, 76:14
Let thank, O God, and give Thee praise, 76:14
Let thank, O God, and honor Thee, 69:6
Let thanks, O God, be given Thee, 69:6
Let thanks to the Highest resound, 66:3
Let the cunning world be angry, 152:5
Let the doctrine perish, 2:3
Let the evil-tongued revile us, 70:5
Let the mockers' tongues jeer, 70:5
Let the mocking tongues deny it, 70:5
Let the people praise Thee, 69:6
Let the tongues of the mockers, 70:5
Let the whole creation cry, 262
Let them thank God, and Thee adore, 69:6
Let then, O beloved father of the country, 215:8
Let Thine angel ever lead me, 19:7
Let Thine angel, Lord, attend me, 19:7
Let Thine angel with me travel, 19:7
Let Thine angels close attend me, 19:7
Let Thine angels not forsake me, 19:7

Let Thine angels with me journey, 19:7
Let Thy angels travel with me, 19:7
Let Thy blood in mercy poured, 379
Let Thy gracious ears be open, 25:5
Let Thy might descend from Heaven, 126:2
Let Thy praise be sung, 248:43
Let Thy praise, O God, 248:43
Let trumpets clear resound, 128:3
Let us be praising Christ, 121:1; 121:6
Let us but rest awhile in quiet, 93:3
Let us complete the year, 171:6
Let us even go now to Bethlehem, 248:26
Let us even now go even unto Bethlehem, 248:26
Let us even now go to Bethlehem, 248:26
Let us ever walk with Jesus, 481
Let us exult, 16:3a
Let us give praise and honor, 29:8
Let us go now toward Bethlehem, 248:26
Let us go with Jesus, 481
Let us leap with joy, 313
Let us love the faces of the pious, 19:6
Let us love the presence of the holy angels, 19:6
Let us not divide (rend) it, 245:54
Let us not tear and divide, 245:54
Let us now even unto Bethlehem, 248:26
Let us now go even unto Bethlehem, 248:26
Let us, O highest God, finish the year, 41:2
Let us, O highest God, the year accomplish, 41:2
Let us, oh highest God, complete the year, 41:2
Let us, oh highest God, the year complete, 41:2
Let us rejoice, 16:3a
Let us rend not nor divide it, 245:54
Let us share in Jesus' fate, 481
Let us sing from the depths of our hearts, 187:7
Let us strive to be like our Savior, 481
Let us take care; let us keep watch, 213:1
Let us take care; let us watch, 213:1

Let us the countenance of righteous angels, 19:6

Let us the year accomplish, 190:7

Let us the year forthcoming, 190:7

Let us the year fulfill in praise, 190:7

Let us then not cut or tear it, 245:54

Let us then with lowly fear, 115:6

Let us therefore not divide it, 245:54

Let us this year complete then, 171:6

Let us triumph, 16:3a

Let us walk as Jesus willeth, 481

Let us ward him, e'er protect him, 213:1

Let us watch him; let us guard him, 213:1

Let us watch then, pray with heed, 115:6

Let us with joy our voices raise, 377

Let who will in Thee rejoice, 301

Let who will receive thy pleasure, 56:5; 301

Let wish to itself the world, 190:4

Let Your angels travel with me, 19:7

Let your hearts and ears be open, 175:6

Let your thanks with love outpouring, 110:2

Lie before your Savior prostrate, 182:5

Life is but a paltry measure, 39:3

Life is distasteful to me, 170:5

Life is well nigh done for me, 381; 488

A life of steadfast piety, 459

Life's burdens and sorrows with gladness I share, 75:5

Life's last moment, quickly come, 31:8

Life's radiant sun to rest is sinking, 321

Life's sun, light of the senses, 180:5

Life's true sunlight, light of feeling, 180:5

Life's weal and woe, 156:3

Lift high your heads aloft, 70:8

Lift thy head and proudly sing, 40:6

Lift up, my soul, forget all pain, 246:68

Lift up your heads and be comforted, 70:8

Lift up your heads on high, 70:8

Lift up your heads, ye mighty gates, 321

Lift your head high and be assured, 70:8

Lift yourself with joy, 36:1

The light along the ages, 287

The light and glory of the sun, 446

Light as is flying chaff, 166:5

The light of day is flying, 448

The light of highest majesty, 91:2

Light of light, enlighten me, 124:6; 373

Light up my heart, 248:47

Light-minded, fickle persons, 181:1

The lightnings and thunders, 244:33c

Like a father pitieth his little children, 17:7

Like a shepherd, 208:9

Like a wayward sheep and wandering, 330; 331

Like as a father bendeth, 225:2

Like as a father bendeth in pity, 17:7

Like as a father pities, 225:2

Like as a father pities the children, 17:7

Like as a father pitieth, 225:2

Like as the hart, 148:3

Like as the rain-sent water, 166:4

Like as the raindrops and snow from heaven fall, 18:2

Like as the savage ocean waters, 178:3

Like as the showers and snow from heaven fall, 18:2

Like as the wild waves of the sea, 178:3

Like hungry beasts they rage and roar, 178:5

Like Peter I am not presumpt'ous, 68:3

Like rough and angry waves of ocean, 178:3

Like Thee the grave will not hold me, 15:9c; 95:6

Likeness of false hypocrites, 179:3

Likewise also the chief priests, 244:67c

Likewise also the cup after supper, 246:14

Likewise Amor seeks his pleasure, 202:4

Likewise, the Spirit also helpeth, 226:1

The lips of the foolish say, 308

List and mark, ye erring mortals, 7:2

List now, the flutes' melodious choir, 206:9

List our harps and tuneful voices, 1:5

List, ye people, God is calling, 76:3

Little does this world's damnation, 123:5

The little grain of wheat brings no fruit, 114:4

Little Jesu, heart's beloved, 248:9

Little worth's found on Earth, 64:5

Live Augustus! Live our King!, 207a:9

Live steadfast; die with faith, 198a:6
Live, sun of this Earth, 208:11
Lo, a table Thou for me hast spread, 112:4
Lo, as the hart, 148:3
Lo, God is here, 377; 416
Lo, God's almighty power and hand, 147:8
Lo here, there lies in stable dark, 248:17
Lo here, there lies in the dark stall, 248:17
Lo, I am with you always, 182:3
Lo, I come; I am with you, 182:3
Lo, I come now; I stand before the door, 61:4
Lo, I come now unto you, 182:3
Lo now, I come now, 182:3
Lo, the day of days is here, 262
Lo, there is no soundness within my body, 25:1
Lo, there is none, 227:2
Lo, we hail Thee, dearest King, 245:34
Lo, when the last great trump shall thunder, 127:4a
Lo, who is this I see, 121:5
Lock, my heart, this blessed wonder, 248:31
Long as fleecy flocks shall wander, 208:13
Long expected festal day, 194:1
Long life to you, sun of this Earth, 208:11
Long live August, 205:15; 207a:9
Long live Kortte!, 207:11
Long live the sun of the Earth, 208:11
Long may the lindens of Sax'ny, 214:9
Long my spirit waiteth for the Lord, 131:4a
Long since a tempest hath been brewing, 46:3
A longed-for day, 31:3
Longed-for joy-light, 184:1
Look down, Holy Dove, Spirit, 226:4
Look down in pity, 131:2b
Look down in pity on my need, 113:2
Look down, O God, 244:60
Look down, O Lord, from Heav'n behold, 2:6
Look indeed and see then if there be a grief, 46:1a
Look on my will, I know, 17:6

Look on Thy Son's most bitter death, 101:6
Look there; there lies in the dark stable, 248:17
Look up, faint heart, 454
Look up, faint heart, exult with joy, 248:12
Look up, O fearful heart, 168:4
Look up to thy God again, 40:6
Look upon me, my guardian, 244:21
Look upon my will, I know, 17:6
Look upon us, blessed Lord, 373
Look where Jesus beckoning stands, 244:70a
Look with contentment, 202:9
Look ye, behold what love is on us, 64:1
Look ye, I stand before the door, 61:4
Look ye, Jesus waiting stands, 244:70a
Look ye now, 46:1a
Look, ye sinners, 408
Look ye then and see if there be any sorrow, 46:1a
Look yonder, O my soul, 245:31
Loose Him; do not hold, 244:33b
Loose Him; halt ye, bind Him not, 244:33b
Loose Him; leave Him; bind Him not, 244:33b
Lord, a child am I, 78:3
Lord, all my heart is fixed on Thee, 149:7; 174:5; 245:68; 340
The Lord Almighty stands forever, 45:2
Lord, are not then Thine eyes on unbelievers, 102:1a
Lord, are not Thine eyes upon the truth, 102:1a
Lord, are Thine eyes not searching, 102:1a
Lord, as far as clouds are stretching, 171:2
Lord as far as clouds in heaven, 171:2
Lord, as far as the clouds go, 171:2
Lord, as far as the clouds move, 171:2
Lord, as Thou willst, 72:2b; 73:4
Lord, as Thou willst, so send it to me, 156:6
Lord, as Thou wilt, 73:4
Lord, as Thou wilt, deal Thou with me, 73:1a; 156:6
Lord, as Thou wilt, do unto me, 73:1a
Lord, as Thou wilt, so be it ever, 156:4

Lord, as Thou wilt, so deal with me, 73:1a; 156:6; 339

Lord, as Thou wilt, so do with me, 73:1a

Lord, as Thou wilt, so may it be, 73:1a; 156:6; 339

Lord, as Thou wilt, so must themselves all things, 72:2b

Lord, as Thou wilt, so ordain it, 73:1a; 156:6

Lord, as Thou wilt, so send it to me, 73:1a

Lord, as Thou wilt, teach us to do Thy bidding, 72:2b

Lord, as Thy name is, so Thy praise resounds, 171:1

Lord, as wide as heaven is spacious, 171:2

The Lord ascendeth upon high, 388

Lord, at all times doth my soul, 329

Lord, behold, here are two swords, 246:22c

Lord, blessings rich in plenty, 17:5

The Lord bless thee and keep thee, 323

The Lord bless you all now, 196:4

The Lord bless you, yea now, 196:4

Lord, by Thy will shall I be guided, 156:4

Lord, can it be, 244:60

The Lord cares for us, 196:2

The Lord careth for us, 196:2

Lord, chastise not in Thy wrath, 246:74

Lord Christ above, to Thee I pray, 166:3

Lord Christ, by God engendered, 96:1; 96:6; 601; 698; A55; A75; A77; A156:1

Lord Christ from death is ris'n today, 306

Lord Christ, God's only Son, 164:6

Lord Christ, He is my being, 95:1a

Lord Christ, of God eternal, 164:6; A156:1

Lord Christ, of God supernal, 22:5; 96:6; 164:6

Lord Christ, of God the Father, 601

Lord Christ of old to Jordan came, 7:1

Lord Christ, reveal Thy holy face, 332; 632; 655; 655a; 655b; 655c; 709; 726; 749; A56; A172

Lord Christ, the only Son of God, 22:5; 96:1; 96:6; 164:6; 601; 698; A55; A75; A77; A156:1

Lord Christ, the Son of God alone, 96:1

Lord Christ, Thou art the heavenly light, 766

Lord Christ, Thou art the Prince of Peace, 67:7; 116:1; 143:2

Lord Christ, we here Thy praises sing, 121:1

Lord Christ, we now Thy praises sing, 121:1; 611; 696

Lord, do not Thine eyes turn on unbelievers, 102:1a

The Lord doth choose a holy dwelling, 34:4

Lord, enter not into judgment, 105:1a

Lord, enter not into wrath, 105:1a

Lord, every heart doth know, 34:2

Lord, fain I'd be in Heaven, 146:4

The Lord for ever bless and keep us, 324

Lord, for Thee my spirit longs, 150:2

Lord, from Thee have I been parted, 55:5

The Lord gives love, and grants His blessing, 186:8

Lord, go not into judgment, 105:1a

Lord, go Thou not into court, 105:1a

Lord God, before Thy feet we fall, 130:1

Lord God, creation owns Thee alway, 120a:1

The Lord God ever be unto you, 120a:7

Lord God, Father, my champion strong, 37:3

Lord God, Father, my strong hero, 37:3

Lord God, great master of creation, 120a:1

Lord God, heavenly king, 232:7a; 233:3; 234:3; 236:4

Lord God, Heaven's gate unlock, 617

Lord God, in anger smite me not, 338

The Lord God is my pastor, guide, 112:1

Lord God, King of Heaven, 232:7a

Lord God, my Father, strength and shield, 37:3

Lord God, my heart gives Thee thanks, 521

Lord God, now be Thou praised, 601

Lord God, now open Heaven wide, 617

Lord God, now open wide Thy Heaven, 617

Lord God, now we praise Thee, 601

Lord God of Hosts, of glorious might, 10:2

Lord God of Hosts, whose mighty hand, 416

Lord God, our praise we give, 16:1; 24:6; 725

Lord God, our praise we render, 601

Lord God prosper you; yea, more and more, 196:4

Lord God, the Holy Ghost, 466

Lord God, the Lord of all creation, 120a:1

Lord God, Thee praise do we, 16:1; 190:2; 328; 725

Lord God, Thee praise we sing, 725

Lord God, Thy Heaven now open wide, 617

Lord God, Thy mercy great extends beyond, 17:3

Lord God, Thy praise we sing, 16:1; 190:2; 328

Lord God, we all give praise to Thee, 130:1; 130:6.1

Lord God, we all praise Thee, 130:1

Lord God, we all Thee praise, 130:1

Lord God, we do praise Thee, 16:1

Lord God, we give Thee praise, 16:1; 190:2

Lord God, we praise Thee, 16:1; 130:6.2; 328; 725; A31

Lord God, we praise Thee, all of us, 130:1; 326

Lord God, we praise Thee ev'ry one, 130:1

Lord God, we praise You, 16:1

Lord God, we thank Thee ev'ry hour, 178:7.1

Lord, grant me grace to do, 45:7

Lord, grant that I Thine honor, 107:7

Lord, grant that I Thy honor, 107:7

Lord, guide my heart and will, 5:7; 148:6; 163:6

The Lord has come, our poor flesh, 61:2

The Lord hath all these wonders wrought, 248:28

The Lord hath dealt bountifully with us, 69:4

The Lord hath good for us achieved, 119:7

The Lord hath holpen, 10:5

The Lord hath lain Him down to rest, 244:77a

The Lord hath mighty things for us achieved, 69:4

The Lord hath mighty things for us fulfilled, 69:4

The Lord hath shewed strength, 243:7

Lord, have mercy (on us), 232:1; 232:3; 233:1a; 234:1a; 235:1a

Lord, have mercy (upon us), 232:1; 232:3; 236:1a

The Lord, He is my shepherd kind, 112:1

The Lord, He is my shepherd true, 85:3; 112:1

Lord, hear my deepest longing, 161:6; 244:72

Lord, hear my supplication, 131:1b

Lord, hear my voice, 131:1b

Lord, hear my voice's crying, 131:1b

Lord, hear the voice of my complaint, 177:1; 185:6; 639; A73

Lord, hearken to my crying, 131:1b

Lord, here on Earth my soul prepare, 153:9.1

Lord, here we stand consumed with longing, 249:8a

Lord, how plenteous is Thy bounty, 462

Lord, how wondrous, 462

Lord, I am poor, oppressed by heavy sorrow, 138:1

Lord, I am thinking of that time, 329

Lord, I believe; aid me in my weakness, 78:7

Lord, I believe; help me, weak one, 78:7

Lord, I believe; help Thou mine unbelief, 78:7

Lord, I have faith; help my frailty, 78:7

Lord, I have transgressed, 330; 331

Lord, I have trusted in Thy name, 244:38

Lord, I hope e'er Thou wilt all those, 184:5

Lord, I hope ever that Thou will not leave, 184:5

Lord, I hunger for Thy spirit, 180:3b

Lord, I need Thee; come Thou, heed me, 148:4

Lord, I ready am to die, 160:5

Lord, I sing Thy name, 142:7

Lord, I trust Thee and adore Thee, 78:7

Lord, I trust Thee; help my weakness, 78:7

Lord, I trust Thee; I adore Thee, 78:7
Lord, I wait for Thy salvation, 60:1b
Lord, I wait now for Thy help, 60:1b
Lord, if proud enemies rage, 248:54
Lord, if Thou wilt, 73:4
Lord, if Thou wilt, all follows Thy direction, 72:2b
Lord, if Thou wilt, all is disposed and guided, 72:2b
Lord, if Thou wilt, must all things be, 72:2b
Lord, I'm waiting for Thy grace, 60:1b
Lord, in me do Thou abide, 148:5
Lord, in our hearts we hold in sooth, 34:2
Lord, in our inmost hearts we hold, 34:2
Lord, in peace depart I, 337
Lord, in Thee have I put my trust, 640; 712
Lord, in Thy love look down on us, 76:7; 311; 312
Lord, in Thy mercy grant us peace, 42:7; 126:6
Lord, in Thy wrath oh, chide me not, 338
Lord, instead of on our good works, 9:5
Lord, instead of regarding good works, 9:5
The Lord is a sun and shield, 79:1
The Lord is and shall remain the best, 197:2
The Lord is bountiful to us, 119:7
The Lord is close alway at hand, 117:5
The Lord is ever at my side, 112:5
Lord, is it I, 244:15c
The Lord is just, 20:5
The Lord is King, 428; 429; 430
The Lord is king eternally, 143:5
The Lord is king everlastingly, 143:5
The Lord is king now evermore, 143:5
The Lord is mindful of us, 196:2
The Lord is my faithful shepherd, 85:3; 104:6; 112:1; 112:5; 260
The Lord is my shepherd, 112:1
The Lord is my sun and shield, 79:1
The Lord is my true shepherd, 85:3; 104:6
The Lord is not and never was from His own, 117:5
The Lord is now my shepherd true, 112:1
The Lord is ours; He will not fail, 117:5

The Lord is reigning evermore, 143:5
The Lord is sovereign everywhere, 143:5
Lord Jesu, blessed Prince of Peace, 67:7
Lord Jesu Christ, I cry to Thee, 177:1
Lord Jesu Christ, I turn to Thee, 655; 655a; 655b; 655c; 709; 726; A56; A172
Lord Jesu Christ, in Thee alone, 33:1
Lord Jesu Christ, Lord Prince of Life, 43:11.1
Lord Jesu Christ, man's surest stay, 48:7
Lord Jesu Christ, pure source of good, 113:8
Lord Jesu Christ, the Prince of Peace, 67:7
Lord Jesu Christ, Thy power display, 6:6
Lord Jesu Christ, true man and God, 127:5; 336
Lord Jesu Christ, turn Thou to us, 655; 655a; 655b; 655c; 709; 726; 749; A56; A172
Lord Jesu Christ, with us abide, 6:1; 253
Lord Jesu, conqueror of death art Thou, 67:3
Lord Jesu, Thou Thy mercy show'st, 48:7
Lord Jesu, who as man wast born, 127:1
Lord Jesus, ah, Thy bitter pain, 245:32
Lord Jesus, bid me go, 22:3
Lord Jesus, bitter was the woe, 487
Lord Jesus by thee stands, 72:4
Lord Jesus, call to me, 22:3
Lord Jesus Christ, appear to us, 632
Lord Jesus Christ, be present now, 332; 632; 655; 655a; 655b; 655c; 709; 726; 749; A56; A172
Lord Jesus Christ, I cry to Thee, 48:7; 185:6
Lord Jesus Christ, I turn to Thee, 332; 632; 749
Lord Jesus Christ, in Thee alone, 33:1; 33:6; 261
Lord Jesus Christ, light of my life, 335
Lord Jesus Christ, Lord Prince of Life, 43:11.1
Lord Jesus Christ, man's surest stay, 48:7
Lord Jesus Christ, my highest good, 113:8; 168:6

Lord Jesus Christ, my life, my light, 118; 153:9.3; 335
Lord Jesus Christ, my only help, 48:7
Lord Jesus Christ, my only stay, 48:7
Lord Jesus Christ, my sovereign good, 113:1; 168:6; 334
Lord Jesus Christ, only begotten Son, 235:4
Lord Jesus Christ, our Lord most dear, 122:6
Lord Jesus Christ, pure source of all, 113:1
Lord Jesus Christ, sole comfort, 48:7
Lord Jesus Christ, the Prince of Peace, 67:7
Lord Jesus Christ, Thou fount of grace, 113:1; 334
Lord Jesus Christ, Thou hast already, 333
Lord Jesus Christ, Thou hast in love, 333
Lord Jesus Christ, Thou hast prepared, 333
Lord Jesus Christ, Thou highest good, 48:7; 113:1; 113:2; 168:6; 334
Lord Jesus Christ, Thou highest possession, 168:6
Lord Jesus Christ, Thou prepared a meal, 333
Lord Jesus Christ, Thou Prince of Life, 43:11.1; 454
Lord Jesus Christ, Thou prince of love, 11:6; 43:11.1
Lord Jesus Christ, Thy might display, 6:6
Lord Jesus Christ, Thy pow'r make known, 6:6
Lord Jesus Christ, true man and God, 127:1; 336
Lord Jesus Christ, turn Thou to us, 632
Lord Jesus Christ, turn towards us, 332
Lord Jesus Christ, unto us turn, 632; 709
Lord Jesus Christ, with us abide, 253; 649
Lord Jesus, dearest Master, 25:4
Lord Jesus, draw me unto Thee, 22:2
Lord Jesus, fare Thee well, 244:77b
Lord Jesus, God's dear Son, 151:4
Lord Jesus, in the days of old, 416
Lord Jesus lay in death, 15:2
Lord Jesus, let me not appear in unbefitting, 162:4

The Lord Jesus lifted His hands on high, 11:2
Lord Jesus lives, 145:6
Lord Jesus, my repose, 21:7
Lord Jesus, ne'er will I into Thy feast, 162:4
Lord Jesus raised His hands, 11:2
Lord Jesus, rest in peace, 244:77b
Lord Jesus stoopeth in my sorrow, 38:3
Lord Jesus, take me too with Thee, 22:2
Lord Jesus, the only Son, 601
Lord Jesus, Thee we bless, 244:77b
The Lord Jesus then lifted up His hands, 11:2
Lord Jesus, Thou alone art mine, 75:3
Lord Jesus, Thou art going forth, 500
Lord Jesus, Thou the sting of death hast drawn, 67:3
Lord Jesus, Thy dear angel send, 149:7; 245:68
Lord Jesus to me calls, 49:3b
Lord Jesus, we give thanks to Thee, 623
Lord Jesus, when we come to die, 245:68
Lord Jesus, when we stand afar, 253
Lord Jesus, with Thy children stay, 6:1
Lord keep us steadfast in Thy word, 6:6; 126:1
Lord, lead us by Thy guiding hand, 90:5; 101:7
Lord, let in me Thy true love, 180:6
Lord, let in me Thy faithful loving, 180:6
Lord, let me never be confounded**, 244:38
Lord, let not all Thy loving kindness, 180:6
Lord, let Thy blessed angels come, 149:7; 245:68
Lord, let Thy steadfast love for me, 180:6
Lord, let us love to gaze, 19:6
Lord, Lord, oh vouchsafe the vision quickly, 249:8b
Lord, Lord, the oxen daily comfort know, 138:3b
Lord, may the love from Heaven, 180:6
Lord, may Thy hand, 41:3
Lord, may Thy love be ever with me, 180:6
Lord, mighty Lord, we Thee acclaim, 10:2

Lord most high, Thy mercy show, 63:7

Lord, my evil deeds are many, 247:89; 330; 331

The Lord my faithful shepherd is, 85:3; 104:6; 112:1

Lord, my God, if Thou shouldst mark iniquity, 131:2a

Lord, my God, my heart and soul, 21:2

The Lord, my God, my shepherd is, 85:3; 112:1

Lord, my God, my spirit was in heaviness, 21:2

The Lord my guide vouchsafes to be, 85:6; 104:6

Lord, my heart I gladly grant Thee, 244:19

Lord, my love is all unworthy, 77:5

Lord, my love so poor remaineth, 77:5

The Lord my pasture shall prepare, 321

The Lord my shepherd deigns to be, 112:1; 112:5

The Lord my shepherd e'er shall be, 104:6

The Lord my shepherd is, 878

The Lord my shepherd is and guide, 112:1

The Lord my shepherd is and true, 104:6; 260

The Lord my shepherd is; my need, 112:1; 112:5

Lord, my soul doth thirst for Thee, 150:2

Lord, my thanks to Thee, 142:5

Lord, my weeping, tears, and sighing, 13:1

The Lord never forsakes His people, 117:5

Lord, never me abandon, 23:2

Lord, not I, 244:15c

Lord, now let Thy servant pass in peace, 337

Lord, now lettest Thou this Thy servant in peace, 83:2a

Lord, now lettest Thou Thy servant depart, 83:2a

Lord, now lettest Thy servant depart in peace, 83:2a

Lord, now lettest Thy servant hence to depart, 83:2a

Lord, obtain what Thou wilt for me, 156:6

Lord of all majesty and might, 416

Lord of all things dead and living, 8:6

Lord of life, and King all glorious, 8:6

Lord of Life, I pray Thee hear me, 180:7

Lord, of life I'm weary, 337

The Lord of might, from Sinai's brow, 2:1; 9:1; 308; 638

Lord of our life, 245:7

Lord of our life, and God of our salvation, 244:3; 244:55; 275; 400

Lord of the heavens, hear our halting voice, 248:24

The Lord of time hath to thy house accorded, 134a:6

Lord, oh, hearken to my calling, 131:1b

The Lord on high maketh plain, 45:2

Lord, on this Thy Passiontide, 159:5

Lord, ordain what Thou wilt for me, 339

Lord, our Creator, 245:1

Lord, our Governor, 245:1

Lord, our hearts hold Thy word, 34:2

Lord, our Master, 245:1

Lord, our Redeemer, 245:1

Lord, our souls with zeal inspire, 194:5

Lord over death and life, 8:6

Lord, permit now in peace Thy servant to depart, 337

Lord, pour not Thy vengeance, 463

Lord, prosper my endeavor, 343; 624

Lord, punish me not in Thy wrath, 338

Lord, rebuke me not, 105:1a; 198:1

Lord, remember Thou the Savior, 463

Lord, salvation is my hope, 60:1b

Lord Savior Christ, my soverign good, 113:1

Lord, send not Thy vengeance, 463

Lord, send Thy grace and breathe a blessing, 120a:6

Lord, set not revenge on me, 463

The Lord shall preserve thee, 71:7

Lord, shall we smite with the sword, 246:32b

Lord, shall we with the sword among them smite, 246:32b

Lord, speak to me, that I may speak, 377

Lord, strengthen Thou my heart, 5:7; 148:6

Lord, strong and mighty, God, 10:2

Lord, strong and powerful alone, 10:2

Lord, take my heart, 174:5

Lord, take my heart into Thy keeping, 229:4

Lord, take my heart; it beats for Thee, 245:68

Lord, teach me now a song, 134:5

Lord, teach us to consider, 106:2c

Lord, the door wide open standeth, 61:5a

Lord the only begotten Son, 232:7b

The Lord then said, 246:22a

Lord, these our hearts hold out to Thee, 34:2

Lord, Thine eyes look towards faith, 102:1a

Lord, Thine eyes look towards the faith, 102:1a

Lord, Thine hand, Thy blessing, 41:3

Lord, Thine own eyes see after true believing, 102:1a

Lord, Thou art my creator, 464

Lord, Thou hast been our dwelling place, 321

Lord, Thou has been Thy people's rest, 178:7.1

Lord, Thou lookest instead of good works, 9:5

Lord, Thou look'st past our good labors, 9:5

Lord, Thou my God and Father art, 138:7

Lord, Thou our Master, 245:1

Lord, Thou that art strong and mighty, 10:2

Lord, Thou wast born for my salvation, 68:4

Lord, Thou who art judge of all, 105:1a

Lord, Thou who art strong and mighty, 10:2

Lord, Thou who strong and mighty art, 10:2

Lord, Thou wilt justly judge all the ungodly, 102:1a

Lord, though awhile in tears of sorrow, 244:78

Lord, Thou'st shown us bounteous favor, 63:3

Lord, through my faith, 77:6

Lord, through Thy goodness, 600

The Lord thus saith: Yea, o'er my people I rejoice, 28:3

Lord, Thy cherubim, oh, send us, 130:5

Lord, Thy compassion, 248:29

Lord, Thy defense, 41:3

Lord, Thy goodness, 248:29

Lord, Thy goodness reaches, 17:3

Lord, Thy goodwill extends as far as Heaven is, 17:3

Lord, Thy hand, Thy blessing, 41:3

Lord, Thy mercy, 248:29

Lord, Thy mercy and Thy pity, 189:5

Lord, Thy pity, 248:29

Lord, Thy praises hear us voicing, 63:3

Lord, Thy regard, Thy blessing, 41:3

The Lord thy share of joy will send, 93:4

Lord, Thy word have I believed, 78:7

Lord, 'tis by Thy wondrous favor, 14:4

Lord, 'tis not man's deeds Thou seest**, 9:5

Lord, 'tis Thy care, Thy blessings, 41:3

Lord, to Thee, 150:2

Lord, to Thee I make confession, 330; 331

Lord, to Thee my heart I proffer, 244:19

Lord, to Thee my heart is given, 244:19

The Lord to us great things has done, 69:4

Lord, to us Thyself be shewing, 6:5

Lord, truth and right Thy word imparts, 34:2

Lord, unto highest Heav'n, 17:3

Lord, we give to Thee, 190:2

Lord, we thank Thee for Thy bounty, 193:3

Lord, weigh Thou and judge us not, 105:1a

Lord, weigh us and judge us not, 105:1a

Lord, what Thou willst shall be (please), 156:4

Lord, what Thou wilt shall be (me), 156:4

Lord, what vicious agony, 487

Lord, when haughty enemies snarl, 248:54

Lord, when our haughty foes assail (rejoice), 248:54

Lord, when our proud enemies pant, 248:54

Lord, when proud enemies do thwart us, 248:54

Lord, when the stiff-necked foes do rage, 248:54

Lord, wherefore hidest Thou, 81:2

Lord, who art strong and mighty, 10:2

Lord, who shall sit beside Thee, 281; 282

Lord, whose name is Love, 33:5
Lord, why art Thou so far from me, 81:2
Lord, why dost Thou not now protect us, 81:2
Lord, why dost Thou remain so distant, 81:2
Lord, why remainest Thou so distant, 81:2
The Lord will hear the faithful calling, 115:5
The Lord will help the poor and needy, 186:8
The Lord will not desert His folk, 117:5
The Lord will not suffer thy foot to be moved, 71:6
Lord, with Thee our works awaken, 9:5
Lord, You have from every path called us, 76:6
Lord, Your goodness extends as far as the heavens, 17:3
Lord, Your goodness extends throughout, 17:3
The Lord's hand, 109:2
The Lord's majesty is also worshipped, 36:7
The Lord's name be praised for ever, 30:3
The Lord's own hand, 109:2
The lot of God's ordaining, 97:7
Love divine, all loves excelling, 462
Love draws with gentle steps, 36:3
Love guides with gentle steps, 36:3
Love is a feeling hard to beat, 212:4
Love of love and light of light, 145:1
Love one another; let this be, 57:8
Love slowly draws with tender steps, 36:3
Love surpassing brought Thee, 182:4
Love thou thy God, this is the first, 77:1
Love unending, 'twas for love, 182:4
Love, ye Christians, in your works, 76:12
Loving God, oh, pity me, 179:5
Loving Shepherd, hope of mortals, 184:6
Lowly bend before the (thy) Savior, 182:5
Lowly bent and full of repentance, 199:4
Lull to sleep all care and sorrow, 197:3
Luscious fruits to autumn reddening, 205:7

M

Mad hireling slave, think on thy sin, 246:3
Magnify the Lord, O my soul, 10:1
Maidens all are stubborn creatures, 211:6
Maidens of a stubborn nature, 211:6
Maidens who have stupid tempers, 211:6
Maidens, you are all pigheaded, 211:6
Maintain my heart pure in the faith, 3:6
Maintain us, Lord, within Thy word, 126:1
Make a joyful noise unto God, 51:1
Make a reck'ning, thund'rous word, 168:1
Make a reckoning, thunder-word, 168:1
Make, Lord, Thy holy Gospel manifest, 126:5
Make manifest Thy might, O Christ, 6:6
Make manifest Thy might that Thou, 6:6
Make me a captive, Lord, 466
Make me as well, my God, 77:4
Make me strong with Thy spirit's joy, 168:6
Make our mouth full with laughter, 110:1
Make ready, Lord Jesus, the highway to Heaven, 147:5
Make ready, O Jesus, to Thee now the way, 147:5
Make ready the pathways; make ready the road, 132:1
Make ready the pathways; the highways prepare, 132:1
Make ready the ways; make ready the route, 132:1
Make ready, you heavens, 249:10c
Make thee clean, my heart, from sin, 244:75
Make thyself clean, my heart, 244:75
Make thyself, my spirit, ready, 115:1
Make yourself ready, Zion, 248:4
Man by God regenerated, 80:2a
Man is dirt, dust, ashes, 47:3
The man who leaves to God all power, 93:1
The man whose heart on Earth is set, 94:7
Mankind, believe then in this grace, 7:6
Mankind, believe then in this mercy, 7:6
Mankind, do believe this grace, 7:6
Mankind is clay, dust, 47:3

Mankind is dirt, stench, 47:3
Mankind, trust now in this mercy, 7:6
Man's favor and might, 126:3
Man's heart's rebellious, and perverse too, 176:1
Man's nature's foul, 47:3
Man's puny power and might, 126:3
A mansion at His side, 43:10
Many other things, 246:43a
Many will say to me, 45:4
Many will say unto me on that day, 45:4
Many women were gathered there, 244:73c
Marching with the heroes, 317
Mark and hark, ye mortal children, 7:2
Mark and hear, O mankind's children, 7:2
Mark and hear, ye children of men, 7:2
Mark and hear, ye men's children, 7:2
Mark, mark, it snaps; it breaks, 92:3
Mark my heart, constantly only this, 145:5
Mark, now watch ye if Elias, 244:71e
Mark, O my heart, evermore only this, 145:5
Mark thou, my heart now, for ever, 145:5
Mark well God's mighty love, 85:5
Mark ye and hark ye; forget ye not, 145:5
Mark ye how great a love, 64:1
Marvel, O men, at this great mystery, 62:2; 62:4
A marvel 'tis to mortal minds, 152:5
Mary immaculate, 485
Master, all my living follows, 39:5
The master is good, 212:5
Master kind and true, 212:8
Master, pray with pity view, 63:7
May all cares and sorrows slumber, 197:3
May divine providence and eternal goodness, 206:11
May God all-bountiful, 192:2
May God be gracious to us, 76:7
May God be merciful to us, 311; 312
May God be prais'd henceforth, 322
May God His grace to us convey, 76:7; 311; 312
May God let thee still sustain us, 225:3
May God smile on you, 196:4

May God to us His mercy show, 76:7
May God unto us gracious be, 311; 312
May God wish to be gracious to us, 76:7
May good fortune and happiness, 249a:11a
May good luck and prosperity, 249a:11a
May He seek from my error, 97:5
May Heaven befriend you, 208:15
May Heaven now grant to you two gracious ones, 212:18
May heavenly bounty and goodness eternal, 206:11
May heavenly providence guard and protect, 206:11
May honor be sung to Thee, 248:43
May I ever be content, 204:6
May little Zschocher, 212:14
May my body and spirit pine away, 3:4
May my soul be contented, 204:6
May our mouth be full of laughter, 110:1
May peace be unto you, 158:1
May peace now be with thee, 158:1
May pleasure and joy, 197:8
May plenty be such you'll be laughing, 212:20
May plenty be such you'll be with you, 212:20
May prosperity attend you, 36b:8
May squire find a purseful of ducats, 212:16
May the chamberlain take in ten thousand, 212:16
May the coming years before us, 207a:7
May the ever-rich God, 192:2
May the grace of Christ our Savior, 248:53
May the people thank and praise Thee, 76:14
May they have many fine sons, 212:18
May Thine angels close attend me, 19:7
May this new year before us, 190:7
May to us God His mercy show, 76:7
May we complete this year, 41:2
May what my God wills come to pass, 65:7; 103:6; 144:6; 244:31
May ye see in contentment, 202:9
May you e'er contentment know, 202:9
May you ever, ever prosper, 207a:9
May you find in the contentment, 202:9
May you live in sweet content, 202:9

May you see in contentment, 202:9

May your chaste love's e'er sacred union, 202:8

May your future abound with laughter, 212:20

May your increase be steady, 212:20

May your increase be sure, 212:20

May your name go like suns, 173a:7

May your prosperity be enduring, 212:20

May'st thou to the foe not deliver, 71:6

The meaning was hidden from them, 22:1b

Meanwhile consider thy soul, 114:6

Meanwhile, God gives a good conscience, 75:6

Meanwhile, I beg you know, 211:9

Meanwhile I live with You in happiness, 84:5

Meanwhile, show God a blameless conscience, 75:6

Meanwhile we sigh with burning desire, 249:8a

Meanwhile we sigh with burning eagerness, 249:8a

The meek shall not go empty, but be filled, 75:1a

Melt, my heart, 245:63

Members of Christ, ah, consider, 132:5

Members of Christ, oh consider, 132:5

Members of Christ, remember what the Savior, 132:5

Men are but clay, dust, 47:3

The men, however, that held Jesus, 246:41a

Men teach a doctrine false and vain, 2:2

Men, whose boast it is, 262

Merciful Father, Highest God, 103:6

Merciful God, 244:60

Merciful heart of eternal love, 185:1

Mercifully grant us peace, 42:7; 126:6

A merciless judgment will certainly be, 89:3

Mercy's immeasurable being has not confined, 121:3

A mere wave of His hand casts down, 248:57

The merry chase, the hunt is my delight, 208:1

Methinks I mark Thee, shepherd, coming, 175:4

Methinks we all can learn a goodly lesson, 42:5

Mid laughter and jesting, 216:5

Might and power be now sung to, 149:2

Might and power rise victorious, 149:2

Might and power Thee be offered, 149:2

The might of man availeth not, 188:4

The might of the world loses itself, 188:4

Mighty and strong art Thou, Lord, 10:2

The mighty can by stubbornness be blinded, 147:4

Mighty cedars oft are battered, 150:5

A mighty fortress is our God, 80:1; 302; 303; 720

The mighty God casteth down from their seat, 10:4

Mighty God, His own time is ever best, 106:2a

The mighty guardian cares for me, 104:2

The mighty He hath dethroned, 243:8

Mighty Lord, and king all-glorious, 248:8

Mighty Lord of all creation, 248:8

Mighty love that Thee, great Son of God, 182:4

The mighty ones fall from their seat, 10:4

The mighty ones from off their seats, 10:4

The mighty ones He hurls down from their thrones, 10:4

The mighty ones hurls He from their throne, 10:4

Mighty patron, we would charm you, 210:8

Mighty warrior, prince of princes, 31:4

The mighty works our God hath wrought, 64:2

Mighty, yet lowly, 846

Mind and soul become confused, 35:2

A mind that exquisitely feeleth, 36c:2

Mindful of His mercy, 10:5

Mine eye hath seen the Savior, 66:4b

Mine eyes beheld our blessed Lord, 66:4b

Mine eyes behold the Savior, 66:4b

Mine eyes ever turn to God, 150:6

Mine eyes ever upward look to the Lord, 150:6

Mine is Jesus; what a blessing, 147:6

The mire of sin has so bespotted, 5:2

The mire of sin hath put me in sore plight, 5:2

A miserable mortal I, 131:4b

The miserable shall eat, 75:1a

Miserere, 244:47

Misfortune here on Earth, 20:2

Misfortune ne'er unbrokenly, 20:2

Misfortune strikes on all sides, 139:4

Misfortune wraps from all directions, 139:4

Misfortune wraps on all sides, 139:4

Mister Tax Collector, 212:6

Moaning and most piteous weeping, 13:5

A moment I've forsaken thee, 103:6

The moon's pale beams are shining, 367

More than all we are possessing, 263

Moreover, do well also, 169:6

Moreover wisdom and understanding, 92:4

The morning light is breaking, 245:52

Mortal, remember Jesus Christ, 403

Mortify us by Thy goodness, 22:5; 132:6

Mortify us by Thy grace, 22:5; 132:6; 164:6

Mortify us through Thy goodness, 96:6; 164:6

Most blessed day of refreshment, 70:10a

Most eternal, whom one yet Father calls, 173:5

Most High, make Thy goodness, 51:3

Most High, renew Your goodness, 51:3

Most Holy Trinity, great God, 172:3

Most potent Leopold, 173a:1

Most righteous God, will you recall, 89:5

Most serene Leopold, 173a:1

Most serene one, whom Anhalt calls Father, 173a:5

Most wretched of men, oh, who shall deliver me, 48:1

Motet mourning Count von Flemming, 118

Mourn and worry not, O soul, 489

The mournful bells that toll, 198a:4a

Mouth and heart stand open to Thee, 148:4

Mouth and heart stands* to Thee open, 148:4

The mouth of fools doth God confess, 308

Move into Thy gates, 183:5

Murmur not, beloved Christian, 144:2

Murmur not, Christian soul, 144:2

Murmur not, man of Christ, 144:2

Murmur not, O my soul, 144:2

Must I be sad, 87:7

Must I be so troubled, 87:7

Must I be sorely troubled, 87:7

Must I be troubled, 87:7

Must I then tread this gloomy vale, 198a:7b

Must Pales' sacrifice be the last, 208:8

Must Thou now thus, my Jesus, say good night, 412; 501

Must thus Thou part, my Lord, 501

Mute sighs, silent lamentations, 199:2

My all in all, my everlasting good, 22:4

My all to God do I submit, 351; 707; 708; 708a

My anguish and need, 156:3

My assistance is always there, 60:2b

My bailiwick did you invade, 216:2

My being I behold, 17:6

My belief itself has dressed me, 49:5a

My believing heart, be glad, 68:2

My believing heart, rejoice, 68:2

My beloved is mine, 140:6

My beloved now is Lord, 248:52

My beloved rules already, 248:52

My best beloved already rules, 248:52

My blessed benefactor, for ever my friend, 22:4

My blessed Savior gone forever, 154:1

My body and spirit may languish, 3:4

My brow may run with honest sweat, 84:4

My care and grief increase, 13:4

My cause is God's, and I am still, 351; 707; 708; 708a

My cause is God's; I too am His, 707; 708; 708a

My chosen spouse is Christ the Lord, 1:6; 49:6a

My comforter is not by me, 247:59

My companions, worthy muses, 214:5
My courage falters low, 8:3
My course is set to Heaven above, 31:9
My cross of trouble glad I carry, 56:1
My cross with gladness I carry, 56:1
My cross with gladness on I carry, 56:1
My days of sorrow, 457
My dear Jesus, Thou, 157:3
My dear Redeemer comforts me, 5:4
My dear Savior, 245:60a
My dear, you said it, 212:23
My dearest father weepest still, 198a:8a
My dearest God, ah, grant me yet Thy mercy, 153:2
My dearest God, ah let Thee on it take pity, 153:2
My dearest God allow me still in vain to cry, 13:2
My dearest God allows me to call, 13:2
My dearest God still lets me call, 13:2
My dearest Jesu, I have lost Thee, 154:1
My dearest Jesu now hath left me, 154:1
My dearest Jesus is lost, 154:1
My dearest Jesus, Thou, 157:3
My dearest Lord hath let me, 13:2
My dearest Savior, Thou, 244:9
My dearest Savior, wilt Thou answer, 245:60a
My dearly beloved already rules, 248:52
My dearly beloved Bridegroom, 248:3
My desire is my Savior to embrace now, 161:3
My desire is to see my Savior, 161:3
My doubting heart is stilled, 75:12
My earthly afflictions with gladness, 75:5
My end has been set down, 161:4
My eye sees the risen Savior, 66:4b
My eye sees the Savior arise, 66:4b
My eye sees the Savior awakened, 66:4b
My failings are so great, 89:6
My faint heart indeed feels fear, 8:3
My fainting soul, be not so fearful, 8:2
My faith again has won me, 49:5a
My faith has me myself so clothed, 49:5a

My faith it is which glorious, 49:5a
My faith itself has clad me thus, 49:5a
My faith now holds me, 49:5a
My faithful heart, exult (rejoice), 68:2
My faithful Savior comforts (consoles) me, 5:4
My faithful shepherd is the Lord, 85:3
My Father, as Thou wilt, 246:25
My Father, Thy will be done, 246:25
My Father's love mine truly is, 92:2
My faults I hope He pardons, 97:5
My fear and need, 156:3
My feast is now prepared, 49:3a
My feast is prepared, 49:3a
My final bed would bring me terror, 60:3
My final sickbed will terrify me, 60:3
My foes so proud may try to frighten, 248:62
My friend and I sit here at leisure, 515
My friend is mine, 140:6
My friend is my own, 140:6
My friend, that's just the wind, 201:3
My gaze will turn for ever, 95:2b
My God and judge, 33:2
My God, be merciful to us, 69:6
My God, behold me lying before Thee, 244:63.1
My God, cast me not away, 33:4; 105:2
My God, cast me not out, 33:4
My God, condemn me not, 105:2
My God, do not cast me away, 33:4
My God, forsake me not, 105:2
My God, here my heart will be, 18:3a
My God, here shall my heart abide, 18:3a
My God, here will my heart be, 18:3a
My God, how long, 155:1
My God, hurry the moment, 82:4
My God, I give myself to Thee, 65:7; 92:7a
My God, I love Thee from my heart, 77:3
My God, I love Thee well with all my heart, 77:3
My God, I will openly confess Thee, 132:4
My God, into Thy hand I joyfully now yield me, 65:7
My God is true, 52:4

My God makes ready to relieve me, 321
My God, oh, let me now depart, 82:4
My God, oh, speed the moment, 82:4
My God, open for me the gates, 32:6
My God, open me the portals, 32:6
My God, open to me the gates, 32:6
My God, reject me not, 33:4; 105:2
My God, to Thee I bring my heart, 18:3a
My God, when at last will you give me, 82:4
My God, when comes that blessed Now, 82:4
My God, when comes the beautiful Now, 82:4
My God, when shall the great moment, 82:4
My God, when Thou shalt call me home, 149:7
My God, when will the beautiful, 82:4
My God, when wilt Thou, 98:2
My God, when wilt Thou call me, 82:4
My God, who hast possessed my heart, 18:3a
My God, with all my heart I love Thee, 77:3
My guardian, deign to own me, 244:21
My guilt and sin, 87:4
My heart and my flesh cry out, 727
My heart, behold how all, 245:62
My heart believes and loves, 75:12
My heart doth love Thee so, O Lord, 174:5
My heart, ever faithful, 68:2
My heart, ever trusting, 68:2
My heart in my Savior rejoices, 68:2
My heart is bathed in blood, 199:1
My heart is deep distressed, 199:1
My heart is drowned in grief, 199:1
My heart is ever well content, 112:2
My heart is ever yearning, 727
My heart is filled with faith, 75:12
My heart is filled with fear and joy, 180:4
My heart is filled with joy and terror, 180:4
My heart is filled with longing, 161:6; 727
My heart is filled with love, 75:12
My heart is full, and I must sing, 43:11.1
My heart now knows content, 204:1
My heart, O Lord, is sore distressed, 48:7
My heart possesses God alone, 169:2a; 169:3

My heart rejoiceth, 243:2
My heart, see all the world, 245:62
My heart, see how the world around, 245:62
My heart swims in blood, 199:1
My heart that believest, 68:2
My heart, the whole world suffers, 245:62
My heart was deeply troubled, 21:2
My heart, whilst all the world suffers, 245:62
My heart will put aside, 89:4
My heart with grief doth swoon, 199:1
My heart with joy now raises, 269
My heart within feels fear and gladness, 180:4
My heart's delight is unsurpassed, 1:6
My heav'nly shepherd cares for me, 104:2
My help is already there, 60:2b
My helper standeth near, 60:2b
My highest prize is God's dear word, 18:4
My hope is built on nothing less, 377
My hope is in Almighty God, 52:5
My hope on Earth, Lord Jesus Christ, 33:1
My hopeful hero, thou, of one blood, 213:6
My hopeful hero, to whom I am truly kin, 213:6
My house stands open, 207:5
My inmost heart now raises, 269
My Jesu, fare Thee well, 244:77b
My Jesu, what affliction, 487
My Jesus, at Thy command, 486
My Jesus cares for me, 72:4
My Jesus, draw me after You, 22:2
My Jesus, draw me on, 22:3
My Jesus, draw me, so shall I run, 22:3
My Jesus, draw me unto Thee, 22:2
My Jesus, farewell, 244:77b
My Jesus, fear of death didst Thou dispel, 67:3
My Jesus, good night, 244:77b
My Jesus has arisen, 67:2
My Jesus has by now, 43:5
My Jesus has now completed, 43:5
My Jesus has risen, 67:2
My Jesus hath henceforth, 43:5
My Jesus holds his peace, 244:40

My Jesus, how great anguish of soul, 487
My Jesus I do not leave, 70:11; 124:1; 154:8
My Jesus I leave not, 98:5
My Jesus is arisen, 67:2
My Jesus is risen, 67:2
My Jesus is speaking of me, 49:3b
My Jesus keeps silence, 244:40
My Jesus keeps silent, 244:40
My Jesus leave I not, 98:5; 124:1; 124:6;
    154:8; 157:5
My Jesus, let me not come to the wedding,
    162:4
My Jesus, let me not without a robe ap-
    proach, 162:4
My Jesus lives, 145:6
My Jesus, my helper, my port, 15:9b
My Jesus, my Savior and shield, 15:9b
My Jesus now for aye, 43:5
My Jesus now is taken, 244:33a
My Jesus shall be all I own, 75:3
My Jesus shall be my everything, 75:3
My Jesus shall my all be, 75:3
My Jesus speaks of me, 49:3b
My Jesus, Thou art called death's poison,
    67:3
My Jesus, Thou art called the bane to death,
    67:3
My Jesus, what agony of soul, 487
My Jesus, what distress of soul, 487
My Jesus who was dead, 15:2
My Jesus, whom the seraphim serve, 486
My Jesus will do it, 72:4
My journey through life, 56:2
My journey through the world, 56:2
My joy is all in Thee, 133:1; 465
My judge and master, 33:2
My last bed will frighten me, 60:3
My last halting-place will me frighten, 60:3
My last request is that I may expire, 502
My life at peace with God proceedeth, 84:5
My life has no other aim, 27:2
My life in the world, 56:2
My life is but a burden, 170:5
My life is ebbing away, 457

My life is hid in Jesus, 95:1a; 281; 282
My life is now almost gone, 457
My life is over now, 457
My life is sweet with gracious blessing, 84:1
My life on Earth is a voyage, 56:2
My lifetime hath no other goal, 27:2
My longing is the Savior to embrace, 161:3
My Lord and God, I'm in Thy might, 464
My Lord and master, 33:2
My Lord, cast me not away, 33:4
My Lord, grant it, 291
My Lord, here will my heart now be, 18:3a
My Lord is king alone, 248:52
My lord, it's all the wind, 201:3
My Lord Jesus I won't forsake, 124:1
My Lord Jesus, what pain befell Thee, 487
My Lord o'er death triumphant rose, 95:6
My love, exactly, 212:23
My love for Jesus is constant, 468
My love is mine, 140:6
My love, well said, 212:23
My loving Savior gives me hope, 5:4
My loving Savior, how have you offended,
    244:3
My majestic Jesus, before whom, 486
My Master and my Lord, 244:9
My master Jesus now hath left me, 154:1
My master Jesus reigns, 248:52
My meal is prepared, 49:3a
My mind can conceive of naught, 245:27.2
My mouth and heart are open, 148:4
My one delight, 208a
My one delight is close to view the chase,
    208:1
My one delight is in a lively hunt, 208:1
My open grave I see before me, 156:2a
My peace I give to you, 158:1
My pious heart, be full of glee, 68:2
My poor heart so weak and weary, 248:53
My precious Jesus now hath vanished, 154:1
My purpose now regard, 17:6
My Redeemer and preserver, 69:5
My Redeemer and preserver watch Thou,
    69:5; 69a:5

My Redeemer and sustainer, keep me, 69:5
My reporting gun of cannons, 214:4
My Savior bless'd, my peace, 247:130
My Savior calls to me, 49:3b
My Savior, does Thy name instill, 248:39
My Savior falls low before His Father, 244:28
My Savior, I cannot forget You, 247:27
My Savior is arisen, 67:2
My Savior is at hand, 60:2b
My Savior Jesus now is taken, 244:33a
My Savior lets Himself be seen, 186:5
My Savior lives, 145:6
My Savior, never part from me, 247:27
My Savior now appeareth, 186:5
My Savior now is risen, 67:2
My Savior oft appeareth, 186:5
My Savior, take me, take Thou me, 22:2
My Savior, why must all this ill, 244:25b
My Savior, why should agony befall, 244:25b
My Savior will be true to me, 92:2
My shepherd is the Savior dear, 85:3
My Shepherd, now receive me, 244:63.2
My shepherd true, with mighty arm, 85:6
My shepherd's gone and I'm so lonesome, 104:3
My sighs, my tears, 13:1
My sin it is which binds Thee, 244:16; 246:48
My sin it was which binds Thee, 244:16
My sin it was which bound Thee, 244:16
My sins and evildoing, 246:17; 247:20
My sins He will erase them, 97:5
My sojourn in the world, 56:2
My sorrow ever grows, 13:4
My sorrow grows amain, 13:4
My sorrow grows greater and robs me, 13:4
My sorrow increases and robs me, 13:4
My soul, arise, 69:3
My soul, awake and render, 194:12
My soul, do not be troubled, 522
My soul doth exalt the Lord God, 10:1
My soul doth glorify and worship, 189:1
My soul doth magnify the Lord, 10:1; 10:7; 243:1; 324; 648

My soul doth rest in Jesus' keeping, 127:3
My soul, exalt the Lord, 29:8
My soul exalts the Lord, 10:1; 10:7; 324; 648
My soul extols and praises, 189:1
My soul glorifies and praises, 189:1
My soul is ever in Thy hand, 156:2b; 245:40; 377
My soul is His forever, 13:6
My soul magnifies the Lord, 10:1; 243:1
My soul, now praise thy Lord God, 17:7; 28:2; 29:8; 389; 390
My soul, now praise thy maker, 17:7; 389; 390
My soul, oh praise the Lord thy God, 28:2
My soul praises and exalts, 189:1
My soul rejoices however God, 204:6
My soul shall rest in Jesus' bosom, 127:3
My soul shall rest in Jesu's keeping, 127:3
My soul, there is a country, 161:6; 244:63.1; 281
My soul, to God resign thee, 44:7
My soul waiteth for the Lord, 131:4a
My soul waits for the Lord, 131:4a
My soul will rest in Jesu's hands, 127:3
My soul will rest in Jesus' keeping, 127:3
My soul's delight, His holy word, 18:4
My soul's delight is God's command, 18:4
My soul's delight is God's own word, 18:4
My soul's delight is God's word, 18:4
My soul's own treasure is God's word, 18:4
My soul's treasure is God's word, 18:4
My soul's treasure is the word of God, 18:4
My soul's true treasure is God's word, 18:4
My spirit be joyful, 146:7
My spirit comprehends the sweetness, 76:11
My spirit doth rejoice in Christ, 76:11
My spirit Him descries, 43:9
My spirit how joyful, 146:7
My spirit on Thy care, 878
My spirit was in heaviness, 21:2; 21:3
My sponsor is at hand, 60:2b
My steps Thy spirit loving guideth, 108:3
My table is prepared, 49:3a

My tears flow while the heart is fearful, 146:5

My thank,* God and praise Thee, 69:6

My time has come; my life is ended, 457

My treasure of treasures, mine infinite store, 22:4

My treasured Savior, let me ask Thee, 245:60a

My trust I place in God's good grace, 255

My trust is bold, Thou'lt still uphold, 184:5

My trust's in God indeed, 188:5

My wandering in the world, 56:2

My way is Thine, O God, 128:5

My weary heart is faint, 8:3

My yoke has been broken, 56:3

Myself to God resigning, 107:6

Mysterious act of love is here unfolded, 244:55

Mysterious acts of God's almighty mercy, 244:55

A mystic light fills the whole sphere, 125:4

N

Nations, listen to God's calling, 76:3

Nature of unbounded favor, 121:3

Naught against the (Thy) power, 248:57

Naught could me deliver, 74:7

Naught is lovelier than Thou, 246:11

Naught is too late or early, 97:2

Naught on Earth is lasting, 227:7

Nay, for then no man alive may Thou acquit, 105:1b

Nay, God is ever prompt and ready, 88:3

Near Thee would I be staying, 244:23

'Neath: see also Beneath

'Neath his purple mantle bright, 173a:4

'Neath Thy care I rest me, 81:7

Ne'er: see also Never

Ne'er feel shame, O heart of mine, 147:3

Ne'er frightened be, 42:4

Ne'er from Jesus will I part, 379

Ne'er I'll repine when death's upon me, 157:4b

Ne'er will I cherish, 30:8

Ne'er yet have ye asked a favor in Mine own name, 87:1

Neither Hell's despite nor Satan, 107:4

Never: see also: Ne'er

Never fear, never fear, 52:3

Never Jesus will I leave, 98:5; 124:1; 124:6; 154:8; 157:5; 244b; 380

Never, Jesus, will I leave Thee, 70:11

Never will I part with Christ, 379

Never will my heart refuse Thee, 244:19

Nevertheless Thy healing word, 113:4

New kindness of the Lord, 10:3

The new-born Babe, 122:1; 122:6

The new-born Child, the dearly beloved, 122:1

The new-born Child this early morn, 122:1

The new-born little Child, 122:1

The newly born, the tiny Child, 122:1

The newly born little Child, 122:1

Night has come, 296

The night is falling, 296

The night our Savior was betrayed, 265

Night's darkness falleth, 296

No brief hour vanishes, 477

No child of man dwells here on Earth, 74:8

No child of man here on the Earth, 74:8

No child of man upon this Earth, 74:8

No doctor is to be found except Thee, 103:3

No doubt can disturb me, 108:2

No doubt can now divert me, 108:2

No earthly gloss, no fleshly light, 1:4

No easy task it is to be a Christian, 459

No fiend of Hell can e'er devour me, 123:4

No fiend of Hell can now confound me, 123:4

No foe I fear, 149:3

No fruit the grain of wheat will bear, 114:4

No fruit the seed of wheat can bear, 114:4

No fruit the wheat grain brings, 114:4

No, God hath planned and e'er intendeth, 88:3

No, God is all the time intending, 88:3

No, God is always diligent, 88:3

No, God is ever anxious to know us, 88:3
No greater grief afflicts the heart, 209:2
No Hell-foe can me devour, 123:4
No hellish foe can ensnare me, 123:4
No hour ever passes, 477
No hour goes ever by, 477
No idle promise this, 207:8
No longer life delights me, 170:5
No man can prevail over death, 4:3
No man could conquer death, 4:3
No matter, let what may ensue, 111:2
No misfortune is to be found, 20:2
No more can Hell's dark force avail, 248:63a
No more here peace of Eden reigneth, 198a:3a
No more, pale Death, thy grim face can affright me, 114:5
No more shall sin or death prevail, 248:63b
No more the fear of death affects me, 183:2
No more to sigh, no more to weep, 416
No mortal child here upon the Earth, 74:8
No mortal man could prevail, 4:3
No mortal man upon the Earth, 74:8; 108:6
No mortal will or might, 126:3
No, never, 246:22b
No, not on the feast, 244:5
No one such virtue hath, 46:6
No one was able to overcome death, 4:3
No other end in life have I, 27:2
No physician except Thee is to be found, 103:3
No powers of Hell can now ensnare me, 123:4
No, royal Queen, thou shalt not die, 198:10
No shepherd seeks with such devotion, 246:37
No tongue can tell the story, 128:4
No wit of man nor mortal, 178:2
No word He speaks, my Lord, 244:40
A noble man is like, 204:7
Nobody could overcome death, 4:3
Nobody is like unto Thee, Lord, 110:3
None for me cares, 138:2
None is like Thee, Lord, 110:3

None, Lord, is like to Thee, 110:3
Nor dread nor doubt disturbs me, 108:2
Nor for Heaven, nor for Earth, 70:11
Not after the world, not after Heaven, 70:11
Not an hour passes, 477
Not by angel hosts attended, 30:6
Not by Earth or Heaven bright, 70:11
Not for Earth's vain joys I crave, 70:11
Not for Heaven nor the world, 70:11
Not for the Earth, not for sky, 70:11
Not for world, for Heaven not, 70:11
Not for world or Heaven's might, 70:11
Not in anger, Mighty God, 115:6
Not in wrath, O Lord, e'er judge me, 101:2
Not on the feast, 244:5
Not only where God's free winds blow, 151:5
Not so sadly, not so deeply troubled, 384; 489
Not this man, but Barabbas, 245:29
Not this man here, but Barabbas, 245:29
Not this man, no, not Him, 245:29
Not this man, not this one, 245:29
Not this man, rather Barabbas, 245:29
Not to fathom is the manner, 188:3
Not upon the feast, 244:5
Note and hear, you children of men, 7:2
Nothing, 246:22b
Nothing but hot air, but mighty little brains, 201:13
Nothing can compare, 212:4
Nothing can save me, 74:7
Nothing is lovelier than Thou, 246:11
Nothing is more lovely than Thee, 246:11
Notice, my heart, constantly only this, 145:5
Nourish me; make me full, 246:9
Now again be thou joyful, O my spirit, 21:9
Now again upon Thy birthday, 142:3
Now all give thanks to God, 79:3; 657
Now all is o'er; my Savior and my friend, 159:3
Now all lies beneath Thee, 11:6
Now all men thank Thee, God, 79:3
Now all men thank ye* God, 79:3
Now all thank and bring honor, 195:6

Now all thank God, 79:3; 192:1
Now all the fiends may I defy, 160:4
Now all the forests are at rest, 13:6; 44:7; 244:16; 245:15.2; 392
Now all the woods are sleeping, 244:16; 392; 756
Now all the world is but a hospital, 25:2
Now all to God give thanks, 79:3
Now all torments vanish, 32:5
Now all troubles disappear, 32:5
Now am I prepared to go, 160:5
Now angry is the clever world, 152:5
Now Annas had had Jesus bound, 245:16
Now Annas had sent Him bound, 245:16
Now Annas ordered Jesus bound, 245:16
Now Annas sent Him bound, 245:16
Now are ye well avenged, 248:64
Now are you well avenged, 248:64
Now are you well revenged, 248:64
Now as I live, of old God spake, 102:7
Now at length the hour is near, 381
Now at that feast the governor, 244:54a
Now at the manger here I stand, 248:59
Now at Thy feet creation lies, 11:6; 116:6
Now at Thy manger here I stand, 469
Now awake, my soul, my senses, 244:48
Now Barabbas was a murderer (robber), 245:30
Now be glad, O thou my spirit, 70:7
Now be still, languid music, 210:4
Now behold and tell me if grief be found, 46:1a
Now behold the Paschal Lamb, 4:6
Now bless, my soul, the Lord God, 28:2; 389; 390
Now bless the Lord, oh bless Him, 28:2
Now blessed be the Lord God of Israel, 167:2
Now blessed be Thou, Christ Jesu(s), 91:1; 314; 604; 697; 722; 722a; 723
Now blessed Thou, O Christ, 306
Now came the first day of th' unleaven'd bread, 246:8a
Now cheer our hearts this eventide, 253; 414

Now Christ doth end in triumph, 248:64
Now Christ hath taken vengeance, 248:64
Now Christ is risen, Alleluia, 15:7
Now Christ is risen to God on high, 128:1
Now claim, Moses, what thou wilt, 145:4
Now come, let us hasten, 249:3
Now come, Lord Jesus, 106:2f
Now come, Redeemer of our race, 61:1
Now come, Savior of the Gentiles, 36:8; 61:1; 62:1; 62:6; 659; 659a; 660; 660a; 660b; 661; 661a
Now come, Savior of the heathen(s), 36:2; 61:1; 62:1
Now come, the Gentiles' Savior, 36:2; 61:1; 62:1
Now come, the heathens' Savior, 62:1
Now come, the world's salvation, 36:2
Now comes from God's great majesty and throne, 62:3
Now comes the gentle Savior, 699
Now comes the Savior of mankind, 659; 659a; 660; 660a; 660b; 661; 661a
Now comfort take, good Christians all, 114:7; 256
Now dance and sing, ye Christian throng, 388; 734; 734a; 755
Now dawns for us a glorious day, 67:4; 629
Now daylight's youthful glory, 448
Now, dear Midas, 201:14
Now dear soul, it is time, 248:46
Now, dear Spirit, I follow Thee, 175:7
Now dedicate yourself to Him, 31:5
Now disappear all troubles, 32:5
Now do as your father tells you, 211:7
Now do we pray God, the Holy Ghost, 197:5; 385
Now do what your father says, 211:7
Now does our deep distress, 450
Now doth the Antichrist, 44:5
Now doth the Lord in peace recline, 244:77a
Now doth the Lord in peace repose, 244:77a
Now every morning doth our God, 90:2
Now everything lies below You, 11:6
Now everything lies beneath Thee, 11:6

Now, false world, now I have nothing, 95:2a
Now fear and dread are cast aside, 160:4
Now firm is my resolve, 161:4
Now forty days since Easter morn, 266
Now fourscore years am I, 71:2a
Now from the sixth hour, 244:71a
Now give the year good ending, 190:7
Now give ye thanks, both old and young, 187:7
Now God be with us, 296
Now goodnight, existence, 64:8
Now grant that I with heart sincere, 177:3
Now grant us concord graciously, 42:7
Now guide, O Lord, the lips, 134:5
Now, hark ye what I'm going to tell, 211:7
Now has the hope and the strength, 50
Now, hasten impatient, 249:3
Now hath salvation and strength, 50
Now hath salvation come to us, 638
Now hath the grace and the strength, 50
Now He came to His disciples, 244:30
Now hear the flutes' soft choir, 206:9
Now, hearken to my last word, 211:7
Now Heaven's sweet delight, 123:2
Now help us, Lord, these servants Thine, 120:6
Now, honored Spirit, I follow Thee, 175:7
Now I am fourscore year, 71:2a
Now I close my eyes, 378
Now I have found the ground, 122:6
Now I know in Thee confiding, 105:6
Now I know that Thou art loving, 105:6
Now I know that Thou wilt quiet, 105:6
Now I know that Thou wilt still, 105:6
Now I know Thou shalt make quiet, 105:6
Now I know Thou wilt calm, 105:6
Now, idlers, list to me, 207:10
Now in my God am I made glad, 162:5
Now in readiness I wait, 160:5
Now is my Jesus bound and taken, 244:33a
Now is our salvation come, 638
Now is salvation come (unto us), 638
Now is salvation come to Earth, 9:1
Now is the health and strength, 50

Now is the mournful time, 450
Now is the salvation and the strength, 50
Now is to us salvation come, 9:1
Now it came to pass in those days, 248:2
Now Jesus Christ, the Son of God, 4:4
Now, Jesus, grant me, 190:6
Now Jesus, grant that with, 190:6
Now Jesus, grant Thou, 190:6
Now join we all in praise to Thee, 41:1
Now join we all to praise Thee, 41:6; 171:6; 190:7; 362
Now joyful is my heart, 199:8
Now, judges, what have you to say, 201:8
Now laud and praise with honor, 29:8; 51:4; 167:5
Now let all praise God's mercy, 391
Now let all thank God, 79:3; 252; 386
Now let all the heavens adore Thee, 140:7
Now let every tongue adore Thee, 140:7
Now let no joy nor fear from Thee, 177:4
Now let our songs to Heaven wing, 145:7
Now let the world desire, 190:4
Now let Thy gracious spirit shine, 116:6
Now let trouble swiftly vanish, 32:5
Now let us all to God, 79:3
Now let us beg true faith of the Holy Ghost, 169:7; 385
Now let us pray to God and Holy Ghost, 169:7
Now let us pray to God, Holy Ghost, 385
Now let us pray to the Holy Ghost, 169:7; 197:5
Now let us singing, praise God, 391
Now let us to God the Lord, 165:6
Now let us to God the Lord give thanks, 194:12
Now let us to the bagpipe's sound, 212:24
Now lieth all beneath Thy feet, 11:6
Now listen to me, 211:7
Now listen to your father talk, 211:7
Now, Lord, govern my mind, 158:3a
Now love doth draw with gentle paces, 36:3
Now make ready, Jesu, the way, my Savior, 147:5

Now make your judgment, 201:8

Now may the will of God be done, 144:6; 244:31

Now may the world with all its pleasure, 186:9

Now may the world with its pleasures, 186:9

Now may thy proud foes flee in terror, 248:62

Now may ye proud foes be affrighted, 248:62

Now may you proud foes be affrighted, 248:62

Now, Midas dear, 201:14

Now, Miecke, give me your lips, 212:3

Now, Molly, won't you give me, 212:3

Now, mortals all, your voices raise, 195:6

Now must all Christendom unite to do God honor, 76:13

Now must Thou then, my Savior, say farewell, 412

Now must we Jesus laud and sing, 121:6; 611; 696

Now my Jesus is taken, 244:33a

Now, my Jesus, will I grieve for Thee, 159:3

Now, my soul, praise the Lord, 28:2

Now notice, and your sire obey, 211:7

Now, now we truly know, 119:6

Now old Schlendrian goes and (out), 211:9

Now on that day, the first of Unleavened Bread, 244:13

Now on the first day, 244:13

Now open stands the once-closed door, 151:5

Now order, Moses, as thou wilt, 145:4

Now order thine house, 106:2d

Now order thy house, 106:2d

Now, Pan, tune up your throat, 201:6

Now, people all, your voices raise, 195:6

Now Peter sat without in the palace, 244:45

Now Pilate said unto Him, 245:28

Now play no more, 210:3

Now praise God on the highest throne, 33:6

Now praise, my soul, the Lord, 17:7; 28:2; 29:8; 167:5

Now praise, my soul, the Master, 28:2

Now praise the Lord, my soul, 17:7; 29:8; 389; 390

Now praise the Lord on high, 79:3

Now praise we all our mighty Lord, 130:1

Now praise we Christ, the Holy One, 121:1; 611; 696

Now praise we God almighty, 79:6; 165:6

Now praise we great and famous men, 255

Now praise ye the Lord, 30:3

Now praised be Almighty God, 602

Now praised be the God of Israel, 167:2

Now praised be the Lord, my God, 129:1; 129:2; 129:3

Now praised be the Lord, the God, 129:4

Now praised be Thou, Jesu Christ, 64:2; 91:1; 91:6

Now prophesy, who is't that smote, 246:41b

Now quickly I end all my earthly existence, 57:7

Now rejoice, all ye children of God, 387

Now rejoice, dear Christians, together, 388

Now rest, Redeemer, in the tomb, 246:78.1

Now rest Thy members worn and holy, 245:67

Now save us, Heavenly Father, save us, 18:3c

Now see my teardrops falling, 146:5

Now shall I hold fast to Him, 187:6

Now shall my beloved Bridegroom, 248:3

Now shall my Bridegroom, 248:3

Now shall the grace and the strength, 50

Now shall vanish ev'ry torment, 32:5

Now shall we all praise Christ, 611

Now shalt be known, 203:2

Now should we be praising Christ, 696

Now slay us through Thy kindness, 164:6

Now sorrow and doubting forever I banish, 8:4

Now spare your woe, I pray, 216:4

Now, Spirit, dear, I'll follow Thee, 175:7

Now teach our hearts, O Spirit, 183:5

Now tell us, Thou Christ, 244:43b

Now thank the Almighty, 15:9a

Now thank we all God, 79:3

Now thank we all our God, 79:3; 120a:2a; 192:1; 252; 386; 479; 657; A164:1

Now thank we our God, 79:3

Now thank we the Highest, 15:9a

Now thank ye all and bring your praise, 195:6

Now thank ye all our God, 79:3; 192:1

Now thank your God and praise His name, 195:6

Now thank your God in songs of love, 195:6

Now thanks to Thee, Lord God in Heaven, 350

Now thanks to Thee, O God in Heaven, 350

Now that disciple was known unto the high priest, 245:14

Now that is well, 212:10

Now that same disciple was known, 245:14

Now that the daylight fills the sky, 332

Now that the sun doth shine no more, 396

Now the day is over, 407

Now the eternally contracted bond, 99:4

Now the Feast of Unleavened Bread, 246:2

Now the first day of the Feast of Unleavened Bread, 244:13

Now the from-eternity-made covenant, 99:4

Now the governor, at that feast, 244:54a

Now the hour of our salvation, 30:5

Now the husbandman rejoices, 206:5

Now the Lord is** brought to rest, 244:77a

Now the Lord is laid to rest, 244:77a

Now the Lord's eternal kingdom, 162:6

Now the sheep secure are grazing, 208:9

Now the Spirit of Him who raised Jesus, 227:10

Now Thou willst still my conscience, 78:6

Now Thou wilt this my conscience quiet, 78:6

Now to my heart sweet peace is given, 78:6

Now to rightward, now to leftward, 96:5

Now to the right, now to the left, 96:5

Now to Thy servants help afford, 120:6

Now, treach'rous world! Now I'll have nothing more, 95:2a

Now tremble, all ye hardened sinners, 70:2

Now tremble, stony-hearted sinners, 70:2

Now 'twas upon the Feast of Unleavened Bread, 244:13

Now upon that feast, the governor, 244:54a

Now vanish, my sorrows, so noisily storming, 8:4

Now vengeance hath been taken, 248:64

Now wake my heart, and all my soul, 268

Now wast thou not also with Jesus, 244:46a

Now we acknowledge this, 119:6

Now we ask the Holy Spirit, 169:7; 197:5

Now we can understand, 119:6

Now we sing as one, 208:10

Now welcome, precious joy, 36:5

Now we're off to our tavern, 212:24

Now when at supper they were met, 285

Now when Jesus sojourned in Bethany, 244:6

Now when Jesus was born in Bethlehem, 248:44

Now when Jesus was in Bethany, 244:6

Now when King Herod had heard, 248:48

Now when Pilate heard, 245:43

Now when Pilate heard this (what), 245:39

Now when the centurion saw, 246:73

Now when the morning came, 244:49a

Now will I, myself, my Jesu, 159:3

Now will I show to all men, 203:2

Now wilt Thou my conscience quieten, 78:6

Now wilt Thou quieten my conscience, 78:6

Now with the choir unite, 386

Now woods and fields are sleeping, 244:16

Now woods and wolds are sleeping, 244:16; 244:44

Now would the Highest, 43:2

Now yield we thanks and praise, 45:7; 64:4; 94:8

Now you are well avenged, 248:64

Now you proud foes may be afraid, 248:62

Now you will quiet my conscience, 78:6

O

O: *see also* Ah

Oh anguish of heart; oh fear, 400

Oh anguish; oh dread and trepidation, 400

Oh, awesome marriage feast, 162:2

O beautiful day, beloved time, 210:1

Oh, beautiful, my country, 244:63.1

Oh, beautiful place, come gentle death, 157:4b

O beggar, happy is your lot, 75:13

O beloved Son of God, 151:4

O beloved soul, turn your senses away, 494

O best beloved land of ours, 193:4

Oh, bide with us, Lord Jesus Christ, 6:3

Oh, bide with us, Thou Savior dear, 6:1; 6:3

Oh bleed, thou loving heart, 244:12

Oh, bleeding head, and wounded, 244:63.1

Oh, blessed are the pious, 495

Oh, blessed are those lips, 147:2

O blessed Christ, once wounded, 244:63:1

O blessed Christ, who always His will in God's, 72:2a

Oh, blessed day, 63:2; 119:2

O blessed Jesu, how hast Thou offended, 244:3; 244:55

O blessed Jesu, Thou alone, 16:5

O blessed Jesus, what is Thy transgression, 244:3

Oh, blessed land, 119:2

Oh, blessed lips, Mary made known, 147:2

O blessed Lord, to do the Father's will, 72:2a

O blessed rest, O welcome heart's delight, 170:1

O blessed rest, thou giv'st, 170:1

O blessed Savior, grant, 244:9

O blessed Savior, hear, 244:9

O blissful day, 63:2

O calm majestic features, 244:63.2

O charming day, wished-for time, 210:1

O child of God, consider, 80:3

O child of man, cease quickly, 20:10

O child of man, now cease forthwith, 20:10

O child of man, reflect a span, 20:10

O child of man, reflect awhile, 20:10

O child of man, thou diest not, 198a:10a

O child of man, thou shalt not die, 198a:10a

Oh, children of your God, rejoice, 387

O Christ, comfort of the world, 670; 673

O Christ, Lamb of God, 23:4

O Christ, my all in living, 95:1a; 281; 282

O Christ, our Lord, Thy people guide, 119:9

O Christ, protect us, us Thy faithful, 275

O Christ, strong champion of all souls, 275

O Christ, that art the light and day, 274

O Christ, the healer, 6:6

O Christ, the only Son of God, 698

O Christ, Thou art our lamp and light, 273

O Christ, Thou art the beauteous day, 766

O Christ, Thou art the heavenly light, 766

O Christ, Thou art the light and day, 766

O Christ, Thou art the light of day, 273; 766

O Christ, Thou Lamb of God, 619

O Christ, what consolation, 244:63.1

O Christ, which art the light and day, 274

O Christ, who art the light of day, 274

O Christ, who on the tree, 300

O Christ, whose love has sought us, 122:6

O Christendom, awake, 91:4

O Christendom, rejoice, 91:4

O Christian blessed who always doth His own will, 72:2a

O Christian soul, subject thy will entirely, 72:2a

O Christian world now rise, 91:4

O city of our sires beloved, 193:4

Oh, cold hearts of men, 249:4

Oh, cold mind of men, 249:4

Oh, come and mourn with me awhile, 274

Oh, come, Lord Jesus, come, 106:2f

O come, Thou longed-for Savior, 36:2

O come to Me, saith God's dear Son, 108:6

O come, ye souls today, 479

Oh, comfort sweet, 138:4

Oh, contain thyself, 109:4

O countenance almighty, 244:63.2

Oh, cure me, Thou practitioner, 135:2

Oh, cursed knave, how dare you, 246:3

O darkened night, when will your shadow, 492

Oh, darkest woe; ye tears, 404

O day of bliss, appointed hour, 210:1

Oh, day of pain, the saddest, 224:21
O dear Lord Jesu, watch o'er me, 166:3
O dearest Jesu, 245:7; 245:27.2
O dearest Lord, do not in anger scorn, 153:2
O dearest Lord, let not my crying, 13:2
O dearest Savior mine, 244:9
O Death, none could lay thee low, 4:3
O Death, none could thee subdue, 4:3
Oh, don't pass us by, 23:2
O echo, ye heavens; O earth be thou gladdened, 134:6
O enter Lord, Thy temple, 183:5
O, enter thou, blithe sprite of gladness, 73:2
O eternal fire, O source of love, 34:1
O eternal word, Jesus Christ, 409
O eternity, fateful word, 513
O eternity, thou terrifying word, 60:1a
O eternity, thou thunder-word, 20:1; 20:11; 513
O eternity, thou word of fear, 20:1
O eternity, thou word of thunder, 20:1; 20:7; 60:1a; 397
O eternity, word of God, 513
O eternity, word of thunder, 513
O eternity, you word of thunder, 20:1; 20:11; 60:1a
O ever faithful God, 24:6; 45:7; 398; 399
Oh, ever-gracious melody, 210a:1
O ever-righteous God, 192:2
O everlasting God, 194:2
O faith, thou art a pledge to treasure, 37:2
Oh, faith undoubting grant me, 37:6
O faithful Echo, 213:5
O faithful God, so great, 46:6
Oh, farewell, thou worldly tumult, 27:5
O Father, hear our humble prayer, 74:8
O Father, here before Thee, 22:5
O Father in the Heaven who art, 636; 682; 683; 683a
O Father, in Thy mercy blest, 198a:1
O Father, let Thy will be done, 65:7; 72:5; 103:6; 111:1; 144:6; 244:31
O Father, may Thy will be done, 244:31
O Father, our Creator, 73:5

O Father, send the spirit down, 74:8; 108:6
O Father, Thou Almighty God, 758
O Father, unto Thee I fly, 2:6; 77:6; 469
O favored town on Neisse, 216:1b
O fearful darkness, when will you end, 492
O fearsome Aeolus, 205:4
O feeling heart, 245:7
O fill now, ye flames, both divine and celestial, 1:3
O fire ever flaming, O love's fount eternal, 34:1
O fire everlasting, O fount (fountain), 34:1
O fire everlasting, O wellspring, 34:1; 34a:1
O food of exiles lowly, 244:16
O food to pilgrims given, 393; 394; 395
O fool that withdraws from God, 111:3
O foolish man who would shun God, 111:3
O foolish one! Almighty God, 111:3
O foolish one, who doth from God withdraw, 111:3
Oh, foolish one, who himself from God, 111:3
O foolish world, 94:4
O foolish world, for ever now we part, 95:2a
Oh, for Thy name's sake let me prove, 113:7; 168:6
O fortunate Christians, O flock, 184:2
O fount of love unbounded, 244:21
O friend of souls, what joy, 517
O friend, Thou'rt mine, 140:6
Oh, frigid mind of men, 249:4
O generous love, 245:7
O gentles, may fair sons be born to you twain, 212:18
O glittering morn, 31:3
O gloom of sin, when wilt thou pass over, 492
O gloomy night, when com'st thou, 492
O gloomy night, when with thou, 492
O God Almighty, Father, Son, 290
O God and Lord, 692; 692a; 693; 714
O God, banish me not, 105:2
O God, be merciful to me, 305; 721
O God, do not condemn, 105:2

O God, enthroned in Heaven high in splendor, 350

O God, eternal source of love, 45:7

O God, from Heaven look below (Thou), 2:1

O God, here shall my heart be found, 18:3a

O God, Holy Ghost, 671; 674

O God, how deep, how dread His agony, 244:25a

O God, how grievous is the woe, 3:1; 44:4; 58:1

O God, how long afflict ye, 155:1

O God, how many a heartache, 58:1

O God, how many a pain for the heart, 3:1

O God, how many heart-pains, 44:4

O God, how many pains of heart, 3:1; 44:4; 58:1

Oh, God, how much sorrow, 153:9.3

O God, how much sorrow afflicts me, 58:1

O God, in all my woes, 188:5

O God in Heaven, we praise Thee, 601

O God in Heav'n, safeguard Thine own, 225:3

O God, let the people praise Thee, 69:6; 76:14

O God, look down from Heaven, 2:1

O God, my faithful God, 45:7; 398

O God, my heart doth love Thee only, 77:3

O God of justice, when Thou shalt call, 89:5

O God of love, O king of peace, 290

O God of power and might, 46:6

O God, our faithful God, 45:7; 465

O God, our Father, throned on high, 248:12

O God, our Lord, Thy holy word, 184:5

O God, rebuke me not, 105:2

O God, reject me not, 33:4

O God, the champion of our race, 37:3

O God, the rock of ages, 287

O God, the straightest way, 79:4

O God, Thou champion of our race, 37:3

O God, Thou faithful God, 24:6; 45:7; 129:5; 398; 399; 767

O God, Thou good God, 398; 399

O God, Thou holy God, 24:6; 398; 399; 767

O God, Thou just God, 767

O God, Thou just Lord, 767

O God, Thou pious God, 45:7

O God, Thou righteous God, 24:6

O God, to Thee I bring my heart, 18:3a

O God, to whom we turn, 94:8

O God, we pray Thee, bless and consecrate, 120:5

O God, what manifold distress, 3:1

O God, when Jesus Christ doth chance, 172:6

O God, when Jesus mine doth chance, 172:6

O God, when wilt Thou say to me, 82:4

O God, who art the only light, 316

O God, who art Thyself the light, 316

O God, who plenteous founts of love, 219:5.2

O God's Spirit, my comfort, 175:7

O Good Shepherd, help Thy people, 184:6

Oh, goodly city much beloved, 119:4

O gracious God, 244:60

Oh, grant me faith unswerving in Jesus, 37:6

Oh, grant that I may willingly do, 45:7

O grant Thy strength and spirit, 18:3b

O grant us, mighty God, 41:2

O great and mighty God, 46:6

O great God of might (truth), 46:6

O great King, 245:27.1

O great Lord, most mighty King, 248:8

O great love, O love, 245:7

Oh, great wedding feast, 162:2

Oh, grief, here throbs the rack'd and bleeding, 244:25a

Oh, grief, how throbs His, 244:25a

Oh, grief, how trembles His overladen heart, 244:25a

Oh, grief, now pants His agonizing heart, 244:25a

Oh, grief of heart; oh bitter smart, 404

Oh, guard my heart; sustain, Thine own, 3:6; 153:9.3

Oh, guide my heart and will, 5:7; 148:6; 163:6

Oh, guide us, Lord, with Thy right hand, 90:5

O guiltless Lamb of God, 618; 656; 656a

Oh, hail this brightest day of days, 294; 605; 719

O happy couple, pure bliss, 197:6

O happy day, 210:1; 290

Oh, happy, happy they whose lips, 80:7

Oh, happy land, 119:2

O happy town on Pleiss, 216:1a

Oh, happy we, in God confiding, 122:4b

Oh, hard road, 60:2a

Oh, haste thee, my soul, from the world, 124:5

Oh, haste ye, then, ye shepherds, 248:18

Oh, he who trusts in God's protection, 88:7

O head, all bruised and wounded, 244:63.1

O head, all scarr'd and bleeding, 244:63.1

O head, bloody and wounded, 244:21; 244:23; 244:63.1; 244:72; 248:5

O head, covered in blood and with wounds, 244:63.1

O head, full of blood and wounds, 244:63.1

O head, so full of bruises, 244:63.1

O head, so pierced and wounded, 244:63.1

O head, with blood e'er flowing, 244:63.1

Oh, heal me, Lord, 135:2

Oh, heal me, Thou healer, 135:2

Oh, hear, my God, my pray'r and sore complaining, 254

Oh, hearken to Thy children's crying, 115:5

O heart filled with mercy and love, 185:1

Oh, heart of mine, 482

O heavenly ardor, sweetest comfort, 226:4

Oh, heavy going, 60:2a

Oh, heavy way, 60:2a

Oh, help, Christ, Son of God, 245:65

Oh, help me, Lord, to praise Thee, 343; 624

Oh, help us, Lord, Thy servants crowned, 120:6

O highest God, let us bring about the year, 41:2

O holy ardor, sweet comfort, 226:4

O holy city, seen of John, 403

O holy day, 63:2

O holy font that washeth white, 165:1

O holy fountain, sanctified, 165:1

O Holy Ghost and water bath, 165:1

O Holy Ghost, Thee we pray, 175:7

O Holy Spirit, 165:1

O Holy Spirit, by whose breath, 122:1

O Holy Spirit, counsel sweet, 175:7

O Holy Spirit, enter in, 1:6; 436

O honor o'erwhelming, 59:2

Oh, how artful Cupid has deceived me, 524:8

Oh, how blessed are ye above all, 198a:8b

Oh, how blessed are ye beyond our telling, 405; 406

Oh, how blessed are ye whose toils, 405; 406; 495

Oh, how blessed ye are, ye faithful, 405; 406; 495

Oh, how cheating; oh, how fleeting, 26:1; 26:6; 644

Oh, how dear is Jesu's loving, 147:6

Oh, how fleeting; oh, how cheating, 26:1

Oh, how full of glad tidings is to me, 157:4b

Oh, how futile, how inutile, 26:6; 644

Oh, how good for us it is, 194:10

Oh, how I feared the tomb's forbidding prison, 66:5

Oh, how my heart beats full of anxious dreading, 400

Oh, how my weary soul is filled, 516

Oh, how shall I receive Thee, 248:5

Oh, how sweet the coffee tastes, 211:4

Oh, how sweetly tastes the coffee, 211:4

Oh, how that word gives comfort, 104:4

Oh, how vain, oh, how fleeting, 644

Oh, how well it has happened to us, 194:10

Oh, I am a child of sin, 78:3

Oh, if only I were seeing, 439

Oh, I'm longing; how I'm longing, 161:3

Oh, indeed, what silly stuff, 212:4

O inexhaustible source of blessing, 125:5

O infinite, whom yet we Father call, 173:5

O Israel, hope in the Lord, 131:5a
O Israel's shepherd, 104:1
Oh, it does feel so good, 212:4
O Jesu, beloved Master, 25:4
O Jesu Christ, man's surest stay, 48:7
O Jesu Christ, my heavenly Lord, 335
O Jesu Christ, my life and light, 118
O Jesu Christ, Thou Prince of Peace, 67:7; 116:1; 143:2
O Jesu Christ, we bless Thy name, 103:6; 244:31
O Jesu, dear Master, I flee, 25:4
O Jesu, Lord of heav'nly grace, 153:9.1
O Jesu, Master mine, 128:5
O Jesu, our Redeemer, do Thou save, 25:4
O Jesu so meek, O Jesu so kind, 493
O Jesu so sweet, 493
O Jesu, welcome, gracious guest, 43:11.1
O Jesu, welcome, gracious name, 248:12
O Jesu, what a grievous loss, 247:59
O Jesus Christ, light of my life, 118
O Jesus Christ, my life and light, 118
O Jesus Christ, my life, my light, 118; 335; 750
O Jesus Christ, Thou dearest Lord, 43:11.1
O Jesus Christ, Thou highest good, 113:8
O Jesus Christ, Thou Prince of Peace, 116:1
O Jesus, dearest Master, 25:4
O Jesus Lord, my light and life, 118
O Jesus most sweet, O Jesus most mild, 493
O Jesus, my comfort and joy, 247:130
O Jesus, my joy, 128:5
O Jesus, now be praised, 41:1
O Jesus, O dear Master, 25:4
O Jesus so gentle, Jesus so sweet, 493
O Jesus sweet, O Jesus mild, 493
O Jesus, Thou my bridegroom, 335
O Jesus, Thou my heart's delight, 335
Oh, join with me in praising God's goodness, 613
Oh, joy; Christ our Savior for us fighteth, 67:6b
Oh, joy; God veils His majesty, 133:2
Oh, joy; I have my lord for ever, 157:4a

Oh, joy; Jesus for us fighteth, 67:6b
Oh, joy; Jesus helps us battle, 67:6b
Oh, joy; Lord Jesus speaks, 81:6
Oh, joy; oh, rapture, 205:12
Oh, joyful day of our salvation, 83:1
Oh, joyous day of the new order, 83:1
Oh, joyous transformation, 206:2
O King of Glory, 245:27.1
O King on high who leads us, 164:6
O Lamb of God, 232:24
O Lamb of God all blameless, 244:3
O Lamb of God, all holy, 618; 656; 656a
O Lamb of God, all spotless, 401
O Lamb of God, innocent, 401
O Lamb of God, most holy, 401; 618; 656; 656a
O Lamb of God, most stainless, 401; 618; 656; 656a
O Lamb of God, once wounded, 244:63.1
O Lamb of God, our Savior, 401
O Lamb of God, pure and holy, 656; 656a
O Lamb of God, pure, spotless, 401; 618; 656; 656a
O Lamb of God, Savior, 401; 618; 656; 656a
O Lamb of God, still keep me, 281
O Lamb of God that died, 455
O Lamb of God, unspotted, 401; 618; 656; 656a
O Lamb of God, who, bleeding, 401
O Lamb of God, without blemish, 401
O Leipzig, favored town, 216:1a
O Leipzig, New Jerusalem, 193:4
Oh, let me sing God's praises, 107:7
Oh, let not this be my life's dying hour, 439
Oh, let Thy spirit us inflame, 116:6
Oh, let Thy watchful angel band, 219:5.1
Oh, let us ne'er, Thy vengeance feeding, 116:5
Oh, let us praise the Lord, 79:3
O light everlasting, O love never failing, 34:1
O little Jesu, my heart's love, 248:9
O little one sweet, 493

Oh, longed-for day, 31:3

Oh, longed-for, joyous light, 184:1

O Lord Almighty, 245:27.1

O Lord, arise, come help me now, 321

O Lord, as I have trusted Thee, 52:6; 640; 712

O Lord, as long ago the Wise Men, 30:11

O Lord, be merciful to us, 225:3

O Lord, conduct us by Thy hand, 90:5; 101:7

O Lord, confirm and guide me, 194:12

O Lord, continue still, 29:6

O Lord, continue to care for us, 225:3

O Lord, direct and guide Thou me, 158:3a

O Lord, dissolve my heart's unpitying mood, 164:4

O Lord, do not pass judgment upon Thy servant, 105:1a

O Lord, forgive our sins so great, 127:5

O Lord, forgive us all our sin, 127:5

O Lord God, 233:3; 234:3

O Lord God, heavenly king, 232:7a; 236:4

O Lord God, I ponder in great heaviness, 21:2

O Lord God, through Thy mercy's grace, 101:3

O Lord God, Thy godly word, 184:5

Oh, Lord, how many miseries, 3:6; 153:9.3

O Lord, I love Thee from my heart, 174:5

O Lord, I pray Thee from my heart, 18:5

O Lord, I pray Thee heartily, 18:5

O Lord, in faith to Thee we pray, 184:5

O Lord, inaugurate our government, 120:5

O Lord, incline us to consider, 106:2c

O Lord, it is enough, 82:1; 82:2

O Lord, it is my one desire, 27:2

O Lord Jesus Christ, the only begotten Son, 235:4

O Lord Jesus, let my life, 470

O Lord, let Thy dear angel, 245:68

O Lord, my conscience wilt Thou quiet, 78:6

O Lord, my darkened heart enlighten, 248:47

O Lord, my God, forgive me (Thou), 113:7

O Lord, my God, from You alone, 501

O Lord, my God, I cry to Thee, 639

O Lord, my God, Thou wilt not now forget, 30:7

O Lord, now govern all my thoughts, 158:3a

O Lord of heav'n and earth and sea, 452

O Lord of life and glory, 244:63.2

O Lord, our Father for evermore, 371

O Lord our God, from Heaven look down, 2:1

O Lord our God, Thy holy word, 184:5; 757

O Lord our God, Thy sacred word, 757

O Lord our God, to Thee we raise, 130:1

O Lord, rebuke me not in Thy anger, 135:1

O Lord, rebuke not a poor sinner, 135:1

O Lord, relent, I pray Thee, 135:1

O Lord, search me out and examine my heart, 136:1

O Lord, so consecrate this government, 120:5

O Lord, so order my heart, 158:3a

O Lord, so teach us to remember, 106:2c

O Lord, stretch forth Thy mighty hand, 90:5; 101:7

O Lord, teach us to reflect, 106:2c

O Lord, teach us to remember, 106:2c

O Lord, the Father for ever more, 371; 669; 672

O Lord, the only begotten Son, 232:7b

O Lord, there's none like Thee, 110:3

O Lord, this grieving spirit, 135:1

O Lord, Thou crown'st the year, 187:3

O Lord, Thou God of truth, 46:6

O Lord, Thy dearest angel send, 245:68

O Lord, Thy little angel send, 245:68

O Lord, Thy love's unbounded, 244:21

O Lord, Thy will is like a fast-closed book, 73:1d

O Lord, 'tis enough, 82:1; 82:2

O Lord, to Thee in faith we pray, 184:5

O Lord, we come to praise Thee, 41:1

O Lord, we praise Thee, 322

O Lord, we pray at our last day, 184:5

O Lord, we welcome Thee, 133:6; 197a:4; 398
O Lord, we worship Thee, 45:1
O Lord, what is a child of man, 110:4
O Lord, when may my troubles cease, 82:4
O Lord, who dares to smite Thee, 244:44; 245:15.1
O love divine! What hast thou done, 122:6
O love, how deep, 377
O love, naught with thee can vie, 174:3
Oh, love of my love, 491
O love of wondrous power, 96:2
O love that cast out fear, 466 and 45:7
O love, which has no equal, 174:3
O love, which has no peer, 174:3
O love, whose perfect path, 290
O lovely day, awaited long, 210:1
Oh, luckless souls, perverted, 181:2
O man, accomplish thy salvation, 20:6
O man, behold Jesus Christ, 403
O man, bemoan your great sin, 622
O man, bewail the grievous fall, 244:35
O man, bewail thy great sin(s), 244:35; 402
O man, bewail thy greivous fall, 402; 622; A61
O man, bewail thy grievous sin, 244:35; 402; 622
O man, bewail thy heavy sin, 622
O man, bewail thy mortal fall (sin), 622
O man, bewail thy sin so great, 244:35
O man, bewail your great sin, 244:35
O man, Christ Jesus now behold, 403
O man, deliver this thy spirit, 20:6
O man, give up this world's vain pomp, 20:9
O man, lament thy huge transgressions, 244:35
O man, list to his sighing, 244:16; 244:44; 245:15.2; 393; 394; 395
O man, make haste to save thy spirit, 20:6
O man, save thy (your) soul, 20:6
O man, this day in darkest gloom doth lie, 341
O man, thy grevious sin(s) bemoan, 244:35; 402; 622; A61

O man, thy heart is cold, 249:4
O man, thy heavy sin lament, 244:35
O Master, dearest, best, 157:3
O Master, give us ev'ry season, 181:5
Oh, may that bright angelic band, 130:6.2
Oh, may this righteous God, 192:2
Oh, may Thy church and our dear land, 219:5.1
Oh, may Thy love constrain me, 244:63.2
Oh, Maytime's the gay time, 202:7
O men of feeble heart, 249:4
O men so cold of heart, 249:4
O men, ye who daily sin, 122:2
O men, you who daily sin, 122:2
Oh, merciful and mighty God, 32:4
Oh, mighty God, 35:6
O mighty God of truth, 46:6
O mighty King, 245:27.1
O mighty love, 245:7
Oh, mild, sweet Jesus, 493
Oh, Mister Tax Collector, 212:6
O morning star, how fair and bright, 1:1; 1:6; 36:4; 172:6; 436; 739; 764
O mortal child, cease quickly, 20:10
O mortal world, 95:2a
O mortals, Death will surely call us, 198:2
O mortals, if with me ye do desire, 37:4
O mortals, ye each day transgressing, 122:2
O mortals, ye who face damnation, 122:2
Oh, most blessed refreshment day, 70:10a
O most holy Three-in-One, 172:3
O most Holy Trinity, 172:3
Oh, most lovely feast of joy, 194:1
Oh, most unhappy band of wayward spirits, 181:2
Oh, must Thou say good night, now, Jesus mine, 412
O my dearest Jesu Babe, 248:9
O my deir hert [English dialect], 122:6
O my God, forsake Thy people nevermore, 79:5
O my Savior, doth Thy name inspire, 248:39
O my Savior, doth Thy name now wash, 248:39

O my soul, arise, proclaim, 69a:3

O my soul, be glad and joyful, 19:7; 25:6; 70:7

O my soul, be thou rejoicing, 19:7

O my soul, prepare to meet Him, 180:1; 180:7

O my soul, right joyful be thou, 70:7

O my soul, where wilt thou find, 245:19

Oh, my soul, why doest thou grieve, 384

O my spirit, be content, 204:6

O my spirit, rise, 69:3

O my spirit, wake, prepare, 115:1

O my treasure rich and fair, 197a:1

Oh n'er be dismayed, 15:4

O never failing source of blessing, 125:5

Oh, never to foemen deliver the soul, 71:6

Oh, nevermore, Jesus, Thy servant will leave, 154:7b

O night of gloom, when wilt thou, 492

O pain, affliction torture me, 48:2

O pain and grief, His heart throbs, 244:25a

O pain, here trembles the tortured heart, 244:25a

O pain, O misery which strikes, 48:2

O paradise of bliss (souls), 172:4

O paradise of the soul, 172:4

O paradise, who doth not crave, 478

Oh, pardon me, my God, 244:47

O peace and serenity, for which the soul, 170:1

O people, who commit sin daily, 122:2

O pleasant rest, beloved soul's delight, 170:1

O poorness which no wealth can match, 75:13

O poverty that no riches equal, 75:13

O poverty, which no wealth equals, 75:13

Oh, praise and honor God our King, 117:1; 117:4; 117:9

Oh, praise Him, for he never forgets, 220:1

Oh, praise the God of our salvation, 510; 511; 512

Oh, praise the king supreme in might, 137:1

O praise the Lord, 30:2

Oh, praise the Lord, all ye heathens (nations), 230:1

Oh, praise the Lord for all his mercies, 28:1

Oh, praise the Lord; His name extol, 129:1

Oh, praise the Lord; my Savior lives, 160:3

O precious love, the King of Earth, 198a:9a

O quickly come, dread Judge of all, 416

Oh, rejoice, ye Christians, loudly, 40:8

O righteous God, ah, judgest Thou, 89:5

O righteous God, pray count aright, 89:5

O sacred day, 63:2

O sacred head, encircled, 244:63.1

O sacred head, now wounded, 244:63.1; 244:72

O sacred head, once wounded, 244:63.1

O sacred head, so wounded, 244:63.1

O sacred head, sore wounded, 244:63.1

O sacred head, surrounded, 244:63.1; 270; 271; 272

O sacred spirit's water bath, 165:1

Oh, sadness; oh bitter pain, 404

Oh, save us, dearest Father, 18:3c

O saving Victim, 332

O Savior mine, what agony, 487

O Savior mine, who dareth to smite Thee, 244:44

O Savior sweet, O Savior kind (mild), 493

O Savior, Thou who wearest, 379

O Savior, why must all this ill, 244:25b

O shepherd of Israel, give ear, 104:1

O shield of truth, 16:4

Oh, show me, dear Savior, Thy sweetness undying, 152:6

O sinful world, now have I done with thee, 95:2a

Oh, sing and be joyful, 206:1

Oh, sing unto the Lord a new song, 225:1

O sinner bear with patience, 114:3

O sinner, bear with patient heart, 114:3

O sinner, patient bear the load, 114:3

O sinner, raise the eye of faith, 469

O slaughtered Lamb, 455

Oh, sorrow, here trembles the anxious, 244:25a

O soul beloved, withdraw thy mind (senses), 494
O soul, let no sadness, 186:10
O soul, the paradise, 172:4
O soul within me, why art thou so distressed, 435
Oh, soul's paradise, 172:4
O spirit of life, 493
O spirit of the living God, 332
O spirit pure of joy and gladness, 73:2
O spotless Lamb, 455
O spotless Lamb of God, 618; 656; 656a
Oh, stay with us, Lord Jesus, 6:3
O strangled Lamb, 455
Oh, strive ye with ardor in years still before us, 134a:4a
O sweet Child Jesus, O gentle Child Jesus, 493
O sweet content, in our life, 144:5
O sweet content, thou'rt of man, 144:5
Oh, sweet, enchanting melody, 210a:1
O sweet Immanuel, 123:1
O sweet Jesus, gentle Jesus, 493
O sweetest joy, pour on us thy grace, 169:7
O sweetest love, grant to us alway, 169:7
O sweetest love, help us two to feel, 197:5
O sweetest love, to us grant alway, 197:5
O sweetest love, unto us grant alway, 169:7
O sweetest Name, 171:3
Oh, take my willing heart, 80:4
Oh, taste and see, 34:3
Oh, teach me, Lord, my days to number, 27:1; 166:6
Oh, teach our hearts, Spirit divine, 183:5
Oh, tell us now, Thou Christ, 244:43b
Oh, tell us, thou Christ, 244:43b
Oh, that it soon might happen, 249:8b
Oh, that my life's final hour may not strike today, 439
Oh, that the bell may toll my last hour, 439
Oh, think, my soul, 509
Oh, think on us with Thy compassion, 29:5
O thou by God exalted creature, understand, 121:2

O thou charming bridal pair, 197:6
O thou consoling fire, gift divine, 226:4
O thou creature exalted by God, 121:2
O thou creature made higher by God, 121:2
O thou holy fire, Paraclete, 226:4
O thou love of Christ, 439
O Thou love of my love, 491
O thou most blessed voice, 147:2
O Thou my Savior, give me answer, 245:60a
O Thou of God the Father, 164:6; 601; 698; A55; A75; A77
O thou pleasing couple, 197:6
O Thou sweetest source of gladness, 8:6; 246:68; 483
O Thou true Son of Mary and of God, 1:2
O Thou who camest from above, 122:6; 245:40; 377
O Thou who dost accord us, 244:16; 392
O Thou, who 'mid the watr'y sea, 18:5; 65:7
O thou whom God created and extolled, 121:2
O Thou whose head was wounded, 244:63.1
O Thou with hate surrounded, 244:63.1
O Thou, with whom in sweet content, 321
O thou world so fairly builded, 301
Oh, toilsome road, 60:2a
O treacherous love, you deceive me, 203:1
O treasure of treasures, O goodness divine, 22:4
Oh, tremble, all ye hardened sinners, 70:2
O Trinity of blessed light, 293
O trusting heart, 68:2
Oh, unbelieving hearts, 249:4
O undying fire, O love's fount eternal, 34a:1
O unexhausted store of kindness, 125:5
Oh, unfortunate condition, 181:2
Oh, walk the heavenly way, 152:2
Oh, we poor sinners, 407
Oh, we wretched sinners, 407
O welcome day, 31:3
Oh, welcome, dearest love, 36:5
Oh, welcome, joyous light, 184:1
Oh, welcome light of joy, 184:1
Oh, welcome, will I utter, 27:3

Oh, well for us that we believe in Him, 122:4b
Oh, well for us who believe in Him, 122:4b
Oh, well for ye, all bliss possessing, 34:3
Oh, well for you, all bliss possessing, 34:3
Oh, well for you, ye souls elected, 34:3
Oh, well is me! New born in Thee am I, 165:4
Oh, what an honor thus, 59:2
Oh, what are then these honors, 59:2
Oh, what are these honors, 59:2
Oh, what great honors are these, 59:2
Oh, what great things do I encounter, 189:4
Oh, what great things do I find, 189:4
Oh, what great things I find, 189:4
Oh, what stupendous wonders, 189:4
Oh, when will the time be ripe, 248:51
Oh, when will the time come, 248:51
Oh, where is He that is born king, 248:45
Oh, wherefore does Thine anger rise, 101:4
Oh, whither in this vale of sorrow, 114:2a
Oh, whither shall I flee, 5:7; 136:6; 148:6; 646; 694
Oh, whither shall I fly, 5:1; 5:7; 89:6; 136:6; 646; 694
Oh, why art thou cast down, my soul, 424
Oh, why such sad behavior, 107:1
Oh, wicked child, 211:3
Oh, woe and grief beyond belief, 404
Oh, woe and misery is mine, 48:2
Oh, wonder, that a heart (soul), 125:3
Oh, wonder, that one's heart, 125:3
Oh, wonder-power of love, 96:2
Oh, wonderful coffee, lovlier than a thousand, 211:4
Oh, wondrous feast of love, 162:2
O wondrous love, 245:7
O wondrous love, such judgment harsh, 244:55
O wondrous love, such punishment endureth, 244:55
O wondrous love, that suffers this correction, 244:55

O wondrous love, the king who reigns, 198a:9a
O wondrous love, this sacrifice to offer, 244:55
O wondrous love whose depths no heart hath found, 244:3
O wondrous type, 290
Oh, wondrous wedding feast, 162:2
O word of God most holy, 153:5; 244:21
O word, that heart and soul alarms, 87:2
O word, that shakes the heart and soul, 87:2
O word, that soul and body awes, 87:2
O word, that spirit and soul affrights, 87:2
O word, to terrify the soul, 87:2
O world, behold thy life, 393; 394; 395
Oh, world, behold upon the tree, 393; 394; 395
O world, leave me in contempt, 123:5
O world, so vain, I leave thee, 95:2b
O world, thy life doth languish, 244:44; 393; 394; 395
O world, thy life is ended, 244:16; 393; 394; 395
O world, thy life is ending, 393; 394; 395
Oh, would a thousand tongues were mine, 69a:2
Oh, would my faith were not so weak, 38:4
Oh, would the hour were close, 95:3
Oh, wretched man I, 48:1
Oh, wretched man that I am, 48:1
O ye heavenly bodies, 476
O ye of little faith, why are ye so fearful, 81:4
O ye righteous, glad (joyful) be, 195:1b
O ye righteous, sing and praise, 195:1b
O ye stars, you atmosphere, 476
Oh, ye unhappy band of mortals, 181:2
Oh, yes, just so, 201:3
Oh, you may get ten thousand ducats, 212:16
O you sweet delightful pair, 197:6
O you thoughts, 524:4
O Zittau, happy town, 216:1b
Object of my first desire, 357
Obstinacy can the mighty delude, 147:4

Ode of mourning, 198a,
O'er death no man can prevail, 4:3
O'er death no man could prevail, 4:3
O'er death no one could prevail, 4:3
O'er field and forest stealing, 244:16
O'er mountain and valley, 201:7
O'er us no more fears of Hell, 248:63a
O'er us no more shall fears of Hell, 248:63a
O'erpowered I stand, 35:3
O'erwhelm us with Thy kindness, 96:6
O'erwhelm us with Thy mercy, 22:5
Of death is He guilty, 244:42b
Of death this man is guilty, 244:42b
Of fear and pain, 248:35
Of flowers the fairest, 212:14
Of His mother Christ took care, 245:56
Of Jesus all my soul is singing, 147:9
Of Jesus am I ever singing, 147:9
Of Jesu's blood the flow with might, 136:6
Of Jesus' wonders I'll be singing, 147:9
Of judgment be thou not afraid, 127:4d
Of my sighing, of my crying, 13:1
Of our own power can we do naught, 80:2b
Of Sabaoth Lord, 120a:5
Of the factor you had best beware, 212:6
Of this world I ask for naught, 64:7
Of what avail our bitter sorrow, 93:2
Of what avail our cares and sorrows, 93:2
Of what avail the hosts of Hell, 139:6
Of woman born He came, 167:4
Of woman was He born, 167:4
Of woman's seed came, 167:4
Off we go then to where the bagpipes play, 212:24
Off with Him; crucify Him, 245:36
Oft had I longed for death, 57:3
Old Adam once, with anguish riven, 133:3
Old Adam's fall corrupted all, 637; 705
The old dragon burns with envy, 130:3
Old Schlendrian is searching, 211:9
The old year has passed, 614
The old year has passed away, 288; 289
The old year hath passed, 614
The old year is past, 614,

The old year now hath passed away, 288; 289; 614
On all men close the grave's grim portals, 198a:2
On Christ ascended to the skies, 128:1
On Christ's ascension alone, 128:1
On Christ's ascent to Heav'n alone, 128:1
On Christ's journey to Heaven alone, 128:1
On contentment, 204
On Earth below distress and woe, 48:3
On Earth has dawned the day of days, 145:7
On Earth has dawned this day of days, 67:4; 629
On Easter-morn He rose again (agen), 306
On every side misfortune gathers, 139:4
On God my hope is surely stayed, 138:5
On God my trust I surely place, 188:1
On God stands my confidence, 138:5
On high where God abideth, 189:3
On Him am I depending, 97:8
On Him believing, thou are* free from judging, 68:5
On Him mayst thou it venture, 107:3
On him's not a stain, 212:8
On Jesus all my love is cast, 1:6; 49:6a
On Jesus Christ's ascent on high, 128:1
On Jesus lay thy sorrow, 244:53
On my behalf was Thy revealing, 68:4
On my beloved God I rely, 188:5
On my dear God I trust, 188:5
On my Shepherd I rely, 92:8
On my wings you shall soar, 213:7
On our new council here, 71:7
On Sinai Mountain Moses trod, 298; 635; 678; 679
On that day that Christ our Lord predicted, 310,
On the doors of Heaven yonder, 146:8
On the evening of that same Sabbath, 42:2
On the righteous must the light, 195:1a
On the wood His arms are stretch'd, 40:6; 245:21; 245:56
On Thee alone, Lord Jesus Christ, 33:1
On Thee I have set my hope, O Lord, 52:6

On Thee mortal eyes wait, Lord, 23:3
On Thee, O Lord, my hopes I lean, 244:38
On them, Lord, a blessing breathe, 193:5
On this Earth must Christ's disciples, 44:3
On this glad day ascend in joyous strain, 16:2
On this great day, 214:2
On this new year shed Thy blessing, 344
On this painful repentance, 199:5
On us indeed fall the sin's stains, 136:5
Once He came in blessing, 318; 337; 600; 703; 724
Once I loved from Thee to wander, 244:48
Once in sin from Thee I parted, 55:5; 244:48
Once more, dear Lord, I Thee entreat, 111:6
Once more, O Lord, I ask of Thee, 111:6
One can from this a fine example, 42:5
One can from this see a beautiful example, 42:5
One can see here a good example, 42:5
One day, one day shall my yoke, 56:3
One, however, in their number, 17:4
One man may but for belly care, 18:3e
One moment, please, 212:13
One of Jesus' twelve disciples, 244:11
One of them, however, as He saw, 17:4
One of them that were healed, 17:4,
One of these afflicted lepers, 17:4
One should take care, 166:5
One sings with joy of the victory, 149:1
One thing alone a Christian's purpose, 75:9
One thing alone us anxious makes, 36c:6
One thing is needful, O Lord, 304
One thing is needful, O Lord, this one thing, 453
One thing, Lord, alone I covet, 304
One thing, Lord, to me is needful, 304; 453
One thing more, O Lord, 111:6
One thing needful, then, Lord Jesus, 304
One thing only, Lord, I need, 304; 453
One thing's needful, 453
One understands what sorrow means, 209:2
The one who guides his soul, 144:4
One's creator while on Earth, 39:3

Only a gesture from His hands, 248:57
Only be still; wait thou His leisure, 93:3
The only begotten Son, 232:7b
Only bleed, dear heart, 244:12
Only bleed, thou dearest heart, 244:12
Only hate, really hate me, 76:10
Only in Thee, Lord Jesus Christ, 33:1; 33:6; 261
Only Jesus is my life, 490
Only my Jesus is my life, 490
Only one thing ails a Christian mind, 75:9
Only prevent, true Father, prevent, 18:3c
Only stay, dearest love of my life, 11:4
The only thing that pleases me is the merry hunt, 208:1
Only through great tribulation can we enter, 146:2
Only through love and through pity, 164:3
Only to each his due, 163:1
Only to God on high be glory, 104:6; 112:5; 260
Only to God on high be honor, 112:5
Only to my temple shrine, 207:5
Only to the father-hands of Jesus, 114:2b
Ope the gates of Zion before me, 32:6
Open both ears, for Jesus has solemnly, 175:6
Open, Lord, to me the portals, 32:6
Open my eyes, O Lord, 453
Open now, my heart, to Jesus, 61:5a
Open the gates of Zion before me, 32:6
Open thou, my heart entire, 61:5a
Open thou, my heart, to Jesus, 61:5a
Open thyself, my whole breast, 61:5a
Open to my poor songs, Jesu, 25:5
Open to my songs so meager, 25:5
Open unto me the portals of Thy goodness, 32:6
Open up, my whole heart; Jesus comes, 61:5a
Open up, O heart of mine, 61:5a
Open wide for me the portal, 32:6
Open wide, my heart and spirit, 61:5a
Open wide, my heart; Jesus is coming, 61:5a
Open wide, my heart, thy portals, 61:5a
Open wide the gates of mercy, 32:6

Open wide Thy gates before me, 32:6
Open ye both ears and listen, 175:6
Open ye both your ears, 175:6
Open, ye heavens, 249:10c
Open your two ears, 175:6
Oppressed with weary sighing, 135:4
Others provide only for their bellies, 18:3e
Our blessed Lord, when he had suffered, 7:5
Our chamberlain is a kindly man, 212:8
Our Christian faith is ever safe, 44:6
Our excellent and beloved, 212:8
Our excellent, dear chamberlain, 212:8
Our Father, by whose servants, 287
Our Father, clothed with majesty, 416
Our Father high in Heaven, 28:6
Our Father in Heaven, 102:7; 636; 760;
  761; 762
Our Father in the Heaven who art, 245:9;
  416; 636; 682; 683; 683a; 737; 760; 761;
  762
Our Father in the heav'ns above, 245:9
Our Father, Lord of Heaven and Earth, 416
Our Father, Thou in Heaven above, 90:5;
  102:7; 636; 682; 683; 683a; 737
Our Father, thron'd in Heaven high, 416;
  636; 682; 683; 683a; 737; 760; 761; 762
Our Father, we have wandered, 270; 271;
  272
Our Father, which art in Heaven, 636; 682;
  683; 683a; 737; 760; 761; 762
Our Father, who art in Heaven, 90:5; 102:7;
  245:9; 416
Our fathers' God, 120a:5
Our fathers' God from out whose hand, 377
Our first unsullied innocence, 198a:3b
Our foes are all in Your hand, 178:7.1
Our foes, great God, are in Thy hand, 178:7.1
Our foes, O God, are in Thy hand, 178:7.1
Our foes press on us far and wide, 178:5
Our fondest wish is that you will have, 212:18
Our freedom, Son of God, arose, 245:40
Our God and Father, Mighty Lord, 37:3
Our God has chosen as His dwelling, 34:4
Our God in Heaven reigning, 16:6; 28:6

Our God is just, 20:5
Our God provides with open hand, 197:2
Our God to whom we turn, 45:7; 465
Our grievous sins beset us sore, 101:5
Our hearts ever yearn for the treasures, 26:4
Our hearts, O Lord, are overcome, 246:1
Our hearts rejoice in no false light, 1:4
Our hero battles on, 245:58
Our Holy Christ is ris'n today, 306
Our hope awaits the fitting time, 186:6
Our hope awaits the proper time, 86:6
Our humble role, our need, 186:2
Our Jesus hath for aye, 43:5
Our journey through the world, 56:2
Our joy is turned to bitterness (mourning),
  26:3
Our joy to mourning turneth, 26:3
Our joy will be to sadness turned, 26:3
Our lips are mute, our wisdom dumb, 280
Our Lord commanded you, 169:6
Our Lord has come to save us, 61:2
Our Lord is God of endless pow'r, 302; 303
Our master is good, 212:5
Our master thinks of old and young, 212:9
Our master we all respect, 212:5
Our might alone do nothing can, 80:2b
Our might counts for nothing, 80:2b
Our most excellent chamberlain, 212:8
Our mouth and sound of the strings, 1:5
Our mouths and sounding strings, 1:5
Our mouths and sounds of strings, 1:5
Our new squire is the chamberlain, 212:2
Our New Year greeting bringing, 190:7
Our offering we view askance, 36c:6
Our own might is far too weak, 14:2
Our own strength is called too weak, 14:2
Our praise, Lord God, give we, 328
Our Savior by this pow'r divine, 48:5
Our Savior Christ once knelt in prayer, 122:6
Our sin hath us corrupted much, 101:5
Our sins, O Lord, do Thou forgive, 127:5
Our sovereign's weal, 207a:4
Our strength is too weak, 14:2
Our strength proves too weak, 14:2

Our tiny city, 212:14
Our utmost might is all in vain, 80:2b
Our vanity begets conceit, 185:4
Our weak voice falters, 51:2b
Our whole salvation doth depend, 86:6; 155:5; 638
Our youth, like springtime, soon must pass, 206:11
Ours was the obligation, 244:16; 246:48
Out, all ye evil spirits, 135:5
Out from their church will they cast you, 44:1
Out from their temples they cast you, 44:1
Out of darkness call I, Lord, to Thee, 131:1a
Out of deep distress I cry to Thee, 38:1
Out of love my Savior is willing to die, 244:58
Out of the deep call I to Thee, 38:1
Out of the deep have I called unto Thee, 131:1a
Out of the deep I cry to Thee, 38:1; 686; 687
Out of the deep to Thee I tell, 38:6; 156:6
Out of the depths I call, 246:40
Out of the depths I cry, Lord, to Thee, 131:1a
Out of the depths I cry to Thee, 38:1; 38:6; 686; 687
Out of the depths I cry to Thee, O Lord, 131:1a
Out of the depths, O Lord, 38:1
Out of the depths to Thee I raise, 38:6
Out ye, idolatrous mob, 76:5
An outcast of men, who now shall deliver my body, 48:1
Overcome wretched fear at last, 209:5

P

The pain of my death be but a gentle slumber, 249:7
Pan is a master; mark it well, 201:11
Pan is master, 201:11
Pan is victor, 201:11
Pan, lift your voice and sing, 201:6
Pan, now stir your throat, 201:6
Pan, 'tis thy turn to sing, 201:6
Pardon, elders, mighty rivers, 206:8
Pardon us, gracious Lord, 144:2
The parting hour has come, 161:4
The Paschal Lamb before us see, 158:4
The Paschal Lamb here we see, 158:4
The Paschal Victim here we see, 4:6
Pass ye swiftly, happy hours, 208:11
The passing year is ended, 28:1
The Passion according to St. John, 245
The Passion according to St. Luke, 256,
The Passion according to St. Mark, 247
The Passion according to St. Matthew, 244
Passion chorale, 244:63
The Passion of our Lord according to St. Matthew, 244
Past is the old year, 614
Pasture for the soul, my joy, 497
The path of faith now run, 152:2
Patience, even when false tongues sting, 244:41
Patience; not far is the day, 30:11
Patience; the acceptable day, 30:11
Patience, when false tongues, 244:41
Patient be thou, bear thine affliction, 93:3
Patient muses, my members, 214:5
Patron revered, 210a:9a
A pauper our Lord chose to be, 91:5
Peace be over Israel, 34:5
Peace be unto all mankind, 34:5
Peace be unto Israel, 34:5; 34a:4
Peace be unto thee, 158:1
Peace be unto you, 67:6a; 158:1
Peace be upon Israel, 34:5
Peace be with thee, 158:1
Peace be with you, 67:6a
Peace; fear thou not, and fear not, 178:6
Peace of mind and sweet contentment, 204:2
Peace of mind and true contentment, 204:2
Peace over Israel, 34:5
Peace, peace be within thy walls, 34:5
Peace, peace, thou perturbed sea, 81:5

Peace, peace, thou unruly sea, 81:5
Peace, peace, trouble-laden sea, 81:5
Peace, ye pipers; peace nor plead ye, 210:6
Peace, ye pipers; singers, cease ye, 210a:6
Peaceful shall be my departure, 249:7
Peal out, ring out, judgment-call, 70:10b
Peal, shattering fanfares! Loud trumpets, 207a:1
Peal, shattering fanfares of loud trumpets, 207a:1
Peasant cantata, 212
Penance and remorse, 244:10
Penitence, fearful pain, 244:10
The people He upstirreth, 246:49b
The people who in darkness walked, 375; 376
Perhaps you're right, 212:19
Perish all vain teachers, 2:3
Permit, beloved father of our land, 215:8
Permit, O mossy source of mighty streams, 206:8
Persecutes thee even now the evil world, 58:2
Perverseness oftentimes will blind, 147:4
Peter answered and said, 244:22
Peter answered eagerly, 244:22
Peter, faithless, thrice denies, 245:20
Peter heedlessly denies his God, 245:20
Peter in forgetfulness thrice denied, 245:20
Peter sat in the palace court, 244:45
Peter then gave Him answer, 244:22
Peter, thoughtless, Christ denies, 245:20
Peter, unreflecting, 245:20
Peter was sitting without in the court, 244:45
Peter, while his conscience slept, 245:20
Peter, who denied his Lord, 245:20
Peter, who doth not recall, 245:20
Phoebus, all thy melodies, 201:9
Phoebus and Pan, 201
Phoebus drives his horses prancing, 202:3
Phoebus drives his prancing horses, 202:3
Phoebus hastens on his swift steed, 202:3
Phoebus hastens with speedy horses, 202:3
Phoebus hurries with swift horses, 202:3

Phoebus speeds with swift horses (steeds), 202:3
Phoebus, thy sweet melody, 201:9
Phoebus with swift horses races, 202:3
Phoebus, your fine melody, 201:9
Phoebus, your melody has given birth, 201:9
Phoebus, your melody was born, 201:9
Physician none I find to cure me, 103:3
Pilate answered, 245:51
Pilate said to them, 244:76d
Pilate said unto them, 244:76d
Pilate saith unto them, 245:37
Pilate then said to the high priests, 246:47
Pilate therefore said unto Him, 245:28
Pilatus saith unto them, 245:45
A pilgrim here, I gaily journey, 111:4
Pious muses, my associates, 214:5
A pitiless judgment will certainly fall, 89:3
Pity me as I bear, 131:2b
Pity me with such a burden, 113:2
Pity Thou me, O Lord my God, 721
Pitying heart of eternal love, 185:1
Play, soul-inspired songs, 210:2
Play the well-touched flutes that enemy, 214:3
Pleading, pleading draw thou near, 115:4
Pleasant are Thy courts above, 262
Pleasant fields of Wiederau, 30a:1
Pleasant lands of Wiederau, 30a:13
Pleasant rest, beloved soul's desire, 170:1
A pleasant sight and happy, 202:6
Pleasant Wiederau, 30a:13
Pleasant Wiederau, rejoice, 30a:1
Pleasant Zephyrus, 205:9
The pleasures of the world, 190:4
Pluck the strings in Cythara, 36:4
Poised on my pinions shalt thou hover, 213:7
The poor are bewildered, 2:4
The poor forsaken lie, 2:4
A poor man am I; who will set me free, 48:1
Poor me, human being and sinful, 55:1
The poor ones are troubled, 2:4
Poor souls who are inclined, 204:3
The poor will the Lord embrace, 186:8

A poor wretch I, a servant unto sin, 55:1
Poor wretched man, a slave of sin, 55:1
Pour forth thine abundance, thou fountain, 5:3
Pour out richly, Thou divine source, 5:3
Pour out thyself richly, thou divine spring, 5:3
The poverty that God assumes, 91:5
The poverty which God on Himself takes, 91:5
The power of sin is doom'd to fail, 248:63b
The pow'rs of darkness here, 6:4
Praise and bless Him, ev'ry one, 63:5
Praise and fame with honor, 51:4
Praise and glory and might, 21:11b
Praise and glory and pow'r, 21:11b
Praise and glory and thanks, 21:11b
Praise and glory, blessing, honor, 106:4a
Praise and glory to the fount of goodness, 117:1
Praise and honor and fame (glory), 21:11b
Praise and honor be to God the Father, 10:7
Praise and honor to the Highest Good, 117:1; 117:4; 251
Praise and thanks be sung to Thee, 146:8
Praise and thanks be to God who did not allow, 14:5
Praise and thanks ever, Lord, 249:10b
Praise and thanks remain, Lord, 249:10b
Praise and thanks shall be, Lord, 249:10b
Praise and thanks to God, 14:5
Praise and thanks unto Thee we raise, 249:10b
Praise and thanks we sing to You, 249:10b
Praise and thanks would we be singing, 146:8
Praise be done to God the Father, 62:6
Praise be God the Father done, 62:6
Praise be the Lord, 129:1
Praise be Thou, Jesu Christ, 604
Praise be to Almighty God, 602; 704
Praise be to God! All is well, 29:4
Praise be to God the Father, 62:6
Praise be to the Father done, 36:8; 62:6
Praise be to Thee, Jesus Christ, 604

Praise, glory and honor unto God, 231
Praise, glory, thanks to Thee be paid, 121:6
Praise God, all ye Christian men, 732; 732a
Praise God, all ye Christians, 609
Praise God Almighty, our king and our ruler, 137:1
Praise God, enthroned above the sky, 375; 376; 609; 732; 732a,
Praise God! For all is well, 29:4
Praise God for His grace to you, 195:3
Praise God, for now the year is ending, 28:1
Praise God from whom all blessings flow, 130:6.1; 326
Praise God in all His splendor, 11:1
Praise God in all lands, 51:1
Praise God in His kingdom, 11:1
Praise God, man knoweth the narrow path, 79:4
Praise God! The beast is felled, 19:2
Praise God! The beast lies low, 19:2
Praise God! The dragon's low, 19:2
Praise God the Lord, ye sons of men, 151:5; 375; 376; 609; 732; 732a,
Praise God; the year draws to its closing, 28:1
Praise God; the year is nearly ended, 28:1
Praise God, thy Father, for His loving-kindness, 374
Praise God upon His heavenly throne, 33:6
Praise God! We are so blessed, 29:4
Praise God, we know now the certain road, 79:4
Praise God with hands and voices, 220:1
Praise God, ye Christians, all as one, 609
Praise God, ye Christians, all together, 151:5; 375; 376
Praise God, ye people, for His love is boundless, 286
Praise God, ye people, one and all, 151:5; 375; 376
Praise God, you Christians, all together (altogether), 609
Praise Him; praise the great Creator, 207:11

Praise Him, the highest, omnipotent, King, 137:1; 137:5

Praise Him, the Lord, for He in His own image, 137:3

Praise Him, the Lord, O my soul, praise His name, 137:5

Praise Him, the Lord, the Almighty, the King, 137:1

Praise Him, the Lord, who all blessings, 137:4

Praise Him, the Lord, who in all things is ever, 137:2

Praise, honor, and thanks be said to Thee, 121:6

Praise, honor, and thanks to Thee be said, 121:6

Praise, honor, thanks to Thee be said, 121:6

Praise Jehovah all ye people, 51:1

Praise Jehovah in His splendor, 11:1

Praise, Jerusalem, the Lord, 119:1

Praise, joy, and gladness be blended in one, 248:1

Praise, late future and kind fate, 207a:7

Praise, late posterity, 207a:7

Praise, O Jerusalem, the Lord, 119:1

Praise, O Jerusalem, thy God (Lord), 119:1

Praise, O my soul, thy maker, 17:7

Praise, O Zion, praise Thy God, 190:3

Praise, O Zion, your God, 190:3

Praise our God in all His splendor, 11:1

Praise our God, so good and true, 195:3

Praise our God who reigns in Heaven, 11:1

Praise the Almighty, all that's in me, 137:5

Praise the Almighty God; reverent bow ye, 137:5

Praise the Almighty, our king and our ruler, 137:1

Praise the Almighty, the powerful king, 137:1

Praise the Almighty, who all things so gloriously, 137:2

Praise the Almighty, who doth with His splendor, 137:3

Praise the Almighty who fair in His image did make, 137:3

Praise the Almighty who hath so manifestly blessed, 137:4

Praise the Almighty, who thine estate clearly, 137:4

Praise the Lord, all heathens, 230:1

Praise the Lord, all that is within me, 137:5

Praise the Lord, all ye heathen, 230:1

Praise the Lord, all ye nations, 230:1

Praise the Lord, for He is most gracious, 374

Praise the Lord for His mighty acts, 225:4

Praise the Lord in His deeds, 225:4

Praise the Lord, my soul, 69:1; 143:1

Praise the Lord, O Jerusalem, 119:1

Praise the Lord, O my soul, 69:1; 143:1

Praise the Lord, O my spirit, 69:1

Praise the Lord; praise His holy name, 30:3

Praise the Lord; rise up rejoicing, 263

Praise the Lord, the Almighty, the King, 137:1

Praise the Lord, the mighty king of honor(s), 137:1

Praise the Lord; the year is drawing, 28:1

Praise the Lord through every nation, 140:7

Praise the Lord; what is in me praise His name, 137:5

Praise the Lord, who all things so gloriously, 137:2

Praise the Lord, who has created you artfully, 137:3

Praise the Lord who has set you up so well, 137:3

Praise the Lord, who has visibly blessed your, 137:4

Praise the Lord, who rules over all, 137:2

Praise the Lord who thy state visibly blessed, 137:4

Praise the Lord who skillfully and beautifully, 137:3

Praise thou the Lord, Jerusalem, 119:1

Praise thou the Lord, O Jerusalem, 119:1

Praise thou the Lord, O my spirit, 69:1; 143:1

Praise thou the Lord, the omnipotent monarch, 137:1
Praise thou Zion, praise the Lord, 190:3
Praise thy creator, for He owns and loves thee, 374
Praise thy God, O Zion, 190:1a
Praise to God here, ev'ry one, 62:6
Praise to God in every land, 51:1
Praise to God on high in Heaven, 11:1
Praise to God sing ev'ry one, 36:8
Praise to God the Father be (given), 36:8; 62:6
Praise to Jehovah, the almighty King, 137:1
Praise to the Highest who all things, 137:2
Praise to the Highest, who makes thee, 120a:8.1; 137:4
Praise to the Highest who maketh thy way plain, 137:3
Praise to the Lord, 650
Praise to the Lord; He is king over all, 137:1
Praise to the Lord! Oh, let all that is, 120a:8.2; 137:5
Praise to the Lord, the Almighty, 57:8; 137:5
Praise to the Lord, the Almighty, the King, 120a:8.2; 137:1
Praise to the Lord, the omnipotent, 57:8; 137:1
Praise to the Lord, who with His love befriends, 286
Praise to Thee and adoration, 32:6
Praise waiteth for Thee, O God, in Zion, 120:1
Praise ye Almighty God, 602
Praise ye Almighty God; reverent bow, 120a:8.2; 137:5
Praise ye God, all men, adore Him, 51:1
Praise ye God in all the lands, 51:1
Praise ye God in ev'ry nation, 51:1
Praise ye God throughout creation, 51:1
Praise ye God's good will, 195:3
Praise ye Jehovah all ye people, 51:1
Praise ye Jehovah with anthem of praise, 137:1

Praise ye the Highest, all people now living adore, 137:5
Praise ye the Highest, yea, all people living, 137:5
Praise ye the Highest; yea, all that it is in me, 120a:8.2
Praise ye the Lord, 230:2
Praise ye the Lord, all ye nations, 230:1
Praise ye the Lord for acts so mighty, 225:4
Praise ye the Lord God for His loving-kindness, 374
Praise ye the Lord God who hath so manifestly, 137:4
Praise ye the Lord; His acts are mighty, 225:4
Praise ye the Lord in all His greatness, 225:4; 225:5
Praise ye the Lord in gladsome chorus, 321; 434
Praise ye the Lord, O my soul, 143:1
Praise ye the Lord, O my spirit, 69:1; 69a:1; 143:1
Praise ye the Lord; praise Him, 225:4
Praise ye the Lord who so clearly has favored, 120a:8.1
Praise ye the Lord who so mightily rules all, 137:2
Praise ye thy fortune, fair Saxony blessed, 215:1
Praise your good fortune, blessed Saxony, 215:1
Praise your good luck, blessed Saxony, 215:1
Praised be Almighty God, 704
Praised be God; praised be His name, 30:3
Praised be God; praised His name, 30:3
Praised be God the Father, 36:8
Praised be God the Lord who lives, 129:4
Praised be the Lord God, my light, 129:2
Praised be the Lord God of Israel, 167:2
Praised be the Lord, my God, my comfort, 129:3
Praised be the Lord, my God, my light, 129:1

Praised be the Lord, my God, my salvation, 129:2

Praised be the Lord, my God, who ever lives, 129:4

Praised be the Lord, my God, who lives, 129:4

Praised be Thou, Jesu Christ, 91:1; 697; 722; 722a; 723

Praised be Thou, Jesus Christ, 64:2; 91:1; 248:28; 314; 604

Praised be Thou, O Jesu Christ, 91:1

Praised be Thou, O Jesus Christ, 64:2; 314; 604; 697; 722; 722a; 723

Pray be quick, 211:8

Pray silence; list to me, 211:1

Pray though even now as well, 115:4

Pray ye, ever watch and pray, 115:4

Pray yet also in the midst of watching, 115:4

Prayer for peace, 164:6

Precious gift beyond compare, 197a:1

The precious gift of peace, 119:5

Prepare for Thy coming the way to our hearts, 147:5

Prepare the way; prepare the course, 132:1

Prepare the ways; prepare the road, 132:1

Prepare Thee, Jesu, then now the way, 147:5

Prepare Thy way, O Jesu, now, 147:5

Prepare thyself, Zion, 248:4

Prepare ye the highway, the way of the Lord, 132:1

Prepare ye the paths, prepare the highways, 132:1

The presence of the blessed angels, 19:6

The present Christendom, 179:2

The present is full of the promise of glory, 134a:4b

Preserve my faith from error free, 3:6

Preserve us, Lord, by Thy word, 6:6

Preserve us in the true path, 79:6

Preserve us, Jesus Christ, our Lord, 119:9

Prevent it, righteous Father, 18:3c

Prince eternal, strong defender, 31:4

A prince his people rules as Pan, 208:7

A prince in his country's Pan, 208:7

A prince is the Pan of his country, 208:7

A prince must be another Pan, 208:7

Prince of being, mighty warrior, 31:4

Prince of life, heavenly warrior, 31:4

Prince of life, strong champion, 31:4

The princeling builds him palaces, 94:3b

The princes of Sheba hither came, 65:1; 65:2; 603

Principal and interest also, 168:3

Print Thine image pure and holy, 32:6

The promise of our fathers given, 10:6

The promise which He made to our fathers, 10:6

Prone at Thy feet creation lies, 11:6

Prophesy unto us, Thou Christ, 244:43b

Prophesy, who is it that smote Thee, 246:41b

Prostrate yourselves with thanks, 248:36

Protect us, Lord, and be our guide, 120:6

Protected by Thee, I am free, 227:3

The proud man buildeth palaces, 94:3b

Prove Thy might, Lord Jesus Christ, 6:6

Prove Thy power, Lord Jesus Christ, 6:6

Puffed-up pride, but little understanding, 201:13

Puffed-up pride expanding, lacking understanding, 201:13

Punish me not in Thy wrath, 115:6; 246:74

Purge thyself, my heart, 244:75

Pursue thee though the wicked world, 58:2

Put all fear and doubt behind thee, 32:6

Put far from us, O faithful God, 101:1; 101:7

Put forth abundantly, thou divine spring, 5:3

Put from thee, my spirit, the world and its tears, 124:5

Put from us, O faithful God, 90:5

Put thou thy trust in God, 466

Put thy faith in God the Lord, 197:1

Put to sleep all worrisome cares, 197:3

Put your house in order, 106:2d

Put yourselves the Savior under, 182:5

Q

Queen and pearl of royal ladies, 214:7
Queen o'er all our land's extent, 214:6
Queen of hearts, who o'er us reigns, 214:6
The queen of our country whom Heaven, 214:6
Queen of queens and peerless peeress, 214:7
Quickly as the swift stream flowing, 26:2
Quickly, Christ my Lord, restore me, 244:51
Quickly, quickly, you whirling winds, 201:1
A quiet end I would attain, 502
Quiet, Lord, my froward heart, 384
Quiet now, faint music, 210:4
Quiet now, moving music, 210:4
The quiet river sings, 207a:2

R

Rage and toss, ye billows stormy, 153:6
Rage on; rage, insensate swarm, 215:5
Rage then, bold swarm, 215:5
Rage then, insolent swarm, 215:5
Rage then, presumptuous swarm, 215:5
Rage ye on, ye wanton band, 215:5
The raging of the harsh winds, 92:6
The raging of the winds so cruel, 92:6
Raise the viols in Cythera, 36:4
Raise to the Highest a song of thanksgiving, 66:3
Raise yourselves up joyfully, 36:1
Rare comfort, dearest Lord, 153:4
Ready am I; come, call me hence, 128:2
Ready be, my soul, alway, 115:1; 115:6
Receive me, my Redeemer, 244:21
Receive, then, ye heavens, 249:10c
Recitative and chorale, 95:2a, 95:2b
Recognize me, my keeper, 244:21
Recover now, O troubled feelings, 103:5
Recover yourselves, troubled minds, 103:5
Recover yourselves, troubled voices, 103:5
A redeemed and hallowed spirit, 173:2
Redeemer of His folk, 248:27
Redouble then your strength, 63:6

Redouble, therefore, you hot flames, 63:6
Redoubled may they rise, 63:6
Reflect on Jesu's bitter death, 101:6
Refresh the heart, you charming strings, 201:15
The refuse of sin has not only stained me, 5:2
Regard me, then, my Master, 244:21
Regard me then, my Savior, 244:21
Reject it not, Thou who'rt my soul's delight, 65:5
Rejoice all ye Christians, 40:8
Rejoice, all ye spirits, 66:1a
Rejoice, all ye, the chosen spirits, 34:3
Rejoice and be merry, 243:14
Rejoice and give welcome, 207:2
Rejoice and sing with might, 243:14
Rejoice and sing; your gracious king, 248:35
Rejoice and sing; your heav'nly king, 248:35
Rejoice, be glad! Up, praise thy days, 248:1
Rejoice, exult! Up, glorify the days, 248:1
Rejoice, for joined is here a bond, 195:4
Rejoice, for my Redeemer lives, 160:3
Rejoice, God's children, 387
Rejoice good Christians, raise the strain, 155:5
Rejoice greatly, good Christians, 734; 734a
Rejoice greatly, O my soul, 19:7; 25:6; 30:6; 32:6; 39:7; 70:7; 194:6; 246:68
Rejoice, holy flock, rejoice, 30:12
Rejoice, if ye be reproached, 244:41
Rejoice in God in all lands, 51:1
Rejoice, legion of the redeemed, 30:1; 30:12
Rejoice meanwhile that thy salvation, 248:35
Rejoice, my heart, for the sorrow, 151:2
Rejoice my soul, rejoice my heart, 21:10
Rejoice now, all ye Christians, 734; 734a; 755
Rejoice now, Christian souls, 734; 734a; 755
Rejoice now, Christians young and old, 387
Rejoice now in gladness, 66:1a
Rejoice, now, O Heaven, and Earth, 134:6

Rejoice, O heart, for now is all the pain, 151:2

Rejoice, O my soul, and forget, 70:7

Rejoice, O my spirit, and comfort now take, 15:5

Rejoice, O my spirit, in thy consolation, 21:10

Rejoice, O my spirit; my heart sing, 21:10

Rejoice, O my spirit; rejoice in thy gladness, 21:10

Rejoice, redeemed flock, rejoice, 30:1

Rejoice, rejoice, for now we know, 249:10a

Rejoice soul; rejoice heart, 21:10

Rejoice; the old year now is ended, 28:1

Rejoice; the passing year is ended, 28:1

Rejoice the while that our Savior, 248:35

Rejoice the while that the Savior, 248:35

Rejoice thee greatly, O my soul, and forget, 70:7

Rejoice thee, my spirit, and be of good cheer, 15:5

Rejoice thee now, my heart, 151:2

Rejoice thee, redeemed host, 30:1

Rejoice thee, soul; rejoice thee, 21:10

Rejoice then, O my heart, 151:2

Rejoice, ye Christians all, 40:8

Rejoice, ye Christians, loudly, 313

Rejoice, ye faithful, rejoice, 30:1; 30:12

Rejoice, ye hearts, 66:1a

Rejoice, ye heav'ns, and all therein, 311

Rejoice, ye holy host, rejoice, 30:12

Rejoice ye, my spirit, 21:10

Rejoice, ye souls, elect and holy, 34:3

Rejoice, ye souls, His vessels chosen, 34:3

Rejoice, ye who in Christian faith, 184:3

Rejoice, you hearts, 66:1a

Rejoice, you joyful voices, 120:2

Rejoicing do I greet my death, 82:5

Rejoicing, exultant, with Thee ever dwelling, 158:3b

Release, O my spirit, 245:63

Remain also my God in me, 148:5

Remain faithful to me, 467

Remain likewise, my God, in me, 148:5

Remain to Jesus true, 75:11

Remain true to Jesus, 75:11

Remain with us for the evening will come, 6:1

Remember Jesu's (Jesus') bitter death, 101:6

Remember, Lord, my Savior true, 30:7

Remember me, and take me, 244:21

Remember me, my Savior, 244:21

Remember me that I may not forget Thee, 504

Remember now, O Jesus, 116:3

Remember then, O Jesus, 116:3

Remember thou, my soul, and ponder, 509

Remember though, O Jesus, 116:3

Remember us in Thine affection, 29:5

Remember us in Thy love, 29:5

Remember us with loving kindness, 29:5

Remember us with Thine affection, 29:5

Remember us with Thy love, 29:5

Rememb'ring His mercy, 10:5

Remove from us, O faithful God, 90:5; 101:1; 101:7

Rend, my heart, the chains of Mammon, 168:5

Repent in time! Death cometh quickly, 90:1

Repentance and remorse, 244:10

Resist sin or else its poison, 54:1

Resist staunchly all temptation, 54:1

Resist then sin, 54:1

Resound all creation; rejoice ev'ry nation, 134:6

Resound now, ye lyrics, 172:1

Resound, ye Heaven; rejoice, Earth, 134:6

Resound ye heavens; rejoice thee Earth, 134:6

Resound, ye songs; ring out, 172:1; 172:7

Rest content in Him and rest tranquil, 460

Rest content in the Lord, 460; 510; 511; 512

Rest easy, heart, and worry not, 111:2

Rest here in peace, Redeemer, 245:67

Rest here, languid tones, 210:4

Rest in peace, weary spirits, 210a:4

Rest now, dear Savior, in Thy tomb, 246:78.1

Rest now, Redeemer, in Thy tomb, 246:78.1

Rest thee now, weary spirit, 210a:4

Rest thy faith on God the Lord, 197:1
Rest well, beloved, 245:67
Rest well, holy limbs, 245:67
Rest well, O Savior, 245:67
Rest well, ye holy limbs, 245:67
Rest ye here, wearied spirits, 210a:4
Retain only, O world, my belongings, 8:5
Retire thee quickly, my heart, from the world, 124:5
Return from gloomy caves of death, 480
Return from out the darkened grave, 480
Return now, return now, 205:11
Return, return, you whirling winds, altogether, 201:1
Return ye, return ye, 205:11
Return ye, return ye, ye whirling tornadoes, 201:1
Reveal Thy might, Lord Jesus Christ, 6:6
The riches and treasures that men seek, 26:4
Right honored sir, 210:9
Right sore my conscience doth reproach, 131:4b
Right welcome! All hail!, 30a:3
Right welcome will I greet him, 27:3
Right well hath God the world ordained, 187:7
Righteous God, ah, dost Thou reckon, 89:5
Righteous God, ah, reckonest Thou, 89:5
Ring out, all ye trumpets, 207.2
Ring out all ye trumpets in gayest staccato, 207a:1
Ring out, ring out, O final trumpet, 70:10b
Ring out, songs, resound, 172:1
Ring out with clarion call, 128:3
Ring out, ye songs, resound, 172:1
Rise, festive sounds, 207a:1
Rise, my soul, to watch and pray, 115:1; 115:6
Rise, O Shepherds; rise and praise Him, 248:15
Rise, O soul, this happy morning, 180:1
Rise, that we may now all as one, 176:6
Rise up my heart, in (with) gladness, 441
Rise up, the hour will not await, 440

Rise, ye of faith, sing ye the songs, 134:2
Risen is the Holy Christ, 628
The robbers also, which were crucified, 244:68
Rock, beyond all else my treasure, 152:4
Rock, beyond all treasures shining, 152:4
Rock of ages, cleft for me, 384
Rock of ages, never failing, 152:4
Rock of ages, truth divine, 384
Rock yourselves to sleep, 249a:7
Rock yourselves, you contented sheep, 249a:7
The rod of Moses smote the rock, 246:39
Roses will I freely pick me, 86:2
Round me falls the night, 409
Rouse thee up, my soul, from slumber, 146:8
Rouse thyself, my soul, and gather, 244:48
Rouse thyself, my weak spirit, 43:11.2; 248:12; 454
Rouse yourselves, fearful and timid minds, 176:5
Ruler art Thou of earth and sky, 11:6
Ruler of Heaven, hark, 248:24
Ruler of Heaven, hear, 248:24
Ruler of Heaven, regard our poor praise, 248:24
Ruler of Heaven, though weak be our voices, 248:24
Ruler over dead and living, 8:6
Ruler over death and life (living), 8:6
Run where, 245:48b
Run, ye souls, 245:48a
The rushing of the raw winds, 92:6
The ruthless world arraigneth me, 244:38

S

Sacrament, 244:17, 244:21
Sad that the curse, 136:2
A safe stronghold our God is still, 80:1; 302; 303; 720; A49
The sages of Sheba, 65:1
St. John Passion, 245

St. Luke Passion, 246
St. Mark Passion, 247
St. Matthew Passion, 244
Saints and sinners to the banquet all are bidden, 162:1
Salvation and blessing, 120:4
Salvation has come to us, 9:1; 86:6; 155:5; 186:6
Salvation hath come down to us, 9:1
Salvation is now come to us, 638
Salvation now is come to Earth, 86:6; 155:5; 186:6; 638
Salvation sure has come to man, 9:1; 638
Salvation unto us has come, 9:1; 638
A sanctified mind sees and tastes, 173:2
Sanctify us by Thy goodness, 22:5
The sapphire halls of God's fair house, 198:8
The sapphire house of eternity, 198:8
A saving health to us is brought, 638
The Savior accepts the sinners, 113:6
The Savior bowed before His father bendeth, 244:28
Savior, breathe an evening blessing, 439
The Savior comes, 30:4
The Savior comes to Earth, 152:3
Savior, constant shower upon us, 51:3
The Savior falleth low before His Father, 244:28
The Savior falling down before His Father, 244:28
The Savior falls before His Father kneeling, 244:28
The Savior falls down before His Father, 244:28
The Savior has come, has taken, 61:2
The Savior has descended, His glory, 61:2
The Savior helpeth all who love Him, 109:5
The Savior is come and has taken, 61:2
The Savior is in charge in Israel, 152:3
The Savior is set for the fall and rising, 152:3
The Savior is the sinner's friend, 113:6
The Savior knows, indeed, His people, 109:5
The Savior knows, yea, His own, 109:5

The Savior low before His Father bending, 244:28
Savior, make me all Thine own, 244:19
Savior mine and dearest Master, 69:5; 69a:5
The Savior now appeareth, 61:2
The Savior now is set for the fall and rising, 152:3
The Savior now is set in Israel, 152:3
Savior of my soul from death, 165:5
Savior of the Gentiles, come, 599; 659; 659a; 660; 660a; 660b; 661; 661a
Savior of the heathen, come, 599; 659; 659a; 660; 660a; 660b; 661; 661a; 699
Savior of the nations, come, 62:1; 62:6; 599; 659; 659a; 660; 660a; 660b; 661; 661a; 699
The Savior sendeth forth the faithful, 139:3
The Savior sendeth out His faithful, 139:3
The Savior sends, indeed, His people, 139:3
The Savior sends, yea His own, 139:3
Savior, shepherd, 92:8
The Savior sinners doth accept, 113:6
Savior was He of others, 244:67d
Savior, when in dust to Thee, 159:5; A57
The Savior's voice to sinners calls, 113:6
Say, art thou, cruel Aeolus, 205:8
Say, beauteous goddess, 208:3
Say, my Savior, tell me rightly, 248:39
Say not they die, those martyr souls, 122:6
Say, sweetest Jesu, what law Thou hast broken, 244:3
Say yes to my endeavors, 194:12
Scarce tongue can speak, 176:6
Scatter good seed while you may, 185:3
Scatterbrained and shallow people, 181:1
Schlendrian goes off on his search, 211:9
Scion of Habsburg, noble, glorious, 206:7
Scion of Hapsburg's lofty family tree, 206:7
Search me, God, and learn my heart, 136:1
Search me, God, and learn of my heart, 136:1
The searcher of hearts ever knoweth, 226:3
See, dear God, how my enemies, 153:1
See, dearest God, the many foes, 153:1

See Him now, the Righteous One, 245:56
See how breaks, how tears, how falls, 92:3
See how fiercely they fight, 19:1
See how in happiness this day, 202:9
See how the righteous perish, 362
See how weak, how frail, how vain, 92:3
See in contentment a thousand bright days, 202:9
See, Jesus has His hand, 244:70a
See Judah's hero, 245:58
See, Lord, behold, here are two swords, 246:22c
See, Lord, my good intent, 17:6
See, love beyond compare, 85:5
See my dwelling bare and lowly, 61:5b
See my heart, Lord, open, loving, 148:4
See, my thoughts are Godward given, 166:2
See now, how poor, how weak, how frail, 92:3
See now, I stand before the door, 61:4
See now, I will send out many fishers, 88:1a
See now the Bridegroom, 248:3
See now, we must go up to Jerusalem, 159:1a
See now, we're going up to Jerusalem, 159:1a
See now what great affection, 64:1
See now what love, 64:1
See our flocks with wooly fleeces, 208:13
See, see, what kind of wonder, 248:17
See the destined day arise, 36:8; 62:6
See the Easter Victim, 4:6
See the land is decked with flowers, 206:7
See the Lord of life and light, 245:21; 245:65; 283; 620; 620a; 747
See the Lord of light and life, 245:21
See the Savior's outstretched arm, 244:70a
See to it that thy fear of God, 179:1
See to it that thy God-fearing, 179:1
See, we greet Thee, mighty King, 245:34
See what a love the Father has shown, 64:1
See what His love can do, 85:5
See what His love hath wrought, 85:5
See what His love will do, 85:5
See what love does, 85:5

See, world, thine own life's token, 244:16; 393; 394; 395
See, world, thy Lord in anguish, 245:15.2; 393; 394; 395
See ye, behold what love, 64:1
See ye, for many fishermen send I, 88:1a
See ye not the ruddy splendor, 205:7
See ye, see the Savior's outstretched hands, 244:70a
See ye, that shall thus be blessed, 34a:3
Self-love deceives, 185:4
Self-love doth vain delude itself, 185:4
Send down, Lord, Thy blessing here, 193:5
Send down Thy great strength from Heaven, 126:2
Send, Father, send Thy holy light, 198a:1
Send in, Lord, Thy blessing, 193:5
Send Thy might from above, 126:2
Send, we pray Thee, help from Heaven, 126:2
Serenade for the birthday of Prince Leopold, 173a
Serene and at peace with oneself, 204:2
Serpent benighted, art not affrighted, 40:4
Serpent, Hell-horror, dost not feel terror, 40:4
Serpent in Hell, there, 40:4
The serpent, that in Paradise, 40:5
The serpent, who in Paradise, 40:5
The servant forms, the need, 186:2
A servant's lot, distress, 186:2
Serve thy God with fear, nor show hypocrisy, 179:1
Servitude, distress, want, 186:2
Set in order thine house, 106:2d
Set in order thy house, 106:2d
Set not thy heart on the things of the world, 26:4
Set ready thine house, 106:2d
Set thine house in order, 106:2d
Set thy house in order, 106:2d
Set your house in order, 106:2d
Shady hollows, ye're my pleasure, 205:5
Shake thy head, 40:6

Shake you now your head and say, 40:6
Shake your head and say, 40:6
Shall I my life's path, 153:8
Shall I not exalt my Maker, 413
Shall I not loud praises sing Thee, 413
Shall I not my God be praising, 413
Shall I then in this world, 71:2b
Shall I then likewise death's ways, 92:9
Shall it, yea, then be that punishment, 48:3
Shall Pales be the last thus, 208:8
Shall Pales' offering (sacrifice), 208:8
Shall Pales, then, alone, 208:8
Shallow natures, flighty creatures, 181:1
Shame! 'Tis no Christian's part, 186:4a
The shape of vile transgression, 54:2
Shed, Lord, on this new year blessing, 248:42
Sheep and lambs may safely graze, 208:9
Sheep can graze in safety, 208:9
Sheep can graze in safety, 208:9
Sheep can safely graze, 208:9
Sheep may safely graze (pasture), 208:9
Sheep may safely, while their shepherd, 208:9
Shepherd cantata, 249a
Shepherd ne'er through byway going, 246:37
Shepherd of Israel, hear us, 104:1
The shepherd on high cares for me, 104:2
A shepherd true am I, 85:1
The shepherds keep their flocks by night, 122:6
Shine forth, O beauteous morning light, 248:12
Shine on, fair sun, o'er this pasture, 208:11
Should e'er His face seem turned from thee, 9:7; 155:5; 186:6
Should I remain in the flock, 503
Should Jesu's love my sins forgive me, 48:6
Should not this august occasion, 207:9
Should Satan league his forces, 153:5
Shout joyfully to God in all lands, 51:1
Shout now, shout to the Lord, A160:1a
Shout, rejoice! Up, praise the days, 248:1
Shout ye, all ye joyful voices, 120:2
Shout ye exultant this day of salvation, 248:1
Show pity, Lord; O Lord, forgive, 305

Show thy reckoning, word of doom, 168:1
Show us Thy way, O God, 878
Show your love by what you do, 76:12
The shuddering clamor of the bells, 198:4
Sickness and death now terrify me, 60:3
Sighing, crying, sorrow, need, 21:3
Sighing, tears, distress, grief, 21:3
Sighing, weeping, sorrow, 21:3
Sighing, weeping, trouble, 21:3
Sighs, tears, sorrow, distress, 21:3
Sighs, tears, worry, need, 21:3
Sighs unspoken, silent grieving, 199:2
Silence, Hell's host, 5:5
Silence, silence is the answer, 246:7
Silent sighing, mute laments, 199:2
Silent sighing, quiet mourning, 199:2
Silent sighing, soundless grieving, 199:2
Silent, you flutes; quiet your melodies, 210:6
Silly fond lover, fate has become, 203:3
Silver is made pure through fire, 2:5
Simeon's song of praise, 95:1c; 125:1
Simon Peter also followed, 245:12
Simon Peter answered and said, 244:22
Simon Peter followed Jesus, 245:12
Simon Peter sat without the palace, 244:45
Sin brings but grief, 40:3
The sin brings sorrow, 40:3
Sin brings us grief, 40:3
Sin brought us grief, 40:3
The sin has sorely destroyed us, 101:5
Sin sore besets us everywhere, 101:5
Sin still besets us everywhere, 101:5
The sin-begotten birth of Adam's cursed offspring, 165:2
Since Christ doth own my being, 95:1a
Since Christ is all my being, 95:1a
Since Christ is gone to Heaven, 128:1
Since Jesus hath my sins forgiven, 48:6
Since Thou art risen, 15:7
Since Thou didst leave the grave again, 15:9c; 95:6
Since Thou from death arisen art, 95:6
Since Thou from death art ris'n again, 95:6

Since Thou from death hast risen again, 15:9c; 95:6

Since Thou from death once rose, 95:6

Since Thou hast risen from the grave, 15:9c; 95:6

Since Thou, Lord, hast said, 171:5

Since Thou, Lord, will count up sins, 131:2a

Since Thou my God and Father art, 138:7

Since time began the covenant was sealed, 99:4

Since we have finished, 212:23

Since with Thee there is no living person just, 105:1b

Sincerity, a gift it is, 24:2

Sincerity is one of God's gifts, 24:2

Sincerity is one of God's most gracious blessings, 24:2

Sincerity's the gift of God, 24:2

The sinful birth of Adam's, 165:2

Sing a new song to the Lord, 411

Sing for joy, ye ransomed band, 30:1

Sing joyful songs to God, 243:11

Sing, my soul, to God, 413

Sing now to God new songs of praise, 225:1

Sing out ye voices, loud and clear, 122:6

Sing praise and thanks to God, 192:3

Sing praise to Christ, 142:4

Sing praise to God who dwells on high, 117:1; 117:9; 251

Sing praise to God who reigns above, 9:1; 117:1; 251; 307; 388; 480

Sing praises to God, the Lord God, 30:3

Sing praises to God who dwells on high, 117:1; 172:1

Sing praises! Your voices, 172:1; 172:7

Sing, pray, and follow God unceasing, 88:7; 93:7

Sing, pray, and follow God unswerving, 88:7

Sing, pray, and go in God's ways, 88:7; 93:7

Sing, pray, and keep His ways unswerving, 88:7; 93:7; 197:10

Sing, pray, and walk at God's direction, 93:7

Sing, pray, and walk in God's own pathway(s), 88:7; 93:7

Sing, pray, thy faith in Him confessing, 93:7

Sing the Lord a new song, 411

Sing to God a new-made song, 190:1a; 225:1; 411

Sing to the Lord a glad, new song, 190:1a

Sing to the Lord a new song, 190:1a; 225:1

Sing to the Lord a new-made song, 190:1a; 225:1

Sing to the Lord, O my spirit, 69:1

Sing unto the Lord a new song, 225:1

Sing we all, thy faithful subjects, 213:13

Sing we from our inmost hearts, 187:7

Sing we the birth of God's dear Son, 122:1; 122:6

Sing ye; be joyful this day of salvation, 248:1

Sing ye the Lord a joyful song, 190:1a

Sing ye the Lord a new refrain, 190:1a

Sing ye to God a joyful song, 190:1a

Sing ye to God with heart and voice, 187:7

Sing ye to the Lord a new song, 225:1

Sing ye to the Lord a new-made song, 225:1

Sink not yet, my soul, to slumber, 55:5; 146:8; 244:48; 359; 360

Sink to rest, languid strains, 210:4

Sink to rest, strains enchanting, 210:4

A sinner and a soul most wretched, 179:6

A sinner, Lord, I pray Thee, 135:1; 135:6

Sinners, guilty, 408

The sins' dirt has not only stained me, 5:2

Sin's dull grief bids my erring heart, 244:10

Sin's wage is death, 40:3

Sir, we bear it in mind, 244:76b

Sir, we remember it well, 244:76b

Sir, we remember that that deceiver, 244:76b

Sire, Lord and Master, 245:1

Sit down beneath His shadow, 281

Slaughtered Lamb, 455

The slave of sin must serve the devil, 54:3

Sleep, my beloved, 213:3; 248:19

Sleep, my dearest, 248:19

Sleep now, weary spirit, 82:3

Sleep Thou, my dearest, 248:19

Sleepers, awake! A voice is calling, 140:1; 645

Sleepers, awake, calls the voice, 140:1
Sleepers, awake! raise your voices, 140:1
Sleepers, awake! the voice is calling us, 140:1
Sleepers wake! A voice astounds us, 140:1; 140:7
Sleepers, wake; a voice is calling, 645
Sleepers, wake, for night is flying, 140:1; 140:7
Sleepers, wake! Loud sounds the warning, 140:1
Sleepers, wake! Sounds are falling, 140:1
Sleepers, wake! The voice is calling, 140:1
Sleepers, wake! The watch-cry pealeth, 140:7
Slumber, all ye; care and sorrow, 197:3
Slumber, beloved, 248:19
Slumber, child, 34:5
Slumber, my dear one, 213:3
Slumber, my lov'd one, 248:19
Slumber now, O weary spirit, 82:3
Slumber now, weary eyes, 82:3
Slumber now, ye eyes so weary, 82:3
Slumber now, ye weary eyelids, 82:3
Slumber on, O weary eyes, 82:3
Slumber on, O weary spirit, 82:3
Slumberers, wake! The bridegroom cometh, 140:1
So all my mortal life along, 117:7
So all of you may know, 212:22
So all our sins will also slumber, 244:26b
So all our sins will fall asleep, 244:26b
So angels, rejoice and fittingly sing, 248:22
So appears Thy natal day, 142:3
So arise then, thou God-devoted soul, 31:5
So art Thou then, my Savior, 30:7
So be 't! I needs must then obey, 206:10
So be 't; I rest in peace, 138:6
So be it then, 119:8
So be it, then I say, 148:6
So be it; thus spoke Jesus, 458
So be it; Thy name shall alone, 248:40a
So be now, my soul, Thine, 44:7
So be now, soul, His, 13:6; 97:9
So be now, soul, Thine, and trust Him, 13:6

So be, O spirit, be contented, 155:3
So be the bond of chaste love, 202:8
So be thou still, patient, abiding, 93:3
So becomes Thy word, 126:5
So believe now, 72:3
So choose your path, ne'er backward looking, 207:4
So come before His countenance, 117:9
So come thou unto Me, 140:5
So come to Me, you My chosen, 140:5
So come whate'er betide, 133:6
So come whate'er betide, on Jesus will I stay me, 197a:4
So come within to Me, 140:5
So come ye now before His face, 117:9
So come ye now into His courts, 117:9
So Cupid also seeks his pleasure, 202:4
So departs from God's glory and throne, 62:3
So do not wonder, O Master, 176:4a
So eager I follow, 245:13
So, fair and lovely Wiederau, 30a:12
So falter not, 72:3
So fan ye hotter yet the flames, 63:6
So far as Thou the noble peace, 41:4
So farewell, Earth's vain distractions, 27:5
So follow God and His persuasion, 197:4
So forth I'll go to Jesus Christ, 31:9
So go I with courageous steps, 111:4
So go in to Me, 140:5
So go then hence, ye (you) shepherds, 248:18
So go ye thence, ye shepherds, go, 248:18
So go ye there, ye shepherds, go, 248:18
So God lets Himself not be untestified, 76:2
So, good Christian, be thou found, 115:6
So happy walk where God shall lead, 197:10
So has God loved the world, 173:4
So has the Lord our God fulfill'd, 30:7
So henceforth, happy Wiederau, 30a:12
So I give myself into Thy hands, 229:4
So I go with encouraged steps, 111:4
So I yield myself into Thy hands, 229:4
So I'll entrust my soul into Thy hands, 229:4
So is my Jesus captured now, 244:33a

So is there now no damnation, 227:2
So issues forth from God's majesty and throne, 62:3
So join in and let the pleasure, 208:10
So join with me that this glad day, 208:10
So journey glad on God's true pathways, 197:10
So journey I thither to Jesus Christ, 31:9
So joyous enter we this house, 30a:2
So joyous, go ye forth, 36c:1
So just as I pay duty, 30a:11
So keep we all this holy feast, 4:7
So keep we this high festival, 4:7
So let me sing God's praises, 107:7
So let our songs to Heaven wing, 145:7
So let our voices all the wide world, 214:8
So let our voices with accord, 176:6
So let the bond of chaste love, 202:8
So let the people praise Thee, 69:6
So let Thy spirit us inflame, 116:6
So let us go forth that Salem of gladness, 182:8
So let us go into joyful Salem, 182:8
So let us go into the Salem of joy, 182:8
So let us hail this happy year, 122:6
So let us have the Easter feast, 4:7
So let us keep the Easter feast, 4:7
So let us keep the great high feast, 4:7
So let us keep this holy feast, 4:7
So let us observe the Easter feast, 4:7
So let us then hasten to Salem rejoicing, 182:8
So let whate'er betide, 133:6
So let whate'er betide, on Jesus will I stay me, 197a:4
So long a God in Heaven dwells, 20:7
So long as a drop of blood in my heart, 124:2
So long as a God in Heaven lives, 20:7
So long as a God lives in Heaven, 20:7
So long as in me there is breath, 124:2
So Love searches out, 202:4
So marvel then, O Master, not, 176:4a
So may I kneel before Thee, 107:7

So may my soul be Thine, Lord, 13:6
So may this day with joy ablaze, 173a:6
So mourn thou, destroyed God's city, 46:2
So must I say, my Jesus, Fare Thee well, 412; 501
So must it be, 77:2
So my Jesus is taken, 244:33a
So ne'er let Earth's vain, empty pleasure, 204:4
So now believe, 72:3
So now go in with Me, 140:5
So now good-bye, my Jesus, Thou must say, 501
So now I will, my Jesus, 159:3
So now, my Jesus, Thou must go, 500
So now, O soul, let Him be thine, 13:6
So now the law, the law that is of the Spirit, 227:4
So now the Lord in peace doth bide (dwell), 244:77a
So now, ye angels, rejoice and sing, 248:22
So, O betrothed pair, 202:8
So, O soul, be content, 155:3
So our sins fall to sleep, 244:26b
So place thee 'neath thy Savior's blood-bespattered, 80:6
So rejoice, ye chosen souls, 184:3
So remains My heart to thee, 49:5b
So sets He forth from God the Father's throne, 62:3
So shall all Christendom commend God's love, 76:13
So shall all Christendom the love of God, 76:13
So shall Christendom praise the love of God, 76:13
So shall it be, 77:2
So shall my heart be satisfied, 150:3
So shall our sins to sleep be laid, 244:26b
So shall the word, 126:5
So shall your subjects rejoice, 249a:11b
So sing we in this glad time, 16:2
So slumber shall our sins befall, 244:26b
So speak the souls that trust the Lord, 92:7b

So stand beside Christ's blood-red banner, 80:6

So stand by Christ's bloodstained flag, 80:6

So stand then beside Christ's blood-bespattered, 80:6

So stand then under Christ's own blood-stained flag, 80:6

So stand where Jesus' crimson banner, 80:6

So swept away today, 63:4

So take thy stand with Jesus' blood-bespattered, 80:6

So teach us, Lord, 246:50

So that the prophecy, 245:8

So that the saying, 245:8

So that the saying be fulfilled, 245:26

So that the Scripture might be, 245:55

So that the word, 245:8

So that we, all with one accord, 176:6

So that we thus altogether, 176:6

So that you all know, 212:22

So the avenging judge extinguishes, 90:3

So the Lord, after He with His disciples, 43:4

So then, as long as life shall be, 153:9.1

So then double your hot flames, 63:6

So then, forlorn one, patience, 155:3

So then let us hasten to Salem, rejoicing, 182:8

So then my heart and voice, 45:6

So then, prepare thyself for Heaven, 114:6

So there is no damnation, 227:2

So there is now no condemnation, 227:2

So there is now no damnation, 227:2

So therefore now, O soul, 31:5

So thou with thy mouth, 145:2

So, though I tread death's cheerless ways, 92:9

So, though misfortunes fall, 186:4b

So, though thy heart be clouded dark, 83:4

So today, darling Father, 211:8

So truly God His world did bless, 68:1

So turneth on this day, 63:4

So walk happily on God's ways, 197:10

So we celebrate the high feast, 4:7

So we shall raise upon this joyful day, 16:2

So whatever you wish, 24:3

So when by death at last, 111:5

So when death comes, 111:5

So will I hold to Thee, O Jesus, 133:6

So will then heart and mouth, 45:6

So wilt Thou also Lord, 128:5

So wonder not, O Master mine, 176:4a

So wondrously God loved us, 96:2

So, worthy Midas, 201:14

So yield now, ye foolish and purposeless sorrows, 8:4

So you won't have to suffer shame, 246:42

Soar joyfully aloft, 36:1

Soar joyfully on high, 36:1

Soar upwards to thy God, 40:6

Sobbing and pitiful weeping, 13:5

Sobs and sighing, tears and crying, 13:1

Soft pleasure beckons slyly, 213:8

Soft pleasure is indeed seductive, 213:8

Soft shall be my troubles in death, 249:7

The soldiers plaited then, 245:33

Some care only for their stomachs, 18:3e

The Son of God did come, 600

The Son of God doth condescend, 152:5

Son of God, enthroned on high, 6:2

The Son of God has come, 318; 600

The Son of God is come, 703; 724

The Son of God, the word divine, 152:5

Son of God, to whom highest praise, 6:2

Songs of thankfulness and praise, 262

Sonnets sung with sweet devotion, 210:2

Soon my journey will be done, 31:8

Soon our final hour will be sounding, 310

The sorrow of death shall be, 249:7

Sorrow shall no longer vex me, 249:5

Sorrow, sighing, trouble, crying, 12:2

The sorrows Thou art bearing, 244:16

Sorrows, vanish, 187:5b

Soul and body bend before Him, 35:2

Soul and spirit are bewildered, 35:2

Soul, array thyself with gladness, 180:1; 180:7

Soul, be contented, 460

Soul, break free from Mammon's fetters, 168:5
Soul, for your fragrance myrrh will do no longer, 249:5
The soul hath learned to treasure, 246:5
The soul in Jesu's hands reposes, 127:3
The soul knows how to judge, 246:5
The soul knows how to value, 246:5
Soul of mine, be not ashamed, 147:3
The soul of the Christian within, 456
The soul on faith moves upward, soaring, 37:5
The soul rests in Jesu's (Jesus') hands, 127:3
A soul that loves God purely, 24:1
The soul that truly knows his risen Lord, 134:1
Soul, thy spices shall no more be myrrh, 249:5
Soul, upraise ye, 69:3; 69a:3
Soul with spirit is bewildered, 35:2
Soul, your spices shall no longer be myrrh, 249:5
Sound and blast, O last trump, 70:10b
Sound and crack, O final stroke, 70:10b
The sound of rejoicing is heard, 149:1
Sound, ye flutes, your notes so thrilling, 214:3
Sound ye, ye drummers! And blow ye, ye buglers, 214:1
Sound, you drums! Resound trumpets, 214:1
Sound your knell, blest hour(s) of parting, 53
The sounds of the bells, 198:4
Source of all good, 445
Sov'reign Lord and king almighty, 248:8
The spacious firmament on high, 72:5; 244:31; 311; 312
Speak now, melody enchanting, 210a:2
The Spirit also helpeth us, 226:1
Spirit and soul are in tumult, 35:2
Spirit and soul become confused, 35:2
Spirit and soul becomes* disordered, 35:2
Spirit blessed, comfort rare, 183:4
The Spirit helpeth our infirmities, 226:1

The Spirit helps our infirmities, 226:1
The Spirit helps our weakness, 226:1
The Spirit helps us in our weakness, 226:1
Spirit of love, now our spirits bless, 197:5
A spirit pure and holy, 24:1
Spirit, these thy costly spices, 249:5
The splendid day is dawning, 629
The splendor of August's birthday, 207a:3
The splendor of the highest glory, 91:2
Spotless robes of white enfold me, 162:6
Spread open, ye heavens, 249:10c
Spring comes laughing o'er the hill, 212:4
Spring is the year's pleasant king, 206:9
Spurn me now; hate me right well, 76:10
The squire is fine, 212:5
Squire, long may you flourish so jolly and free, 212:20
The squire's all right, 212:5
Stablish me upon the rock of trust, 150:4
The staff and rod of mighty God, 184:5
The staff of Moses smote the rock, 246:39
Stand steadfast against transgression, 54:1
Stand thou fast, 12:6
Standing alone are we undone, 80:2b
Starry aisles and heavenly spaces, 248:53
Stars above in heaven shining, 366
Stars above in myriads shining, 366
Stars of the morning, so gloriously bright, 514
The state of Christendom, 179:2
Stay, my beloved, 508
Stay thou near by, 508
Stay with us for it will evening become, 6:1
Stay with us; the evening approaches, 6:1
Stay, ye angels, stay, 19:5
Stay, you angels, stay with me, 19:5
The stem of Jesse hath flowered, 243:16
Step on the path of faith, 152:2
Still, be still; by word defiling, 246:7
Still doth my spirit quiet know, 150:3
Still faithful I remain, 466
Still He planned for others' good, 245:56
Still I am and remain content, 150:3

Still Jesus stands when strife is pending, 46:5

Still nigh me, O my Savior, stand, 122:6

Still, O thou tow'ring sea, 81:5

Still shall they leave that word His might, 80:8

Stir, Almighty, now our souls, 173:6

Stir Thou, Lord, our hearts this day, 173:6

Stone, above all others precious (treasured), 152:4

Stone, beyond all jewels shining, 152:4

Stone surpassing ev'ry treasure, 152:4

Stone, which is above all treasures, 152:4

Stop, you sad eyes, stop your weeping, 98:3

Storm and rage, ye seas of trouble, 153:6

The storm of wrath was long in coming, 46:3

Storm, only storm, ye trouble-tempest, 153:6

Storm then, storm afflictions' tempests, 153:6

The story famed is told, 264

Stream forth in abundance, ye fountains, 5:3

Stream of salty tears, torrents, 21:5

Streams of salt tears, floods rush, 21:5

Streams of salt tears flow ever forth, 21:5

Streams of salty tears are welling, 21:5

Strength and might be sung to God, 149:2

Strengthen for service, Lord, 255

Strengthen me with Thy joy-spirit, 113:8; 168:6

Strengthen my faith, from doubting free, 3:6; 153:9.3

Strife and conquest are united, 12:4

Strike at last, thou hour desired, 53

Strike my hour, so long awaited, 53

Strike, oh strike, awaited hour, 53

Strike strong the strings on lute, 36:4

Strike then, long-awaited hour, 53

Strike, thou hour so long expected, 53

Strike, wished-for hour; break forth, 53

The strings attune, the organs sound, 36:4

Strive and conquer, hero bold, 62:4

Strive to sow the seeds of love, 185:3

A strong castle is our Lord, 80:1

A strong citadel is our God, 80:1

Strong compassion which, O mighty Son of God, 182:4

Strong in faith, hold ye fast, 174:4

Strong in Thy strength, 478

A stronghold is our God, 80:1; 80:8; 302; 303

A stronghold sure is God our Lord, 80:1; 302; 303; 720; A49

A stronghold sure our God is, 80:1; 80:8

A stronghold sure our God remains, 80:1

Stubbornness can blind the mighty, 147:4

Students are very gay, 524:12

A sturdy fortress is our God, 80:1

Subdue us by Thy goodness, 22:5

Succor Thy people, Lord Jesus Christ, 119:9

Such is the Christian's task, 185:5

Such is the law, 77:2

Such pain, such sorrow strike at me, 48:2

Suffer not Thou my soul to remain in Hell, 15:1

Suffer Thou not my soul, 15:1

Sufficiency is a treasure in this life, 144:5

Sun, diffuse thy brightest beam, 176:3

The sun has set; all radiance has descended, 297

The sun in its splendor has set, 297

The sun is set; in purple clouds descended, 297

The sun is setting; the day with its joys, 447

The sun is sinking in the west, 446

The sun is sunken in the west, 446

Sun of Heaven, shine upon me, 180:5

Sun of life, light of the senses, 180:5

Sun of life, my spirit's radiance, 180:5

Sun of life, thou light revealing, 180:5

Sun, thy clear beloved light, 176:3

The sun with its golden rays, 451

Sunbeams down streaming, 451

Sunk deep in sin, 198a:4b

The sun's bright splendor, 451

The sun's light and splendor, 446

Suppose the torments of the damned, 20:4

Suppose the torture of the damned, 20:4

A sure stronghold our God is He, 80:8; 302; 303; 720
Sure the heart's own humble dwelling, 248:53
Surely God must be merciful to me, 199:3
Surely such a heart's low dwelling, 248:53
Surely, surely, I say to you, 86:1
Surely this day thou'lt be with Me, 106:3b
Surely thou also are* one of them, 244:46a
Surely thou also art a (His) disciple, 244:46a
Surely thou also art one of them, 244:46a
Sustain my faith to act aright, 153:9.2
Sustain my heart by faith divine, 3:6
Sustain my heart in faith pure, 3:6
Sustain us in the truth, 79:6
Sustain us, Lord omnipotent, 126:1; A50
Sweep our hearts, O fingers golden, 201:15
Sweet and balmy Zephyrus, 205:9
Sweet Child, Thou'rt mine, 197a:2
Sweet comfort, my Jesus comes, 151:1
The sweet content of Heav'n, 123:2
Sweet Jesus, joy of my heart, 473
Sweet rest can refresh me, 207a:5
Sweet Savior, bless us ere we go, 321
Sweet slumber, my weary eyes, 82:3
Sweet solace, my Jesus cometh, 151:1
Sweet spring is advancing, 212:18
Sweet the moments, rich in blessing, 147:6; 147:10
Sweet the rose is; let me pluck it, 86:2
Sweet voices harmonious of strings, 207:2
Sweet will be my death and gentle, 249:7
Sweetly sound, ye strains enchanting, 210:2
Swing up joyfully, 36c:1
Swing yourself up to your God, 40:6
The swirling waters drag me downward, 9:3
A symbol is this child in Israel, 152:3
Symphony from the Christmas oratorio, 248:10

T

Take cheer, there is holiness, 133:2
Take comfort; know, His body torn and bleeding, 245:32
Take courage, my weak spirit, 248:12
Take courage now, 109:4
Take courage now, my weary soul, 454
Take fright, 102:5
Take from us, Lord, Thou faithful God, 101:1
Take from us, Lord, Thou true God, 90:5; 101:1
Take heart, and tremble not, 168:4
Take heart, O feeble spirit, 454
Take heart, our mortal frame, 133:2
Take heart; our spirits live, 198a:5
Take heed, I say to you, 127:4b
Take heed of fortune's wiles, 166:5
Take hope, a holy body holds Almighty God's, 133:2
Take it now; clasp your hope, 174:4
Take me for Thine own alway, 65:6
Take me for Thine own now hence, 65:6
Take me from myself and give me, 163:5
Take me, Jesus, take Thou me, 65:6
Take me, Savior, for Thine own, 65:6
Take me to Thee for Thine own, 65:6
Take me to Thyself as Thine own, 65:6
Take me to You as Your own, 65:6
Take my heart and make it Thine, 163:5
Take possession of thyself, my soul, 13:6
Take that thine is, and go thy way, 144:1
Take, then, mighty prince, our praise, 173a:8
Take then, O world, all I have gathered, 8:5
Take Thou me, Thine own to be, 163:5
Take up thy cross, the Savior said, 295
Take us, too, O mighty lord, 173a:8
Take us up also, great prince, 173a:8
Take warning, ye obdurate sinners, 70:2
Take what is thine and go away (hence), 144:1
Take what is thine, and go thy way, 144:1
Take what thine is, and go thy way, 144:1
The tares in the harvest, 181:3
The task the Father planned, 43:5
Te Deum, Lord, we sing, 328
Teach me, O Lord, to recognize, 453
Teach Thou our hearts, O Spirit, 183:5

Tear up, blow up, shatter the cave, 205:1
Tell me, if thou knowest, 249:9
Tell me quickly and truly, 249:9
Tell me quickly; hear me, 249:9
Tell me quickly; tell me (where), 249:9
Tell me quickly where I may find, 249:9
Tell then, tell me quickly, 249:9
Temporal honor will I gladly forgo, 47:5
Tempting conflict of the Gods, 208a
Ten thousand ten thousand of chariots, 43:3
Ten thousand times thousand, 43:3
Terrestrial treasure the heart may not dote on, 26:4
Than Thee no healer can I find me, 103:3
Thank God, it now is almost over, 321
Thank God! Now all is well, 29:4
Thank God, now the year goes to its end, 28:1
Thank God! The dragon fell, 19:2
Thank God, their throat He did not yet, 14:5
Thank God, we know it, 79:4
Thank God, we now know the certain road, 79:4
Thank goodness, that is over, 212:15
Thank we Thee, Lord, that Thou afford, 349
Thank ye the Lord, for He is very gracious, 286
Thank your good fortune, ye thrice-blessed, 215:1
Thanks and praise joyful, Lord, 249:10b
Thanks be to God, my end is near me, 321
Thanks be to God on high, 287
Thanks be to God, who from the pit, 14:5
That all of you may know, 212:22
That blood which through my guilt doth stream, 78:4
That death no one could subdue, 4:3
That disciple took her, 245:57
That disciple was known unto the high priest, 245:14
That evil draw me not astray, 244:26b
That God at last might do, 264

That God doth love the world we know, 68:1
That God has blessed His people, 248:28
That God has ever blessed us thus, 64:2; 91:6; 248:28
That God who gave me the promise, 13:3
That He is the aid of my brow, 21:6b
That He is the help of my countenance, 21:6b
That He of my countenance the comfort, 21:6b
That Heaven waits for me is sure, 64:6
That is fine, but don't let's talk, 212:10
That is polite; no one speaks, 212:10
That is the art of Christians, 185:5
That is the Christian's art, 185:5
That is the Father's will, 73:5
That is too clever for you, 212:15
That is why My heart feels for you, 49:5b
That Jesus lives do I rejoice, 66:4a
That Lamb that was slain for us, 21:11a
That man a godly life might live, 298
That my countenance's help, 21:6b
That night when Jesus Christ, 265
That other disciple to the high priest, 245:14
That other disciple was well known, 245:14
That same Jesus Christ, 246:72
That so might be fulfilled, 245:26
That sounds just la-dee-dee-da, 212:17
That sounds too coarse, 212:17
That sounds too crude, 212:17
That takest away the sins, 232:8
That the saying might be, 245:8
That the saying of Jesus might be fulfilled, 245:26
That the Scripture might be fulfilled, 245:55
That, the wind does, 201:3
That Thou might to the word Thy spirit add, 18:3b
That thou mightst shun eternal woe, 246:42
That Thou wilt keep me pure, 2:6
That thus might be fulfilled, 245:26
That we may therefore all at once, 176:6
That which affrights us mortals so, 83:2b

That which God did speak and promise, 10:6

That which God of old spake, 10:6

That which God promised Abraham, 248:14

That which Isaiah prophesied, 65:3

That which my God wills should always happen, 111:1

That wilt Thou, God, preserve pure, 2:6

That word shall still in strength abide, 80:8

That word they must allow to stand, 80:8

That wouldst Thou, God, untainted keep, 2:6

That's a fine idea, 212:10

That's far too clever, 212:15

That's far too fine for us, 212:15

That's much too clever, 212:15

Thee, dear Lord, I'll ever cherish, 248:33

Thee, dear Lord, with heed I'll cherish, 248:33

Thee have I ever and ever loved, 49:6b

Thee have I loved and loved for ever, 49:6b

Thee have I loved with love eternal, 49:6b

Thee I greet, Thy love I treasure, 410; 499; 768

Thee I shall not leave until Thou bless me, 157:1

Thee, Lord, I love with sacred awe, 340

Thee, Lord, is no one like, 110:3

Thee, Lord, our God, we praise, 16.1; 190:2

Thee, my Master, faithful serving, 248:33

Thee, Prince of Peace, Lord Jesu Christ, 67:7

Thee we adore, O hidden Savior, 519

Thee will I diligently preserve, 248:33

Thee with tender care I'll cherish, 248:33

Their bright appearance, 130:2

Their brilliant throng, 130:2

Their countenance is more obstinate, 102:1c

Their delight in love, 202:7

Their doctrines are false and vain, 2:2

Their faces are harder 'gainst Thee, 102:1c

Their faces are harder turned against Thee, 102:1c

Their glory bright, 130:2

Their grinning jaws are open wide, 178:5

Their radiance and lofty wisdom, 130:2

Their splendor bright, 130:2

Their tongues in specious words, 308

Then ah, what heavy calamity, 124:4

Then answered Peter and said, 244:22

Then, as is meet, we now will sing, 145:7

Then assembled the chief priests, 244:4

Then assembled the elders with the scribes, 244:4

Then assembled together all the chief priests, 244:4

Then assembled together the chief priest(s), 244:4

Then at evening of the same Sabbath, 42:2

Then be of good cheer, my soul, 13:6

Then began he to curse and to swear, 244:46b

Then bowed He His head, 245:59

Then bring forth Thyself thanks, 134:5

Then came Jesus with them, 244:24

Then came the day of unleavened bread, 246:8a

Then close beside thy Savior's blood-besprinkled, 80:6

Then come, and tie for them the knot, 195:4

Then come before His countenance, 117:9

Then come ye all into His courts, 117:9

Then cometh Jesus with them, 244:24

Then cried they out all the more, 244:59a

Then cry aloud, thou fallen town of God, 46:2

Then delivered he Him therefore, 245:47

Then delivered he Him unto them, 245:47

Then did he send forth Barabbas free, 244:59e

Then did Herod privily call the Wise Men, 248:55

Then did Jesus lift up His hands, 11:2

Then did they spit in His face, 244:43a

Then do not imagine to yourselves, 46:4

Then fittingly, you angels, rejoice, 248:22

Then go your ways as God shall guide you, 197:10

Then God obey and do His bidding, 197:4

Then hast Thou, Jesu, Thy countenance altogether, 57:8
Then he cast the silver pieces, 244:50
Then he released Barabbas to them, 244:59e
Then Herod called the Wise Men, 248:55
Then Herod, when he had privily called, 248:55
Then Jesus said unto the chief priests, 246:34
Then John, in joyful welcome springing, 121:4
Then John's own glad and joyful leaping, 121:4
Then led away they Jesus, 245:22
Then led they Jesus from Caiaphas, 245:22
Then let the world and all its pleasures, 186:9
Then let us go onward to Salem with singing, 182:8
Then let us keep the feast today, 4:8
Then let us put all fear behind us, 92:5
Then My heart shall keep its affection, 49:5b
Then, O my god, be mine to stay, 65:7
Then one of the twelve, called Judas, 244:11
Then one of the twelve disciples, 244:11
Then our mouth filled with laughter, 110:1
Then our sins go to sleep, 244:26b
Then pass forever now, all empty pleasure, 123:6
Then Pilate delivered Him, 245:47
Then Pilate said unto Him, 245:28
Then Pilate said unto them, 245:24
Then released he Barabbas unto them, 244:59e
Then said Pilate to the chief priests, 246:47
Then said Pilate unto them, 245:24
Then seize, O world, all my possessions, 8:5
Then shall this past'ral, 208:8
Then shall thy light break forth, 39:1b
Then so wilt Thou be at Thy right-hand place, 128:5
Then spat they on Him, 244:43a
Then stand beside the bloodstained flag of Christ, 80:6

Then straightway the soldiers of the governor, 244:62a
Then straightway thy light shall break forth, 39:1b
Then the band and the captain, 245:10
Then the disciples worshipp'd Him, 11:9
Then the Lord, when He in this wise, 43:4
Then the same day at evening, 42:2
Then the soldiers, 245:53
Then the soldiers of the governor, 244:62a
Then they began to spit, 244:43a
Then they spat on Him, 244:43a
Then toll for me soon, 95:4
Then unto them saith Pilate, 245:37
Then vanish, you mad fruitless cares, 8:4
Then went one among the twelve, 244:11
Then went one of the twelve, 244:11
Then were they exceeding grieved, 244:15b
Then when Pilate heard, 245:43
Then while I live this life of care, 153:9.1
Then yield, ye foolish, vain cares, 8:4
Then your heart shall live on for ever, 75:1b
There a voice of one is crying, 30:6
There and hither, yonder, thither, 96:5
There appear'd unto Him an angel, 246:26
There ariseth now a light, 195:1a
There arose a conflict, 19:1
There arose a fight, 19:1
There arose a great fight (strife), 19:1
There arose a strife, 19:1
There came unto Pilate Joseph, 245:66
There comes a day when secrets are disclosed, 136:3
There comes a day which judges, 136:3
There comes a day which the hidden, 136:3
There comes the Antichrist, 44:5
There comes the day to bring concealment, 136:3
There comes the heroes' hero, 43:6
There cometh, yea, the time, 44:2
There has the darkness on many sides, 6:4
There I remain; there I have delight, 158:3b
There is a blessed home, 516
There is a daring and a shy thing, 176:1

There is a defiant and despondent thing, 176:1

There is besides Thee no physician, 103:3

There is but one thing cannot fail, 92:2

There is naught destructible, 74:6

There is naught of soundness, 25:1

There is neither language nor nation (speaking), 76:1b

There is neither speech nor discourse (language), 76:1b

There is no condemnation, 74:6

There is no greater sadness (woe), 209:2

There is no language or speech, 76:1b

There is no more soundness in all my body, 25:1

There is no other physician to be found, 103:3

There is no wholeness in my body, 25:1

There is not a speech or a language, 76:1b

There is not a speech or language, 76:1b

There is nothing damnable, 74:6

There is nothing healthy in my body, 25:1

There is nothing late and early, 97:2

There is now nothing condemnable, 227:2

There is something obstinate yet weak, 176:1

There is then no punishment, 74:6

There is therefore now no condemnation, 227:2

There lives no child of man on Earth, 74:8

There now is no, there's no condemnation, 227:2

There ripens a dreadful ending, 90:1

There ripens fast for you destruction, 90:1

There ripens for you a dreadful end, 90:1

There seeks the Antichrist, 44:5

There shall be many saying to me, 45:4

There shall I bide where I long to dwell, 158:3b

There shall no doubt deter me, 108:2

There should to Christ be praises sung, 121:1

There stand before God's throne, 309

There uprose a fierce strife, 19:1

There uprose a great strife, 19:1

There wait all things on Thee, 187:1

There was a wondrous war, 4:5

There was also a strife, 246:18

There will be many who say to me, 45:4

There will be many who will say, 45:4

There will I remain; there it is my pleasure, 158:3b

There will the Highest prepare, 43:2

Therefore all things whatsoever, 24:3

Therefore always depart, you vanities, 123:6

Therefore be doubled, ye passionate flames, 63:6

Therefore be ye not anxious, 187:4

Therefore defiance to Hell's army, 139:6

Therefore defiance to the Hell's hosts, 139:6

Therefore do not be anxious, 187:4

Therefore go now away, ye vanities, 123:6

Therefore I cling to Him, 188:2b

Therefore I deliver myself unto Your hands, 229:4

Therefore I do not leave Him, 188:2b

Therefore I go with courageous step, 111:4

Therefore I myself to Him surrender, 107:6

Therefore I place myself in Thy hands, 229:4

Therefore I proceed with confidence, 111:4

Therefore I surrender myself to Him, 107:6

Therefore if death seizes the spirit, 111:5

Therefore let it not surprise Thee, Master, 176:4a

Therefore let us all be found, 115:6

Therefore let us ever be, 115:6

Therefore my breast, 113:4

Therefore, pleasant Wiederau, 30a:12

Therefore resist sin, 54:1

Therefore revive, fearful and timid spirit, 176:5

Therefore shall ye not sorrow, 187:4

Therefore so let us perpetually watch, 115:6

Therefore take no thought, 187:4

Therefore the Spirit for us intercedeth, 226:2

Therefore then shalt Thou me upon Thy right, 128:5

Therefore we also justly joyful are, 145:7

Therefore we justly praise and thank Thee, 130:6.1

Therefore, when death at the end, 111:5
Therefore, when the death at last, 111:5
Therefore will I, because I live still, 153:9.1
Therefore you ought not to worry, 187:4
There's a wideness in God's mercy, 439
There's naught can protect me, 74:7
There's no condemnation, 74:6
There's nothing can befall me, 97:3
Thereupon I place myself in Your hands, 229:4
Thereupon one of the lepers, 17:4
These are my last hours, 488
These are the holy Ten Commandments, 635; 678; 679
These are the holy Ten Commands, 298; 635; 678; 679
These are the sacred Ten Commandments, 298
These mercies we're adoring, 16:6
These mine eyes are looking e'er to the Lord, 150:6
These wait all upon Thee, 187:1
They all are waiting on Thee, 187:1
They all from Sheba shall come, 65:1
They all said, 244:54b
They all shall come from Saba, 65:1
They all shall come out of Saba, 65:1
They answered, 244:54b
They are: see They're
They beset us as if we were heretics, 178:4
They call us heretics, and lie in wait, 178:4
They did beat and scourge and smite, 247:110
They did not comprehend, 175:5
They did not understand what it is, 175:5
They have made their faces harder, 102:1c
They have sorely mocked You, 247:110
They, however, did not see, 175:5
They however worshipped Him, 11:9
They kindled then a fire, 246:36
They knew not the meaning of these words, 22:1b
They lie in wait for us as heretics, 178:4
They lie in wait like heretics, 178:4
They name us heretics in scorn, 178:4

They open their jaws wide, 178:5
They open wide their hungry jaws, 178:5
They open wide their ravenous jaws, 178:5
They ought to let the word stand, 80:8
They peep in each nest, 206:11
They said, 244:54b
They shall cling to the word of God, 80:8
They shall from out Sheba all be coming, 65:1
They shall put you out of the synagogues, 44:1
They shouted, 244:54b
They sing now of triumph with joy, 149:1
They stood there, all His acquaintance, 246:75
They teach a vain and false deceit, 2:2
They teach empty, false deceit, 2:2
They teach us vain and false deceit, 2:2
They teach vain, false cunning, 2:2
They were the more fierce, 246:49a
They who die are blessed, 60:4b
They who would brand me heretic, 178:4
They will all come out of Sheba, 65:1
They will from Sheba all come, 65:1
They will put you under the ban, 183:1
They're foolish who shall waste, 204:3
They're known to all, 164:2
The thieves also, which were crucified, 244:68
Thine accounting, Judgment Day, 168:1
Thine enemies shall all be scattered, 57:5
Thine for ever, mine for ever, 213:11
Thine immortal name and glory, 215:3
Thine is all the honor, 171:6
Thine is alone the glory, 41:6
Thine is alone the honor, 41:6; 171:6
Thine, Lord, be all the glory, 41:6; 171:6
Thine old age be like to thy childhood, 71:3
Thine otherwise bright beloved glow, 176:3
Things born of man's power, 178:2
The things of earth, 1:4
Things of Earth I value not, 64:7
Things of naught are Earth's vain treasures, 56:5; 301
Think about Jesus' bitter death, 101:6

Think, dear heart, on Jesus now, 482

Think, Lord, now on Thy ministry, 143:7b

Think, Lord, on us, Thy grace bestowing, 29:5

Think not amid the hour of trial, 93:5

Think not in all thy tribulation, 93:5

Think not in thy oppression-heat, 93:5

Think not when high thy sorrow swelleth, 93:5

Think not when hot affliction presses, 93:5

Think not when trial thee defieth, 93:5

Think not within thy trial by fire, 93:5

Think, O my spirit, 509

Think of us with Thy love, 29:5

Think you, world, my poor lot scorning, 123:5

The third day He rose again, 480

This a faithful saying is, 141:1

This day hath triumphed God's own Son, 630

This day is so joyful, 294

This day, O man, is one of bitter pain, 341

This day, O mortal, is a great day of sorrow, 341

This day on which your birth occurred, 36c:5

This day shalt thou be with Me, 106:3b

This day, so rich in joy and love, 294; 605; 719

This day surely thou'lt be with Me, 106:3b

This day that is so full of joy, 605; 719

This day to us a Child is born, 253; 414

This day will bring to Israel release, 63:4

This day with joy our hearts hath filled, 36c:8

This Earth below and Heav'n above, 178:7.2

This fellow said, God's temple can I raze, 244:39b

This fellow said, I am able to destroy the temple, 244:39b

This fellow said, I'm able to destroy God's temple, 244:39b

This glorious day is filled with joy, 294

This God has clearly shown, 7:3

This God hath told by word, 7:3

This, God, Thou wouldst preserve pure, 2:6

This great pain is truly too much to bear, 444

This happy day, right honored Hennicke, 30a:4

This has God clearly with word, 7:3

This has He all to us done, 91:6

This has He done for all of us, 248:28

This hath God shown, 7:3

This hath He all for us now done, 64:2

This He did for us all to show, 64:2

This is a day, 122:5

This is a day where all, 214:2

This is now the Gospel truth, 141:1

This is the ancient law, 106:2e

This is the Christian art, 185:5

This is the Christian goal, 185:5

This is the day, 122:5

This is the day when, 214:2

This is the Father's pleasure, 73:5

This is the Father's purpose, 73:5

This is the time of bitter suffering, 450

This is the true, the Paschal Lamb, 158:4

This is the voice of my beloved, 154:6

This is the voice of my Friend, 154:6

This is too citified, 212:15

This Jesus Christ, the same today, 246:72

This joyous light's upright admirers, 195:2

This life is not mine own, 168:2

This man calleth for Elias, 244:71c

This means that ye must too, 169:6

This my Jesus I'll not leave, 124:1; 154:8; 157:5

This my soul exalts the Lord now, 10:1

This my spirit waiteth for the Lord, 131:4a

This our new government, 71:7

This practice of the heart in love, 202:7

This proud heart within us swelling, 248:53

This rebirth of the heart in love, 202:7

This sign do I give you, 248:16

This then, the law of the Spirit of life, 227:4

This thought to thee, 34a:6

This very same Lord Jesus Christ, 246:72

This well I know, 95:5

This will my Savior do, 72:4
This will put you under the ban, 44:1
This world, a house of sin, 170:2
This world I hold for naught, 64:4
This wretch I am, this wretched sinner, 179:6
Thou all I do protecting, 194:12
Thou are* alone, Lord Jesus Christ, 33:1
Thou art a Spirit who teaches, 183:5
Thou art alone, Lord Jesus Christ, 33:1
Thou art alone the truth, 229:3
Thou art alone the way, 229:3
Thou art born for me as good, 68:4
Thou art born for my good, 68:4
Thou art born man to my advantage, 68:4
Thou art gone up on high, 466
Thou art indeed beloved of my soul, 165:4
Thou art my God, of ev'ry gift the giver, 163:2
Thou art my God, the giver, 163:2
Thou art, my God, the source, 163:2
Thou art my helper, 73:1c
Thou art, O God, of all good things, 163:2
Thou art, O God, the life and light, 377
Thou art the King of Glory, 246:44
Thou art the right way, 229:3
Thou art the way of life, 229:3
Thou art the way, the truth, 229:3
Thou art Thyself, O Jesu dear, 77:6
Thou blessed Savior, Thou, 244:9
Thou bliss of earliest innocence, 198a:3b
Thou by whom all love is kindled, 491
Thou canst, O Death, no further now affright me, 114:5
Thou canst restore me soon, 103:4
Thou Child, art mine and I am Thine, 197a:2
Thou child of God consider, 80:3
Thou countenance so noble, 244:63.2
Thou, dear God's Son, now Thou, 151:4
Thou dear Redeemer, Thou (when), 244:9
Thou dear Savior, Thou, 244:9
Thou, dear Son of God, hast, 151:4
Thou dearest Savior, answer give me, 245:60a

Thou didst us, Lord, from ev'ry pathway, 76:6
Thou dost assure, O God, 153:4
Thou dost in glory stand, 119:4
Thou face of God's annointed, 244:63.2
Thou false one, seek but to destroy the Lord, 248:56
Thou false one, seeking but to fell the Lord, 248:56
Thou fervor divine, comfort sweet, 226:4
Thou gav'st me blood, 246:15
Thou give* me blood, 246:15
Thou giv'st me blood, 246:15
Thou God in truth and very God, 1:2
Thou God of might, 35:6
Thou God the Father, God the Son, 290
Thou goest now, my Savior, forth, 500
Thou great man of sorrow, 300
Thou guide of Israel, hear me, 104:1
Thou guide of Israel, hearken, 104:1
Thou hallowed, chosen morn, 377
Thou hast been born for my well-being, 68:4
Thou hast been shewn, O man, what is good, 45:1
Thou hast My heart, 49:5b
Thou hast, O God, from every byway, 76:6
Thou hast smitten, 102:1b
Thou hast stricken them, 102:1b
Thou hast unto Thy word Thy pow'r, 18:3b
Thou hast us, O Lord, from all ways, 76:6
Thou heart of compassion, eternal devotion, 185:1
Thou hidden love of God, 321; 416
Thou hidden source of calm repose, 416
Thou holiest light, comfort sweet, 226:4
Thou holy fervor, comfort sweet, 226:4
Thou holy fire, sweet consolation, 226:4
Thou, Jesus, art my all in all, 75:3
Thou, Jesus, who art far above, 77:6
Thou king of all honor, 246:44
Thou knowest right well, man, what good is, 45:1
Thou life's prince, Lord Jesus Christ, 43:11.1

Thou, Lord, alone dost crown, 187:3

Thou, Lord, Thou alone crownest the year, 187:3

Thou, Lord, Thou alone dost crown the year, 187:3

Thou, Lord, Thou crownest alone the year, 187:3

Thou Lord, Thou dost alone the year crown, 187:3

Thou, Lord, will crown the year, 187:3

Thou love so sweet, give us now thy grace, 197:5

Thou love so tender, give to us thy grace, 169:7

Thou makest me, O Death, now not further anxious, 114:5

Thou man, bethink thee of thy soul, 114:6

Thou man of mighty woe, 300

Thou man of sorrows, hail, 300

Thou man whom God created cannot know, 121:2

Thou most blessed, all-quickening day, 70:10a

Thou must believe; thou must hope, 155:2

Thou must trust now; thou must hope, 155:2

Thou my treasure, soul's true pleasure, 497

Thou name of Jesus, 171:3

Thou, O beautiful structure, 56:5

Thou, O death, makest me no longer anxious, 114:5

Thou, O fair universe, 56:5; 301

Thou, O God, hast surely promised, 13:3

Thou, O Lord, crownest the year, 187:3

Thou of angel hosts the leader, 130:5

Thou of cherubim the master, 130:5

Thou of Hapsburg, high descendant, 206:7

Thou only art Lord, 236:5

Thou precious love, shed o'er us thy grace, 197:5

Thou precious love, shed over us, 169:7

Thou precious Son of God, 151:4

Thou preparest a table for me, 112:4

Thou preparest before me a table, 112:4

Thou preparest for me a table, 112:4

Thou preparest me a table, Lord, 112:4

Thou prince of life, Lord Jesus Christ, 11:6; 43:11.1

Thou Prince of Peace, Lord Jesus Christ, 67:7; 116:1; 143:2

Thou Prince of Peace, to Thee we bow, 67:7; 116:1; 143:2

Thou prophet, Thou Christ, 244:43b

Thou sacred ardor, comfort sweet, 226:4

Thou saucy knave, 201:2

Thou serpent, thou but seek our Lord, 248:56

Thou shalt be with Me today, 106:3b

Thou shalt God, thy Lord, love, 77:1

Thou shalt love God thy maker, 77:1

Thou shalt, O Death, make me no longer anxious, 114:5

Thou shalt thy God and Master cherish, 77:1

Thou shepherd bountiful, hear us, 104:1

Thou shepherd of Israel, hear us, 104:1

Thou sinner, patient bear the load, 114:3

Thou smitest them, 102:1b

Thou son of man, whom God did once create, 121:2

Thou speakest, dearest God, 153:4

Thou speakest even, dear God, 153:4

Thou spirit divine, 671; 674

Thou strikest them, 102:1b

Thou sweet Jesus-name, 171:3

Thou sweet love, bestow thy favor on us, 197:5

Thou sweet love, favor us, 169:7; 197:5

Thou sweet love, give us thy favor, 197:5

Thou sweet love, give us thy grace, 169:7

Thou sweet love, grant us thy grace, 169:7

Thou sweet love, pour over us thy grace, 169:7

Thou sweet name, 171:3

Thou sweetest love, grace on us bestow, 197:5

Thou sweetest love, pray we heartily, 197:5

Thou sweetest name of Jesus, 171:3

Thou that art equal to the Father, 36:6

Thou that destroyest the temple and buildest, 244:67b
Thou that destroyest the temple of God, 244:67b
Thou that life and death ordainest, 8:6
Thou that sittest at the right hand, 232:9
Thou that takest away the sins, 232:8
Thou the Father of us all, 36:6
Thou to whom the sick and dying, 248:53
Thou traitor, thou but seek'st the Lord, 248:56
Thou traitor, who dost seek the Lord to kill, 248:56
Thou true God and David's son, 23:1
Thou true Son of God and Mary, 1:2
Thou true Son of the Lord and Mary, 1:2
Thou very God and David's son, 23:1
Thou very God, the Three-in-One, 293
Thou very Son of God and Mary, 1:2
Thou very Son of God and Virgin, 1:2
Thou wert born for my sake, 68:4
Thou who, a God, as man yet came, 127:1
Thou who, a God, as man yet come, 336
Thou who always help me so, 186:3
Thou who art like Thy Father, 36:6
Thou who art seated at the right hand, 232:9
Thou who art the Father like, 36:6
Thou who art three in unity, 293
Thou who destroy the temple of God, 244:67b
Thou who is* like your* Father, 36:6
Thou who sittest at the right hand, 232:9
Thou who takest away the sins, 232:8
Thou whose praises never end, 6:2
Thou wilt assuage my woe, 103:4
Thou wilt fill my heart's desire, 108:5
Thou wilt give Thy spirit and strength, 18:3b
Thou wilt me after the anguish, 103:4
Thou wilt not let my sin condemn me, 78:6
Thou wouldst not give to the enemy, 71:6
Though a lover fumes and threshes, 208:4
Though all men should forsake Thee, 244:23
Though all the fiends are striving, 153:5
Though body, spirit may decay, 3:4

Though both my flesh and soul may languish, 3:4
Though fiends appear on every hand, 80:5
Though from Thee temptation lured me, 55:5; 244:48
Though God appear at times severe, 186:6
Though God at times may chasten, 155:5
Though God our King from Heaven, His place, 20:7
Though God our King from Heaven's high place, 20:7
Though great my sins and sore my woes, 38:6
Though great our sins and sore our woes, 38:6
Though He may seem His love concealing, 188:2b
Though Heaven above we fain would merit, 70:4
Though Heaven above we would inherit, 70:4
Though Heaven and Earth be destroyed for ever, 127:4c
Though Heaven and Earth into atoms shall vanish, 127:4c
Though Heaven and Earth pass and utterly perish, 127:4c
Though Heaven and Earth perish in the fire, 127:4c
Though here be hellish woe and pain, 3:3
Though hushed and muted voices utter, 36c:7
Though I am but dust and earth, 61:5b
Though I be but a puny thing of earth, 5:6
Though I be but a sinner, 135:1; 742; A47
Though I be but dust and ashes, 61:5b
Though I be but dust and earth, 61:5b
Though I be gone a little time, 103:6
Though I be late retiring, 97:6
Though I essay the road of death, 92:9
Though I feel fear of Hell and pain, 3:3
Though I feel Hell's anguish and pain, 3:3
Though I lapsed, and straying wander, 244:48

Though I may have seceded from Thee, 55:5

Though I must my life's full course, 153:8

Though I now from Thee have fallen, 55:5

Though I soon be earth and ashes, 61:5b

Though I suffer all life long, 153:8

Though I suffer, I will be silent, 87:6

Though I turned away from Thee, 244:48

Though in myself my soul's chief foeman, 139:5

Though it appeared as He would not, 155:5

Though it appeared as if He would not, 9:7; 186:6

Though it may appear that He is not willing, 9:7

Though it should seem He were opposed, 9:7; 155:5; 186:6

Though luxury may well entice, 213:8

Though many false witnesses came, 244:39a

Though must I live all my days, 153:8

Though my feet from Thee have wander'd, 244:48

Though my heart is drowned in tears, 244:18

Though my life be only sadness, 150:7

Though our sins, 87:4

Though prayers be denied to you, 9:7; 155:5

Though prayers should be denied to you, 9:7

Though reviling tongues assail us, 70:5

Though sin brings pain, 40:3

Though sorrow round me presseth, 3:5

Though soul and body faint, despite me, 3:4

Though suffering smart thee, 186:10

Though the evils of the world, 466

Though the mocking tongues revile us, 70:5

Though the world cannot refrain, 58:4

Though Thou wert captive, Lord divine, 245:40

Though to dust my body turneth, 61:5b

Though toilsome the journey, 'twill soon now be, 57:7

Though volatile inconstancy, 30a:8

Though war and conquest, triumphant and glorious, 215:7

Though weak is man, 5:6

Though wicked men, 248:62

Though with unworthy feeble voices, 36:7

Though with us many sins abound, 38:6

Though worms destroy my body, 161:6

Though worms our flesh devour(ing), 161:6

Thoughtlessly fickle persons, 181:1

Thoughts, fearful and haunting, 105:3

Thou'lt ne'er forget, Lord Jesus, 116:3

Thou'rt blest; God mighty things hath done, 134:3

Thousand fears and troubles lowering, 143:4

A thousand ten thousand ride after his chariot, 43:3

A thousand times I think of Thee, 246:66

Thousandfold misfortune, fright, 143:4

Thousandfold misfortune, horror, trouble, 143:4

Thousandfold misfortune, terror, 143:4

Thousandfold on other nations cometh fear, 143:4

A thousandfold renew the ardor, 63:6

Thousandfold than present blessings, 36b:8

Three kings came from Sheba, 65:2

Three kings from the East, 65:2

Thrice-holy name, that sweeter sounds, 443

Thron'd upon the awful tree, 384

Through Adam came our fall, 637; 705

Through Adam's fall debased, 637

Through Adam's fall mankind fell too, 637

Through Adam's fall the soul of man, 637

Through Adam's fall we all were lost, 637; 705

Through bitter tribulation we enter into God's, 146:2

Through Christ our Savior, Amen, 106:4b

Through Christ the Savior, Amen, 106:4b

Through fire silver becomes pure, 2:5

Through fire the silver pure becomes, 2:5

Through Jesus Christ, Amen, 106:4b

Through Jesus Christ, Lord, Amen, 106:4b

Through Jesus Christ our Lord, Amen, 106:4b

Through mighty power, 71:5

Through our Lord Jesus, Amen, 106:4b

Through paths of tribulation must mortals, 12:3

Through power and might, 71:5

Through the blind and zealous use of weapons, 215:7

Through the fire silver becomes pure, 2:5

Through Thee, our guiding light supernal, 198a:7a

Through Thee, the Lord of all creation, 198a:7a

Through Thee, Thou type all types transcending, 198a:7a

Through Thine agony and blood, 246:27

Through this new government, 71:7

Through Thy imprisonment, O Son of God, 245:40

Through Thy Passion, blood, and sweat, 246:27

Through waves and clouds and storms, 153:5

Through weapons inflamed by zeal, 215:7

Throughout my life, O Lord, I pray, 27:2

Throughout the whole Earth's broad expanse, 125:4

Throughout the world, 36b:6

Throw, my heart, do throw thyself, 155:4

Throw, my heart, throw thyself, 155:4

Throw to the ground swollen proud ones, 126:4

Thus all things bear witness of God, 76:2

Thus at last I wish to die in peace, 502

Thus dost Thou die for me, 500

Thus even Cupid seeks, 202:4

Thus faithful to His purpose, 197:7

Thus God His witnesses provideth, 76:2

Thus goest Thou now, my Jesus, thither, 500

Thus has God loved the world, 68:1

Thus hath our God fulfilled the oath, 30:7

Thus He spake to our fathers, 243:11

Thus I go to Jesus Christ, 31:9

Thus I'm to Him devoted, 107:6

Thus in zeal the avenging judge extinguishes, 90:3

Thus is the bond of innocent love, 202:8

Thus Lord, will I endeavor, 246:33

Thus my heart lays aside anger, 89:4

Thus my mouth full of the Queen may fill, 214:8

Thus, my Savior, Thou dost intend, 30:7

Thus ought Christianity the love of God, 76:13

Thus ought the whole wide world, 17:2

Thus saith the Lord: I shall take delight in doing, 28:3

Thus saith the Lord: I will rejoice over them, 28:3

Thus saith the Lord: In them will I be joyful, 28:3

Thus saith the Lord: It evermore shall please me, 28:3

Thus saith the Lord: It shall to me bring pleasure, 28:3

Thus speaks the Lord: It shall be a joy, 28:3

Thus speaks the soul resigned to God, 92:7b

Thus speaks the soul which trusts in God, 92:7b

Thus the light of this charming day, 173a:6

Thus, then, my own heart, 45:6

Thus then, the law of the Spirit of life, 227:4

Thus Thou takest leave of Earth, 501

Thus we are also rightly glad, 145:7

Thus we celebrate the high feast, 4:7

Thus, when your sorrow doth your heart, 186:4b

Thus will I, while I yet have life, 153:9.1

Thus will the heart and mouth, 45:6

Thus will Thy word and truth, 126:5

Thy beauty long desired, 244:63.2

Thy blessings, Lord, accrue, 10:3

Thy blood, elixir pure, contains a potion, 136:6

Thy blood hath so washed away my guilt, 78:4

Thy blood that hath cleansed my guilt, 78:4

Thy blood, that liquid rich, 136:6

Thy blood, the honored essence, 136:6

Thy blood which cancels my guilt, 78:4

Thy blood, which doth my guilt redeem, 78:4

Thy blood, which erases my guilt, 78:4

Thy blood, which my ill-doing spent, 78:4

Thy blood's most precious flow, 136:6

Thy body, manna of my soul, 246:13

Thy bonds, O Christ, have set us free, 245:40

Thy bonds, O God's Almighty Son, 245:40

Thy bonds, O Son of God most high, 245:40

Thy bounty, good and true, 10:3

Thy bounty, Lord, deny me not, 156:2b; 247:44; 377

Thy brightness all the dark consumes, 248:46

Thy brightness does consume all darkness, 248:46

Thy brightness hath devoured all darkness, 248:46

Thy compassion, Thy salvation, 189:5

Thy cross is the kingly throne, 246:64

Thy cross is the royal throne, 246:64

Thy dear light, before so bright, 176:3

Thy dwelling is prepared, 74:3

Thy flesh, that manna of my soul, 246:13

Thy fold, O God, shall bring to Thee, 69:6

Thy folk, Lord Jesus Christ, advance, 119:9

Thy glory drives all gloom away, 248:46

Thy God will not abandon thee, 138:3a

Thy Godly might and majesty, 246:46

Thy goodness overflowing, 17:5

Thy goodness, Thy mercy, 189:5

Thy goodness, Thy pity, 189:5

Thy grief restrain, I pray, 216:4

Thy grieving children, 199:6

Thy healing word restores, 113:4

Thy joyful spirit give me strength, 113:8; 168:6

Thy love is mine, 140:6

Thy mansion is prepared, 74:3

Thy might and glory hallowed, 246:46

Thy mighty pow'r, Lord Jesu(s), show, 6:6

Thy name extends beyond the sun, 173a:7

Thy name I live to praise and honor, 248:41

Thy name, O God, we magnify, 76:14

Thy name, O Lord, we magnify, 69:6; 76:14

Thy otherwise bright beloved gleam, 176:3

Thy people are distressed, 2:4

Thy people help, Lord Jesus Christ, 119:9

Thy people, Lord, give praise to Thee, 76:14

Thy plaint is heard above, 57:4

Thy power and great might, 71:5

Thy power and might, 71:5

Thy prophets, Lord, in ages past, 30:9

Thy rock and shield I'll be, 30a:7

Thy sacrifice has cleansed the stain, 78:4

Thy sacrifice is my reliance, 199:7

Thy Saxons, 198:2

Thy Saxony, 198:2

Thy spirit ever shall direct me, 108:3

Thy spirit God from Heaven sends, 108:6

Thy spirit is a teacher, 183:5

Thy spirit, Lord, from Heaven sent, 108:6

Thy spirit, sent from God above, 108:6

Thy spirit, sent from Heav'n above, 108:6

Thy spirit, which God from Heaven gives, 108:6

Thy spirit will in such wise rule me, 108:3

Thy spirit will me so govern, 108:3

Thy spirit will thus guide me, 108:3

Thy splendor drives the night away, 248:46

Thy storm of wrath was long in coming, 46:3

Thy tempest gathered from great distance, 46:3

Thy tempest gathered in the distance, 46:3

Thy truth Thou wilt preserve, O Lord, 2:6

Thy voice is heard by ev'ry nation, 76:6

Thy ways are dark, a closed and sealed book, 73:1d

Thy will be done, Father, Son and Holy Ghost, 291

Thy will be done, Lord God, 245:9

Thy will be done, O God, 245:9

Thy will be done, O Lord, 245:9

Thy will be done on Earth, O Lord, 90:5; 245:9

Thy will be done the same, Lord God, 245:9

Thy will for evermore be done, 290

Thy will, in truth, is like a book, 73:1d

Thy will must all creation, 245:9
Thy will, O Lord, be done, 245:9
Thy will, O Lord, is as a sealed book, 73:1d
Thy will, O Lord, our God, 245:9
Thy word and blessed blood, 165:6
Thy word, communion, sacrament, 165:6
Thyself be true, O spirit, 13:6; 44:7
'Til: *see also* Until
'Til now ye have asked for nothing in My
    name, 87:1
Till He comes, oh let the words, 384
Till now have ye naught been asking, 87:1
Till then be mindful of thy spirit, 114:6
The time of bitter suffering begins again,
    450
The time of bitter suffering has returned,
    450
Time, that makes days and years, 134a:1
A time to watch, a time to pray, 290
'Tis: *see also* It is
'Tis by acts of love and mercy, 164:3
'Tis clear; God in His Heaven, 215:6
'Tis dancing and singing that gladdens our
    heart, 201:7
'Tis dancing and singing that quickens our
    hearts, 201:7
'Tis dancing and sporting that rouseth the
    heart, 201:7
'Tis deeds of love and mercy, 186:5
'Tis done; the covenant is made, 195:4
'Tis faith lends wings; the soul arises, 37:5
'Tis finished, all, 159:4
'Tis finished now, 245:58
'Tis finished; the strife, 159:4
'Tis for your good that I now leave you,
    108:1
'Tis God who possesseth my heart's deep
    affection, 174:2
'Tis God's rare love His children showing,
    36b:3
'Tis gone, that bright and orbed blaze, 290
'Tis good, Lord, to be here, 878
'Tis hard indeed, 204:5
'Tis He and He alone, 43:7

'Tis He, who all alone, 43:7
'Tis I, my sins betray Thee, 244:16
'Tis I should show contrition, 244:16
'Tis I, 'tis I should languish, 246:48
'Tis I who should, repenting, 244:16
'Tis I whose sin now binds Thee, 244:16
'Tis indeed the Gospel truth, 141:1
'Tis Jesu's love and nothing else, 38:2
'Tis now the hour our prayer to pour, 396
'Tis poverty, yet beyond all wealth, 75:13
'Tis right angels thus should sing, 248:22
'Tis right that angels thus should sing, 248:22
'Tis right to hear the angels' singing, 248:22
'Tis so, thy foemen I will vanquish, 57:5
'Tis sure that awful time will come, 307
'Tis Thee I would be praising, 248:41
'Tis thee we hymn, 36c:4
'Tis Thou, O Holy Spirit, that teachest,
    183:5
'Tis Thou, O Lord, hast said, 171:5
'Tis Thou, O Spirit, teachest, 183:5
'Tis tossing of the airy breezes, 92:6
'Tis well; from out my heart all wrath, 89:4
'Tis well; God ever thinks of thee, 134:3
'Tis well; no more lament, 133:6
'Tis well; now care will cease, 138:6
'Tis well that I reflect, 17:6
'Tis well; the all deserved, 36b:2
'Tis well, the fears of death impart, 133:5
'Tis well, the smart and sting of death, 133:5
'Tis well; Thy name, O Lord, 248:40a
'Tis well! Unto my festival, 205:14
'Tis well with him who on his God, 139:1;
    139:6
'Tis well with him who on the Lord, 139:1
'Tis well with me, for by Thy might, 345;
    464
'Tis well, ye angels; joyful sing, 248:22
'Tis well; your nuptial vows are made, 195:4
To all men Jesus good hath done, 244:57
To all whom it concerns, 212:22
To be a Christian, great the cost, 459
To be at peace and satisfied, 204:2
To be in truth as one appears, 179:4

To be loving one to another, 202:7
To be quiet and content in oneself, 204:2
To be sure, I notice about this world, 169:2b
To be sure, the stains of sin, 136:5
To Christ be now our homage paid, 121:1
To Christ must we give praise and sing, 611
To Christ our peace is owing, 28:6
To Christ we should sing praises now, 121:1
To Christian souls it ever is distressing, 75:9
To die is held in dread by ev'ry mortal, 60:4a
To do good and have compassion, 39:4
To do good and share, 39:4
To do well and to share, 39:4
To dwell there my spirit deep panteth, 158:3b
To each but what's due him, 163:1
To each his own tender, 163:1
To each only his due, 163:1
To earthly treasures the heart to attach, 26:4
To false witness my Savior will not answer, 244:40
To Father, Son, eternally, 106:4a
To feign righteousness, 246:31
To fritter away fifty dollars, 212:12
To give to Thee my heart I strive, 163:4
To God a joyful anthem raise, 117:1
To God Almighty be praises and thanks, 137:1
To God alone be highest praise, 711; 715; 716; 717
To God be praise and thanks, 14:5
To God be praise that my Redeemer lives, 160:3
To God be praise that we escape, 14:5
To God be praise; we know the right way, 79:4
To God commit thy griefs, 244:53
To God give thanks and praise, 79:3
To God I give my heart and soul, 92:1
To God let all the human race, 326; A31
To God, my soul, resign thee, 13:6; 44:7; 97:9

To God on high all glory be, 662; 663; 663a; 664; 664a; 675; 676; 676a; 677; 711; 715; 716; 717; 771; A48
To God on high alone be honor, 662; 663; 663a; 664; 664a
To God on high alone be praise, 260; 662; 663; 663a; 664; 664a; 675; 676; 676a; 677; 711; 715; 716; 717; 771; A48
To God on high be thanks and praise, 260
To God praise and thanks, 14:5
To God the anthem raising, 613
To God thy way commending, 270; 271; 272
To God we render thanks and praise, 602; 704
To God's all-gracious heart and mind, 92:1
To God's all-gracious providence, 65:7; 92:1; 92:9
To hands which are ever open, 164:5
To hang the heart on earthly treasures, 26:4
To heathen folk He hath brought light, 83:5
To Him be all the glory, 117:2b
To Him I am committed, 97:8
To him my laurel crown is owing, 207:6
To Him, my spirit, yield thee, 13:6
To Him who sits at God's right hand, 151:5
To his creator yet on Earth, 39:3
To honor Thee, I dare, all defying, 246:19
To honor Thee I will take any risk, 246:19
To human eye this seems to be, 7:7
To Jesus will I cling, 133:6
To Jordan came our Lord the Christ, 7:1; 684; 685
To Jordan stream came Christ our Lord, 684; 685
To Jordan when our Lord had gone, 280; 684; 685
To Jordan's stream came Christ our Lord, 7:1; 280; 684; 685
To know our God, we mortals, 141:3
To living waters bright and clear, 112:2
To man God nothing oweth, 84:2
To me thy heart awarding, 518
To me to live is Jesus, 95:1a

To me ungrateful, aye, shunned and hateful, 30:8

To me what wealth of favor, 17:5

To mercy, pity, peace and love, 151:5; 375; 376

To mortal eye this seems to be, 7:7

To my beloved God, 744

To my Jesus do I cling, 124:1

To my Shepherd I am true, 92:8

To my Shepherd I remain faithful, 92:8

To my Shepherd I'll be true, 92:8

To our trembling supplication, 372

To practice love, to hearten oneself, 202:7

To practice loving, to enhearten oneself, 202:7

To protect those who hated Him, 246:60

To punish enemies through the blind and zealous, 215:7

To pure water He directs me, 112:2

To rejoice in Jesu's life, 66:4a

To release me from the prison, 245:11

To righteous souls this light upspringing, 195:2

To ruin you an end of terror, 90:1

To Satan never will I yield, 160:4

To save us from eternal shame, 246:42

To shepherds, as they watched by night, 607

To show outward goodness, 246:31

To strife and struggle am I prone, 177:5

To the Father equal, 36:6

To the Father praises, 292

To the hand of vilest sinners, 246:56

To the hands which themselves, 164:5

To the heavens your voices raise, 63:5

To the inn away where bagpipes play, 212:24

To the inn where bagpipes play, 212:24

To the man his burden beareth, 99:5

To the pure water He directs me, 112:2

To the right side, to the left side, 96:5

To Thee all creatures sound their praise, 117:2b

To Thee all my heart is given, 244:19

To Thee alone be glory, 41:6; 171:6

To Thee alone we cling, 133:6

To Thee alone we cling, for Thee all else, 197a:4

To thee be true, O spirit, 97:9

To Thee give thanks the heav'nly host, 117:2a

To thee He hath shown, man, the right way, 45:1

To Thee I cry, Lord Jesus Christ, 639

To Thee I now stretch out mine arms, 31:9

To Thee I send my cry, Lord Jesus, 177:1

To thee I stretch My hand, 57:4

To Thee, Jehovah, come I singing, 299; 452

To Thee, Jehovah, shall I sing, 452

To Thee, Jehovah, to Thee will I sing, 452

To Thee, Jehovah, will I sing, Jehovah, 452

To Thee, Lord Jesus, thanks we give, 623

To Thee, Lord, lift I my soul, 150:2

To Thee, my God, confession frank, 132:4

To Thee, O Father, my spirit I commend, 106:3a

To Thee, O Lord, in loving kindness, 76:6

To Thee, O Lord, our hearts we raise, 248:12

To Thee, O Lord, will I sing praises, 299

To Thee our humble praise we sing, 130:6.1

To Thee, the Lord of Lords, with joy, 129:5

To Thee, the Lord our God, we now pray, 385

To Thee, Thee, Jehovah, I will sing, 299; 452

To thee, thou world of evil, 95:2b; 415; 735; 735a; 736

To Thee, to Thee, Jehovah, will I sing, 299

To Thee we trust; to Thee we sigh, 101:3

To their flocks the shepherds then returned, 248:34

To them in God confiding, 247:120; 369

To this end appeared the Son of God, 40:1

To this end has appeared the Son of God, 40:1

To this my pray'r, O God, give heed, 449

To thy rest now return thee, my spirit, 21:9

To train oneself in loving, 202:7

To truly be a Christian costs a lot, 459

To unbind me from the shackles, 245:11

To us a Child is born, 65:2; 142:2

To us a Child is given, 142:2
To us He hath done all things well, 244:57
To us is come the Savior, 61:2
To us salvation now is come, 9:1; 9:7
To us upon this happy morn, 414
To vain and empty show the world doth give, 94:3a
To water pure He leadeth me, 112:2
To what purpose is that waste, 244:7
To what purpose is this waste, 244:7
To where far Vist'la marges laves, 198:9b
To whom we now the holy let resound, 129:5
To whom we the holy now with joy, 129:5
To witness false my Savior answereth not, 244:40
To You alone belongs all the honor, 41:6
To you has come, 34a:6
To you it has been revealed, O man, 45:1
To You, Jehovah, I shall sing, 299
To You, Jehovah, I will sing, 452
Today alive and in your prime, 102:7
Today all thought of care we bury, 207a:5
Today are the heavens with grace overflowing, 134a:2
Today, dear Father, find me, 211:8
Today God's only-gotten Son, 342; 630
Today God's Son hath triumphed, 630
Today God's Son triumphs, 342
Today He once again opens wide, 151:5
Today He opens new the door, 151:5
Today He opens us the door, 151:5
Today He reopens the door, 151:5
Today He unlocks again the door, 151:5
Today livest thou; today mend thy ways, 102:7
Today shalt thou be with Me, 106:3b
Today the fear and dread, 63:4
Today the Highest His own triumph, 43:2
Today the Lord in triumph reigns, 342
Today then, dear Father, do it, 211:8
Today thou liv'st; repent today, 102:7
Today thou liv'st; today repent, 102:7
Today triumphed God's Son, 630

Today triumphs God's Son, 630
Today triumphs the Son of God, 630
Today's Christianity, alas, 179:2
Together we must ever strive, 176:6
Together with the Holy Ghost, 233:6; 234:6; 235:6; 236:6
The tolling of the trembling bells, 198:4
The tomb is void, 66:2
The torments, nail-scars, 78:5
Touch, Highest, our spirit, 173:6
Touch our senses, Lord most high, 173:6
Toward Thee, my Savior, am I gazing, 125:2
A tower of safety is our God, 80:1
A tower of strength is our God's name, 80:1
Transform us by Thy kindness, 22:5; 96:6; 132:6; 164:6
Transformed be now today, 63:4
The transient honors of the world, 47:5
The treacherous wiles of sin, 54:2
Treacherous world, I trust thee not, 52:2
Tread thou the path of faith, 152:2
The treasure of the wide world, 204:4
The treasures in this wide world, 204:4
Tremble, fear and terror, 15:3
Tremble not, O little flock, 42:4
Tremble ye hardened sinners, 70:2
Trembling and dithering the thoughts, 105:3
Triumph, all ye joyous voices, 120:2
The triumph is completed, 248:64
Triumph, triumph now is mine, 56:3
Triumphs today the Son of God, 342; 630
Troth and truth should be the base, 24:5
Trouble, anguish, sorrow, care, 21:3
Trouble thyself not, O soul, 186:1
Trouble, toil and tribulation, 123:3
Troubled heart, be of good cheer, 247:41
A truce to repining, to mourning, 66:1b
A truce to thy bluster, 15:6
True believers and baptized surely shall be saved, 37:1
True faith to me vouchsafe, Lord, 37:6
True, such a chamber in the heart, 248:53
True will serve you, 30a:7
Truly, I regard the mundane world, 169:2b

Truly love, ye Christians, 76:12
Truly, this was the Son of God, 244:73b
Truly, thou also art one of them, 244:46a
Truly, truly, I say to you, 86:1
Truly, truly, I say unto you, 86:1
Truly, when that occurs to me, 113:3
Truly, when to me that appears, 113:3
The truly worthy man, 204:7
Trumpets uplift ye! Loud drumrolls, now thunder, 214:1
Trust all to God, the Father, 244:16
Trust in the Lord, 174:4
Trust the Lord; come thou to Him with open heart, 179:1
Truth and honor e'er must be, 24:5
Truth and justice must direct, 24:5
Tune all your strings of lute and harp, 36:4
The turf shall be my fragrant shrine, 387
Turn again to thy rest, O my soul, 21:9
Turn not ye back, ye who would follow, 207:4
Turn O Lord, Thine ear to hear me, 372
Turn, Princess, turn a backward glance, 198:1
Turn your ardent thoughts to Heaven, 110:2
'Twas: see also It was
'Twas Christ our Lord after his Passion, 7:5
'Twas from the first decreed, 106:2e
'Twas in the cool of eventide, 244:74
'Twas surely his faint heart, 176:2
The twelve holy disciples, 246:21
Twigs and boughs, 205:13
Twigs and branches, 205:13
'Twill come to pass that on that day, 45:4
The two thieves, also which with Him, 244:68

U

Undaunted stand and bold, and trust, 70:8
Under Thy protection am I, 81:7
Under Thy protection from the foe's, 227:3
Under Thy protection from the foe's subjection, 81:7

Under Thy shelters am I from the storms, 81:7
Under your protection, I am, 227:3
An undisguised intention, 24:1
Unending mighty God, 194:2
Unfathomable is the way, 188:3
Unfathomed lies God's fount, 125:5
Unfold the gates of Heaven, O Lord, 617
An unforgiving word of judgment, 89:3
Unfortunately today's Christianity, 179:2
Unhappy man, 111:3
United discord of the varying strings, 207:2
Unless we sow our seed aright, 181:4
Unless you renounce this habit, 211:5
An unpitying judgment will on thee surely fall, 89:3
An unstained mind, 24:1
Until: see also 'Til
Until now you have prayed for nothing, 87:1
Unto sin oppose resistance, 54:1
Unto the world this happy morn, 122:1
Unto Thee, Lord, is no man equal, 110:3
Unto Thee, O God, do we give thanks, 29:2
Unto us a Child is born, 142:2
Up, arouse thee; give thy heart, 155:4
Up, awake from highest steeple, 140:7
Up, believers; sing the glad songs, 134:2
Up, faithful ones, 134:2
Up, follow where I lead, 213:4
Up, joyous raise your song, 36:1
Up my heart, and give thyself, 155:4
Up, my heart, the day of the Lord, 145:1
Up, my heart; the Lord's day, 145:1
Up, my heart, this glorious day, 145:1; 198a:10b
Up, my soul, arise, 69:3
Up, my soul, gird thee with power, 115:1
Up, my soul, sleep not in sin, 244:75
Up, my soul, the Lord's own day, 198a:10b
Up, my soul; 'tis Christ's great day, 145:1
Up, my soul; 'tis God's great day, 145:1
Up, resounding tones, 207a:1
Up to Heaven will I fly, 146:3
Up to the very stars, 36c:1

Up, up, my heart, and thou my entire being, 268

Up, up, my heart, and thou my mortal mind, 268

Up, up, my heart, with gladness (joy), 441

Up, up, the proper time is here, 440

Up, up, with bright sound, 128:3

Up, up, with clear sound proclaim, 128:3

Up, up, with lively sound, 128:3

Up, up, with trumpet tone, 128:3

Up, up, ye trumpets call, 128:3

Uphold my heart with faith in Thee, 3:6

Uphold us in the true faith, 79:6

Uphold us, Lord, by Thy dread word, 6:6; 126:1

Uphold us Lord, by Thy word, 126:1

Uphold us, Lord, with Thy word, 126:1; A50

Uplift your heads on high, 70:8

Upon earthly treasure the heart to be setting, 26:4

Upon His arm relying, 97:4

Upon His strength relying, 107:3

Upon me God hath deigned to shine, 172:6

Upon my agonized remorse, 199:5

Upon my wings you shall soar, 213:7

Upon that night of murk and gloom, 265

Upon the third day I will rise again, 244:76c

Upon this year begun, O grant Thy blessing, 41:2

Upon Thy holy word bestow Thy strength, 18:3b

Upward where the stars are burning, 263

Urschel, bring me a light, 524:9

Us modify through Thy kindness, 132:6

Us mortify through kindness, 22:5

The usual bright, beloved gleaming, 176:3

V

Vain and fleeting, naught completing, 26:1

Vain Earth's poor vanities, 94:8

Vain foolish men absurdly boast, 308

Vain world, forbear thy pleading, 95:2b

Vainly, world, dost boast thy treasures, 301

Vain's all my toil and striving, 97:2

Valet would I now give thee, 95:2b

Vanish, fear and terror, 15:3

Vanish, gloomy shadows, 202:1

Vanish now, ye winter shadows, 202:1

The variety of evil sin, 54:2

The venemous brambles of pleasure, 181:3

Verdant banks my waters nourish, 30a:11

Verily, I hold on to Jesus, 157:4a

Verily I say to you, 127:4b

Verily I say unto you, 127:4b

Verily, since you have willed, 119:7

Verily, verily, I say unto you, 86:1

The very foundations of Earth tremble, 246:70

Very well, so will I, O Jesus, 133:6

Very well, the terror and sadness of death, 133:5

Vex no more, sad melancholy, 202:1

Vex thyself, O spirit, not, 186:1

The vibrating of the bells, 198:4

Victorious Judah's hero, 245:58

Village gossip, 212

Vivat Mueller! Mueller vivat!, 205:15

Vivat, vivat! Vivat, honored guest, 205:15

Voice and heart to Thee are open, 148:4

A voice is crying in the wilderness, 30:6

A voice makes itself heard in the wilderness, 30:6

The voice of my supplication, 131:1b

The voice of rejoicing and hope, 149:1

A voice resounds throughout the wilderness, 30:6

W

Wailing, crying, mourning, sighing, 12:2

Wailing, sighing, 12:2

Wait, and see if Elijah cometh, 244:71e

Wait, let us see, 244:71e

Wait, let's see if Elias now will come, 244:71e

Wait, let's see now, 244:71e

Wait to see now whether will Elias, 244:71e

Wake, arise! the call obeying, 140:1
Wake, arise! the voice is calling, 140:1
Wake, arise, the voices call us, 140:1
Wake, awake, for night is dying, 140:1; 140:7
Wake, awake! for night is flying, 140:1; 140:7; 645
Wake from sleep! Hark, sounds are falling, 140:7
Wake from sleep! Wake! sounds are falling, 140:1
Wake, my heart, 145:1
Wake, my heart, the night of dread, 198a:10b
Wake, my soul, wake up from sleep, 115:1
Wake, my spirit, 69:3
Wake, oh wake, and sleep no longer, 140:1; 140:7
Wake, oh wake, with tidings thrilling, 140:1
Wake or asleep, in life or death, 114:7
Wake! the watch is crying, 140:1
Wake! the watchman's voice is sounding, 140:1
Wake, the welcome day, 475
Wake, thou beloved linden town, 120:3
Wake up! cries the voice of the watchers, 140:1
Wake up, my heart and sing, 194:12
Wake up, my weak spirit, 454
Wake up; the voice calls to us, 140:1
Wake up, wake up, lost sheep, 20:8
Wake up, wake up, ye straying sheep, 20:8
Wake up, ye nerves and all ye members, 110:6
Wake up, you veins and limbs, 110:6
Wake, wake, wake to gladness, 30:10
Wake, ye maids! Hark, loud resounding, 140:1
Wake, ye maids! Hark, strikes the hour, 140:1; 645; A66
Walk gladly in God's ways, 197:10
Walk in My ways and commandments, 57:8
Walk in the way of faith, 152:2
Walk on the road of faith, 152:2
Watch and pray, pray and watch, 70:1

Watch and pray when trials beset thee (you), 54:1
Watch o'er me, ye heavenly guardians, 149:6
Watch, pray, be prepared, 70:1
Watch, pray, pray, watch; be ready, 70:1
Watch with care lest all thy piety, 179:1
Watch ye, pray ye, be prepared, 70:1
Watch ye, pray ye, ready be, 70:1
Watch ye, pray ye, watch and pray, 70:1
Watch ye, pray ye, keep prepared, 70:1
Watchful, prayerful ever be, 70:1
Watchman, tell us of the night, 262
The waters of Belial their storm-crests are rearing, 81:3
Waver not, O fearful soul, 99:3
'Way: see also Away
The way is hard, 60:2a
The way is long and full of sighs, 58:5
The way of sin is subtle, 54:2
'Way, 'way with Him, 245:44
The ways of God are not as man, 86:4
We adore in the temple, 51:2a
We all believe in one God, 437
We all believe in one God, maker, 765
We all believe in one God, the Creator, 680; 681; 765
We all believe in one God, the Father, 680; 681; 740; A69; A70,
We all believe in one true God, 437; 680; 681; A69; A70
We all believe in one true God, Father, 740,
We all believe in one true God, maker, 765
We all must bear much sorrow to enter into God's, 146:2
We all rejoice, 249:10a
We are at peace, 30:2
We are commanded to be true, 169:6
We are glad, 249:10a
We are going now where the bagpipes whine, 212:24
We are happy, 249:10a
We are now going where the bagpipe hums, 212:24
We are rejoiced, 249:10a

We believe all in but one God, 437; 680; 681

We believe all in but one God, Earth and Heaven, 765

We believe all in but one God, Father, 740

We believe in one God, 765

We bless Thee, Jesus Christ our Lord, 623

We can all learn a goodly lesson, 42:5

We can face tribulation more calmly, 93:3

We celebrate this holy feast, 4:8

We Christian folk, 40:3; 110:7; 248:35; 612

We Christian folk today, 710

We Christian people, 40:3; 612

We Christians may rejoice, 40:3; 110:7

We Christians may rejoice today, 612; 710

We come here Thy great holiness, 195:5

We come here Thy pure holiness, 195:5

We come to praise Thy holiness, 195:5

We did not see You when You came, 122:6

We eat and live well, 4:8

We eat and we live very well, 4:8

We eat now and live indeed, 4:8

We feel in truth the marks of error, 136:5

We found this fellow perverting, 246:45d

We give thanks to Thee, 232:6

We give Thee but Thine own, 878

We give Thee thanks, 232:6; 235:3; 236:3

We give Thee thanks God, we give Thee thanks, 29:2

We go to meet Thee, Savior, 248:5

We had already sunk too deep(ly), 9:3

We had sunk too deep, 9:3

We hail Thee, hail Thee King of the Jews, 244:62b

We hasten with eager yet faltering footsteps, 78:2

We hasten with feeble but diligent footsteps, 78:2

We hasten with feeble yet eager footsteps, 78:2

We hasten with footsteps so eager yet halting, 78:2

We hasten with timid but diligent paces, 78:2

We hasten with weak but diligent steps, 78:2

We hasten with weak yet eager steps, 78:2

We have a fine new master here, 212:2

We have a law, 245:38

We have a new overlord, 212:2

We have a new overseer, 212:2

We have a sacred law, 245:38

We have already sunk too deeply, 9:3

We have an ancient law, 245:38

We have indeed a law, 245:38

We have no king but Caesar, 245:46

We have peace, 30:2

We have rest, 30:2

We have with us a law, 245:38

We hear indeed the words, 164:2

We hear verily what love says, 164:2

We honor here Thy noble name, 62:5

We honor this glory and come now, 62:5

We honor this glory and now come near, 62:5

We honor this great majesty, 62:5

We hurry with weak yet eager steps, 78:2

We in Thy host sing to Thee, 248:23

We laud Thee with the hosts of Heaven, 248:23

We lift our hearts, O Father, 281

We live in comfort and eat the true, 4:8

We make offering at the temple, 51:2a

We may herein a heartening lesson ponder, 42:5

We mortals, scarred by sin's dark blemish, 122:2

We must all bear much sorrow, 12:3

We must enter the Kingdom of God, 12:3

We must go through much tribulation, 12:3

We must in spirit God be ever seeking, 141:3

We must pass through great sadness, 12:3; 146:2

We must pass through great tribulation, 12:3

We must see corruption, 246:78.2

We must through great tribulation enter, 146:2

We must through much tribulation, 12:3

We must through much tribulation enter, 146:2

We must through tribulation, 12:3

We must trust Him; we must heed Him, 155:2

We need no longer be affrighted, 92:5

We needy sinners pray Thee, 246:23

We now have rest, 30:2

We now rejoice, 249:10a

We pay homage to this glory, 62:5

We poor sinners plead, 246:23

We poor, sorry sinners, 407

We praise all such goodness of Yours, 16:6

We praise all this Thy kindness, 16:6

We praise all Thy compassion, 28:6

We praise Thee, 232:5

We praise Thee, all, our Savior, 91:1; 314; 604; 697; 722; 722a; 723

We praise Thee and do Thee adore, 130:6.1

We praise Thee, Lord, and low adore, 130:6.1

We praise Thee now in chorus, 190:7

We praise Thee, O God, 601

We praise Thee, O God, we worship Thee, 29:2

We pray in the temple, 51:2a

We pray that God's angelic band, 130:6.2

We pray Thee Lord, do Thou command, 130:6.2

We pray to the temple, 51:2a

We pray towards the temple, 51:2a

We salute Thee, King of the Jews, 245:34

We salute Thee, of all Jews, 245:34

We saw Thee in Thy balmy nest, 342

We send aloft our praises, 28:6

We shall now no longer hesitate, 92:5

We sing the praise of Him who died, 243:13; 253

We sing Thy praise, Immanuel, 248:23

We sing to Thee all glorious Lord, 248:23

We sing to Thee along with Thy hosts, 248:23

We sing to Thee, Immanuel, 248:23

We sing to Thee in Thy army, 248:23

We sing to Thee in Thy host, 248:23

We sing to Thee within Thy host, 248:23

We set ourselves down in tears, 244:78

We sit by Thee with tears overflowing, 244:78

We sit down in tears, 244:78

We sit down with tears, 244:78

We sit* ourselves down in tears, 244:78

We suffer sore by sin bespotted, 136:5

We thank and praise Thy name, 69:6

We thank Thee and praise Thee for Thy fervent love, 134:4

We thank Thee and praise Thee for Thy warm, 134:4

We thank Thee, dear Lord Jesus Christ, 623

We thank Thee for Thy great glory, 232:6

We thank Thee, God, that they, 479

We thank Thee, God, we thank Thee, 29:2

We thank Thee, Jesu, that indeed, 143:6

We thank Thee, Jesus Christ our Lord, 623

We thank Thee, Lord Christ Jesus, 341

We thank Thee, Lord, for sending, 37:6; 347; 348

We thank Thee, Lord God, we thank Thee, 29:2

We thank Thee, Lord Jesu(s) Christ, 623

We thank Thee, Lord, we thank Thee, 29:2

We thank Thee, O Lord, we thank Thee, 29:2

We thank Thee, we praise Thee for all Thy devotion, 134:4

We thank Thee, we praise Thee who wondrously loved, 134:4

We thank, we praise Thy burning love, 134:4

We thank You, Lord Jesus Christ, 623

We therefore pray Thee, help us, Lord, 120:6

We therefore would no longer falter, 92:5

We thus raise our voices at this joyous time, 16:2

We wake or sleep; we live or die, 114:7

We wake or sleep, yet we are indeed, 114:7

We were already too deeply sunk, 9:3

We were ere then too deeply fallen, 9:3

We will worship toward the holy temple, 51:2a

We worship in the holy temple, 51:2a

We worship in the house of God, 51:2a

We worship in the temple, 51:2a

We worship toward Thy temple, 51:2a

We wretched sinners beg Thee, 246:23

Weak, in that Nicodemus had the courage, 176:2

The weakness which God hath assumed, 91:5

A weary road, 60:2a

Weary with woe, my heart is deep despairing, 400

Wedding cantata, 34a; 120a; 195; 196; 197; 202; 210

Wedding chorale, 250; 251; 252

Weeping, complaining, sorrowing, fearing, 12:2

Weeping, complaining, worries, fear, 12.2,

Weeping, crying, sorrow, sighing, 12:2

Weeping, failing, mourning, fearing, 12:2

Weeping, lamenting, worrying, fearing, 12:2

Weeping, lamenting, worrying, quaking, 12:2

Weeping, wailing, anguish, dread, 12:2

Weeping, wailing, grieving, fearing, 12:2

Weeping, wailing, mourning, fearing, 12:2

A welcome boon were death, 57:3

Welcome, I will say, 27:3

Welcome in prosperity, 30a.3

Welcome, joyous festal day, 194:1

Welcome, my dear love, 36:5

Welcome, precious treasure, 36:5

Welcome, Resurrection's morn, 70:10a

Welcome to Thee, sweet Jesu, 768

A welcome will I give Him, 27:3

Welcome, will I say, 27:3

The welfare of His faithful children, 36b:3

Well for him who on his God, 139:1

Well for him whose help is the God of Jacob, 143:3

Well for him whose help the God of Jacob is, 143:3

Well for me, Jesus is found, 154:7a

Well for me; my Jesus speaks, 81:6

Well for me that I have Jesus, 147:6

Well for thee, God has on thee thought, 134:3

Well for thee, thou people, 119:3

Well for us all, 130:4

Well for us! Jesus helps us fight, 67:6b

Well for us that day, 130:4

Well for you, ye chosen souls, 34:3

Well for you, you chosen souls, 34:3

Well hath our God the world ordained, 187:7

Well I know, ne'er in Hell wilt Thou leave my soul, 15:1

Well, judges, which has won, 201:8

We'll ne'er this happy day forget, 173a:6

Well, pretty daughter, 211:5

Well said, my hero true, 213:6

Well said! My song was bad, 212:19

Well thee, God hath remembered thee, 134:3

Well thee, thou linden people, 119:3

Well then, beloved shepherdesses, 249a:8

Well then, death's fear and pain, 133:5

Well then, my heart lays away wrath, 89:4

Well then, my heart puts anger, 89:4

Well then, my heart will lay wrath, 89:4

Well then, thus I'll as well find, 138:6

Well then, Thy name alone shall be, 248:40a

Well then, to fear and pain of death, 133:5

Well though for us that day, 130:4

Well, what then has He done, 246:54

Were God not with us all the time, 14:1

Were God not with us all this time, 14:1

Were God not with us at this time, 14:1

Were God not with us here today, 14:1; 257

Were God not with us in this time, 14:1

Were God our Lord not on our side, 178:1; 258; A71

Were God the Lord not on our side, 178:1

Were I lost, my hopes all blighted, 55:5

We're off now to the merry stall, 212:24

We've got a new squire master here, 212:2

We've heard, indeed, what love, 164:2

We've said enough, 212:21

We've spent fifty talers, 212:12

We've striven with ardor in years now behind us, 134a:4b

What a wealth of creatures, 187:2

What abundance of goodness, 17:5

What all wisdom in the world, 176:6

What am I to do with thee, Ephraim, 89:1

What an honor Jesus has accorded, 59:2

What are those great castles, 524:1

What art thou, ask thy conscience duly, 132:3

What art thou, ever ask thy conscience, 132:3

What art thou, O my soul, forever grieving, 425

What ask I from the world, 94:1; 94:8

What avail us the heavy cares, 93:2

What avails purple majesty, 75:2

What avails the majesty of purple, 75:2

What better had the guiltless clothed, 246:52

What blessedness is theirs, 80:7

What blessings God to us has brought, 69:2

What bliss, I have now found Jesus, 154:7a

What can delight the soul, 30a:5

What can the terrors of Hell now hold, 248:63a

What can the torments of Hell, 248:63a

What can thee then, in thy conduct, 88:6

What can then thee in all thy dealings, 88:6

What can these anxious cares avail thee, 93:2

What can we do, Augustus, 215:2

What care I for the world, 64:4; 94:1; 94:8

What cause is there for me to be affrighted, 88:6

What childish, stupid folly, 97:2

What concerns you so much, 249a:10

What creatures are contained, 187:2

What creatures contains the great sphere, 187:2

What do all our troubles avail us, 93:2

What do I ask of the world, 64:4

What doth it profit all our sorrow, 93:2

What doth to others dreadful seem, 83:2b

What doth trouble thee, O my spirit, 21:6a

What excess of goodness Thou givest me, 17:5

What excess of goodness You give me, 17:5

What gloom? What tomb, 210:7

What God does, ever well is done, 12:7; 144:3; 250

What God does, He with skill will do, 100:3

What God does is completely done, 75:14; 100:6

What God does is done well, 12:7

What God does is well accomplished, 69a:6

What God does is well done, 12:7; 69a:6; 75:7; 75:14; 99:6; 100:1; 100:6; 144:3; 250

What God does is with justice done, 100:4

What God does is with patience done, 100:2

What God does is with reason done, 12:7; 69a:6; 75:7; 75:14; 98:1; 99:1; 99:6; 100:1; 100:2; 100:3; 100:4; 100:5; 100:6; 144:3; 250; A67

What God does is with wisdom done, 75:7; 75:14; 100:5; 144:3

What God does, surely that is right, 98:1

What God does, that is done well, 12:7; 75:7; 75:14; 99:1; 99:6; 100:1; 100:3; 100:4; 100:5; 100:6; 144:3

What God does, that is finely done, 98:1

What God does, that is rightly done, 98:1; 100:1; 100:2; 100:3; 100:4; 100:5; 100:6

What God does, that is well done, 12:7; 75:7; 75:14; 98:1; 99:6; 100:1; 144:3

What God doth e'er is just and right, 100:2

What God doth, only that is right, 98:1; 99:1; 100:1; 100:4; 144:3

What God doth, sure is wholly right, 100:3

What God doth, surely that is right, 98:1

What God doth, that alone is right, 75:14; 99:6; 100:6

What God doth, that is rightly done, 12:7; 75:7; 75:14; 98:1; 99:1; 99:6; 100:1; 100:2; 100:3; 100:4; 100:5; 100:6; 144:3

What God doth, that is well done, 99:1

What God has done is good indeed, 12:7

What God hath promised Abraham, 248:14

What God hath promised to Abraham, 248:14
What God of old has undertaken, 10:6
What God of old to our forefathers, 10:6
What God of old unto our fathers, 10:6
What God ordains alone is right, 12:7; 69a:6; 75:7; 75:14; 98:1; 99:1; 99:6; 100:1; 100:5; 144:3; 250
What God ordains is best of all, 12:7; 69a:6; 99:6; 100:6
What God resolves will come about, 72:5; 111:1; 144:6; 244:31
What God resolves will He achieve, 72:5; 144:6; 244:31
What God to Abraham had spoken, 248:14
What God to Abraham had sworn, 248:14
What God to Abraham revealed, 248:14
What God to the fathers of old, 10:6
What God told and promised, 10:6
What God wills, that alone is right, 250
What God wills, that is best of all, 12:7
What God's almighty power hath laid, 117:3
What God's splendor doth reveal, 194:3
What gracious God has vowed to do, 86:3
What grief, what anguish, 48:2
What happiness and joy are mine, 66:4a
What has He done, 246:54
What has so, Sarmatia, moved you, 215:4
What, have you, my God, 21:4
What help to us are grievous worries, 93:2
What here may shine I all resign, 47:5
What human pow'r and wit contrive, 178:2
What if the law demand its toll, 145:4
What is base man, the child of Earth, 19:4
What is God's love, 169:4
What is it, soul, which thus with woe, 424; 506
What is it then, Sarmatia, 215:4
What is it troubles thee, my heart, 138:1
What is that to us, 244:49b
What is the cause of all His suffering, 244:25b
What is the cause of all such torment, 244:25b

What is the cause of all such woes, 244:25b
What is the cause of this, 244:25b
What is the love of God, 169:4
What is the world to me, 64:4; 94:8
What is the worthless man, 19:4
What is, then, scornful man, 19:4
What is there, soul, so sorely, 506
What is there to grieve me, 87:7
What is this fragile thing, 19:4
What is this vile thing, 19:4
What is't God's love provideth, 169:4
What joy my Savior brings to me, 1:6; 49:6a
What joy! What rapture!, 205:12
What law, beloved Jesu, hast Thou broken, 244:3
What laws, my blessed Savior, hast Thou broken, 244:3
What love this, which to none is like, 174:3
What makes you grieve, my heart, 423
What man can calculate the love, 248:7b
What men's strength and wit can do, 178:2
What, Midas, are you mad, 201:12
What, most beautiful goddess, 208:3
What multitudes of creatures, 187:2
What my God desires, may it happen, 111:1
What my God will, be done alway, 72:5; 111:1
What my God will, let be alway, 144:6
What my God wills, 244:31
What my God wills be done alway, 72:5; 111:1; 144:6
What my God wills is best alway, 72:5
What my God wills, may that always happen, 144:6
What my God wills, that always happens, 72:5
What my God wills, that happens alway(s), 72:5; 111:1
What my heart desires of Thee, 108:5
What my heart from Thee desires, 108:5
What my heart from Thee desireth, 108:5
What my heart of Thee doth seek, 108:5
What, my heart, so discontents thee, 21:6a; 423

What need I of this world, 64:4; 94:1; 94:8
What need is there to quarrel, 201:4
What need is there to wrangle, 201:4
What need we any further witness, 246:45b
What, no anthem for my Maker, 413
What now of the terrors of Hell, 248:63a
What on Earth seems of worth, 64:5
What once Isaiah had forecast, 65:3
What our God has created, 117:3
What overflow of goodness, 17:5
What plenitude of blessing, 17:5
What profit thus to argue, 201:4
What profiteth pomp's high estate, 75:2
What profits us this world's estate, 75:2
What reason hadst, O Poland, 215:4
What reck I of the world, 64:4; 94:1; 94:8
What salvation and happiness, 498
What shades? What grave is this, 210:7
What shall I, a sinner do Lord, 259
What shall I make of thee now, Ephraim, 89:1
What shall I make out of thee, Ephraim, 89:1
What shall I of thee make, Ephraim, 89:1
What sorrow fills me for these wayward spirits, 170:3
What strangest punishment is suffered yonder, 244:55
What suits me is only the merry hunt, 208:1
What superabundance of goodness, 17:5
What terror now hath Hell for us, 248:63a
What the glow of the Highest fills, 194:3
What the Highest's light hath filled, 194:3
What the world contains must vanish, 64:5
What the world doth contain, 64:5
What the world holds within itself, 64:5
What the world keeps to itself must disperse, 64:5
What then inspired you, Sarmatia, 215:4
What there Isaiah did once foretell, 65:3
What there Isaiah foresaw, 65:3
What Thou, O God, created hast, 117:3
What though blasts of wintry weather, 206:3
What though my mortal body perish, 3:4

What though our foe, 41:5
What though our sins are manifold, 38:6
What though the Earth with rage, 58:2
What though the feeble mouth, 51:2b
What though the foe, 41:5
What though the hand of death, 124:3
What though the world be full of sin, 80:5
What though trials wait me here, 244:29
What time as we in peace, 41:4
What to us as men terrible appears, 83:2b
What to us mortals seems so dire, 83:2b
What tongue can tell, A162:4
What tongue can tell Thy greatness, Lord, 436
What use is purple's majesty, 75:2
What voice is with the tempest blending, 38:3
What will the terrors of Hell do now, 248:63a
What wit and strength of men, 178:2
What wonder is it, 198:9a
What wonder this, 198:9a
What wondrous punishment is this to render, 244:55
What wondrous things for us does God achieve, 69:4
Whate'er befall or ill betide, 177:4
Whate'er God will, let that be done, 72:5; 244:31
Whate'er God wills is best alway, 72:5; 92:9; 111:1; 111:6; 144:6; 244:31
Whate'er I have, O world, 8:5
Whate'er I have or hope to gain, 72:2c
Whate'er may vex or grieve thee, 244:53
Whate'er my God ordains is best, 72:5
Whate'er my God ordains is right, 12:7; 69a:6; 75:7; 74:14; 98:1; 99:1; 99:6; 100:6; 144:3; 250
Whate'er my lot or weal, 72:2c
Whate'er our God created hath, 117:3
Whate'er the task before me, 97:1; 367
Whate'er the task He sendeth, 13:6; 44:7; 97:9
Whatever God does, it is done aright, 100:1; 100:2; 100:3; 100:4; 100:5; 100:6

Whatever God ordains is right, 99:6
What's in the bone the flesh will show, 211:10
What's that I hear, 249a:4
When Adam fell, the frame entire, 637; 705
When Adam fell, the human race, 18:5; 637; 705
When all around is darkling, 245:52
When all at the last hour shudders, 127:2
When all our guilt, 87:4
When along life's thorny road, 423
When angels visit us, 19:6
When anguished and perplexed, 427
When at last I must depart, 244:72
When black despair in chains had bound me, 38:5
When by the law we come to recognize sin, 9:6
When called by Thee, I gain Thy portal, 229:1; 229:4
When cares on me press, 3:5
When cares oppress me, I will sing, 3:5
When cares press upon me, 3:5
When Christ is in you, 227:8
When Christ our Lord was crucified, 621
When Christ sat at the table there, 285
When clanging falls the stroke of death, 124:3
When comes at last our final day, 219:5.2
When comes my hour of parting, 244:72
When comes the day for which we're sighing, 70:3
When comes the day of our deliverance, 70:3
When comes the day when we go out, 70:3
When com'st Thou, my Lord, 140:3
When comest thou, my salvation, 140:3
When comest Thou, my Savior, 140:3
When comfort and help must fail, 117:6
When comfortless we feel our need, 117:6
When conscience tells, 9:6
When dark cares oppress me, 87:7
When dawns the day that man releaseth, 70:3

When death at last my spirit calls, 31:9; 95:6; 428; 429; 430
When death at last with ruthless force, 111:5
When Earth's last hour for us is come, 219:5.2
When everyone is struck with horror, 127:2
When ev'rything at that last hour, 127:2
When finally my hour comes, 428; 429; 430
When forty days after Easter, 266
When, full of dread, the last sad moment, 127:2
When gentle spring breezes wander, 202:5
When God His love on us bestows, 122:4a
When grief my spirit fills, 427
When He, however, truth's very spirit, 108:4
When Heaven and Earth in fire disappear, 127:4c
When Heaven and Earth shall in fire have perished, 127:4c
When Heaven and Earth vanish in fire, 127:4c
When Heaven is itself not pure, 136:4
When help and consolation fail, 117:6
When here on Earth my happy lot, 189:2
When Herod the king had heard these, 248:48
When Herod the king heard these, 248:48
When His life had reached its end, 245:56
When I behold myself, 189:2
When I but recall, 69a:4
When I in anxiety and need, 427
When I repose in Thy love, 517
When I shall go the way, 198a:7b
When I shall meet my life's last day, 502
When I survey the wondrous cross, 126:1
When I to rest betake me, 97:6
When I too am departing, 244:72
When in my deepest woe my gaze I lift, 428; 429; 430
When in our deepest trouble, 641
When in spring the breezes blowing, 202:5
When in the hour of utmost need, 431; 432; 641; 668; A78

When in the hour of uttermost need, 641; 668

When is it then to happen, 11:11

When is the hour approaching, 11:11

When it is my Lord's good pleasure, 161:5

When Jesus, after His Passion, 7:5

When Jesus, after His sufferings, 7:5

When Jesus Christ in the night, 265

When Jesus had finished all these, 244:2

When Jesus had heard them, 244:8

When Jesus now had finished, 244:2

When Jesus on the cross was bound, 621

When Jesus on the cross was found, 621

When Jesus on the cross was hung, 621

When Jesus perceived it, 244:8

When Jesus stood beside the cross, 621

When Jesus then had finished, 244:2

When Jesus there endured His Passion, 7:5

When Jesus understood it, 244:8

When Jesus was born in Bethlehem, 248:44

When Jordan hush'd his waters still, 290

When King Herod heard that, 248:48

When King Herod heard these, 248:48

When King Herod heard this, 248:48

When life begins to fail me, 244:72

When life's last hour shall call me, 244:72

When loud and clear the trumpet soundeth, 127:4a

When man will rest in God's own sight, 339

When merciful God, 264

When mortal aid and comfort fail, 117:6

When Moses smote the rock, 246:39

When my affliction as with chains, 38:5

When my brief hour is come, 428; 429; 430

When my despair as though with fetters, 38:5

When my last hour is close at hand, 428; 429; 430

When my little hour is at hand, 95:6

When my shepherd hides from me too long, 104:3

When my time of departing comes, 244:72

When my trouble as with chains, 38:5

When nothing can save me, 74:7

When nothing could save me, 74:7

When now the day is at an end, 396

When on the cross the Savior hung, 621

When once at last the trumps have sounded, 127:4a

When once I must depart, 244:72

When once my fear is past, 103:4

When one day the trumpet sounds, 127:4a

When one misfortune to another is bound, 38:5

When our guilt, 87:4

When over me the Dreaded Reaper, 127:2

When Pilate had seen, 244:59c

When Pilate heard of Galilee, 246:49c

When Pilate heard that saying, 245:39; 245:43

When Pilate heard their saying, 245:43

When Pilate saw that he, 244:59c

When Pilate therefore heard that, 245:39

When Pilate therefore heard that saying, 245:43

When roaring, stormy winds are blaring, 92:6

When Satan's hosts provoke thee, 153:5

When seraphim must hide their faces, 486

When shall it ever happen, 11:11

When shall my eyes behold Him, 11:11

When sorrow is prevailing, 3:5

When sorrow round me presses, 3:5

When sorrow sore distresses, 3:5

When spring breezes blow and are wafted, 202:5

When spring's gentle scented zephyrs, 202:5

When strength and help must fail, 117:6

When strength one day shall fail me, 244:72; 245:52; 272

When that one, however, the Spirit of Truth, 108:4

When the bitterness of pain struggles, 99:5

When the comfort and help of this world, 117:6

When the cross' bitter sorrows, 99:5

When the day comes for which we are heading, 70:3

When the foul fiend emerges, 107:4
When the hireling is sleeping, 85:4
When the hirelings sleep, 85:4
When the king had privily called, 248:55
When the morning was come, 244:49a
When the spring breezes caress and waft, 202:5
When the spring breezes stroke and waft, 202:5
When the spring breezes wander through, 202:5
When the time comes for my parting, 244:72
When the trumpets shall sound, 127:4a
When the Wise Men heard what the king, 248:58
When they had heard the king, 248:58
When they were come unto a place, 244:67a
When they which were about Him, 246:32a
When thou art with me, 508
When Thou bidd'st me from that slumber, 55:5
When Thou in prison took Thy place, 245:40
When two pure souls are plighted, 202:6
When waft the springtime breezes, 202:5
When we are in deepest need, 431; 432; 641; 668
When we are in utmost need, 431; 432; 641
When we are troubled through and through, 431; 432; 641; 668; A78
When we awake or when we sleep, 114:7
When we have sinned and flouted, 9:6
When we our sin within the law acknowledge, 9:6
When we realize from the law, 9:6
When we shall hear the last trump calling, 127:4a
When we the sin through the law, 9:6
When will God recall my spirit, 8:1; 483
When will it come to pass, 11:11
When will the day be dawning, 11:11
When will the day come when we depart, 70:3
When will the day dawn that we shall depart, 70:3

When will the night be over, 11:11
When will you come, my Lord, 140:3
When will you come, my salvation, 140:3
When will you pass, O darkest night, 492
When you are with me, 508
Whene'er my shepherd too long hideth, 104:3
Whene'er to rest I take me, 97:6
Whenever I have filled my pipe, 515
Whenever I reach for my well-filled tobacco pipe, 515
Whenever I take up my pipe, 515
Whenever You have given peace, 41:4
Where, 244:70b
Where art Thou then, 175:3
Where can I find Thee, 175:3
Where contentment reigns, 144:4
Where does my Savior dwell, 248:52
Where find I Thee, 175:3
Where God the Lord stands with us not, 178:1
Where goest Thou, 166:1
Where goest Thou, Lord, 166:1
Where has thy beloved gone, 244:36b
Where in this vale of tears, 114:2a
Where is He that is born king, 248:45
Where is He that is born the king, 248:45
Where is my lamb, which I love, 507
Where is the image of our God, 102:2
Where is the image that God, 102:2
Where is the image true, 102:2
Where is the lamb I love and cherish, 507
Where is the lamb that willed to leave, 507
Where is the new-born king, 248:45
Where is the sheep I love, 507
Where is then thy friend hence departed, 244:36b
Where is thy friend gone, 244:36b
Where is your God? they say, 45:7
Where man was all to marred, 414,
Where may I find my Lord today, 154:2
Where may I fly; oh, where, 5:1
Where may Thou be, 175:3
Where may wise advice be found, 25:3

Where shall I find my Jesus, 154:2
Where shall I fly, 5:1
Where shall I refuge find, 5:1
Where shall I, then, my Jesus meet, 154:2
Where streams of living water flow, 112:2
Where the Holiest sheds His light, 194:3
Where the Vistula's torrents run, 198:9b
Where they crucified Him, 245:49
Where to dost thou go, 166:1
Where two and three are gathered, 42:3
Where two and three assembled are, 42:3
Where two or three are gathered then, 42:3
Where two or three are gathered together, 42:3
Where two or three forgathered are, 42:3
Where two or three gathered are, 42:3
Where two or three have gathered them, 42:3
Where will be in this valley of lament, 114:2a
Where will in this lamentation vale, 114:2a
Where will within this vale of sorrow, 114:2a
Where wilt Thou, Lord, that we shall all eat, 244:14
Where wilt Thou that we prepare, 246:8b
Where wilt Thou that we prepare for Thee, 244:14
Where wilt Thou we now prepare for Thee, 244:14
Where wilt Thou we prepare for Thee, 244:14
Where? To Golgotha, 245:49b
Where'er I go, whate'er my task, 97:1
Where'er my task may take me, 367
Wherefore grievest thou, O my spirit, 21:6a
Wherefore has appeared the Son of God, 40:1
Wherefore hath appeared God our Savior, 40:1
Wherefore, Lord Jesu, 484
Wherefore, O Savior, 484
Wherefore, soul of mine, art grieving, 422
Wherefore wilt thou be so wasteful, 244:7
Wherefore wouldst Thou so wrathful be, 101:4
Where's my beloved sheep, 507

Wherever moderation rules, 144:4
Wherewith God hath now afflicted my soul, 46:1b
Wherewith God the Lord afflicted me, 46:1b
Whether there is much sinning with us, 38:6
Whether we wake or fall asleep, 114:7
Which the Lord of old upon me hath laid, 46:1b
While God is constant on my side, 85:6
While God's my shield and helper true, 85:6
While His parting spirit sinks, 245:56
While on this mortal Earth I fare, 153:9.1
While shepherds watched, 376
While steadfastly they watched as He rose, 11:7
While the fleecy flocks wander joyfully, 208:13
While the fleecy herds are joyously driven, 208:13
While the hireling is sleeping, 85:4
While they beheld, He was taken up, 11:5
While Thine arms are round me, 81:7; 227:3
While Thine arms around me, 227:3
While yet a single drop of blood, 124:2
While yet one drop of blood doth run, 124:2
While yet the morn is breaking, 41:6; 287
The white-foaming billows of Belial's torrents, 81:3
Whither, 244:70b
Whither am I to flee, 5:1; 5:7; 89:6; 136:6; 148:6
Whither goest Thou, 166:1
Whither has thy beloved departed, 244:36b
Whither has thy dear one departed, 244:36b
Whither has thy friend departed, 244:36b
Whither is thy beloved gone, 244:36b
Whither shall I flee, 5:1; 89:6; 136:6
Whither shall I fly, 5:1; 646; 694
Whither then is thy friend gone, 244:36b
Who a true Christian would be called, 47:2
Who allows only the dear God to rule, 93:1
Who art thou, ask thy conscience, 132:3
Who art thou? Question thine own conscience, 132:3

Who believe and are baptized shall be saved, 37:1

Who believes in Him, he is not judged, 68:5

Who believes that music is seducing, 210:5

Who believeth and obeyeth, 37:1

Who believeth and observeth, 37:1

Who bides in Christ alone, 75:11

Who can extol the love aright, 248:7b

Who can really estimate the love, 248:7b

Who could so rudely smite Thee, 244:44

Who dare now thus to smite Thee, 245:15.1

Who dares to smite Thee, 245:15.1

Who dareth, Lord, to smite Thee, 244:44

Who does not understand Jesus' name, 133:4b

Who for a certain sedition, 246:55c

Who God acknowledges from the true, 45:5

Who God doth own, 45:5

Who has beaten Thee so, my Savior, 244:44

Who has buffeted Thee so, 244:44

Who has struck Thee thus, 244:44

Who hath, Lord, dared to smite Thee, 244:44; 245:15.1

Who himself exalteth, he shall be made to be, 47:1

Who himself exalteth shall be abased again ever, 47:1

Who hopes in God and Him trusts, 109:6

Who hopes in God and holds Him fast, 109:6

Who hopes in God and in Him trusts, 109:6

Who hopes in God and trusts in Him, 109:6

Who in Him trusteth will not be judged, 68:5

Who in love has fate against him, 203:3

Who is both inward and without the same, 179:4

Who is it that afflicts Thee, 245:15.1

Who is it thinks that music is bewitching, 210:5

Who is there rightly can assess, 248:7b

Who is this so weak and helpless, 439

Who Jesu's name hath never known, 133:4b

Who Jesus' name can't comprehend, 133:4b

Who knows how near I am to my end, 27:1

Who knows how near is my end, 27:1

Who knows how near is my last hour, 27:1; 166:6

Who knows how near my end is, 166:6

Who knows how near my end may be, 27:1; 166:6

Who knows how near my latter ending, 27:1

Who knows how near my life's expended, 27:1

Who knows how near the end may be, 27:1

Who knows how near to me is my end, 27:1; 84:5

Who knows how near to me mine end, 166:6

Who knows how near to me my end is, 27:1

Who knows how near will be my ending, 84:5; 166:6

Who knows how soon my end may be, 27:1

Who knows when life's last hour approacheth, 27:1; 84:5; 88:7; 166:6

Who knows when my death approaches, 27:1

Who lives a life most free from error, 198a:6

Who lives a life of adoration, 198a:6

Who loves Me, he will keep My word, 59:1

Who may this love in full extol, 248:7b

Who offers thanks, he praises Me, 17:1

Who on Him believes is not judged, 68:5

Who only in Jesus remains, 75:11

Who only lets the dear God govern, 93:1

Who only lets the dear God rule, 197:10

Who ought then not in lamentation sink, 103:2

Who praise offers, so honors God, 17:1

Who puts his trust in God most just, 433; 434; 494

Who rightly can the love declare, 248:7b

Who shall, therefore, desire, 170:4

Who should accordingly desire, 170:4

Who should not in mourning sink, 103:2

Who sin commits is of the Devil, 54:3

Who sins is the devil's, 54:3

Who takest away the sins of the world, 233:4; 234:4; 235:5a

Who thanks giveth, he praiseth Me, 17:1

Who thanks offers, he praiseth Me, 17:1
Who then is from within, 179:4
Who, though, doth hear, 76:4
Who trusts in God, a strong abode, 244:31
Who trusts in God, a sure defense, 72:5
Who trusts in God has builded well, 433
Who trusts in God, with mirth may mock, 109:6
Who was it dared to smite Thee, 245:15.1
Who was it, Lord, did smite Thee, 244:44; 245:15.1
Who will but let himself be guided, 434
Who will this love in full extol, 248:7b
Who with contented mind, 144:4
Who with high thoughts, 207:3
Who would not in the deeps of sorrow, 103:2
Who would not melt in tears, 103:2
Who would not rather be in Heaven, 27:4
Who would not sink in grief, 103:2
Who would wish to live here, 170:4
Who'd be content to live, 170:4
Whoever acknowledges God, 45:5
Whoever believes and is baptized, 37:1
Whoever commits sin, he is of the devil, 54:3
Whoever commits sin which comes, 54:3
Whoever himself exalteth, he shall be abased, 47:1
Whoever in love has fate as an enemy, 203:3
Whoever is thus from within, 179:4
Whoever just lets dear God govern, 88:7
Whoever loves Me, 172:2
Whoever loves Me will keep My word, 59:1; 74:1
Whoever professes God, 45:5
Whoever raiseth himself, he shall be humbled, 47:1
The whole created world, 17:2
The whole wide world doth run, 25:2
The whole wide world doth worship Thee, 16:6
The whole world is a place of affliction, 25:2
The whole world is but a hospital, 25:2
The whole world must be, 17:2

The whole world must become, 17:2
Whom Jesus deigns His flock to number, 104:5
Whom mighty God will watch and ward, 339
Whom we that holy now with gladness make, 129:5
Whoso bears his load unbending, with his frailty, 99:5
Whoso doth offer thanks, 17:1
Whoso doth rest in God's defense, 339
Whoso offereth praise glorifieth Me, 17:1
Whoso offers thanks, he praises Me, 17:1
Whoso will suffer God to guide him, 93:1; 434; 642; 647; 690; 691; 691a; A68
Whosoever believeth in Him is not judged, 68:5
Whosoever loves Me, 172:2
Whosoever loves Me, he will keep My word, 74:1
Why are nations raging, 262
Why are ye so sore afeared, 248:49
Why are ye so struck with fear, 248:49
Why are ye stricken thus with fear, 248:49
Why are you sad, my heart, 47:5
Why art cast down within me, 107:1
Why art cast down within thee, 107:1
Why art thou cast down, my heart, 423
Why art thou distressed, O my spirit, 21:6a
Why art thou, O my soul, forever grieving, 425
What art thou restless, O my soul, 47:5
Why art thou sad, my heart, 138:1
Why art thou so cast down, my heart, 47:5; 420; 421
Why are thou sorrowful, O my soul, 506
Why art thou, soul, discouraged, 506
Why art thou, soul, so troubled within me, 435
Why art thou thus cast down, my heart, 138:1; 420; 421
Why art thou troubled, my spirit, 21:6a
Why art thou troubled, O my heart, 138:1; 420; 421

Why art thou troubled so, 516
Why art thou yet, O soul, so troubled, 424; 506
Why art within me, my spirit, so downcast, 435
Why cast down art thou, O my spirit, 21:6a
Why cast down, my heart within me, 21:6a; 423
Why do I ask for the world, 64:4; 94:1; 94:8
Why do I ask of the world, 94:1
Why do you grieve, my heart, 47:5; 138:1; 138:3b; 420; 421
Why do you mourn, my soul, 21:6a
Why do you startle and take fright, 248:49
Why do you stop to argue, 201:4
Why do you wish, O my soul, to feel grieved, 425
Why dost Thou flee, 175:3
Why dost thou mourn, O soul, 506
Why grievest thou, my soul, 506
Why hast Thou hidden Thee, Jesus, 57:8
Why hast Thou, Lord my God, 21:4
Why hast Thou, my God, 21:4
Why hast Thou, O my God, 21:4
Why hast thou sought Me, 32:2
Why hast Thou then, my God, 21:4
Why hast Thou then, O God, 21:4
Why hast Thou Thyself, my God, 21:4
Why is it that thou Me sought, 32:2
Why is it that you have sought Me, 32:2
Why is sorrow here, 248:49
Why, Midas, are you mad, 201:12
Why, Midas, art thou mad, 201:12
Why must Thou suffer all these pangs, 244:25b
Why, my soul, art thou so much vexed, 21:6a
Why need ye then to falter, 88:6
Why, O my soul, art thou cast down, 424; 506
Why should I ask for the world, 64:4
Why should I then grieve, 248:33; 422
Why should people still want to live, 170:4
Why should sorrow ever grieve me, 422
Why should sorrow so benumb me, 422

Why should we here on Earth, 170:4
Why shouldst thou then, my soul, 8:2
Why so troubled, oh, my heart, 384
Why, therefore, should one wish, 170:4
Why troublest thou thyself, my heart, 138:1
Why troublest thou thyself, my soul, 21:6a
Why willst thou be fearful, my spirit, 8:2
Why wilt thou be troubled, 107:1
Why wilt thou, my soul, be terrified, 8:2
Why wilt Thou raise Thy dreadful storms, 101:4
Why wilt Thou so angry be, 101:4
Why wilt thou thyself trouble, 107:1
Why wouldst thou then be saddened, 107:1
Why wouldst thou then, my soul, be frightened, 8:2
Why writhest thou in pain, 245c
Wide open stands the once-closed door, 151:5
Will lightning and thunder, 244:33c
The will of God be alway done, 144:6; 244:31
The will of God be always done, 72:5
The will of God have I neglected, 55:2
The will of God is always best, 72:5; 244:31
Will you no longer take delight, 208:4
Willingly will I submit, 244:29
Wilt not now thyself surrender, 208:4
Wilt Thou forgive that sin, 412; 501
Wilt thou no more delight, 208:4
Wilt thou not give, 518
Wilt thou see, O my soul, 159:1b
Wilt thou to me, 518
Wise art thou, 209:4
Wise beyond your years, 209:4
The wise confine their choice in friends, 443
Wise ones, be happy with this Earth, 443
Wished-for light of joy, 184:1
Wist ye not that I must now be about my Father's, 154:5
With all I have and am, 72:2c
With all my heart I love Thee, 174:5
With all my heart, O Lord, I pray, 18:5
With all my power I free, 203:2
With all that I have and am, 72:2c
With all Thy hosts, O Lord, 248:23

With all Thy saints, Thee, Lord we sing, 145:7

With blessings full crowned this happy day's given, 134a:2

With clear conscience, in humble manner, 75:6

With conscience clear, in humble fashion, 75:6

With constant faith and lively trust, 44:6

With cords of affection my soul ever draw Thou, 96:3

With courage never slacking, 107:3

With desiring I press your tender cheeks, 201:5

With eager, ready arms outstretched, 31:9

With eager steps, yet shy and faltering, 36:3; 36c:3

With ev'rything I have and am, 72:2c

With faith never failing, 68:2

With fear the braggart foes are shaken, 248:62

With fear why are ye taken, 248:49

With fire is silver purified, 2:5

With frightened trembling steps I seek Him, 33:3

With gentle steps is love directing, 36c:3

With girded loins I stand and wait, 56:4

With glad rejoicing all life long, 117:7

With gladness will I now depart, 82:5

With gladness, yea with joyful heart, 95:1b

With glory clad, with strength array'd, 121:6; 332

With God my guard and shepherd true, 85:6

With God my refuge, shepherd true, 85:6

With God my shield and surety, 85:6

With God stands all my confidence, 138:5

With God's name on my lips, 378

With grateful hearts we all are met, 4:8

With grateful hearts we come to Thee, 130:6.1

With great longing do I press your cheeks, 201:5

With happy voices ringing, 245:52

With heart free and lightsome I welcome my lot, 84:3

With heavy fetters sin had bound, 38:5

With Him thou canst act boldly, 107:3

With Him you may attempt it, 107:3

With honor, praise, and glory, 51:4

With horrid doubting, Lord, I tremble, 109:3

With humble heart repent thee, 46:4

With Jesus I will watch and pray, 244:26a

With Jesus will I go, 12:5

With joy I greet my death, 82:5

With joy I look forward to my death, 82:5

With joy I near the gates of death, 82:5

With joy I see the gate of death, 82:5

With joy, oh yes, with heart's delight, 95:1b

With joy we come today, 36b:1

With joy we march onward to Zion, 182:8

With joy will I bear the cross, 56:1

With joy, yea, with joyful happy heart, 95:1b

With joyful heart we now surround, 4:8

With joyful, yea, with joyful, 95:1b

With laughing and joking, 216:5

With lavish hand our God on us, 39:2

With longing heart I stand ready, 56:4

With longing heart prepared I stand, 56:4

With longing I press your tender cheeks, 201:5

With love and peace and joy, 255

With loving and sincere affection, 36b:7

With loving heart and admiration, 36b:7

With loving hearts receive now, 4:8

With loving hearts we have today, 4:8

With loving hearts we keep today, 4:8

With loving hearts we observe today, 4:8

With mirth shall I be shaking, 205:3

With my Jesus I will stay, 124:6; 154:8; 157:5

With one accord, we thank Thee, Lord, 346

With open hand, from His abundance, 39:2

With our own might is nothing done, 80:2b

With patience I prepare, 146:6

With patient heart my cross, 146:6

With patient hearts we wait, 249:8a

With peace and joy do I depart, 95:1c

With peace and joy from Earth I go, 616

With peace and joy I depart, 616

With peace and joy I journey hither, 95:1c; 125:1

With peace and joy I journey thither, 83:5; 95:1c; 125:1; 125:6; 382

With peace and joy I travel there, 83:5

With peace and joy I travel thither, 95:1c; 125:1

With powerful might, 71:5

With praises, O Lord, 95:1b

With praises unto God let Heaven's, 129:5

With praises unto the God the courts, 129:5

With quiver and quaking the sinners, 105:3

With sighs Hell's complaining, 15:7

With spirits joyous haste, 36b:1

With sweat of toil upon my face, 84:4

With sweat upon my countenance, 84:4

With tears overflowing, 245:63

With the Father equal Thou, 36:6

With the Holy Ghost, 232:11

With the Holy Spirit, 232:11; 233:6; 234:6; 235:6; 236:6

With Thee away, the wilds alarm me, 104:3

With thee by me, I go joyfully, 508

With this new year we raise new songs, 288; 289

With timid footsteps God I'm seeking, 33:3

With torrents of weeping, 245:63

With us the Lord hath kindly dealt, 248:28

With voices low and awesome rising, 36:7; 36c:7

With what a loving heart, 216.6

With wonderment behold, O people, 62:2

With words of tender love, 216:6

With writhing fury Satan stands, 130:3

With you beside me, I shall go, 508

Withdraw my heart, fast from this world, 124:5

Withdraw quickly, my heart, from the world, 124:5

Withdraw thyself quickly, my heart, from the world, 124:5

Withdraw, you spirits of sadness, 227:11

Within My breast is peace, 57:6

Within my deepest being, 245:52

Within my heart I bear fear, 8:3

Within my heart, O Savior, 245:52

Within my heart of hearts, 80:4

Within my heart's recesses, 245:52; 735; 735a; 736

Within My lap life's peace abideth, 57:6

Within our inmost being, 245:52

Within the breast, 204:7

Within this pleasance here, 30a:2

Within yon gloomy manger lies the Lord, 248:17

Without God's help our pains we lose, 80:2b

Withstand firmly all sin, 54:1

Woe and pain of travail, 246:58

Woe and rue tear my sinful heart, 244:10

Woe that spirit which its mischief, 102:3

Woe, thou spirit, to thy frailty, 102:3

Woe to mortals who their sinning, 102:3

Woe to spirits which, unblushing, 102:3

Woe to the soul which harm no more, 102:3

Woe, woe is me! How great's the burden, 73:1b

Woe, woe is me! Thy will doth bring me, 73:1b

The woman's offspring came, 167:4

The woman's seed did come, 167:4

The wonderful light and splendor of the sun, 446

A wondrous Child, the Virgin-born, 605

The wondrous hand of might sublime, 147:8

Wondrous things will God accomplish, 173:3

The wondrous works of mighty God, 147:8

Word and deed, 147:1

The word as flesh, 40:2

The word became flesh, 40:2

The word Esaias foretold to them, 65:3

The word made flesh, 40:2

The word of God my treasure is, 18:4

The word of God will firm abide, 80:8

The word they shall let abide, 80:8

The word unshaken e'er shall stand, 80:8

The word was flesh, 40:2

The word was made flesh, 40:2

The world abideth not, 64:4

The world accuses falsely, Lord, 244:38

World, adieu; I am weary of thee, 27:6; 158:2

World, adieu; I have grown tired of you, 27:6

World, adieu; I'm tired of thee, 27:6

The world again shall be new, 202:2

The world, alas, sore hates me, 58:4

World, all thy joys are brief, 161:2

The world and all therein, 17:2

World and Heaven, my Jesus cries aloud, 247:126

The world and its delights I hold for nothing, 186:9

The world around's a dreary wilderness, 186:7

The world awakes from sleep, 202:2

The world becomes renewed, 202:2

The world can bring no lasting joy, 94:6

The world can its delight and joy, 94:6

The world can its desire and joy, 94:6

The world, divinely plann'd, 17:2

The world doth boast its lure and joy, 94:6

The world doth spend its wit, 190:4

World farewell! I am of thee weary, 158:2

World, farewell! I am tired of you, 158:2

World, farewell; I now forsake thee, 27:6

World, farewell! I'm tired of thee, 158:2

World, farewell; of thee I weary, 27:6

World, farewell; of thee I'm tired, 27:6

World farewell! Of thee I'm weary, 27:6; 158:2

The world for me hath falsely set, 244:38

The world grieves, 94:5

The world grows new again, 202:2

The world has betrayed me, 244:38

The world has judged me, 244:38

The world has used me deceitfully, 244:38

The world I hold for naught, 64:4; 94:1; 94:8

The world is as a smoke and shadow, 94:2

The world is but a mighty wilderness, 186:7

The world is dressed anew, 202:2

The world is filled with sickness, 25:2

The world is full of wrong, 170:2

The world is like a haze and shadow, 94:2

The world is like smoke and shadow, 94:2

The world is made over new, 202:2

The world is naught but smoke and shadow, 94:2

The world is reborn, 202:2

The world is sore distressed, 94:5

The world is the great wilderness, 186:7

The world is troubled sore, 94:5

The world its desire and joy, 94:6

World, know thy lure's accursed, 161:2

The world may lie in wait, 58:4

The world may vaunt its luring pleasure, 59:4

The world of man is but a wilderness, 186:7

The world pays court to fame, 94:3a

The world renews itself, 202:2

The world seeks honor and glory, 94:3a

The world seeks praise and fame, 94:3a

The world, since time began, 190:4

World so false, I trust thee not, 52:2

The world that God created here, 117:3

The world, that house of sin, 170:2

The world, the house of sin, 170:2

World, thy delights are false, 161:2

World, thy delights are weights, 161:2

World, thy pleasure is burden, 161:2

World, what art thou to me, 94:8

The world will hate and despise you, 183:1

The world with all its kingdoms, 59:4

The world with all its kings and princes, 59:4

The world with all its realms, 59:4

The world, with treachery replete, 244:38

Worldly fame and earthly gain, 426

Worldly honor and temporal good, 426

The world's great might shall disappear, 188:4

The world's vain power will pass away, 188:4

Worship, pray, and walk in God's ways, 93:7

Worthy patron, art and learning, 210a:8b

Worthy patron, at thy wedding, 210:8

Worthy patrons, art and learning, 210a: 8b

Would that the Lord would grant us grace, 69:6; 76:7; 311; 312

Would to God that on the morrow, 439

Wouldst be a child of God, 132:2a
Wouldst thou a son of God, 132:2a
Wouldst thou call thyself a son of God, 132:2a
The wounding, nail-thrusts, 78:5
The wounding, nailing, crown and grave, 782:5
The wounds, nails, crown, 78:5
The wounds, nails, thorns and grave, 78:5
The wounds, the nails, cross, 78:5
The wounds, the nails, the crown, 78:5
The wretched are confused, 2:4
The wretched shall that day become satisfied, 75:1a
The wretched shall that they become satisfied, 75:1a
Wretched sinner, woe to me, 770
Write Him not as our king, 245:50
Write not, The King of the Jews, 245:50
Write thou not, King of Jewry, 245:50
Write thou not, King of the Jews, 245:50
Write thou not, The King of Jewry, 245:50
Write thou not, The King of Jews, 245:50
Write thou not, The King of the Jews, 245:50

Y

Ye are not in the flesh, 227:6
Ye are not of the flesh, 227:6
Ye are the annointed ones of God, 196:5a
Ye are the blessed of the Lord, 196:5a
Ye can now dispel all, 66:1b
Ye cares, away, 210a:3
Ye Christians all, 612; 710
Ye Christians in this nation, 16:6; 28:6; 613
Ye Christians, leave those murky caves, 480
Ye Christians, take your courage up, 114:7; 256
Ye deities, here a picture, 213:12
Ye foes of man, your might is shaken, 248:62
Ye gates in Zion, 193:1; 193:7
Ye gates, lift your heads, 249:10c
Ye gateways to Zion, 193:1; 193:7
Ye happy flocks whom Christ is keeping, 104:5

Ye happy folk, attend, 207a:8
Ye happy souls whom Christ is leading, 104:5
Ye hear how God's great name, 76:2
Ye hearts which have turned, 185:2
Ye hearts which have yourselves, 185:2
Ye heav'ns, oh, haste your dews to shed, 243:13
Ye herds, so blessed, sheep of Jesus, 104:5
Ye holy ones, be joyful now, 194:7
Ye holy ones, rejoice and sing, 194:7
Ye honored patrons, 210a:9b
Ye lightnings, ye thunders, 244:33c
Ye meadows and heather, bright colored, 208:14
Ye members of Christ, remember what the Savior, 132:5
Ye men, extol God's love, 167:1
Ye mortal folk do ye now long, 37:4
Ye mortals all, if on the face of God, 37:4
Ye mortals, desire you with me, 37:4
Ye mortals, extol the love of the Father, 167:1
Ye mortals, praise ye God's affection, 167:1
Ye mortals so blessed, 184:2
Ye mortals, tell of God's devotion, 167:1
Ye of little faith, oh why are ye so fearful, 81:4
Ye of little faith, wherefore are ye so fearful, 81:4
Ye of little faith, why are ye so fearful, 81:4
Ye people, vaunt God's love, 167:1
Ye portals of Zion, 193:1; 193:7
Ye righteous, rejoice in the Lord, 195:1b
Ye shall all weep and lament me, 103:1
Ye shall be weeping and wailing, 103:1
Ye shall from God's house be cast forth, 44:1; 183:1
Ye shall weep and lament, but the world, 103:1
Ye sluggards all, arise, 207:10
Ye sons of man, do ye aspire with me, 37:4
Ye spirits of sadness, depart hence, 227:11
Ye spirits who have gone astray, 204:3
Ye stars, ye airy winds, 366; 476

Ye stubborn hearts, 185:2
Ye that have spent the silent night, 151:5
Ye thoughts and ye meditations, 110:2
Ye thoughts and ye senses, 110:2
Ye three, each one an honored guest, 30a:10
Ye thrice-blessed Christians, 184:2
Ye true of heart, give thanks, 194:7
Ye voices resounding, 172:1; 172:7
Ye watchers and ye holy ones, 449
Ye who are wise will choose your friends, 443
Ye who bear Christ's name, 117:8
Ye who by Christ's own name are known, 117:8
Ye who do own Christ's holy name, 117:8
Ye who on Christ's own name do call, 117:8
Ye who profess to call you* Christians, 164:1
Ye who the name of Christ do bless, 117:8
Ye who the name of Christ have taken, 164:1
Ye who the sons of God dare call ye, 164:1
Ye who would, like Christ, be holy, 47:2
Ye will be weeping and wailing, 103:1
Yea, bear I even the greatest enemy, 139:5
Yea, come, Lord Jesu(s), 106:2f
Yea, come, my Jesus, 106:2f
Yea, deep within me is my greatest foe, 139:5
Yea, God no man forsaketh, 107:2
Yea, God's sore chastisement, 89:2
Yea, had God not allowed it, 14:3
Yea, had not God His folk defended, 14:3
Yea, had not God His power declared, 14:3
Yea, hear; with His protection, 215:6
Yea, I see what here was told me, 162:6
Yea, I will watch with Jesus, 244:26a
Yea, if then God had but allowed it, 14:3
Yea, if thy faith doth see much darkness, 83:4
Yea, Lord, come quickly, even so, 11:8
Yea, now my God, so fall I to Thee, 65:7
Yea, observes thy faith yet much darkness, 83:4
Yea, should thy faith grow faint, 83:4
Yea, some deny the word and faith, 18:3d
Yea, surely oweth God to speak, 89:2

Yea, the time also comes, 44:2
Yea, there cometh the time, 44:2
Yea, this same word is to my soul, 104:4
Yea, those that have their God's law, 70:6
Yea, though I bear my greatest foe within, 139:5
Yea, though I walk through death's dark vale, 112:3
Yea, though I walk through the valley, 112:3
Yea, though many false witnesses, 244:39a
Yea, though many lying witnesses, 244:39a
Yea, though our sin be ne'er so great, 38:6
Yea, thousand times thousand, 43:3
Yea, thousands on thousands, 43:3
Yea, to my feeble soul Thy word is leaven, 104:4
Yea, truly, flesh and blood, 244:65
Yea, truly, to the cross our flesh and blood, 244:65
Yea, verily, God should speak a word, 89:2
Yea, verily, my heart shall guard, 248:32
Yea, we do acknowledge it, 119:6
Yea, yea, I can defeat the foes, 57:5
Yea, yea, I can the enemies strike, 57:5
Yea, yea, my heart shall keep it closely, 248:32
Yea, yea, thine enemy is vanquished, 57:5
Yea, your heart for evermore liveth, 75:1b
The year is past, 614
The year is past and well may we, 288; 289
The year that is passing God richly endowered, 28:5
Ye're blest, His sheep beloved, 34a:5
Yes, a thousand times a thousand, 43:3
Yes certainly, flesh and blood in us, 244:65
Yes, come, Lord Jesu(s), 106:2f
Yes, faith's the pledge that Jesus loves me, 37:2
Yes, gladly is the flesh and blood, 244:65
Yes, I; Lord, show compassion, 244:16
Yes, if God had allowed it, 14:3
Yes, if God had only allowed it, 14:3
Yes, indeed should God pronounce, 89:2
Yes, it is hard, 204:5
Yes, let us praise our God, 110:7; 142:8

Yes, methinks I now behold it, 162:6
Yes, now indeed should God pronounce, 89:2
Yes, surely God may utter, 89:2
Yes, this flesh and blood of ours, 244:65
Yes, this Thy word is nurture to my spirit, 104:4
Yes, this word is food for my soul, 104:4
Yes, this word is my soul's food, 104:4
Yes today, dearest Father, 211:8
Yes, yes; God is still near, 215:6
Yes, yes; God is still our close help, 215:6
Yes, yes, I can strike enemies, 57:5
Yes, yes, I can strike the enemies, 57:5
Yes, yes, I can thy foes destroy, 57:5
Yes, yes, I hold fast to Jesus, 157:4a
Yes, yes, I hold Jesus fast, 157:4a
Yes, yes, I hold Jesus firmly, 157:4a
Yes, yes, I hold to Jesus firmly, 157:4a
Yes, yes, my heart shall guard for sure, 248:32
Yes, yes, my heart shall guard it, 248:32
Yes, yes, my heart will keep and cherish, 248:32
Yes, yes, my heart will keep and ponder, 248:32
Yes, yes, thy foes I soon will conquer, 57:5
Yet appears almost that me, 67:5
Yet doth the eye of God, 90:4
Yet doth the Spirit beseech God, 226:2
Yet God's observant eye regards us, 90:4
Yet had the law's behests, 9:4
Yet hold awhile, 210a:7
Yet how sees it Thee in Thy crib, 121:5
Yet in the midst of this evil race, 70:6
Yet in this wicked generation, 70:6
Yet Jesus shall e'en midst the judgment, 46:5
Yet Jesus will also be at this punishment, 46:5
Yet Jesus will even by the chastisement, 46:5
Yet Jesus will the righteous keep, 46:5
Yet Lord, I know my spirit is oppressed, 67:5
Yet, loved Princess, thou art not dead, 198:10
Yet marvel not, O Master dear, 176:4a

Yet more from Thee, O God, I claim, 177:2
Yet must the law be fulfilled, 9:4
Yet one thing, Lord, will I beg Thee, 111:6
Yet play no more, 210:3
Yet, Queen, thou diest not, 198:10
Yet, Queen, you do not die, 198:10
Yet shall all believers, 124:4d
Yet silence, for thoughtless and vain, 8:4
Yet since the enemy, 41:5
Yet still the Lord His faithful shieldeth, 46:5
Yet, terrified heart, 168:4
Yet when He, the Spirit of Truth, shall come, 108:4
Yield, all ye evildoers, 135:5
Yield, dull shadows, 202:1
Yield, melancholy shades, 202:1
Yield, spirits of mourning, 227:11
Yield, ye sorrows, 187:5b
You all must know, 212:22
You are right, indeed, 212:19
You are the proper way, 229:3
You are the way, the truth, 229:3
You are wise beyond your years, 209:4
You can drive away the mourning, 66:1b
You daughters are so fixed in your ways, 211:6
You evil child, 211:3
You false man, seek only to bring the Lord low, 248:56
You fields and meadows displaying your verdure, 208:14
You fields and meadows, let yourselves be seen, 208:14
You fields and meadows, may you flourish, 208:14
You happy one, come running, 207a:8
You happy ones, come here, 207a:8
You have sowed the seeds of kindness, 207a:7
You, however, are not of the flesh, 227:6
You leave us now, and at your leaving, 209:3
You lovely prospects, you happy hours, 208:15
You most lovely views, 208:15
You naughty child, 211:3

You offer me your heart, 518
You peevish child, 211:3
You should love the Lord your God, 77:1
You souls who are always dashing about, 204:3
You stars and glorious heavens, 476
You stars, you high airs, 248:53
You stars, you high spheres, 476
You stiff-necked foes might well now be, 248:62
You stubborn child, 211:3
You thoughts and meditations, 110:2
You traitor, try then to lay the Lord low, 248:56
You, who name yourselves of Christ, 164:1
You who say Christ's name, 117:8
You who yourselves call after Christ, 164:1
You will they put under ban, 44:1
You will weep and howl, 103:1
You would give your spirit and strength, 18:3b
You wretched child, 211:3
Your ability surpasses, 209:4
Your arm and Your blessing, 41:3
Your blood, which cancels my guilt, 78:4
Your comrades all rejoice, 36b:4
Your happy birthday celebration, 207a:3
Your heart shall everlastingly live, 75:1b
Your knowledge is contrasted, 209:4
Your life has flown, O Jesus, Savior sweet, 501
Your man of wealth a haughty palace, 94:3b
Your name shall stand as doth the sun, 173a:7
Your peace of mind will be secure, 197:9
Your song is too coarse, 212:17
Your song's not quite the thing, 212:17
Your storm comes up from afar, 46:3

Your welcome we hail with joy, 30a:3
Your welfare will I ever serve, 30a:6
Your wisdom goes far beyond, 209:4
Your ability surpasses, 209:4
Your arm and Your blessing, 41:3
Your blood, which cancels my guilt, 78:4
Your comrades all rejoice, 36b:4
Your happy birthday celebration, 207a:3
Your heart shall everlastingly live, 75:1b
Your knowledge is contrasted, 209:4
Your life has flown, O Jesus, Savior sweet, 501
Your man of wealth a haughty palace, 94:3b
Your name shall stand as doth the sun, 173a:7
Your peace of mind will be secure, 197:9
Your song is too coarse, 212:17
Your song's not quite the thing, 212:17
Your storm comes up from afar, 46:3
Your welcome we hail with joy, 30a:3
Your welfare will I ever serve, 30a:6
Your wisdom goes far beyond, 209:4
You're right, by gad, 212:19
You're right, I own, 212:19
You're right, my poppet, 212:23
You're right; that piece, 212:19
Youselves swift multiply, 63:6

Z

Zion hears her watchman crying, 140:4
Zion hears her watchmen's voices, 140:4
Zion hears the guards sing, 140:4
Zion hears the warders sing, 140:4
Zion hears the watchmen calling, 140:4
Zion hears the watchmen sing, 140:4
Zion hears the watchmen singing, 140:4

Bibliography

THEMATIC INDEXES

Payne, May de Forest. *Melodic Index to the Works of Johann Sebastian Bach.* New York: G. Schirmer, 1938.

Schmieder, Wolfgang. *Thematisch-systematisches Verzeichnis der musikalischen Werke von Johann Sebastian Bach.* Leipzig: Breitkopf & Härtel, 1961.

Schmieder, Wolfgang. *Thematisch-systematisches Verzeichnis der musikalischen Werke von Johann Sebastian Bach.* 2d ed. Wiesbaden: Breitkopf & Härtel, 1990.

BOOKS
(Selected Sources Containing
Ten or More Translated Titles)

Bach, Johann Sebastian. *The Bach Chorale Texts in English Translation [by] Henry S. Drinker.* New York: The Association of American Colleges Arts Program, 1941.

Bach, Johann Sebastian. *Texts of the Choral Works of Johann Sebastian Bach in English Translation by Henry S. Drinker.* New York: The Association of American Colleges Arts Program, 1942.

Bach, Johann Sebastian. *Texte zu den Kirchenkantaten von Johann Sebastian Bach.* Neuhausen-Stuttgart: Hänssler-Verlag, 1984.

Emery, Walter. *A Vocal Companion to Bach's Orgelbüchlein.* Sevenoaks, Kent: Novello, 1969-75.

Grace, Harvey. *The Organ Works of Bach.* London: Novello, 1922.

Hodgson, Julian. *Music Titles in Translation.* Hamden, Conn.: Linnet Books, 1976.

Robertson, Alec. *The Church Cantatas of J. S. Bach.* London: Cassel, 1972.

Steinitz, Paul. *Bach's Passions.* London: P. Elek, 1979.

Taylor, Stainton de B. *The Chorale Preludes of J. S. Bach.* London: Oxford University Press, 1942.

Terry, Charles Sanford. *Bach: the Passions.* London: Oxford University Press, 1926.

Terry, Charles Sanford. *Bach's Chorals.* Cambridge: University Press, 1915.

Terry, Charles Sanford. *Joh. Seb. Bach Cantata Texts, Sacred and Secular.* London: The Holland Press, 1964.

Whittaker, W. Gillies. *The Cantatas of Johann Sebastian Bach, Sacred and Secular.* London: Oxford University Press, 1959.

Whittaker, W. Gillies. *Fugitive Notes on Certain Cantatas and the Motets of J. S. Bach.* London: Oxford University Press, 1924.

Young, W. Murray. *The Cantatas of J. S. Bach.* Jefferson, North Carolina: McFarland, 1989.

SCORES

Bach, Johann Sebastian. *Arias from Church Cantatas for Soprano, an Obligato Instrument and Piano or Organ.* Translation by Jane May. New York: E. F. Kalmus, 1949.

Bach, Johann Sebastian. *Ausgewählte Choralvorspiele für Klavier zu 2 Händen.* Übertragen von Max Reger. Wien: Universal Edition [1900?]

Bach, Johann Sebastian. *The Bach Chorale Book: a Collection of Hymns Set Exclusively to Chorales Harmonised by J. S. Bach.* Selected and edited by J. Herbert Barlow. New York: H. W. Gray, 1922.

Bach, Johann Sebastian. *Bach for Beginners in Organ-Playing.* Compiled and edited by Edward Shippen Barnes. Boston: The Boston Music Co., 1919.

Bach, Johann Sebastian. *Chorales.* Selected and edited by Charles N. Boyd and Albert Riemenschneider. New York: G. Schirmer, 1939-41.

Bach, Johann Sebastian. *Complete Organ Works.* Edited by Edouard Nies-Berger and Albert Schweitzer. New York: G. Schirmer, 1954-67.

Bach, Johann Sebastian. *Complete Organ Works.* New York: E.F. Kalmus, 1947.

Bach, Johann Sebastian. *Eighteen Large Chorales for the Organ.* Edited by Albert Riemenschneider. Bryn Mawr, Pa.: O. Ditson Co., 1952.

Bach, Johann Sebastian. *80 Songs & Arias.* Edited and the English words adpated by Ebenezer Prout. London: Augener, [1909?]

Bach, Johann Sebastian. *Eleven Great Cantatas in Full Vocal and Instrumental Score.* New York: Dover Publications, 1976.

Bach, Johann Sebastian. *Eleven Chorale Preludes from The Little Organ Book.* Arranged for two pianos, four-hands by C. H. Stuart Duncan. New York: G. Schirmer, 1949.

Bach, Johann Sebastian. *The Four-part Chorals of J. S. Bach with the German Text of the Hymns and the English Translations.* Edited by Charles Sanford Terry. London: Oxford University Press, 1929.

Bach, Johann Sebastian. *J. S. Bach's Original Hymn-tunes for Congregational Use.* Edited, with notes, by Charles Sanford Terry. London: H. Milford, Oxford University Press, 1922.

Bach, Johann Sebastian. *Johann Sebastian Bach's Organ Works.* Edited by W. T. Best. London: Augener, n.d.

Bach, Johann Sebastian. *The Liturgical Year: Forty-Five Organ Chorals.* Edited by Albert Riemenschneider. Bryn Mawr, Pa.: O. Ditson Co., 1933.

Bach, Johann Sebastian. *185 Four-part Chorales (from the C. P. E. Bach Collection).* New York: Lea Pocket Scores, 1955.

Bach, Johann Sebastian. *131 Chorals in Five Books.* Edited by H. Clough-Leighter. Boston: E. C. Schirmer, 1932-34.

Bach, Johann Sebastian. *Sacred Songs for Voice and Piano.* English translation by Herbert Grossman. New York: International Music Co., 1948.

Bach, Johann Sebastian. *Sacred Songs from Schemelli's Gesangbuch.* St. Louis: Concordia Publ. House, 1958.

Bach, Johann Sebastian. *A Second Book of Chorals.* Selected and provided with suitable English texts by Thomas Whitney Surette. Boston: E. C. Schirmer Music Co., 1922.

Bach, Johann Sebastian. *Selected Arias.* [Selected] by Ernest Walker. London: Joseph Williams, 1901.

Bach, Johann Sebastian. *Six Organ Chorals (Schübler).* Edited by Albert Riemenschneider. Philadelphia: O. Ditson Co., 1942.

Bach, Johann Sebastian. *Ten Bach Chorales, Arranged for Men's Voices (Four Parts).* [Edited] by Bryceson Treharne; with the original texts and new English translations by Willis Wager. New York: G. Schirmer, 1939.

Bach, Johann Sebastian. *Thirteen Chorales from the Church Cantatas and Motets.* London: Novello, n.d.

Bach, Johann Sebastian. *The 371 Chorales of Johann Sebastian Bach with English Texts and Twenty-three Instrumental Obbligatos.* [Edited by] Frank D. Mainous, Robert W. Ottman. New York: Holt, Rinehart and Winston, 1966.

Bach, Johann Sebastian. *371 Harmonized Chorales, and 69 Chorale Melodies with Figured Bass.* Rev., corrected, ed. and annotated by Albert Riemenschneider. New York: G. Schirmer, 1941.

Bach, Johann Sebastian. *Twenty Chorales, a Chorale Prelude, and a Fugue for Use in the School and Community.* Boston: O. Ditson, 1931.

Bach, Johann Sebastian. *Twenty-five Chorales.* Selected, edited, and provided with suitable English texts by Berta Elsmith and Thomas Whitney Surette. Boston: E. C. Schirmer Music Co., 1919.

Chorale Collection, Including 156 Chorales by J. S. Bach, 22 Swedish Chorales, and 20 Norwegian Chorales. Edited by Elvera Wonderlich. Rochester, New York: Eastman School of Music, 1941.

Songs of Syon. 3d ed. Edited by G. R. Woodward. London: Schott & Co., 1910.

SOUND RECORDINGS

Bach, Johann Sebastian. *Bach Arias.* Angel SQ2-37229, 1976.

Bach, Johann Sebastian. *Bach Organ Favorites.* Columbia M32791, 1974.

Bach, Johann Sebastian. *Geistliche Lieder.* Westminster W9613-9616, 1964.

Bach, Johann Sebastian. *Kantaten: Advent und Weihnachten.* Archiv Produktion 222 005, 1972.

Bach, Johann Sebastian. *Kantaten: Sonntage nach Trinitatis I.* Archiv Produktion 2722 028, 1978.

Bach, Johann Sebastian. *Das Kantatenwerk.* Telefunken SKW 1-, 1972-

Bach, Johann Sebastian. *Music of Jubilee: Bach Favorites for Organ and Orchestra.* Columbia MS 6615. [1964?]

Bach, Johann Sebastian. *Orgelbüchlein, BWV 599-644.* Nonesuch HD-73014, n.d.

Bach, Johann Sebastian. *Sacred Songs and Arias from Schemelli's Song Book.* Musical Heritage Society MHS 3871-3872, 1978.

Notebook for Anna Magdalena Bach. Musical Heritage Society MHS 1663-1664, 1973.

Concordance

This concordance explains the variations in BETI listings from those given in BWV 1, Wolfgang Schmieder's *Thematisch-systematisches Verzeichnis der musikalischen Werke von Johann Sebastian Bach* (Leipzig: Breitkopf & Härtel, 1961). It also identifies those numbers from BWV 1 that are different in BWV 2, Schmieder's *Thematisch-systematisches Verzeichnis der musikalischen Werke von Johann Sebastian Bach.* 2d ed. (Wiesbaden: Breitkopf & Härtel, 1990).

Because many printed scores and published librettos make distinctions given in BWV 1 that are not separately numbered there, it is necessary to supply additional identification for those subsections. For example, BWV 18:3 has five separate titles in BETI. Those supplied subdivisions are designated as a, b, or 1, 2, etc., according to the numbering used in similar works. (Do not confuse those with .1, .2, the numbering for stanzas.) Those subdivisions are identified with the briefest possible amount of text to enable the user to link the passsage with the incipits in BWV 1.

The indexing for BWV 2 contains many changes in the numbering of works as well as renumbering or relocating within works. This is especially evident in BWV 244 and 245. Please note that this concordance is concerned only with changes that affect titles listed in BETI. It is not intended to be a comprehensive concordance of changes in BWV 2.

BWV 1/BETI		BWV 2	BWV 1/BETI		BWV 2
11		11/249b	16:3b	Krönt und	
11:7		11/249b:7a	18:3a	Mein Gott	
11:8		11/249b:7b	18:3b	Du wollest	
11:9		11/249b:7c	18:3c	Nun wehre	
11:10		11/249b:8	18:3d	Ach! Viel'	
11:11		11/249b:9	18:3e	Ein And'rer	
15		15/Anh. III 157	21:6a	Was betrübst	
15:9a	Drum danket	15/Anh. III 157:9	21:6b	Dass er	
15:9b	Mein Jesu	15/Anh. III 157:9	21:11a	Das Lamm	
15:9c	Weil du	15/Anh. III 157:9	21:11b	Lob, und	
16:3a	Lasst uns		22:1a	Jesus nahm	

BWV 1/BETI		BWV 2	BWV 1/BETI		BWV 2
22:1b	Sie aber		67:6b	Wohl uns	
36:1		36 (1):1 and 36 (2):1	70:10a	Seligster	
36:2		36 (2):2	70:10b	Schalle, knalle	
36:3		36 (1):2 and 36 (2):3	71:2a	Ich bin	
36:4		36 (2):4	71:2b	Soll ich	
36:5		36 (2):5	72:2a	O sel'ger	
36:6		36 (2):6	72:2b	Herr, so	
36:7		36 (1):4 and 36 (2):7	72:2c	Mit Allem	
36:8		36 (2):8	73:1a	Herr, wie	
39:1a	Brich dem		73:1b	Ach! aber	
39:1b	Alsdann wird		73:1c	Du bist	
46:1a	Schauet doch		73:1d	Dein Wille	
46:1b	Denn der		75:1a	Die Ellenden	
49:3a	Mein Mahl		75:1b	Euer Herz	
49:3b	Mein Jesus		76:1a	Die Himmel	
49:3c	Komm Schönste		76:1b	Es ist	
49:5a	Mein Glaube		77:6		No text given
49:5b	So bleibt		80:2a	Alles, Alles	
49:6a	Wie bin		80:2b	Mit unsrer	
49:6b	Dich hab'		83:2a	Herr, nun	
51:2a	Wir beten		83:2b	Was uns als	
51:2b	Muss gleich		88:1a	Siehe, ich	
53		53/Anh. II 23	88:1b	Und darnach	
60:1a	O Ewigkeit		92:7a	Ei nun	
60:1b	Herr, ich		92:7b	So spricht	
60:2a	O schwerer		94:3a	Die Welt	
60:2b	Mein Beistand		94:3b	Ein Stolzer	
60:4a	Der Tod		95:1a	Christus, der	
60:4b	Selig sind		95:1b	Mit Freuden	
61:5a	Öffne dich		95:1c	Mit Fried'	
61:5b	Bin ich		95:2		95:2/3
61:6a	Amen		95:2a	Nun, falsche	
61:6b	Komm, komm		95:2b	Valet will	
66:1a	Erfreut euch		95:3		95:4
66:1b	Ihr könnet		95:4		95:5
66:4a	Bei Jesu		95:5		95:6
66:4b	Mein Auge		95:6		95:7
67:6a	Friede sei		102:1a	Herr, deine	

BWV 1/BETI	BWV 2	BWV 1/BETI	BWV 2
102:1b Du schlägest		134a:2	Text & music differ
102:1c Sie haben		134a:3	Text & music differ
105:1a Herr, gehe		134a:4a Es streiten, es siegen	
105:1b Denn vor		134a:4b Es streiten, es prangen	
106:2a Gottes Zeit		138:3a Er kann	
106:2b In ihm		138:3b Ach! wie?	
106:2c Ach Herr!		141	141/Anh. III 157
106:2d Bestelle dein		142	142/Anh. II 23
106:2e Es ist der		143:7a Halleluja	
106:2f Ja, ja, ja		143:7b Gedenk', Herr Jesu an dein Amt	
106:3a In deine		(Text not in BWV)	
106:3b Heute, heute		145:1	145:5a
106:4a Glorie, Lob		145:2	145:5b
106:4b Durch Jesum		145:3	145:1
114:2a Wo wird		145:4	145:2
114:2b Allein zu		145:5	145:3
117:2a Es danken		145:6	145:4
117:2b Gott unserm		145:7	145:5
118	118/231	146:8	No text given
122:4a Ist Gott		148:6	No text given
122:4b O wohl		154:7a Wohl mir	
127:4a Wenn einstens		154:7b Ich will	
127:4b Fürwahr		156:2a Ich steh'	
127:4c Wenn Himmel		156:2b Mach's mit	
127:4d Er wird		157:4a Ja, ja	
131:1a Aus der Tiefe		157:4b Ei, wie	
131:1b Herr, Herr		158:3a Nun, Herr	
131:2a So du		158:3b Da bleib'	
131:2b Erbarm dich		159:1a Sehet, sehet	
131:4a Meine Seele		159:1b Komm, schau	
131:4b Und weil		159:2a Ich folge	
131:5a Israel		159:2b Ich will	
131:5b Und er		160	160/Anh. III 157
132:2a Willst du		164.3	Text inadvertently omitted
132:2b Denn dieses			
133:4a Wie lieblich		169:2a Gott soll	
133:4b Wer Jesu		169:2b Zwar merk	

BWV 1/BETI	BWV 2	BWV 1/BETI	BWV 2
171.6	Includes alternative text	198a:1	Lass, Höchster, lass der Hoffnung Strahl
172:7	Mentioned only in note	198a:2	Ach, wehe, weh uns Menschen allen
176:4a	So wundre	198a:3a	Hinweg, entflohn ist Edens Friede
176:4b	Weil Alle	198a:3b	Der ersten Unschuld reines Glück
180:3a	Wie teuer	198a:4a	Der Glocken bebendes Getön, or Von hoch herab durchbebt und hallt
180:3b	Ach wie		
186:4a	Ach, dass		
186:4b	Drum, wenn	198a:4b	Ich armer Mensch
186:10	Text inadvertently omitted	198a:5	Getrost! Erbarmen kam von Gott
		198a:6	Im Leben fromm, getreu im Sterben
187:5a	Gott versorget		
187:5b	Weicht, ihr	198a:7a	Von dir, du Vorbild aller Frommen
187:7	Includes addl. stanza		
188:1	188:2	198a:7b	Soll ich denn auch des Todes Weg
188:2a	Gott meint	188:3	198a:8a	Des ewgen Gottes Vaterhaus zieht
188:2b	Drum lass	188:3	198a:8b	O wie selig seid ihr doch
188:3	188:4	198a:9a	O grosse Lieb! Es hällt uns werth
188:4	188:5	198a:9b	Doch wir, wir geh'n im Pilgerkleide
188:5	188:6	198a:10a	O Menschenkind, du stirbest nicht
189	189/Anh. II 23	198a:10b	Auf, mein Herz! des Herren Tag
190:1a	Singet, singet	207:2	207:1
190:1b	Alles, was	207:3	207:2
191:1a	Gloria in excelsis	207:4	207:3
191:1b	Et in terra	207:5	207:4
194:6	Includes addl. stanza	207:6	207:5
194:12	Includes addl. stanza	207:7	207:5a
195:1a	Dem Gerechten	207:8	207:6
195:1b	Ihr Gerechten	207:9	207:7
196:5a	Ihr seid	207:10	207:8
196:5b	Amen	207:11	207:9
197a:1	197a:4	210a:8a	Grosser Flemming
197a:2	197a:5	210a:8b	Werte Gönner
197a:3	197a:6	210a:9a	Erleuchtet Haupt
197a:4	197a:7	210a:9b	Geehrte Gönner
198:9a	Was Wunder	216:1a	Vergnügte Pleissen
198:9b	So weit der	216:1b	Beglückte Neissen
198a	Not in BWV 1 or 2	218	218/Anh. III 157
		219	219/Anh. III 157

Concordance

BWV 1/BETI		BWV 2
220		220/Anh. II 23
225:1	Singet, singet	
225:2	Wie sich	
225:3	Gott, nimm	
225:4	Loben den	
225:5	Alles, was	
226:1	Der Geist	
226:2	Sondern der	
226:3	Der aber	
226:4	Du heilige	
229:1	Komm, komm	
229:2	Komm, ich	
229:3	Du bist	
229:4	Drauf schliess'	
230:1	Lobet den	
230:2	Alleluja	
231		28/2a
232:4a	Gloria in excelsis	232:4
232:4b	Et in terra pax	232:5
232:5		232:6
232:6		232:7
232:7a	Domine Deus	232:8
232:7b	Domine Fili	232:8
232:8		232:9
232:9		232:10
232:10		232:11
232:11		232:12
232:12		232:13
232:13a	Credo in unum	232:14
232:13b	Patrem omnipotentem	
		232:14
232:14		232:15
232:15		232:16
232:16		232:17
232:17		232:18
232:18		232:19
232:19		232:20
232:20a	Et expecto	232:21

BWV 1/BETI		BWV 2
232:20b	Amen	232:21
232:21a	Sanctus	232:22
232:21b	Pleni sunt	232:23
232:22		232:24
232:23		232:25
232:24		232:26
232:25		232:27
233:1a	Kyrie eleison	
233:1b	Christe eleison	
233a:1	Kyrie eleison	
233a:2	Christe, du Lamm	
233a:3	Christe eleison	
233a:4	Kyrie eleison	
234:1a	Kyrie eleison	
234:1b	Christe eleison	
234:2a	Gloria, gloria	
234:2b	Et in terra	
235:1a	Kyrie eleison	
235:1b	Christe eleison	
235:5a	Qui tollis	
235:5b	Quoniam tu	
236:1a	Kyrie eleison	
236:1b	Christe eleison	
243:12a	Gloria, gloria	
243:12b	Sicut erat	
243:13	Vom Himmel	243a Einlage A
243:14	Freut euch	243a Einlage B
243:15	Gloria, gloria	243a Einlage C
243:16	Virga Jesse	243a Einlage D
244:4		244:4a
244:5		244:4b
244:6		244:4c
244:7		244:4d
244:8		244:4e
244:9		244:5
244:10		244:6
244:11		244:7
244:12		244:8

BWV 1/BETI		BWV 2
244:13		244:9a
244:14		244:9b
244:15a	Er sprach	244:9c
244:15b	Und sie	244:9d
244:15c	Herr, bin	244:9e
244:16		244:10
244:17		244:11
244:18		244:12
244:19		244:13
244:20		244:14
244:21		244:15
244:22		244:16
244:23		244:17
244:24		244:18
244:25a	O Schmerz	244:19
244:25b	Was ist	244:19
244:26a	Ich will	244:20
244:26b	So schlafen	244:20
244:27		244:21
244:28		244:22
244:29		244:23
244:30		244:24
244:31		244:25
244:32		244:26
244:33a	So ist	244:27a
244:33b	Lass ihn	244:27a
244:33c	Sind Blitze	244:27b
244:34		244:28
244:35		244:29
244:36a	Ach nun	244:30
244:36b	Wo ist	244:30
244:37		244:31
244:38		244:32
244:39a	Und wiewohl	244:33
244:39b	Er hat	244:33
244:40		244:34
244:41		244:35
244:42a	Und der	244:36a

BWV 1/BETI		BWV 2
244:42b	Er ist	244:36b
244:43a	Da speieten	244:36c
244:43b	Weisage, weisage	244:36d
244:44		244:37
244:45		244:38a
244:46a	Wahrlich, du	244:38b
244:46b	Da hub	244:38c
244:47		244:39
244:48		244:40
244:49a	Des Morgens	244:41a
244:49b	Was gehet	244:41b
244:50		244:41c
244:51		244:42
244:52		244:43
244:53		244:44
244:54a	Auf das	244:45a
244:54b	Sie sprachen	244:45a
244:54c	Barabbam	244:45a
244:54d	Lass ihn	244:45b
244:55		244:46
244:56		244:47
244:57		244:48
244:58		244:49
244:59a	Sie schrieen	244:50a
244:59b	Lass ihn	244:50b
244:59c	Da aber	244:50c
244:59d	Sein Blut	244:50d
244:59e	Da gab	244:50e
244:60		244:51
244:61		244:52
244:62a	Da nahmen	244:53a
244:62b	Gegrüsset	244:53b
244:63.1		244:54
244:63.2	Du edles Angesichte	
	(This stanza not in BWV.)	
244:64		244:55
244:65		244:56
244:66		244:57

BWV 1/BETI		BWV 2	BWV 1/BETI		BWV 2
244:67a	Und da	244:58a	245:13		245:9
244:67b	Der du	244:58b	245:14		245:10
244:67c	Desgleichen	244:58c	245:15.1		245:11.1
244:67d	Andern hat	244:58d	245:15.2	Ich, ich und meine	245:11.2
244:68		244:58e		(Stanza not in BWV.)	
244:69		244:59	245:16		245:12a
244:70a	Sehet, Jesus	244:60	245:17		245:12b
244:70b	Wohin?	244:60	245:18		245:12c
	(This does not appear in BWV.)		245:19		245:13
244:71a	Und von der	244:61a	245:20		245:14
244:71b	Eli, Eli	244:61a	245:21		245:15
244:71c	Der rufet	244:61b	245:22		245:16a
244:71d	Und bald	244:61c	245:23		245:16b
244:71e	Halt, halt	244:61d	245:24		245:16c
244:72		244:62	245:25		245:16d
244:73a	Und siehe	244:63a	245:26		245:16e
244:73b	Wahrlich, dieser	244:63b	245:27.1		245:17
244:73c	Und es waren	244:63c	245:27.2	Ich kann's mit meinen Sinnen	
244:74		244:64		(Stanza not in BWV.)	
244:75		244:65	245:28		245:18a
244:76a	Und Joseph	244:66a	245:29		245:18b
244:76b	Herr, wir	244:66b	245:30		245:18c
244:76c	Ich will	244:66b	245:31		245:19
244:76d	Pilatus sprach	244:66c	245:32		245:20
244:77a	Nun ist	244:67	245:33		245:21a
244:77b	Mein Jesu	244:67	245:34		245:21b
244:78		244:68	245:35		245:21c
245:2		245:2a	245:36		245:21d
245:3		245:2b	245:37		245:21e
245:4		245:2c	245:38		245:21f
245:5		245:2d	245:39		245:21g
245:6		245:2e	245:40		245:22
245:7		245:3	245:41		245:23a
245:8		245:4	245:42		245:23b
245:9		245:5	245:43		245:23c
245:10		245:6	245:44		245:23d
245:11		245:7	245:45		245:23e
245:12		245:8	245:46		245:23f

BWV 1/BETI		BWV 2
245:47		245:23g
245:48a	Eilt, eilt	245:24
245:48b	Wohin?	245:24
	(This does not appear in BWV.)	
245:49		245:25a
45:50		245:25b
245:51		245:25c
245:52		245:26
245:53		245:27a
245:54		245:27b
245:55		245:27c
245:56		245:28
245:57		245:29
245:58		245:30
245:59		245:31
245:60a	Mein teurer	245:32
245:60b	Jesu, der du	245:32
245:61		245:33
245:62		245:34
245:63		245:35
245:64		245:36
245:65		245:37
245:66		245:38
245:67		245:39
245:68		245:40
245a:1a	Himmel reisse	
245a:1b	Jesu, deine	
246		246/Anh. II 30
246:8a	Es kam	
246:8b	Wo willt	
246:22a	Der Herr	
246:22b	Nie keinen	
246:22c	Herr, siehe	
246:32a	Da aber	
246:32b	Herr, Herr	
246:41a	Die Männer	
246:41b	Weissage	
246:43a	Und viel	

BWV 1/BETI		BWV 2
246:43b	Bist du	
246:43c	Er aber	
246:43d	Bist du	
246:45a	Er sprach	
246:45b	Was, was	
246:45c	Und der	
246:45d	Diesen finden	
46:45e	Pilatus aber	
246:49a	Sie aber	
246:49b	Er hat	
246:49c	Da aber	
246:55a	Denn er	
246:55b	Hinweg, hinweg	
246:55c	Welcher war	
246:55d	Kreuzige	
246:55e	Er aber	
246:61a	Und sie	
246:61b	Er hat	
246:61c	Es verspotteten	
246:61d	Bist du	
248:7a	Er ist	
248:7b	Wer kann	
248:38a	Immanuel	
248:38b	Jesu, du	
248:38c	Komm! ich	
248:40a	Wohlan!	
248:40b	Jesu, meine	
248:63a	Was will der	
248:63b	Was will uns	
249:8a	Indessen seufzen	
249:8b	Ach! ach!	
249:10a	Wir sind	
249:10b	Preis und	
249:10c	Eröffnet	
249a:3		249a:2
249a:4		249a:3
249a:5		249a:4
249a:6		249a:5

BWV 1/BETI	BWV 2	BWV 1/BETI	BWV 2
249a:7	249a:6	A56	Anh. II 56
249a:8	249a:7	A57	Anh. III 172
249a:9	249a:8	A58	Anh. II 58
249a:10	249a:9	A59	Anh. II 59
249a:11a Glück und	249a:10	A60	Anh. II 60
249a:11b So werden sich	249a:10	A61	Anh. III 172
524:1 Was sind		A62a	Anh. II 62a
524:3 Wer in Indien		A62b	Anh. II 62b
524:4 O ihr Gedanken		A63	Anh. II 63
524:6 Ei, wie sieht		A64	Anh. II 64
524:7 Grosse Hochzeit		A65	Anh. II 65
524:8 Ach, wie hat mich		A66	Anh. II 66
524:9 Urschel, brenne		A67	Anh. II 67
524:12 Studenten sind		A68	Anh. II 68
524:13 Wär ich König in Portugal (This text not in BWV.)		A69	Anh. II 69
691a	691a/Anh. II 79	A70	Anh. II 70
692-693	692-693/Anh. III 172	A71	Anh. II 71
		A72	Anh. II 72
746	746/Anh. III 172	A73	Anh. II 73
748, 748a	748, 748a/Anh. III 172	A74	Anh. II 74
		A75	Anh. II 75
751	751/Anh. III 172	A76	Anh. II 76
759	759/Anh. III 172	A77	Anh. II 77
760, 761	760, 761/Anh. III 172	A78	Anh. II 78
		A79	Anh. II 79
771	771/Anh. III 172	A157	Anh. III 157
A31	Anh. II 31	A159	Anh. III 159
A47	Anh. III 172	A160	Anh. III 160
A48	Anh. II 48	A160:1a Jauchzet, jauchzet	
A49	Anh. II 49		Anh. III 160:1
A50	Anh. II 50	A160:1b Kommet vor	Anh. III 160:1
A51	Anh. II 51	A162	Anh. III 162
A52	Anh. II 52	A164	Anh. III 164
A53	Anh. II 53	A171	Anh. III 171
A54	Anh. II 54	A172	Anh. III 172
A55	Anh. II 55		